~~JY 12 '91~~			
~~JE 1 '95~~			

T*he* B*ook of* M*amie*

The Book of Mamie ¶ A novel

by Duff Brenna

University of Iowa Press   Iowa City

University of Iowa Press, Iowa City 52242

Printed in the United States of America
First edition, 1989

Design by Richard Hendel
Typesetting by G&S Typesetters, Austin, Texas
Printing and binding by Thomson-Shore, Dexter, Michigan

Library of Congress
Cataloging-in-Publication Data
Brenna, Duff.
The book of Mamie: a novel/by Duff Brenna.—1st ed.
p. cm.
ISBN 0-87745-244-X
I. Title.
PS3552.R377B6 1989 89-5064
813'.54—dc20 CIP

Do I contradict myself?

Very well then I contradict myself,

(I am large, I contain multitudes.)

– Walt Whitman, "Song of Myself"

For one true heart in the midst

of all my failure –

– Nancy Rae

Contents

The Book of Mamie

Drowd'n Man

Mamie Beaver, she had to come from the moon. Or maybe even the stars. One star, big and fat and fiery. First one at night, star light, star bright. It just seemed that way, seemed natural – more natural than that she was John Beaver's daughter. Except that she had his size, she didn't look a thing like him. They were opposites. They were like two forces of nature, two winds coming from opposite directions, two mountains breeding landslides, two oceans battling it out, making storms like the Atlantic and the Pacific at Cape Horn.

Mamie Beaver, head like a proud pumpkin. Retarded Mamie Beaver. Brain of a five-year-old? Quiet and slow-moving body, with arms held straight down and fingers rigid, like Frankenstein's monster. She was a farmer's daughter, and she was his mule. Her strength was legend throughout the northern country of Wisconsin. Her father would loan her out for harvest work, and it was said she earned him enough in season so that he didn't have to keep but a pig and a steer each year, together with his garden, and that was enough for the two of them to live at Bulls-Knoll independent of the world.

We were farmers too, but there were nine of us all together, with Mama and Pa and six boys and one girl, so we never had any cause to hire Mamie. She was just GIRL, the myth-legend kind, like the Amazons or Wonder Woman. We'd heard stories about her all our lives, and Pa used those stories to put us in our place once in a while, especially if we whined about something he wanted us to do, like putting up bales – a thousand bales in the field, each one weighing fifty to sixty pounds – and having to get them in because rain was expected overnight. "Oh," he'd say, "don't trouble your pampered, puny selves. Mamie'll be by soon and show you how it's done." None of us could stand the thought – a balloon-headed Beaver coming to add notches to her reputation at our expense – so the hay always got up without Mamie.

Back in the days near the end of 1949, she had hopped aboard the school bus each morning and rode with us to Cloverland. They put her in first grade. She was already nine or ten years old, looking like fifteen or twenty. Rumor said that there was some law forcing John Beaver to give her a try at schooling. She was a flop though. She couldn't even learn the ABCs.

In any case, for the few weeks that Mamie went to school, she and I became friends. I did my best to teach her something, sitting with her in the back of the bus and writing the ABCs over and over again, while she watched, fascinated, a trickle of drool running from her mouth. Lots of times I would smack my tablet over her head in frustration and call her stupid, stupid, stupid. She always smiled and nodded when I called her stupid. Yeah, she understood; she got that part.

At school we called her Horsey and rode about saddled to her hips, yelling for her to giddup. She liked it. She would neigh and cry, "Hippa-weee!" and snort and race across the schoolyard, clicking her tongue against the roof of her mouth, making the clippety sound of a galloping horse. There was no wearing her out at recess. We stood in line, elbowing and shoving to get a turn at her. But other than at recess, everyone pretty much ignored her, including the teachers, except when they would watch us spurring her and get so excited they would holler, "Haw, Mamie! Haw!" and look as though they would ride her themselves.

Then one morning, as the bus was climbing the hill that was part of Bulls-Knoll, someone yelled for us to look-see, and we all jammed our noses against the windows to catch every second of seeing Mamie racing down the Beaver road, her arms flailing the air like penguin wings, trying to get the bus to stop. And running behind her, waving for the bus to go on, was John Beaver. He finally managed to tackle her before she reached the mailbox, and the last we saw he was sitting on top of her rapping his knuckles on her head.

I missed her a lot at first, but then she just faded from my thoughts the way things do, to be brought out for a second or two whenever Pa mentioned her, or when we heard some story of her bending horseshoes or throwing a steer or throwing bales around like they were basketballs.

Ten years passed before I saw her again. She had run away from John Beaver. It was a surprise to everyone because none of us thought she would ever be smart enough to do that. One Sunday morning near noon, I was at the Brule, leaning against a log, my line and bobber in the water, having no luck and not minding a bit. Warm June sat on my chest, and everywhere round was the scent of pine and slow water. Trees guarded me on both sides of the river. I felt safe and glued to life, like something that wouldn't ever die – one of the elect. I had decided to become a teacher when I grew up, and I had until milking time to dream of how successful and famous I would be, so mind-penetrating an intellect that no one could resist learning from me. I would always know the right things to say to reach the most stubborn kid, and I would know so much about everything in the world that no one could ask a question to stump me. So my fame would spread far and wide, across the country and around to the far sides of China. Statues would be erected in my honor. Biographies would be written about my humble rise to greatness and my unbelievable genius. And schools throughout every state would fight for the right to be called Christian Peter Foggy schools. My portrait would hang in the entrance halls. Mothers would point to me and tell their children how grand I was, and how they hoped and prayed that their own little ones would follow in my footsteps. "Remember humble Christian Foggy," the mothers would say whenever the children refused to study. Even my own mother would tell at the interviews that she'd never dreamed I was so special. But Pa would say he knew, because Pa knows everything. Ahhh, it was wonderful to be me on the bank of the Brule – to be fifteen and to have such a large future stretching out in front of me.

Then, in the midst of my dreaming, there she was, sudden as an earthquake, lumbering toward me and blotting out the sun. The same though slightly altered Mamie Beaver – taller, broader, with bosoms, large ones, like fists in boxing gloves. Her nose was the same, full of freckles out to her ears, and her nostrils, wide as thumbtips, quivered as she breathed. A wide, thin mouth with upturned corners, like a jack-o'-lantern with big, yellowy teeth; flat eyes, like an astonished fish; the same moon-round face with its cap of Orphan Annie hair. Mamie Beaver, the runaway. John Beaver was furious to have her back. He had even offered a fifteen-dollar reward.

She squatted in front of me. Dollar signs danced in front of my eyes. Fifteen bucks for her! She stared at me, solemn as a bluegill. I stared back. For a time it was a standoff; then she looked away and started searching through the brush and grass around her. She found a wild onion and pulled it up, rubbed it on her pants, and ate it. "Um um um," she said, and she pulled another onion up and handed it to me. I brushed it on my jeans and ate it. "Um um um," I said as I chewed.

"You probably can't remember me, huh?" I asked her.

Her mouth and chin worked away at what she wanted to say, moving up and down and side to side like loose rubber, trying to clamp down on the words and form them into syllables that would fall out right. Finally she managed to say she remembered me, "Yaay, I member." I asked her what my name was.

"Kritch'n," she said, giggling.

"That's wonderful," I said. I was amazed she knew me after so many years, and I told her she was smarter than people thought she was.

"Smma-art," she replied, tapping her forehead.

"And do you know your ABCs yet?"

She nodded her head like she was pounding nails with it. "Yaay!" she said, all excited.

"Well, all right, let me hear them, Mamie!"

Her chin went up. She looked at the sky as if the letters were printed there, and she started out, "Aaa-yay-yay, bee-yee-yee, cee-yee-yee." Then she stopped and sucked at her finger. Her eyes looked off, studying trees or birds or the empty spot where *d* was supposed to be. I could see she was stumped permanent.

Finally she reached across without looking at me and took up my arm, giving it a squeeze. "B-b-bony," she said, changing the subject. I was bony all right, meatless triangles from head to foot, but I didn't appreciate her reminding me.

"You're fat!" I said.

She leaped up like she was spring-loaded and then cried out, "Hippa-weee!" and pointed to her back. I remembered the playground and the fun and the hippa-weee call and forgot the insult of being skinny. I climbed into the saddle of her hips and wrapped my fingers in her fiery red hair. "Haw!" I yelled, and off she flew down the shore a hundred yards or so and back, clicking her tongue like she used to, neighing and snorting. Up the shore she went another hundred yards or more, then returned again. She was panting a little and had lathered around her lips, but there had been no quit in her. Beneath me had been that same sure power I had known before. I swatted her bottom and told her she was a treasure.

"Yaay!" she said to me, nodding her head in agreement, then taking me up in her arms and smashing me spread-eagled and breathless against her.

"You're killin me," I croaked.

"I fix him fish!" she cried.

She let me drop and took up my line from the water, pulling it in and unpinning the bobber, stripping the salmon eggs off. And from her pocket she produced a piece of cheese, which she molded around the hook. Then she found another wild onion, washed it, chewed it, spit the juice over the cheese, and folded it in until it looked like a glistening yellow pearl. She gave a short cast and let the line drift under in the current. In less than thirty minutes, she caught four carp. She handed two to me, took the other two herself, and told me to come with her. Which I did.

We went upriver for half a mile, then followed a path through the woods until we came out on a large meadow surrounded on all sides by trees. The meadow was covered in dandelions and timothy, the dandelions blooming with deep yellow bouquets above the light green of the timothy, and some gone to seed, and the seed blowing and spinning in the air round us, like fairy down. Insects buzzed and flew up as our feet passed over them. And the woody, grassy smell, thick in the warm sun, made me feel quiet inside and lazy.

Tucked in a corner at trees' edge in the shadows was an old cabin. Fresh red chinking shone between some of the logs. The one small window next to the door had no glass in it. The door itself was held in place by leather hinges. Outside was a log bench, planed smooth. A small garden area had been cleared a few feet away.

We went inside, where I saw an old table and a wired-together chair. Pine needles piled in one corner showed where Mamie slept. Out from the wall opposite the bed was a small stove, in which she started a fire to fry the fish. She fried them in a black skillet with strips of bacon, wild onion, and dandelion greens. It was the best-tasting fish I had ever eaten, and I told her that even if she didn't know anything else, she sure knew how to cook. She agreed to that, giggling and nodding and rubbing her belly.

Afterwards I sat on the bench outside and watched her wander among the dandelions, picking one here, another there, picking them according to her fancy, which, watching her, I figured had no rhyme or reason but a rhythm sure enough, like that of a cow or a deer grazing. In the wild, with the meadow and the sun and the flowers, and the river shushing nearby, and the smell of fried fish and bacon hanging in the air like a lazy dew, Mamie blended in as well as anything born to be there. Mamie of the earth and the forest, the river and the meadow, graceful as a bear without walls. I knew it would be a damn shame to send her back to John Beaver. But fifteen dollars . . . it was a lot of money.

When she came back, arms full of yellow and purple flowers, I asked her if she knew her pa was looking for her. She dropped the bouquet in my lap and screwed up her eyes, cocking her head to one side in a heavy think.

"John Beaver," I said. "You remember your pa?"

"I know'm," she replied.

"Well, he's looking all over for you."

"W-w-where?" she asked, rolling her eyes like was he around close by.

"Here and there, high and low. He worries about you."

"Naw," she answered, scoffing at me. Then she whinnied, lips rolling back from her teeth in a dribbly, dobbin-kind of display. She looked so funny I had to laugh at her. We had ourselves a little fit of giggling in each other's faces and haw-hawin like a pair of jackasses. Then suddenly she broke it off and asked me direct and clear if I liked her pa.

"*Your* pa?" I asked. I didn't know anybody who especially liked John Beaver.

She rapped the top of her head with her knuckles and said, "Oooch me."

I knew what she meant. It was no secret that he beat her. But her being retarded, I guess no one thought it necessary to do anything about it. But there she was in front of me, showing me that she knew he treated her wrong and telling me that it hurt. She wasn't just a mule after all, not that it would make it okay to beat her even if she were. Mules have feelings too.

I thought more about her pa, and I remembered a time one winter when I had been running my trap lines along trails I had known since I was six years old and my brother Calvin showed me how to trap. I had been at it for such a while that I thought the trails belonged to me, so it was a shock one day to find out that someone was stealing my catch. I got up extra early the next morning and set out, determined to find out what was going on.

Light was barely seeping over the horizon when I arrived at the spot of my first snare. In the snow were deep boot marks, and I could see where a rabbit had been flicking its hind legs against the pull of the twine. But it was gone and the trail led north. It was at the next spot that I found my thief. I heard a sound that made my blood run cold, the sound of something in hard pain, a sound like nails screeching across a blackboard, high and horrible and pitiful.

Through the bare trees moved John Beaver, an inky shadow swaying and humming, arms busy with the thing that screeched at each flick of the knife. He had a mink hung between two saplings. A wire hook through its nose was holding its head tied to a branch above, and its front and back legs were spread wide, like it was caught midway in doing jumping jacks. For some reason, John Beaver was skinning it alive. I hid myself and watched. I wanted to help the mink, but I was no match for John Beaver. Me and my five brothers would've been no match for him – throw in Pa too. So I was terrified simple and frozen to the spot, feeling my stupid eyes bugging out.

When he finally had the pelt off, he shook it out and threw it over his shoulder, together with the rabbit, and away he walked, humming and happy as a preacher on Sunday morning. I crept out and found the naked mink still alive. Quick as a ferret, I cut its throat and took off. And I set no more traps that winter.

Nope, I didn't like John Beaver any more than Mamie did herself.

I admitted to her how I felt, and I asked her what she would do if he found her. She studied it a moment, her eyes almost closed with the depth of her concentration. Then she slipped her hands together sideways, like cymbals clashing, and told me she would run. I told her I guessed I would do the same if he were coming for me. She patted my shoulder. Then she took the flowers off my lap, and turning away, she arranged them in her hair. When she was done, she looked over her shoulder at me, shy and flirty sort of.

"Aren't you pretty?" I said.

That set her off. She ducked away and whinnied at the air and started running in a zigzag across the meadow. Just for the hell of it, I got up and chased her. The dandelion seeds rose so thick round us it was like the meadow was exhaling snow. That and all the yellow and the green and the butterball of a sun made me feel giddy and full of a joy I couldn't name. I knew I was acting retarded myself, but I sure didn't care.

I followed her back to the river, where she slipped out of her overalls and shirt and then came for me. She picked me up like I was a beachball and threw me into the water. It was cold! I yelped, and she cried out, "Drowd'n man!" and swam out to save me. She soon had me on the shore again. Then, before I could even catch my breath, she picked me up and threw me again into the water. As soon as I yelled, she cried, "Drowd'n man!" and dove in to rescue me. After about the fourth time I decided I better just relax and let her have her way. For at least an hour we played drowning man.

Usually, when I played it with my brothers, I would end up drowning half the time. But Mamie didn't let me drown once. I was proud of her, and when I finally was let to stay on shore I told her she was wonderful strong and I'd never forget feeling like the hands of God were whooshing me out of the water. We lay naked in the sun, the river at our feet, the meadow unseen through the trees but still sending an occasional dandelion seed over us, like a tiny whirling ballerina. My clothes lay drying, spread out like another body next to me.

I thought about what I was doing, lying alongside a naked girl, and I knew it was something I would not dream of doing with any others that I knew, not even Mary Magdalen, my sister; but with Mamie it seemed to be just the right thing. She was almost like one of my brothers, except her arms were bigger, and she was taller, and she had big breasts. As a matter of fact, she was better than my brothers. She was calmer and a hell of a lot nicer. She didn't pick on me like they did. She didn't laugh and let me drown.

I dozed a bit, and when I woke she was curled on her side, head resting on her arm, staring at me with a small, satisfied smile on her face. I asked her what she thought she was doing.

"Savin you fr-from Inians," she said, fighting to keep her mouth and the words in control.

"I bet you would," I told her.

She pointed to my hair. "Sneezeweed," she said, laughing. She had the same fish wonder in her eyes, a happy fish wonder.

"Can you really say the ABCs?" I asked.

"Yaay, Kritch'n," she answered, "Aaa-yay-yay, bee-yee-yee." She quit, blinked her eyes, and repeated the same two letters.

"Hell, you went to *c* before," I said, disgusted. "Look here."

I turned over and wrote the ABCs in the sand, then went from letter to letter with her, having her repeat them. She did all right that way. I told her I was going to be a great teacher someday and that I would teach her to read and write. She nodded solemnly, aware that I was saying some very important stuff. I wrote the word *dandelion* in the sand and told her it was her first word to learn, *dandelion.* I took her hand and made her write it over and over. After several tries, she did it on her own, putting a string of *dandelions* along the shore. But when I made her turn away and write it without seeing the letters, she got no further than *dan.* I wrote it slow for her. She wrote it next to me. After twenty of them, I made her turn away. She wrote *da* and stopped. Worse than before. It was getting me frustrated. "Pretty stupid," I said. "You wrote forty of the goddamn things. Now you can only do *da*?"

"Stuuu-pid," she replied, rapping her knuckles on her head.

Then I felt bad. "I'm the one who's stupid," I told her, rapping my own head. I wrote the word *stupid* in the sand, and she bent low over it, staring at the letters as if she might, through sheer will, unlock their secrets.

"Mamie's just Mamie," I said, petting her hair.

"Yaay, Kritch'n," she answered, murmuring it into the sand.

Then she went back to writing *dandelion*, following one right after the other, extending the row downriver toward Lake Superior. I watched her awhile. Then I dressed and left her, naked and preoccupied, scratching *dandelion* in the sand. Mamie Beaver, worth a fifteen-dollar reward.

I'm a Dirty Ratter

I was late for milking. The old man was standing at the entrance to the barn, hands on hips, tapping his foot, staring at me like Jehovah.

"I fell asleep," I told him.

"You been asleep since you was born," he said. "Five o'clock! We milk at five o'clock."

"Yessir."

"Five!"

"Yessir, Pa."

He showed me his watch. "You know what time it is? It's six o'clock. We done the milking. Done your share, boy. Done."

"I'm sorry, Pa."

He slapped his hands together like he was going to pray. His eyes rolled toward heaven. He pointed his crooked finger at me and said, "You see what I got here, Deity? You see what old Jacob Foggy has to put up with? You see this little ulcer-maker, this torment of my philosophizing heart, this sleeper-by-the-Brule, this dreamer-in-the-sand, this bare bodkin rotting up Denmark? Huh? Huh?"

I couldn't think of anything to do but apologize again. He was in one of his moods. I thought about my brothers and figured they had probably given him an exasperating day.

He shook his finger at me. He had a finger like a gnarled twig of walnut, because it was broken once in an apple press. "I don't want to hear anything from you about sleeping in the woods. I don't want to hear any fairy tales about fishing and sunning. I was fifteen. I know the tricks. All I want you to do is get your bony ass in there and turn them cows out and clean them milkers by yourself. And get it done before supper. You're always late for supper."

"Yessir."

"You're gonna be late for your funeral."

"Yessir."

"You got thirty minutes, Christian Peter."

"Yessir."

"Thirty minutes. No dragging ass."

"I'll get it done, Pa."

"You better. You keep us waiting supper I'll clobber you. You understand my poetry?"

"Yessir."

He caught me as I tried to slide by him into the milkhouse and cuffed me a couple of light ones on the back of the head like he always did to put punctuation in his words. It never hurt. He never hit any of us hard. But I said, "Ow, Pa, ouch!" just to make him feel good.

"No excuses," he said after me. "No sleeping and dreaming when we got milking to do. We got a farm to run. We all got to pull the load like family. We got to be together or we'll end up like Fortinbras marching in to take over Denmark. Savvy?"

"Yessir," I told him. "Fortinbras taking over Foggy Farm. I savvy, Pa."

The old man went toward the house, and I went to let the cows out and clean the milkers. I knew I was a Jobian trial to him, but I also knew my brothers were worse. They were always scheming on him and saying how they were going to get back at him someday for making them work so hard and yelling at them. They would talk trash about beating him up and running away and letting him wear himself out running his own damn farm. They were going to go out and conquer the world and throw him on his ear if he ever came begging. They talked and talked about it all and how tough they were, but when he came around they shut up quick enough and said yessir to him just like I did. He would sometimes stare at my brothers with a snaky grin on his face, like he knew what they talked about. And he'd wink at me like we understood each other and what the rest of them thought about things didn't much matter. So I always felt special to the old man, and when he got mad at me I didn't mind too much because I knew he liked me best.

I got to the house in time for the blessing. My sister and Mama crossed themselves, like Catholics do, but the rest of us just sat with our heads bowed over our plates, while the old man quoted one of his favorite verses: "A wise son maketh a glad father; but a foolish son is the heaviness of his mother." I peeked at him and saw he had his eyes on me. His voice rumbled across the table like wind ruffling a sheet of corrugated tin. He went on a mile about finding wisdom in doing one's duties and one's family share and telling the truth because beauty is truth and truth is beauty and the bread of sincerity is truth and great is truth it shall prevail for it is the lamp that keeps us all from darkness where we would dwell with fanatics and the spiritually unevolved. It was wearing me down, and I knew my brothers would be after me because it was my fault they had to sit and listen so long before Pa would let us eat. But at last he did run out of inspiration and we said amen.

While I was eating, I was thinking about how I could get back on his good side. I wondered if I ought to tell him about Mamie – get his mind off my transgressions and on to her. But then again, I thought, he might just get madder at me for not bringing her back or not saying something sooner so someone could go get her before dark. And of course, contrary to telling on her was the memory of how she fit so fine where she was, doing what she was doing; how for all her size she romped so beautifully, like a deep-chested mare galloping mightily in the wonderful outdoors, a glory to the sight of anyone. But there was also the fifteen dollars to think about, and of course, doing what the old man would call Samaritan righteousness.

So while I was soaking up the last spot of milk gravy on my plate with the last bite of bread, I threw out as nonchalantly as I could that I had happened onto Mamie Beaver at the Brule. Everybody stopped eating and stared at me. Mama touched my arm to stop me from swirling the bread. She took my chin in her hand and looked at me solemnly – which surprised me a bit because she hardly ever touched me or any of the boys. She was always pretty quiet and hardly seemed to have a voice most of the time or to do much thinking about anything. She was just there every day, moving steadily, doing her work, and once in a while saying something about her arthritis or her bladder. One or the other was usually killing her. Seemed like the only fun she ever had was when she brushed and braided my sister's hair. The two of them might spend an hour or more playing hair – Mary Magdalen sitting in a chair, chewing gum and talking up a twister, while Mama would brush and brush till Mary Magdalen's hair would shine like September wheat. And sometimes they would sing, and that would stop us in our tracks; and like hypnotized cows we would gather round and listen.

So Mama took my chin in her hand and leaned close to me and asked me what was that I had said about Mamie Beaver. I repeated to her that I had seen Mamie, and I added that she was fine and dandy. Mama shook her head sadly and said, "Living in those woods all by herself, poor thing." And she looked at Pa and told him he would have to do something. Her voice had a kind of whine in it when she talked to him, so he wouldn't think she was trying to give him orders.

I told her Mamie wasn't a poor thing. "She's got a cabin with a stove and a table and everything. She's got all the outdoors to sprint. She's just fine."

Big brother Calvin had to get his two cents in just then, saying,

"What do you mean she's got a cabin, boy? She break into somebody's place up there?"

"Heck no," I told him. "Mamie's no goddang thief, Calvin."

"Hey hey!" Pa said, pointing his crooked finger at me. "Son, you're walking on egg shells today. You better show some respect at the table and catch that running-off mouth of yours and make it behave."

"Yessir," I answered, and I apologized. I knew better than to say god-anything in front of Mama. Cussing was for outside, where Pa himself never held back, but in the house in front of Mama it was a quick way of getting a cuffing and some extra chores. I went on to mention that Calvin shouldn't call Mamie a thief and that I didn't like him calling me boy all the time either. Then I explained how Mamie had fixed up an old cabin belonging to nobody; that it was old and run down, and some trapper had probably built it when there were beaver in the Brule.

"It still ain't her property to be fixing up," Calvin said.

Mary Magdalen scoffed at him. "Oh, what you think she should do, you old hypocrite, live in a tree?"

"*Ain't*," crooned Mama. "Calvin, you know better than to say ain't."

Pa tapped Calvin's shoulder. "I've told you till I'm blue in the face that only lowlife hicks say ain't."

"Yeah," said Mary Magdalen, "that's you all right, Calvin. A hick. Manure for brains – and an ain't-saying hick."

"Now now, Mary Magdalen," soothed Mama.

"Oh, he makes me tired, Mama. Christian's right. Calvin ought to clean off his own doorstep before he calls others a thief. He's just a big jerk."

Cash took up Mary Magdalen's side. He told how Calvin stole the Hank Snow record at Zimmerman's Five and Dime. "I saw the devil steal it," he declared righteously.

"Ten years ago, or maybe three. I saw him too," said Cutham.

"It was last year," I told him.

"I never!" cried Calvin.

"You did!" we all shouted.

Everybody pointed at Calvin and accused him. It was fun. His ears got red and his lips trembled. He was denying for all he was worth and darting desperate looks at the old man, who was taking deep breaths, puffing himself up as we yelled "Thief!" at Calvin.

"Shut up!" the old man bellowed.

"Now, Jacob," whispered Mama, "remember about your vein."

Pa had once broke something in his throat so that he spit blood for a couple of days. He broke it yelling at Almer Tubb for letting the rope go slack when Pa was castrating Almer's bull and the bull kicked Pa in the gut.

"You let me worry about my own vein, Ruth," he told her in a tight voice. She pulled her head in and looked down, but I could see a faint smile dipping at the corners of her mouth.

Pa tapped the table with his forefinger, as if he were driving home each word. "May the steely-eyed Deity who's got his eye on the dead sparrow have mercy on any child of mine I find out to be a lowbrow thief. That child of mine might just as well give his soul to the Deity cause I'll have his assss."

Mama gasped and shook her head, as she always did when Pa lowered his voice and pronounced his favorite soul-and-ass intentions, adding a little hiss at the end and clutching his fist like he held it, the ass in question, right there.

"I never, Papa," said Calvin feebly. "I never –"

"Don't be getting this boy in trouble, Cash," said Pa, wiggling his crooked finger at Cash.

Cash sank back and tucked his head the way Mama did. Mary Magdalen looked at Calvin, who was looking back at her with goopy eyes. She took pity on him and said it wasn't really him that day who stole the Hank Snow record. It was Ram Brown, her old boyfriend, who stole it and gave it to Calvin. "He gave it to Calvin, and Calvin sat on it in the car and broke it, Papa," she added.

"That's the truth, Papa," said Calvin, laughing nervously. "I'm so dumb I sat on the thing and broke it, ha ha."

"Ram Brown stole it," Cash agreed.

"Ram Brown is body scum," said our sister. She was scraping gravy with her fingernail, running it round the edge of her plate.

"Ram Brown gives you a Hank Snow record that he stole, and you sit on it and break it," said the old man, nodding his head like it all made sense.

"That's what happened, Papa," Calvin answered, putting his hand over his heart.

"The judgment of the Deity for taking from the hands of a thief. There's more in heaven and earth than Horatio can figure out, let alone an ox like you, Calvin Paul Foggy."

"I never liked Ram Brown anyway," said Calvin.

Then the old man looked at me, raising one brow and lowering the other, fixing me with eyes like a cobra. "Now, Christian, what's this Mamie Beaver business all about? What's going on?"

I told him everything that had happened, except the naked swimming.

When I was done, Calvin said, "You know, Papa, John Beaver's got a fifteen-dollar reward out for her."

"Yeah, I know, but that don't mean Christian would get it. I wouldn't trust that ornery son of a farmer any farther than I could throw him. Which wouldn't be far. He's got to weigh two-eighty at least. And he's stronger than any northerner I know. Broke a man's back in a wrestling match once at a carnival. I seen him do it."

"What's fifteen dollars these days anyhow?" said Mary Magdalen.

"Fifteen is fifteen more than Christian has now," he told her.

"I don't care. I wouldn't give that moose John Beaver the time of day." Mary Magdalen tossed her head, her long blond hair shuttering like a horse's mane, her stubborn chin thrusting forward, daring somebody to tell her she was wrong.

"Like Pa says, fifteen bucks is fifteen bucks," I told her.

"It ain't the money I'm thinking about," said the old man, stroking the stubble on his chin.

"*Isn't*," said Mama softly, her eyes happy to have caught him.

"Ruth, I'm talking here," he told her sharply. And then he looked at me. "And you shouldn't be thinking of what you're thinking of doing to Mamie Beaver just to grab yourself a reward, Christian." Now the crooked finger that had made Calvin sweat was wagging at me again.

"Amen," whispered Mama.

And I heard Calvin whisper to Cash that Pa had said ain't. They both sniggered. Pa shut them up with a quick, hard look. Then he went on, "What is at question here is what our Samaritan duty is to John Beaver. Rotten soul that he is, Mamie is still his daughter and she's bats in the belfry. She needs someone to look after her. And at least he does that. Everybody knows he's proud of her."

"Proud of her like you're proud of the Farmall because it can pull five bottoms in clay," said Mary Magdalen. She was pushing it.

"Well, I'll tell you something, Miss know-everything." His finger had left me and was waving at her. "Any tractor that pulls five in clay is a tractor to be proud of, and any daughter who can outpull any five men you can name is also something to be proud of. At least he cares that much for her. He'd never let her starve. He's a rough booger but that's his daughter out there, and we got to do what conscience says is right."

"But he beats her, Papa." Mary Magdalen's chin was quivering, but I had to admire her hanging tough.

"God knows what else," said Mama, not looking up.

"Beats her, pinches her, works her like a dobbin, and probably puts a halter on her and rides her too," blurted Mary Magdalen.

"She's strong enough," said Calvin sniggering.

"Not funny," Pa told him.

I was ready to forget the money. But the old man said no, there was more to it than money. "Mamie Beaver's just a child out there, and we won't abandon her to the elements. Woods are full of bears and full of traps. What if she should get caught in one and eaten by the other? You want that on your conscience, Yorick? It's going to be the winter of discontent out there in a few months. How's she going to live a healthy life? How's she going to get enough to eat when the snow starts flying? If she don't die of starvation, she'll freeze to death. That slow-witted ole thing ain't – isn't – equipped to survive. She's got less brains than a court jester. She's been lucky so far, but it won't last. Ask King Lear about luck. Beaver might abuse the old beefer now and then, but she's still better off with him. Imagine having a gal like that – why, she'd try the patience of Horatio himself. Warm in winter and fed year round, that's the best a Mamie Beaver can hope for in this life."

Mama and Mary Magdalen both made the same gesture, a kind of fluttering of the fingers in front of their faces. It made me think of dandelion ballerinas at the Brule. It was their way of giving in to the old man's superior logic.

The old man was finished, the decision made. I went outside and got a gunnysack from the granary and went out back to my pickle patch. I figured as long as I was going to have to ride with John Beaver in the morning, I might as well take along a hundred pounds of cucumbers and get five cents a pound at the railyard on the way. I was kneeling on my haunches and studying the cucumbers for the finger-sized ones the buyers liked when my brothers came up behind me. They were standing shoulder to shoulder, each one a tad shorter than the other, like stairsteps, staring at me in a way that said they were looking for trouble.

"You oughtta know to be home on time for the milking, boy," said Calvin.

"I did my share," I said. "And Pa already cuffed me, so there's no need for your two cents."

"Oh yeah, cuffed him like this." He gave Calah a light rub on the top of his head. "He never hits you nothing, Christian."

"You're his pet!" said Cush.

"His pet!" said his twin, Cutham.

"I never been his pet," whined Cash.

"You're gonna make me throw up," I told them.

"Oh yeah?" Calvin snarled. "Well, listen up, beanpole. Every time you screw up the old man gets on us, and we're sick of it."

"The old man gets on you for you, not cause of nothing I do."

"Oh yeah?" said Cutham.

"Not cause of nothing I do," said Cush in a high voice like a parrot.

"Screw up," said Cash.

"Duh!" I shot back.

"Duh!" the twins replied.

I told them they looked like cretins. They did, too. Both had big wet lower lips always hanging and glistening like lips on chimps. My other brothers were just barely more tolerable to look at. I was thankful to the Deity that he had given me a spoonful more of brains and no hanging wet lip. "Cretins, all of you!" I shouted.

"Creature yourself!" Cutham fired back.

"Cretin, Cutham," I explained, "*C-r-e-t-i-n*."

"Oh yeah?" Cutham scratched his head and looked at the rest, his eyes wondering if they were going to take this kind of crap from a runt like me.

Cush mumbled something about my watching it. Calah said I was a bony twit. Cash said I thought reading books made me better than them. Calvin added that I was trying to be like the old man, who had read a bunch of Shakespeare and Emerson once and thought it made him smarter than everybody else.

"Pa *is* smarter than everybody else," I said.

"Duh!" they answered.

Calvin switched tactics. "What you and big Mamie do all day out in them woods?" he asked, his lips twisty like a wet worm.

"Get your ugly face out of the toilet," I answered.

"Mamie show you how?"

"Ick!"

He laughed at me. I threw a cucumber at him and hit him in the gut.

"Ooof! Goddamn, threatening body harm, huh?" He reached down for a dirt clod. Then they all reached down.

"Stone him," said Cutham.

"Stone him," said Cush.

It was a little ritual we often went through. "You throw those at me and this time I'm telling," I promised.

"Ah, fork you, Christian!" they shouted.

Calvin raised his arm. "You gonna tell us what you and Mamie done in them woods?"

"Tell us," said Cash, "or we'll stone you to death."

Calah, his eyes greasy, pleaded with me to tell. "Come on, Christian. Did you do it, huh?"

"None of your goddamn business!" I hollered.

"That's the last insult I'm taking from you," said Calvin, and he let fly the dirt clod, which hit my knee, exploding in a puff of dust. I rolled to my feet and headed across the pickle patch out to the pasture, dirt clods disintegrating all around me. I gave them my usual hunkered-down, foot-flying best, but I could hear them hounding in, especially Calah, who had a pair of thighs on him like Hercules. I might have done better had my stomach not been so heavy with supper and the milk gravy boiling up inside me. Calah caught me by the hair halfway across the pasture. "Gotcha, buttface," he yelled, whirling me around to him. Without meaning to, I threw up on him. "You goddamn booger!" he screamed and shoved me down. Calvin jumped in and put me in a half nelson while Calah kept hold of my hair, shaking it and my head and threatening to make me lick vomit off his shirt. Calvin thought that was a good idea, unless I wanted to tell what Mamie and I did in the woods. Cash, Cush, and Cutham joined in prodding and pinching me, calling me as many names as their tiny minds could think of – turd, piss-ant, puck-eater, asshole. Finally their imaginations ran out, and I gave in and told them Mamie and I swam naked. They squealed and punched each other. I described how she looked and how we had played drowning man and how she had never once let me drown like they always did. I told them they were pussies compared to Mamie.

"Pussies," said Calvin breathlessly. "You must've been naked body to naked body when she saved you every time."

"Naked body to naked body," repeated Cush in awe.

"How'd it feel?" they wanted to know.

"What a stupid question," I answered. "Felt like nothing."

"But her things must of been rubbing on you. You telling us you didn't feel her things?" asked Cush, cupping his hands like he had Mamie's things all to himself.

I told them her things felt about like Cutham's blubber belly. It wasn't what they wanted to hear. "Naw!" they said.

"Maybe a little more solid," I added.

Cush reached over and grabbed a handful of Cutham's stomach. "Mamie's boobs," he said, and they all got hysterical. Even Cutham giggled for a second; then he decided that he had been insulted and slapped Cush's hand away. They started wrestling and forgot about me. Calvin told them to knock it off, but they just kept rolling over each other and grunting like a pair of hogs. Calvin said to hell with them and turned back to me.

"You touch it?" he asked.

I told him I didn't know what he was talking about.

"Oh sure, I bet," he said. "I bet you did more than you're letting on."

"Like what?"

"Like what," he repeated, grinning and sniggering. "Don't play dumb with me, dummy."

"I mean it, Calvin – like what?"

"You know. You know." Then he laughed straight up into the sky and said, "You know, oh boy," and laughed some more. But it seemed to me that for all his being the oldest and the leader, he was making himself embarrassed. His ears were red and he was grinning crookedly and looking away. Fact is, only Calvin and Calah had ever gone out on real live dates. And the girls they took were a couple of our cousins, both modest and upright as nuns, coming from Mom's Catholic side of the family. So I knew that my brothers had never gotten anywhere with them, and I figured they were dumber than I was about girls. I figured they were retarded. They talked about almost nothing else but boobs and butts and what they would do with this girl or that one, and if any one of them got hold of a magazine picture of a naked girl, they all slobbered over it so much it would be ruined before the day was out. But that was as far as it went. If any girl in town even looked at them, they'd get all tongue-tied and practically faint. I didn't see much hope for them, except maybe if they just stuck with Pa and learned farming well enough to make a life of it after he was gone. So Calvin's laughter barked at nothing but air; there was no bite in it.

He and Calah finally let me up, though they punched me a bit more and told me what they would have done with Mamie if they had been me, naked in the river with her. Calvin pulled my nose and said that I was too young to appreciate the knock of opportunity. Calah pounded his big thighs and said that that was where they felt the power. Cash giggled and rolled his tongue round his lips. Cush and Cutham still rolled over each other in the pasture, giggling and cussing. I was left to go back and finish picking my cucumbers.

The old man was waiting for me at the patch. He said, "Work it out with your brothers?"

I said, "Yep." He smiled and dusted off my shoulders.

"John Beaver'll be by at five in the morning to pick you up. So looks like you'll get out of chores again and have to settle up with them boys once more. Every day they get more like your ma's family, like them oddball brothers of hers, Hem and Shem."

I offered to do all the night-milking by myself. He said there wasn't any need for it, that what I was doing was a legitimate excuse to miss a milking. Then, while I squatted on my heels and put pickles in the gunnysack, Pa squatted across from me and told me a few things.

"You're feeling low about what you're doing to Mamie, aren't you, son? I can tell by your face you're feeling yourself a real crapper, crapping out on her."

I told him he was right enough. It was nagging in my heart.

The sky was turning dark blue about the old man's head, and I saw a faint star open its eye. I made a wish on it that I would wake up in the morning with the strength of Samson and beat hell out of Calvin and Calah.

"When you're ratting on Mamie like that, you got to figure it won't feel right in your heart. It's only natural. I'd have it too, if I was giving her away like you. Yeah, you know because of you she's going to get caught and probably get her ass whipped good." Pa sighed and shook his head and looked at me like he couldn't believe I could be such a rat.

"Makes you feel like you're rotten in Denmark for sure," he continued, "and Horatio's philosophy don't help. Yep, it's a hell of a thing you're going to do, son. Let me see if I can't make you feel better about it."

Squatting over those cucumbers while he talked, I felt suddenly long of claw and tooth, a little varmint tugging at the vines, a thing of twitchy nose and whiskers. I wanted to spit myself out. Fifteen dollars, holy shittin Judas. And Mamie would get her ass whipped.

Pa had lit his pipe and was puffing hard to get himself up a good cloud of smoke. The air smelled like spoiled hay. "But," he said, "though you feel like a lowlife shit, let me tell you something. It's one of them mixed truths of high principle that Shakespeare likes to tell about. You know, to be or not to be, and stuff like that. I've read him cover to cover, and I'll tell you he knew as much as the Bible about it. Take comfort that men back in the days of swords and battle-axes were going through the same thing you're going through – and some of them went through a hell of a lot worse. But listen, you're doing something that's got a hair's fineness for moral weight. The Deity looks down and sees you trying to figure it out. He looks to see which side you're going to put the hair on. Should you be the Good Samaritan? Pour oil and wine on her wounds and bring her in out of the cold?"

He puffed and puffed, getting a grip on the pipe and his words, settling into them, happy and satisfied with what was coming out. "That's you, son, the Good Samaritan – the one who showed mercy – your brother's keeper fighting the conscience that's slipping the rat style to you. To be or not to be. Moment of truth. Emerson might say to you, 'Doubt not, O Christian, but persist. Ever the winds blow, ever the grass grows, and ever are men and women atoms of the wind and the grass and each other.' You are Mamie's keeper because you're your own keeper. Pay attention now," he ordered. "Ignorance wants to make its own laws – anarchy, nihilism. It's awake and full of tricks – making you think you're a rat doing wrong instead of right, aah, hmmm, yes. Ignorance." His face was fogged in purple pipe-smoke. It was like he was speaking to me from a cloud. "Awake and full of tricks. What shall I do to inherit the Deity's respect? Get smart. Be a thinker. Figure out the truth I tell you, free of charge – that Mamie is in you and you in Mamie, and both of you are limbs of the organ of life, and the organ is the Over-Soul, the Deity under your feet and over your head and in every breath you take. And if you allow him, he'll guide you to the truth and the Samaritan righteous thing to do. He'll have his bond with you and burn it into your ignorant heart."

Pa paused again. His pipe was going out. He struck a match on his pant leg and relit it. "Mercy is to Mamie Beaver, the Good Samaritan righteousness come forth from Christian. Listen to your Pa. Don't give it another thought. Have I ever steered you wrong? Hmmm? Gather those cucumbers while you may. It's getting dark, son of mine."

Even though I knew he meant well, the old man's philosophizing didn't help get rid of the sense of whiskers and tail and rattiness I felt. I could tell he had a righteous glow in his mind. He had opened his mouth and believed that the truth fell out and that everything was solved for me. But I, wavering over what was really the true Samaritan righteousness, wanted answers a bit more solid than a mixture of Pa's version of Emerson and Shakespeare. Pa was wrapped up again in his pipe-cloud, the Over-Soul blowing smoke. So I looked up and picked out the star I had wished on, and I changed my wish – wishing with all my rodent heart that Mamie would be gone when John Beaver and I got there in the morning.

A Moment of Truth

John Beaver was there before five o'clock, before milking had scarcely got started. My brothers' looks would have killed me if they could. I was getting out of chores twice in a row – unheard of – and I could see they would make me pay. Dirt clods and dirty names, hammerlocks and hair-pulling were in my future. I scurried out the barn door, already sick of the day and wishing it was over and I was back in bed with the lights out. I put my sack of cucumbers in the bed of Beaver's pickup and climbed in next to him, squeezing myself up tight to the door. It was narrow in there with all his bulk, and I didn't want to touch him. The ghost of the mink was between us.

"Where to, Foggy?" he asked, facing around in the gray light, so that all I could see was a bluish face with a lump of tobacco in its cheek. The breath of wet Redman and splow and armpit and hot clutch stuck like hartshorn in my throat. I told him in a whisper where he should go, and he growled, "Good boy," and ruffled my hair. I rolled the window down and breathed in the barnyard flower.

On the way he kept pumping me for information about Mamie. I did my best to answer politely, but it got harder and harder with the questions he asked. First it was just how she was and what she looked like and did she have much to say. Then he wanted to know about more personal things.

He said, "How can that big dummy know nuff to get on so good out there, Foggy? How you figure that? What's her secret, heh?"

"She's smarter than you think," I told him.

"Smarter than I think? Naw," he said. He laughed wetly and spit juice on the floor between his legs. "Maybe she is, maybe she ain't, heh?" He reached a thick finger over and poked me in the ribs. I always hated someone to do that. Skinny as I was, my ribs were tender. He went on, "And maybe somebody been he'pin that moose, heh?" He looked slyly at me and chuckled. He spit some more on the floor and jammed another wad of Redman in his mouth. "Heh?" he kept saying over and over and grinning brown teeth and razor lips at me. My throat and belly felt sour, like acids were melting my insides.

"Not me, Mr. Beaver," I finally managed to say to him. "Not me, sir. Nosir."

"Heh? Course not, course not. That good little Christian Fluppy wouldn't even think of such a thing. Some would though. Some would like to take a'vantage of that lunkhead. But not you, not you. Some would, uh-huh, some would just for the fun of it, know what I mean? She wouldn't know the difference. She'd think you was playin a game, just sportin her. You been sportin my Mamie, Fluggy?"

"Nosir, honest. Not me."

"Course not. Not you, good Fuggyboy." He flicked my ear with his fingernail. It stung like a spider had bit me. "Come on over here," he said, reaching out and grabbing a hunk of my hair.

"Yeow!" I hollered. "Let go! Let go!"

"Shet yer face, you little pile of crap!" He pulled my head round like it was attached to a rag. He gave me a hell of a shake.

"Pleeease sir, pleeease sir," I stammered. My voice sounded as high as a little girl's to me, higher even. "I'll shut my face, sir."

"Damn right you will, Fuzzybutt. Now, when you hear bout my givin out with a reward, heh?"

"Ouch, oh, I don't know, sir. Maybe a week ago. Don't know."

"A week ago?"

"Yessir. Fifteen dollars."

"Greedy little pecker. Maybe you heard it yestiday."

"Nosir, before yesterday."

"But maybe yestiday and you decided she wasn't worth givin up no fifteen bucks, heh? I got yer number."

My mind was offtrack. I didn't know what he meant or what I was supposed to say. I told him I didn't know.

"You know," he growled. "You know what I'm talkin bout, Foggy. You the one kept Mamie out there so you could play house, heh? And she done some things for you, Foggybottom, heh? Didn't she? Mamie knows how." He shook my head again until I thought the roots of my hair were going to let go.

"Yeow, oh, goddamn!" I cried. "Nosir, nosir!" He shook harder still and I couldn't stand it. It seemed better to switch to yessir, yessir, so I did.

"Uh-huh," he answered, satisfied. "That's what I thought, that's what I fuck'n well knew."

He let go of my hair and I tried to rub the roots back in. Jesus, but it hurt.

He was talking. “Ain’t nobody put one over on this badass Beaver yet. I see right through ’em, goddammit, don’t I though? I know what makes ’em tick. You pimply boys is all the same – full of sap, full of nasty sap. Sap makes you tick. And Mamie’s easy. You wanted her to yourself for a while. Ain’t it so?”

“Yessir.”

“Best not to try lyin to the Beaver, Foffybuns.”

“Yessir!”

“You and Mamie, right? Keepin her in the woods, heh?”

“Me and Mamie, yessir.”

His hand swept backward across my mouth. I was too stunned to yell or even to feel anything for a moment. Then my front teeth started aching and my lips pounded like my heart had leapt up inside them. I tasted blood. It was all I could do to keep from bawling. I was terrified of John Beaver. He was as much a horror as the mink had said he was. I wanted my Pa and my brothers. I wanted Calah to hammerlock the sonofabitch and Calvin to pull his hair and Cush and Cutham to stomp him and pinch him. But even as I thought it, I wondered if even all of them were any match for someone so huge and thick and wild and dinosaurlike.

“That’s only a taste of what you deserve for all that nasty sap of yers!” he shrieked. Brown spittle flew from his mouth, raining on the windshield. Then his voice got low and sly again. “She do the no-rain for you?” he asked.

“The what?”

“You want to play dumb again, heh? You gonna tell me you don’t know what her no-rain dance is? You don’t wanna tell me that, son. She done it for you, didn’t she?”

“Yessir, the no-rain dance.”

“Nasty boy,” he said. He was quiet for a while. We drove slowly, the truck rattling and belching up toward the highway, where we turned east and passed the yard where I could have sold my cucumbers. But I wasn’t about to ask John Beaver to stop. I was in no mood to do anything but point the way and keep my mouth shut, let him collect Mamie, and take me home. I was sick right down to my boots that I was leading him to her, but it seemed that there was just nothing else I could do.

“Heh heh heh, I got the goods on you, don’t I, Fluffybum?” he said suddenly. “You little poontang monster. Ha ha ha, got the goods, got the goods. I bet yer sayin to yerself, ‘Fuck that reward money, I want my mama.’ Is that what yer sayin, baby boy?”

"Yessir."

"You just tell ole upright Jacob Foggy that you couldn't take no reward for he'pin a worried-sick papa get his little girl back. A good neighbor just wouldn't wanna take a reward for somethin like that, would he?"

"Nosir."

"Yessir, gotta keep a step ahead in this life, got to, uh-huh."

We came up to the dirt road to go north where Mamie was, and Beaver pulled over. He wanted to know how far, and when I told him it wasn't more than a hundred yards he said we'd walk in. By the time we arrived at the ridge just above Mamie's little valley, the sun was up above the horizon and I could smell the dew rising. There were bees and dragonflies getting warmed up and going places. It was a perfectly natural day. As I walked a short way in front of Beaver, a monarch landed on my arm. It was a big one, with black-veined wings, orange and black, spreading out to catch the sun. John Beaver tried to catch it, but I waved my arm and it got away.

"Pretty, ain't it?" he said, as it fluttered over our heads.

Pretty? I took a long look at Beaver as he watched the butterfly, but I couldn't figure out how the word *pretty* could come out of his mouth.

I pointed the way, and he followed me down the path through the pines. In a few feet we came out on Mamie's meadow. Just then a lark gavc warning and flew away, and a whole flock of crows flew up with it. Mama would have crossed herself if something had startled her so. And there, with John Beaver pushing his way in front of me and a six-inch lump of buck-knifc suddenly in his hand, I felt like maybe there was nothing left to do but put a hex on him, so I crossed myself and whispered, "In the name of the Father, Son, and Holy Ghost, let Mamie be gone." And I didn't feel silly about it. My spirit was warm for heaven's help.

The cabin came into view. There wasn't any smoke from the stovepipe yet, so it seemed Mamie was still asleep. Beaver turned round and gave me a shove that set me on my hindend. He put his finger to his lips and glared at me. I got the messagc. Hc wcnt hunched over, slinking like an overfed Indian. I saw the blade of his knife catch a ray of sun and flash for a second. My mouth wiggled with the need to yell out and give Mamie a warning, but no noise came from it; all my courage was just dead in me. I couldn't help but think of him whirling round and coming after me and splitting me open like he would a rabbit, skinning me like he would a mink. What a yellow streak I had. It was my moment of truth, and I was failing it. I couldn't have been more disgusted with myself.

He got alongside the cabin and peeked in the window. Mamie must have been standing right there, because suddenly I heard a scream come curdling out of the center of that cabin, a scream as haunting as the cry of a loon. John Beaver jumped back from the sound, got his legs all tangled up in firewood, and fell head over heels, yelling, "Yaaaa," on his way down. Despite my own fear, the look of him bowling over made me laugh out loud. Mamie came tearing out the door, running like flame over the meadow, her big legs winging effortlessly along, hardly seeming to touch the ground.

"Go, Mamie, go!" I cried in admiration. She was so artful and pure, like a grass-fat antelope.

Beaver was up and after her. He didn't leap and wind-breeze like she did. His way was to tear through the flowers and grass, and he had a kind of relentless power, like a bull ripping along. They ran in wide circles, edge to edge round the meadow, Mamie flying, Beaver plowing. From a distance they seemed almost like two children, a brother and sister playing with each other, both grinning and cavorting, having the time of their lives. But as they came round the circle close by me, I could tell that Mamie's grin was a grin of terror. And Beaver's smile was the smile of a wolf.

She might have run him to ground had she just kept smooth earth under her, but on one of her leaps she came down on something that threw her off balance, and over she went in a somersault, arms and legs flailing like a shot goose. Beaver was on her before she even stopped rolling. He grabbed her hair and flipped her over on her stomach so he could shove her face in the dirt. He was gasping and spitting Redman all over her.

"Gotcha," he panted. "Gotcha!"

Mamie didn't say anything. She lay like the dead.

Finally, when he had enough puff to tell her, he said, "I ought to skin you alive, runnin out on me who fed your fat ass all yer goddamn ungrateful life!" He pulled her head back and showed her the knife. "You think I won't?" he added, and then pushed her head down and wacked off a handful of hair. "I'll cut it all off," he promised. Then he cut off a couple more handfuls and threw them into the air. They sparkled in the sun like ghostflame.

Not satisfied with gouging her hair, he started pinching her and rapping the knife hilt on her head. Mamie said nothing, did nothing, didn't even move. I think it made him madder that he couldn't make her cry or anything. He put the knife blade right on the back of her neck and said he was going to scalp her first, then skin her, then tack her hide and scalp to the side of the barn and let it dry in the sun. He pulled the hair on the back of her neck and got himself set to scalp. I can't say if he would have done it or not. But the sight of him wiping the blade on his pants back and forth, like he was warming it up, and of Mamie spread-armed and spread-legged, helpless beneath him, then of him touching the back of her neck once more, pulling hard on her hair, and slicing the skin just slightly, so the finest, faintest trail of blood followed along – and then hearing Mamie screech. Mamie screeched the like of which only naked mink could match. And all that together made something snap in my head. I grabbed the first clubby-looking piece of wood I could find and laid it hard across the back of John Beaver's head. He lifted his hands to the spot and turned to look at me.

"What!" he yelled, half-rising, so I had to hit him again and again. "Ughh," he groaned as he toppled over. He lay there gurgling Red-man, blood dripping on a pillow of dandelions, arms and legs spread like a tanner in the sun. His knife lay beside him, the blade dull in the shade of his belly.

I stood over him, trembling and gawking at the bloodletting from my own little hand holding a piece of gnarled pine – and I was amazed at myself, amazed and afraid and proud. I couldn't figure out where it had come from – the nerve to swing and to smack him on the head. And down he had gone, like he was human after all, no harder to kill than a goat. A two-pound hammer between Ferdinand's eyes wouldn't have dropped him so easy as I had dropped John Beaver. Why, he just fell over so fine and awful, let the light go out like a burned-out bulb, instead of coming after me like a nightmare should, in which no matter how hard you swing you can't do him in. Not John Beaver. Three good smacks on the noggin and he was nice and neat, snoring Redman deep in his throat, one of his eyes a bit open and glazed, looking like a pinto bean. It was better than anything I could have imagined. My bony arm dropping the likes of him!

Mamie picked herself up and stood next to me, gawking at him. "K-k-kilt him," she whispered.

"No, no," I protested. "He's still breathing. Didn't kill him."

She wiped the blood from the back of her neck and looked at her hand. "Blood," she said simply, and then she kicked John Beaver in the leg. He groaned. She kicked him again.

He blinked, and his eyes rolled into focus and looked at us. "Ehhh, shit, what'd you do to me?" he said. He raised himself on his elbows and spit, then looked at the stick of wood in my hand. "Ehhh, goddamn, you hit me with that, Fartbottom?"

"I'm sorry, Mr. Beaver," I said.

"Gonna be a damn sight more'n sorry. I'll get you in jail for this. I'll see they send you to reform school, you fuck'n delinquent. And you too, Mamie. Bonnie and Clyde come again, that's you two." He jerked his head at her and blood spattered down on his chest. "What's this? Goddamn, I'm, I'm b-bleedin! Lookit all the blood!"

He sat up and held his palms out to us full of blood. Blood was trickling slowly down the sides of his head and neck and blotting itself on his shirtcollar, turning it from blue to maroon. "Where's my goddamn knife?" he growled. "Where's my goddamn knife? I'm sure as hell gonna kill you sonsabitches, makin me bleed!" He found the knife next to him and started to get up with it in his fist. I felt the pine club being jerked from my hand. I saw Mamie raise it and bring it down across John Beaver's head – whump! blasted him, slaughtered him. I just knew that no mortal head could stand what Mamie had done to his. He wasn't gurgling Redman anymore. His eyes were fixed and bulging, like she had driven them halfway out of their sockets – startled white balls on which the pupils looked like two dark beebees.

"Boo's-eye," said Mamie proudly.

"I think he's dead this time," I told her.

"Yaay, Kritch'n," she answered.

"He's dead, he's dead, he's dead," I could hear myself repeating over and over. I had never seen a dead person before. And I didn't know, but I think I wanted something more profound from Mamie than "Yaay, Kritch'n."

But that was the extent of her concern. She tossed the club in the air and took my hand and led me off to the river. She stuck her head in the water and washed. I did the same. The water was wonderful. I wetted my hair and the back of my neck, splashing with both hands to keep the cool running over me, and finally my brain got clearer and I saw what we had to do. I wiped my eyes on my shirtsleeves and looked at the sun edging the tops of the trees.

Mamie came over and picked me up. "Drowd'n man," she cried.

"No, no!" I pleaded. "Please, Mamie – no!"

She stopped, lowered me into her arms, and cradled me like a baby, looking down into my face, blinking slowly, expecting God knows what. For just a second it did seem possible to play. The air smelled inviting, insects bumbled about, birds argued, flowers stretched in the sun, and the river mumbled along like a shy old man. Nothing had changed. Everything had changed. There beneath it all, crushing dandelions and timothy, was dead John Beaver, dead as a doornail, with four good bumps on his head, three of them given to him by me. I was a criminal, and so was Mamie.

"We got no time for drowning," I told her. Her breath was on my face. It smelled of earth and sweet blood. I asked her to put me down. She stood me upright and petted my arms. Her head was cocked to one side, puppylike, smiling and smiling. "Oh, Mamie, you got to understand," I said. "We're in deep shit, Mamie."

"D-d-dip shit."

"We got to get away from here."

Her voice matched mine, low and solemn. "Yaay, Kritch'n."

There wasn't a whole lot of thinking to do whether to stay or go. My mind kept turning over the sound of the club hitting Beaver's head. I wanted to get away from that sound, far away. I had visions of the police coming for me, putting handcuffs on me, leading me away in chains, while my parents and brothers and sister watched, dumbfounded. Christian Peter Foggy getting hauled to prison, locked up for the electric chair. It was wrong to run, but the dream-power of my fears and visions wouldn't let me stay. Prickles of the itch to run rose up my legs and back. Every voice in me was screaming, "Go!" And I was powerless not to listen.

R*unning* A*way*

Mamie followed me out to the highway, where the Beaver pickup was, but John Beaver had the keys in his pocket. We needed those keys, but I couldn't make myself go back and touch a dead body to get them. I told Mamie she would have to do it. I told her to get his money too. She didn't seem to mind. Off she went at a jog, while I sat on the fender to wait. The whump of pine on Beaver's head echoed in my ears. I talked to it, told it I was sorry. I said it was an accident, a pure little accidental murder happening before I could even begin to understand what I was doing – and the difference between just killing the man or putting him to sleep for a while was probably no more than a pound, or maybe even less than an ounce. Besides, Mamie did it, not me, not Christian Peter Foggy, who was a good boy and should be sent home to do his chores and to get beat up by his brothers. He should be let out of something that wasn't his fault. He should be let to go home and slip the Surge milker on a cow and stand there in the peaceful barn, knowing that such nightmares as the whump of the pine on Beaver's head didn't happen in the hearing of such a dull old farmboy. Only the double pulse of the milkers was real, and only the cow standing quiet, letting her milk down, was real; only the farm and the family were real. But I couldn't convince the whump. It pounded over and over inside my head, until I saw the patrol car come up the highway and pull in behind the pickup and a cop got out and the door slammed behind him. "Oh no," I thought. "What else can happen to this poor boy today?"

He straightened his gun on his hip and his smoky-bear hat on his head and strolled over to me like I was an old buddy of his.

"So what's up?" he said. "Need a tow?" He was a moonish-looking kind of man, with deep, dark eyes like craters and an *o* for a mouth and tiny pockmarks all over his nose and cheeks. His face was round, and he had a small, round stomach that pushed out over his belt. His shoulders pushed forward, and they were round too. He put his hand on top of the pickup and patted it.

"Just waiting on somebody," I said.

He kept patting the pickup like it was a friendly dog. "You got yourself an antique here," he said.

"Yeah, it's pretty old," I answered, trying to smile and keep my voice from shaking.

"What year is it?" he asked.

"Well, I don't know, I guess."

"Must be a thirty-nine or a thirty-eight."

"Yeah, it's pretty old," I repeated.

His *o*-mouth made a smile that looked a bit horsey, like he was going to open up and neigh at me. "So, you're waiting on somebody," he said. "I thought maybe you were broke down."

"Nope, just waiting."

"Yeah, I thought maybe you needed a tow truck."

"Nope, my friend went into the woods there to take care of some business. You know?" I chuckled so he would know what I meant.

"Oh," he said, bobbing his head. "See a man about a dog."

"Yeah, I guess so."

We laughed softly at the idea. He had a nice laugh. I liked him, even if he did have a funny mouth.

"So how's the old truck run?" he asked.

"Runs good. Belches some, but runs good."

"Yeah, built 'em to last. So, you from round here?"

I told him who I was and where I lived and that I was going to sell my pickles up in Iron River.

"You're one of the Foggy boys, huh? Yeah, I know your dad." He paused and looked around. I had the feeling he wanted to wait and see who was going to come out of the woods. "So, how is your dad?" he asked.

I said everything was fine with Pa, just the same as ever.

"You know, I haven't seen him in six or seven years. He used to come in and shoot the breeze with us at the feed store, the one that closed down. I remember Jacob Foggy all right. Does he still quote Shakespeare all the time? Everything was 'rotten in Denmark' with him and 'Horatio knows more in heaven than earth,' or something like that."

"'There are more things in heaven and earth, Horatio, than are dreamt of in your philosophy.' Pa still says it all the time."

"Yeah, that's it. What the hell's that mean, anyway?"

"Pa only knows," I answered, and we both laughed. We both knew that Pa was an odd sort of fellow.

"You read that stuff?" asked the cop.

I told him I liked to read but I wasn't up to Shakespeare. I liked Jack London. "I'd like to be able to write like him, only I'd write about cows instead of dogs."

"You'd write about cows?" His eyebrows arched in surprise.

"Cows are more interesting than people think."

"God," he said laughing, "you're Jacob Foggy's son all right. Listen, I'll tell you what, I was raised on a farm over near Turtle Lake, and I'll tell you what, I've never come on anything dumber or duller than a cow, except maybe some hunters I've known who don't know a cow from a deer. But no, I'll tell you, nothing much can touch a cow for plain stupidity. I've seen cows that would let you beat them to death before they would step across a sixteen-inch barn gutter, and I've seen some that would leap across the same gutter like an antelope, when really all they had to do was take one tiny step across. In fact, I've seen them do dumber things than that."

"But geez," I said, interrupting him, "you got to understand their thinking. You got to be able to think like they do, and then they don't seem so dumb. You know, they just get confused easy. If you ask them to step across a sixteen-inch gutter for the first time, they got to decide if they can maneuver all that big belly and four legs and tail over it without some part falling in and causing a thousand pounds' worth of grief. Things look different to cows than they do to people. Why should they trust us to get them across? Half the time we're petting them, half the time we're smacking them. If I was a cow, I sure wouldn't trust a human. Would you? How many'd you send to Packerland when you were farming? Every cow knows someday you're going to do something bad to her, shoot her or send her to Packerland. Every cow knows it in her bones. Heck, to them maybe Packerland is just across that sixteen-inch gutter, know what I mean?"

The cop had his lips pressed together in a smile. "Jacob Foggy's written all over you," he said.

"We got a cow at home," I told him. "Her name is Sugar. And you know what? I'm never ever going to ship her – never in this life. She's mine, and she did sixteen thousand pounds in her first lactation. She's just like a pet dog, following me round and wanting me to pet her all the time. I've told her I'd never ship her. I've been there, to that slaughterhouse. That place would turn your feelings to concrete if you stayed there long. I bet if everybody had to see those cows smelling blood and slobbering on the floor because they're so scared, we'd all be vegetarians."

"You a vegetarian?" he asked. I had to admit I wasn't, though I wanted to be, but it was hard to be eating meat all your life and then just stop. "I'll tell you what," he said. "You can show us all the slaughterhouses you want and all the cows smelling blood and slobbering on the floor, and you can show us that guy with the explosive rod rapping those cows between the eyes, and you can show us the cows falling dead and getting hauled up by their heels and gutted and skinned and shipped off in trucks to Safeway. And you know what? We'll still eat 'em. It's nothing. Hell, I'm a cop, and I've seen enough to know that if it wasn't for the law keeping us from each other's throats, we'd kill and eat each other. It's real thin, Christian, this idea of civilization. You grow up and become a cop and you find that out real soon. Anybody could be a killer. You could be a killer." He patted me on the shoulder. I swallowed hard and felt my knees tremble. Then he said, "I wish you and Sugar luck. I hope you never do have to ship her, but soft-hearted farmers end up as shovel-jockeys, you know."

"I don't care. I won't ever ship her," I said.

It was about then that I heard Mamie coming back. She was stomping herself a path through the brush and the trees and making a racket.

"That must be your friend," said the cop, looking over his shoulder.

"I guess so," I answered, my ears feeling on fire as Mamie came into view. I could see even from across the road and with her five yards deep in the woods that she had blood on her forehead. She waved as she saw me. I jumped off the fender and ran to meet her. Out loud I said, "Mamie, what happened to your head? You fall down?"

I met her at the edge of the trees. She shook the keys at me and said, "G-g-got'm."

"Shhh," I whispered. "Cop, cop, cop." I added that he would hang us if she didn't keep her mouth shut. "You got John Beaver's blood on your head. I got to make a reason for it." So I pretended to examine her head and at the same time I dug my thumbnail into her and made a little cut. She didn't flinch.

We went back to the pickup and the cop asked us what happened. He took out his handkerchief and dabbed Mamie's cut to stop the bleeding.

"She walked into a low branch," I explained. "She gets clumsy."

"I've done it myself," he said. "When I was a boy, one winter I was out cutting wood and I walked right into the end of a branch. It knocked me cold, tore up my mouth so bad I had to have my teeth pulled and some plastic surgery. This is scar tissue all round my mouth. I can't open it far like most people. It pulls into an *o*. Yeah, I know what a branch can do. Come on, I'll give you a bandaid."

We went to his car, and he took out a first-aid kit and put a dab of iodine on Mamie's cut, then covered it with a bandaid. As he put it on, he seemed to suddenly notice that he was looking up at Mamie. He checked where he was standing, like to see if he was in a hole. "My god, you're a hell of a big girl," he said. "You two aren't brother and sister, are you?"

"Nosir," I told him. "She's my girlfriend."

"You mean she's . . . like your . . . like you take her on dates?"

"Sort of. We don't go on real dates exactly. But I like her."

"Yeah, well," he scratched his hair and smiled his round smile, "you don't look like any couple I ever saw, but what the hell, love is blind, right?" He felt her arm and whistled. Then he seemed embarrassed and his tone turned apologetic. "Well, she is kind of pretty," he said.

"She's a hard worker," I told him. "You should see her in the field. She's beautiful then."

He winked at me. "Hey, she's all right. I like the way she looks. She's different."

"She makes up for what I'm short on. Nobody wants to pick on me when she's around."

"I bet they don't," he said, and he burst out laughing so hard that Mamie and I couldn't help but join in.

When we had laughed ourselves out, he said he had to get going but he hoped to see us around and he wanted me to tell my dad hello from Ken Maydwell. He got in his car and pulled out, then stopped and rolled down the window. "Tell your dad I get lonesome for Shakespeare," he said, and he drove off laughing.

THe was a nice guy, but I was happy to see him go. We waved him down the road, then got in the pickup and went in the opposite direction, heading west. We took Highway 13 until it ran out and then just stayed on the backroads, zigzagging around but still going west mostly, almost all the way to the Minnesota line. Before we got there, the radiator boiled over and we had to stop. The truck sat on an uphill, surrounded on both sides by miles of woods. There were no farms or anything else, just lots of thick trees and underbrush.

As we sat there, smelling steam and leftover John Beaver, I started wondering again what on earth I was doing. I closed my eyes and leaned back and said to myself, "Be a dream, be a dream, be a dream." Then I opened my eyes and there was Mamie hovering over me, her whole face beaming with happiness, and I knew that whatever might be a dream, Mamie wasn't. She was a sight – gappy-toothed; eyes like floating islands of sky; chopped-up, frizzy red hair; shoulders that filled the entire space from dashboard to seatback. All I could do was think of Orphan Annie and Paul Bunyan having a daughter and naming her Mamie.

"Mamie Bunyan," I said to her.

Her mouth was working away, like it was on rubber hinges. She was trying to tell me something important. "La-la-la," she stammered.

"Easy, Mamie," I coaxed. "Say it slow."

Instead she pointed to me, then pointed to herself.

"Yeah," I agreed. "You and me, Mamie. You and me. But what're we gonna do now? You got any ideas?"

She hit the dashboard with her fist. The whole truck rattled and yelped from the blow. A dent appeared in the dash, and a lightning crack ran up the windshield. "G-g-g – !" she hollered. "G-go!"

I turned the engine over until the battery ran down. Then I coasted backward and tried to pop-start it, but when I let the clutch in something snapped underneath and the shift lever flew into neutral and wouldn't go back into gear. While I was trying to force the lever, grinding the gears to dust, the pickup was still rolling backward, and it slowly rolled right off the gravel and into a ditch. Mamie's side came up and hung in the air for at least ten beats of my heart before finally rolling on over slowly, like it was unsure if it was doing the right thing or not. Mamie fell on me, and the sound our heads made coming together reminded me of the whump of Beaver's head. I saw a black hole full of white dots. I heard Mamie giggling. She was giggling and slobbering on my cheek and saying, "La-la-la," her mouth working on my skin the way a snake's mouth works to swallow an egg. Finally she got out the words *love* and *Kritch'n.* She loved me.

I opened my eyes. The steering wheel floated in front of me, the dash rose and fell in waves, and everything was shimmering and shifting from one to two to one to two. I blinked a dozen times but couldn't make my eyes focus. My head was throbbing. Mamie was crushing me, slobbering on me, la-la-la-ing me. It occurred to me that the pickup was on its side and that gas was probably leaking onto a hot manifold, which could start a fire and fry us both. I even imagined for a second that I heard it whoosh into life, but then I figured out it was just the steam hissing up against the hood. It was making things all misty in front of us. I closed the eye that Mamie was drooling on and everything got steadier. Loving me some more, she began digging her fingers into my ribs, which about drove me crazy. I could have killed her,

I was getting so mad. I screamed at her to knock off the bullshit and get off me and get out of the truck before the whole thing blew up. She stopped la-la-ing long enough to ask me if I was scared. "Keer'd, Kritch'n?" she said, her voice tender. I told her I was scared, yes.

She stood up, popped open the door above us, and jumped out like she had springs in her boots. Then she reached back in, grabbed me by the ankle, and lifted me out as smooth and easy as if I was made of marshmallows. She gathered me up in her arms and jumped with me to the ground. For a few seconds, she couldn't help herself – she had to hug me half to death and kiss the bump on my forehead. But finally I managed to groan loud enough to make her stop. Gently, like I was her baby, she carried me off into the woods.

"Oh, dammit all," I told her, as she bundled me along, "this is no game, Mamie. I'm not your baby boy. We're both in bad trouble. They put kids like us in prison. It's just deep, bad trouble. It's just awful. We're in it over our heads."

"Shush," she said, soothing, me. "Shush, shush."

I felt the soft spikiness of a pine branch sweep across my side, then another, and then Mamie laid me down within a tent of evergreen boughs. A huge tree, like a steeple above us, blotted out the sun and let in a soft gray light. I lay beneath it on dry needles, my head throbbing with pain.

I thought to myself right then that I was going to have to ditch Mamie. I'd never be able to stand her. Tinkerbell with a gland problem. Then I thought about the way she stuttered and stammered her la-las to me until she finally managed to say "love Kritch'n," and about the way she cradled me, kissed me, and the sense of safety in her arms. Fact was, I cared for her more than I wanted to, and I knew that without her I would be turning in circles like a calf roped to a tree. For better or worse, it really was Mamie and me. I moaned aloud at the thought. She patted my arm to comfort me.

I eased into sleep and sometime later had a nightmare: John Beaver was sitting on my chest, hitting me over and over with the butt of his knife on the same sore spot on my forehead. "Skin you, Fuggy, skin you, Fuggy," he kept promising. It took a million stars to wish on to make him quit. Damp night air was cool on my face. The smell of pine was thick. Mamie held me spoon-fashion against her, a leg and an arm wrapped over me. The rise and fall of her chest against my back was like an endless wave in a powerful river.

The No-rain Dance

I opened my eyes and saw pine branches like giant fans spread out over me. It seemed like the tree was breathing in my face. It had a cool breath that smelled piny sweet. The forest all around was alive with singing birds. I lay quiet for a while and just listened to how pretty they sounded. Then I started thinking about home and how worried my folks would be. I knew I'd have to get a hold of them and let them know I was okay. And I thought about John Beaver, but I couldn't take thinking about him long, so I forced my mind away and onto something else, namely Mamie. I didn't know where she was. I got up and looked for her. On the ground next to the tree was my sack of cucumbers, but no Mamie. I got a bit scared and started yelling her name as loud as I could. Soon as I yelled, all the birds quit singing. It was suddenly so quiet it made me shiver. I felt like I better not call out again. Then in the stillness I heard a sound far off, a machine of some kind clattering away out toward the road.

I went toward the sound, and soon it got louder. Along with it I could hear the voices of men trying to make themselves heard above the roar of a truck.

"Let's turn her by hand," one of them was yelling.

"That's that blasted gear again. Listen to the sucker clatter," said another somebody.

"Let's just get her over by hand, and then we'll work on that goddamn cable, Red. Come on."

"Well, shit, Tony, it's probably gonna pop my back out again. I'd ruther use the cable."

"Come on, Red. These guys'll help us."

"Aw well, what the hell. Let's do it."

I got within sight and stayed behind a tree to watch. There were four of them. Two of them wore greasy overalls and baseball caps. The other two were from the Highway Patrol. One was Ken Maydwell. The four of them grabbed the pickup and started rocking it. Then one hollered, "Heave!" and they bulled it back over onto its tires.

"Shit, I told you we could do it, Red," said the one called Tony.

"Let's get the cable working," Red said back to him. "I don't want to try and push this dog up to the road."

They went to work on a tow truck that had been sitting there the whole time with its engine roaring and the sound of a loose gear coming from beneath it. Ken Maydwell reached inside the pickup and pulled out a slip of paper. He showed it to the other cop and said, "It's John Beaver's all right."

"Big surprise, huh?" said the other.

"Looks like they rolled backwards and over. Wonder why?" said Ken. "Maybe the old antique just quit on 'em at the top of the hill. Yesterday the boy, Christian, told me what a good truck it was. Sure didn't get far, did they? What you think happened, Frank?"

"I think they're not going to come back and tell us. That's what I think."

"If John Beaver was after you, would you come back?"

"Hell no! I might be a dumb cop, but I ain't crazy."

"God, what a pistol. Mad! You ever see a guy so mad?"

"He was foaming at the mouth! You know, that bastard should of never lived through what they did to his head. You and me'd be dead as doornails. That old boy has the skull of an ape."

Both of them laughed a bit. Then Ken said, "You see he had an *x* on his head? The kid must have hit him one way, then hit him the other and made a neat little *x*."

"*X* marks the spot, haw haw! It was hard to keep a straight face."

"He'd've killed you if you'd laughed!" roared Ken.

"Funny though, wasn't it? And he kept saying, 'I'm a-gonna kill that kid! I'm a-gonna kill that kid!'"

"I heard him. He means it too," said Ken seriously. "We'll be after him for murder one of these days. Mark my words."

"Yeah, that kid's in trouble, more ways than one."

"He was an innocent-looking little pecker, Frank. Real tender-hearted about cows going to slaughter. Beaver must've done something pretty rotten to make a boy like that pick up a club and clobber him. More than what Beaver said about him plankin his daughter and getting caught, huh?"

"What did he call him, a little poontang monster?"

"Poontang monster, yeah!"

"Haw haw haw, poontang monster. I don't know how I kept from falling on the floor."

"And when he said, 'Who'd a ever thought a punk like him could down a Beaver,' that was funny too."

"Brave little shit."

"He had to be. That man's a grizzly. You see his arms, Frank?"

"Crush that boy like straw."

"I'll be the first to say it – God help that boy if that bastard gets a hold of him."

I didn't listen to any more. My whole body was trembling. My heart was beating like I had run a mile. John Beaver was alive! I wasn't partners in murder after all! But then I thought about what they'd said about him crushing me like straw, and I wasn't sure if I was thankful not to have killed him. Why couldn't he at least have amnesia? That would have made it so I could go home. The way things were, I was between a rock and a hard place – John Beaver or jail. Assault with a deadly weapon. Fingerprints and a record. Why me? Why me? I just wanted to go home and mind my own business. I wanted cows to milk and hay to bale. And I wanted eggs and potatoes for breakfast. Damn the Mamie Beaver!

I uncupped my ears and heard the driver of the tow truck yelling down to Ken and Frank that they should come help Tony pull on the cable. They climbed onto the road and all three of them started yanking away, while Red gunned and gunned the engine and pulled on the PTO lever, trying to get the gears to match.

"It's no go, Red!" yelled Tony.

"Hang on! Hang on!" Red yelled. "Gimmee a chance!"

Just then I heard the gears clunk into place. "You did it!" cried Red, and with the engine still roaring he threw another lever, and the cable suddenly started flying from the reel. None of the three men was expecting it. Backward they went, tripping over each other and going down in a heap, tumbling like boulders back down the ditch, yelling, "Ooh, oww, ooh!" all the way to the bottom.

Red jumped out of the truck and hollered, "Oh shit, fellas!"

"Goddamn you, Red!" said Tony, shaking his fist.

Red was looking down and trying to apologize, saying he didn't know how he could've been so stupid. But then he suddenly slapped his knee and burst out laughing. He apologized for laughing, but he just couldn't help himself and laughed some more. He started howling and pointing down at the three of them and slapping both his legs and screaming that he was sorry but they should've seen themselves skittering.

"Shut up!" said Tony, which only made it worse for Red, who finally had to sit down and hold his stomach and moan.

I was giggling myself and so caught up in what was happening in front of me that I didn't hear Mamie coming up behind. When she put her hand on my shoulder I jumped like she'd stuck me with a pin.

"Whoa, Kritch'n," she whispered.

"Where you been?" I asked her. "Look at this." I pointed to the men below us.

She grinned ear to ear. "F-f-funny," she said, pointing.

"Let's get out of here," I said. I took her hand and led her back through the trees. We came to the pine and crawled back under its boughs. Mamie brought the cucumbers with her.

"What are you doing with those?" I wanted to know. "You can't eat 'em, Mamie. They're too young, too bitter."

She looked at me a second and shrugged, then folded the open end of the gunnysack under, and smoothed the cucumbers down and lay with her head on it for a pillow.

"Well, it's a hell of a lumpy pillow," I told her, but when I put my head on it, I found it wasn't half bad.

We lay there for some time and could hear, far off, the tow truck hauling Beaver's pickup out of the ditch. Then things got quiet and the birds started singing again. It was normal woods, but I was in the dumps, sorely depressed. John Beaver was alive and wanting to kill me. The law wanted to put me in jail for assault. I was hungry, and the bump on my head had started to hurt again, and I was lying next to a retarded girl who thought pillows were made of cucumbers. I didn't see how things could be any worse. I put my hands over my face and started to cry. Mamie turned on her side, put an arm around me, and hummed in my ear.

"Get off me, you nut!" I said, throwing her arm back and sitting up. "Anybody ever tell you you're crazy?"

"Uh-huh," she answered.

I grabbed a stick and shook it at her. She looked at me with curious eyes; then she smiled. It was like a baby smiling at me, and I couldn't stay mad. "Dammit, Mamie, what the hell you want?" I asked her.

With her hands she cleared a place in the needles. Then she took my hand and pressed the stick down until it touched the dirt. She scratched lines back and forth and said, "Aaa-yay-yay, bee-yee-yee, cee-yee-yee."

I made her let go of the stick, and then I wrote *h-o-m-e* and said to her, "Home."

Her mouth worked around the word and out it came clearly, "Home." She took the stick and made letters below mine. Satisfied, she sat up and pointed to her letters. Then she pointed to herself, then at me, and said it again, firmly, "Home."

"Yeah," I answered. "You and me – home."

"Hippa-weee!" she cried, jumping up and pulling me with her and having me mount her back. And off we went through the trees, deeper into the woods, Mamie neighing and hollering and moving with that powerful, dobbinlike grace that I had come to expect from her, dodging trees and leaping ferns and barely swishing through the sudden grasses, until we came to a clearing and a large pond. She set me down and held out her arms to the sky, wide to embrace it, like an Indian praying to the Great Spirit.

I looked around. There was a low spot behind us, edged with a thousand tangled vines full of huckleberries, blue and purple and black. The sun's rays hit the jagged leaves and made them shine and made the huckleberries glow invitingly.

Mamie pointed at a rabbit-run coming down to the water. "Bunbuns," she said, grinning.

"That'd be good," I told her. "But how we gonna catch 'em?"

From her farmeralls she pulled John Beaver's buck-knife, then a coil of shoestring rawhide, then an old, leather sling, and finally a fistful of kitchen matches. She shook her treasures at me. I could see the possibilities all right.

But for the moment the berries would do. I hurried to the vines, stripped handfuls of fruit, and crammed them into my mouth. After a few piggy minutes I slowed down and started getting picky. The dark purple berries were the sweetest, so I went for them, plucking them off and popping them into my mouth one by one. My palms and fingertips turned blue, and I could feel the syrup sticking to my lips and chin. It was huckleberry heaven. I ate and ate, squishing and swallowing and feeling like a free animal being natural, a mouse or a squirrel or a bear cub, chomping vine-food and living on the land and no one to tell me what to do, no Pa, no brothers. Not half-bad, I told myself, and suddenly I realized that I wasn't so anxious to go home anymore, and I was even anticipating what might come next. We would catch rabbits and fish, pull up wild onions, eat roots and berries, sleep and wake when we wanted to, lay in the sun, swim in the pond, make the best of what was necessary. Me and Mamie, a home.

When I turned round to see where she was, I found her naked in the pond. Her arms were elbow-high in the water, her body bent forward just enough at the waist so her nipples were under water. She was fishing. In her face was an intense concentration, like she had switched her brain to automatic so it could decide when it would be best to make a move. Her head was down, her eyes fixed and unblinking, as the curious bluegill came to nibble at her nipples and fingers. She kept so still she seemed to be one of those marble statues that some long-ago Greek or Roman had carved, except for the wild-red, hacked-up hair blowing back and forth in the breeze. She was made to fit nature – chunky, solid, wide-shouldered, with just a touch of softness to keep her from looking too much like a man.

The juice on my face and hands had dried like tar. I wanted to wash, but I didn't dare go near the water and scare the fish. So I sat and rested my chin on my knees and waited. By the time Mamie finally threw the first fish on shore, I was all but asleep. The noise woke me, and I saw the surface of the water broken into a bubbly wave with a fat bluegill on top flying toward me. I caught it and tapped its head with the butt of Beaver's knife. I sliced its belly neatly and cleaned it out. Before I was done another fish landed at my feet, then another. Mamie was in stride and had the timing down. Within an hour or less, we had a fire built and a dozen fish to fry. We draped them on green sticks through the gills and gave them no more than five minutes over the flame. They were tasty, flavored with smoke and ash, and the flaky meat pinched from the bones just sighed away in our mouths.

Mamie sat beside me, smacking her shiny lips and licking her fingers and burping profoundly. Round the nipples of her breasts were tiny reddish blue marks where the perch had come to feed. I asked her if they hurt. She shook her head no and told me in her stammering way that the fish just took tiny bites, but we took big bites, we eat 'em all. She laughed at her joke, spraying my face with bits of fish.

"Jesus, Mamie," I said, "You ever learn any manners?"

"Nup," she said, giggling, and to prove it she broke wind.

I had to laugh, and I gave her one right back. We thought we were pretty funny all right. We went crazy with laughter and ended up rolling on our backs and howling the way Red had howled when he tumbled the three guys in the ditch. Farts are funny when you're a kid.

After a time we sobered up, and then I got around to asking Mamie how it was she knew to angle for fish that way with her nipples and fingers. She tapped her head and said, "Smma-art."

"I'll say it is," I answered. "Damn smart. I'd have never thought of it in a million years."

"Yup," she agreed, patting her head in pride.

Then she told me in her slow way that raspberry leaf makes good tea, that fireweed tastes like asparagus and dandelions taste like spinach. She said you catch frogs with forksticks, but you only eat the legs. Slingers are for picking birds off limbs, and snares are for the bunnies.

"Mamie," I said when she finished, "your Pa don't really know you. He told me you were too stupid to make it on your own in the woods. He said I had to be helping you all the time. How come he thinks you're so dumb?"

She raised her eyebrows and looked at me like I knew the answer.

"Maybe you've been fooling everybody, huh?" I said. "Maybe you're so smart you figured it was best to play dumb. Is that it?"

She tapped her head again. "Smma-art, Kritch'n."

"Yeah, you might be ignorant, but you're not stupid."

"Aaa-yay-yay, bee-yee-yee, cee-yee-yee," she said and gave a heavy sigh of sadness.

"Forget that," I said. "Learn this." And I took the knife and carved her name in the sand. She was happy about it. She got down on all fours, her butt shining in the sun, and using her right elbow and forearm to brace herself, she carefully wrote *Mamie,* and again *Mamie,* and again and again. I rocked back on my heels and watched her. She was like some bulky animal come out of the water to scratch and grub in the dirt. She was what the caveman might have been some long years ago – heavy bone and heavy muscle, thick neck and hungry mouth, and a round face with a forehead climbing out of darkness, growing broad and shiny like the new earth, and seeing things fresh in time that way, seeing things through eyes wondrous large, like the eyes of an owl. I wished she were smarter, that she could really learn from me. But I figured that inside her brain was probably a constant fog that could never be cleared away. I told myself it was better to just take her for what she was, pretty smart in some things, after all.

I took a nap, and when I woke the sun was far west. Mamie was a hundred feet or so downshore, still printing her name. I stood and looked at dozens and dozens of *Mamie*s lined up in a row at the water's edge. The wind had picked up and was sending in little waves that had rubbed out a *Mamie* here and there and were lapping at the rest. The sky was clouding over in the southwest and tumbling toward us. The smell of woods and water was getting heavier in the air – a sure sign of rain. I called to Mamie, telling her we had to get back to our tree cause a storm was coming. She looked up at me, her eyes funny, narrow and curious, like she didn't know quite who I was.

"It's me," I said. "What's the matter with you? What you looking at me so funny for?"

She stood up, her knees and shins and forearms covered with damp sand. Her eyes blinked slowly at me, watching me like a lazy wolf. The wind played through her hair. Her mouth drooped, and spit had hardened on her lower lip in ridges white like foam. I swallowed hard as I stared back at her and thought, *God, what a creature! What a scary thing it is.*

"It's gonna rain," I told her.

"Yup," she answered dully.

"We better get back to the tree."

"Hiya," she said.

"Let's go."

But she just stood there, pinning me with her eyes.

"Mamie," I said, nervous as hell, "what you doing? You're looking like a nut. You got foam on your mouth. Hey! Wake up!"

"Hiya, hiya, hiya," she began to sing. "No-rain, no-rain, no-rain." Her voice was deeper, almost mannish, and there wasn't a trace of stammer or stupidness in it. "Hiya, hiya, no-rain, no-rain . . ."

I was jumpy and I was scared, but I was fascinated too. I watched her lift one leg, then the other, slowly singing hiya no-rain, hiya no-rain, as she started to dance. Her body quivered and jiggled in time to the beat of her hiya no-rain song, her breasts bouncing, her huge thighs leaping and red with blood-gorged muscle. She held the knife over her head pointing to the sky and passed it back and forth from one hand to the other. Then she tossed it straight up, twirling it so the point flashed like a mirror going round. And she caught it when it came down, and all the while she sang, "Hiya no-rain, hiya no-rain, hiya no-rain."

She started turning in circles, stomping her legs harder and harder and moving toward me. I watched her coming and tried to read her face as it whirled round and round, but I saw nothing there to give me any confidence. I wondered if she was having some kind of fit, or if she had just finally gone off her rocker and was going to kill me. Fuwump, fuwump, fuwump! Her feet sounded on the ground, closer and closer, until she was close enough to smell. A smell rose from her, a musty smell like damp cow. I tried to wave it away, but it was all over me. I didn't know how I was supposed to act, so I began to move my legs up and down with hers and to sing hiya no-rain too. Her face was inches from mine; her breath blew into my mouth as she sang the hiya no-rain faster and louder and faster and faster. We were dancing together, thumping the sand, packing it harder and harder with the pounding of our heels, and all the time the hiya no-rain covering my face and I breathlessly screaming it back at her.

It went on and on and on, and Mamie's face became lit with an inner fire. Her skin was wet pink; her eyes gleamed like blue flame. Her mouth drew back until it nearly seemed to touch her ears (hiya no-rain), making her look more than anything like a fat, pink-faced frog grinning at me. She jabbed the knife up and up and up. I was sweating buckets and gasping for air. My legs got heavier and heavier. Lumps of lead couldn't have been harder to lift. I couldn't sing hiya anymore. My throat and chest burned. My thighs trembled. The knife poked above my head. Finally I dropped like a rag and tried to say, "Don't," to Mamie as she came for me, her legs parting, leaping on top of me, straddling my waist, her huge bottom grinding me into the sand. Her mouth covered mine, sucking my breath away. I felt like I was going to throw up. Then the working of her hips and the wetness coming from her sliding up and down on me made the lower half of me feel stronger than the upper half. Mamie felt it too and put me inside her. And I stared up into her eyes amazed and full of wonder.

She unglued her lips from mine and sang softly, "Hiya no-rain," into my face, slowing the pace, drawing it out, moving her hips in time slower and slower, until she finally stopped for a moment, just rocking and crooning and sighing above me. Then she was moving faster and pounding harder, picking up the pace until she seemed to be a blur in front of me. The knife came down, slicing the sand beside my head. Mamie's nose touched mine. She shuddered like an earthquake. Her eyes closed, and mine closed too. When I opened them she was smiling and looking like her old, silly self.

"Hiya," she said.

I moved my lips.

"Yaay, Kritch'n!" she hollered.

"Yaay, Mamie," I whispered.

She pulled off of me and grabbed my hand. "Drowd'n man," she cried, dragging me to the water and throwing me in. The shock of the water woke me up. I let her toss me around and rescue me a half-dozen times, till she was ready to put me back on shore. And there we lay in the wind while the water dried from us, and I asked Mamie what was it all about, the dancing and singing and "doing it." She pointed to the sky. It was cloudless, the storminess gone.

"No-rain dance."

"To make the rain go away?"

"Yup."

Then I thought about what John Beaver had asked me – if Mamie had done the no-rain dance with me – and I understood a lot more about him and how he felt about her.

"You really think it works?" I asked her.

"Yup, Kritch'n." She pointed to the sky again.

"Where you think the rain went?"

She cocked her head and thought for a moment. Then she fingered her belly.

"The rain's in there?" I asked.

She shook her head yes and rubbed her belly round and round. "Hmmm," she hummed, "hmmm." Then she cupped herself and rubbed some more and raised her fingers to her nose. She sniffed. "Ahhh," she sighed, smiling hugely and thrusting her fingers in my face.

"Ick, Mamie," I cried. "You're gonna make me barf." I rolled away and stood up. She giggled and came after me, chasing me with her fingers. I ran into the water and shouted, "Drowning man!" And on she came like a tornado. And for the rest of the daylight left, we played drowning man.

Nightmare Beaver

Sleep and wake, sleep and wake, and the sun went from there to there and the moon went from this to that, and I notched a tree and planted sticks to know what day it was, but one day I didn't know anymore and I found out that it wasn't important. It felt nice not to care about what day it was, or what time, the hours filled up by themselves without clocks. I just slept and woke and fed my face. It was hot, even the nights didn't cool off much, and I was always sweaty. The pond was the best place to be, just floating on the surface, if Mamie would leave me alone.

Though the woods were full of game, we had practically no luck with our snares. We did catch a skunk one day. We would have let him go, but he wouldn't let us near enough to cut the noose. He overpowered us and kept us out of his air, so we finally gave up. The next day he was dead, and we could smell him on the wind.

One day we searched the shore all the way round the pond, and on the opposite side we found an old campsite. In the ashes we dug out a rusted grill and a big tin pot with a hole in it about the size of a nickel. We also found some cans with jagged lids peeled back for handles. We cleaned them out and used them to drink from and for boiling raspberry-leaf tea. The hole in the pot we plugged with clay and baked hard in the fire.

Once we got a routine going, we were able to make up all kinds of recipes, not just fried fish and huckleberries. Our favorite was a soup of dandelion greens and wild mustard with red squirrel. Squirrels were nearly as plentiful as bluegill perch, and Mamie was deadly with her sling, whirling it overhead round and round in a blur, the humming of it like a nest of bees, and then fwap! letting it go and plucking a squirrel off a branch as easy as plucking an apple. The Wisconsin woods seemed so easy and helpful with their bounty. And even the mosquitoes weren't bad, as long as we stayed in the shade or close to the campfire smoke or in the water. Our arms and legs did get bitten now and then and itched a lot, but we figured out that a coat of mud did wonders. Some days we would smear it on each other head to toe. It would dry and become light gray in the sun, so we looked like Africans, the ones who go naked and chase giraffes. Or maybe we didn't look that good, but we felt like they did – like mighty hunters, mighty free. At night we always took a bath. We slept beneath the tree on fresh leaves and pine needles piled high.

When we weren't hunting for food or playing in the pond, we pretended we were in school. I was the teacher, of course, and Mamie the pupil. With just a little help she could write her first name. I would scratch *Ma* into the sand and she would complete it. Then I would write *Bea* and she would complete that, only sometimes if she didn't pay close attention the letters would come out backward. I worked on her speech problems. They baffled me. It seemed almost like there were two Mamies. One stuttered and stammered and took forever to get a sentence out, her mouth betraying her, wrapping itself all up in a word. The other was quick to say a perfect hippa-we, or sing a hiya norain, or blurt out a sentence like, "The water's gray today" – which she said once in a normal voice that wasn't *her* normal voice, that had me stuttering and stammering trying to ask her what she was doing saying something that sounded like a real, live human being. She looked at me like I was crazy.

One day I heard her down by the pond yodeling, "Odelaytee tooo, odelaytee tooo," and listening to the echo come back. It sounded good, and it gave me an idea. I would teach her a song.

I sat her down facing me, and I sang to her, "Your cheat-ing hea-art will tell on you." She watched me as I went through my whole Hank Williams imitation, bobbing her head in time and smiling. Then I told her to sing it with me. I started out, "Your cheat-ing hea-art will tell on you," and she answered, "Odelaytee tooo." Actually, I thought we sounded pretty good. But it wasn't what I wanted. I tried some other cowboy songs I knew. To each of them she wanted to yodel. Then, more in frustration than anything else, I sang something Pa always liked to sing in the barn when we were milking cows – "Fig-a-row, Fig-a-row, Fig-a-row!"

When I finished, Mamie threw her head back and burst out in a voice that sounded exactly like my own, "Fig-a-row, Fig-a-row, Fig-a-row!"

"Perfect!" I cried. "Wonderful!"

"Fig-a-row, Fig-a-row, Fig-a-row!" she repeated, throwing my voice right back at me.

"This is it!" I told her. "This is how we're gonna get you talking straight. We're gonna sing you straight."

We got interrupted then by the sound of one of our snares going off. We jumped up and ran for it and found ourselves a rabbit jumping at the end of the noose.

"By god, we finally caught one!" I said.

Mamie lifted the rabbit up and slipped the noose off its head. It was a cottontail, brown and white, about half-grown. Its nose was twitching, its legs were trembling, its eyes were wide as quarters. Mamie felt along its belly and back.

"Poo," she said, shaking her head.

"It isn't much," I agreed.

"Nup nup."

We looked at it together. "Heck, we got plenty to eat," I said.

"Kritch'n eat the bunny?" she asked.

"Nup nup," I answered.

She put it down, and it ran back into the woods. We stood awhile staring at the close columns of trees that kept the woods in permanent shades of purple and gray, and I for one imagined what they would be like in winter all ghosted with snow. I asked Mamie what we were going to do when summer was over. "Things'll get a lot tougher then," I added.

"Yup," she said, looking at me like I had the answer.

At that moment I decided I had to do something about our situation. I had two dollars and fifty cents in my pocket, which was what Mamie took off John Beaver. I knew it would pay for a long-distance call home, if I could find a phone. I told Mamie that I wanted to call my folks. I told her to stay right by the pond till I got back.

"Why call'm?" she asked.

"Because this isn't the Garden of Eden, and my pa will know what we should do."

I went out to the road and headed west for a mile or so, till I came to a town called Plato. WELCOME TO PLATO read an old sign, VACATIONLAND OF THE NORTH – ACCOMODATIONS – LAKE HARMONY – FISH! – BOAT – SWIM – HIKE – STAY WITH US AWHILE FOLKS! The letters were faded. The sign itself hung at an angle. Someone had written at the bottom in messy black letters, *Contemplate your navel, Soc.*

Plato was a tiny place, a wrinkle in the road. It had a café and general store–gas station combined. The gas pump out front was one of those old pump-handle kind. The store was painted a tombstone gray. Some boats were down by the water, overturned, the keels gone to peeling from too much sun and rain. A half-dozen tiny cabins lined the shore. The door to one of them was open, the curtains drawn back. I could see the silhouette of a man as he backed away from the window. The bumper of his pickup barely peeked around the corner of the cabin.

I ignored him and went into the store, where the same kind of laziness sat on the shelves as sat on the boats and cabins outside. Dusty cans with yellow labels, three loaves of Wonder Bread, Twinkies and chocolate cupcakes, different kinds of candy bars, a refrigerator with a round cooler on top that buzzed, and walls covered with wooden signs that said things like HOME SWEET HOME IS WHERE YOU HANG YOUR HAT, LOVE IS A TWO-FOOT MUSKIE, DEATH IS LIFE'S WAY OF TELLING YOU TO SLOW DOWN, A CONTENTED MIND KNOWS PEACE AT ANY AGE, and WHERE THE HELL IS PLATO WISCONSIN? Unlit signs advertised beer and soda pop. Behind a counter lined with toadstool seats sat a bald man with a beard. The beard was white and long enough to rest on his chest. He stroked it like he was petting a cat. Behind him was a grill and a coffee pot and a glass case that was supposed to have pies and cakes in it but was empty. I sat on one of the toadstools and asked the man if I could have a hamburger and a cup of coffee. He jumped a little and shook his head at me like I had said something crazy. His eyes were sad like a hound's.

"We got no meat," he said. "Got no buns. Got scrambled eggs."

Eggs sounded fine to me. He lit the grill and scrambled two, put them on a plate, and handed it to me along with a cup of coffee. I handed him a dollar. He stuck it in his pocket and sat down. The eggs tasted like air. The coffee felt like it was eating my tongue. Raspberry tea was a gourmet drink compared to Plato's coffee. And I was out a dollar.

"You got a phone I can use?" I asked.

"Out of order," he answered.

"Where's a phone I can use?"

"What you want a phone for?"

"Never mind," I said. It wasn't any of his business, but I could see he was a nosy fellow who wouldn't leave it alone. So to change the subject, I asked him if things were always so quiet in Plato.

"Quiet as dust on a door ledge," he answered. He petted his beard and told me there was no justice, just lots of cutthroats. Fancy places up in Millacs and north of Duluth sucked vacationers out of Wisconsin, so only the oldest of the old-timers came to Plato anymore, those with a vision of the way resorts should be, those who didn't like no cluttered-up nature.

"I sort of like it here," I told him. "It's peaceful."

"Peaceful as a cave," he agreed. His voice was moody. "Lots of quiet, lots of time to sit and think. All the time to ask yourself who you are and what you're doing in the backwater of the world. Time to wonder about how smart you've been chasing rainbows all your life. Time to wonder if maybe less appetite and more spirit would have given you a better sense of yourself. It's how you get when you're old. Body gets dull, so all you've got left is your mind. Can't even enjoy a woman anymore, and you make the best of it and say good riddance. Now you can get peaceful inside; now you can work on the inner light. Be all right if you had no memory of what women looked like naked and what they feel like when you slip them on. Don't let anybody kid you, sonny – old age is like being chained up in a pit, and the pit is you staring at your memories like shadows on a wall. And nobody comes to see you because you talk too much. You know you're talking too much, but you can't help it. You see an ear and you've got to bend it. But nobody comes to listen, because people like gadgets. No gadgets here. Just old age and a grumpy old man who won't shut up. Fish don't even bite, they're so bored. Had one customer since I opened this spring. He's out there now. All he does is prowl the woods all day. Won't even rent a boat. He buys beer and potato chips. Ugly mug. Tells me to shut up when I try to talk to him about things. Hate people who won't listen." He was talking to the walls as much as he was talking to me. I got up to look around.

I walked in and out of the shelves. The bald man raised his voice. He wanted me to know about solitude, that it was tolerable if you didn't think about long legs and soft lips. What you had to learn was meditation, to go into a trance for hours and probe the mysteries of life, and to come to understand that only a decent set of ethics made life worth the trouble, because the mysteries never talked and nobody ever knew anything but that nobody ever knew nothing.

While he rambled on, I decided to buy some candy bars to take back to Mamie. I picked some up, but then I thought about only having a dollar and a half left because the old man had charged me a dollar for eggs and coffee. So I said to myself that I ought not be a fool, and I stuffed the candy bars in my pockets. I stuffed Twinkies and cupcakes into my shirt. The man was talking about dying being just the best sleep ever and getting to wake up and talk to your long dead friends, so what was to fear about dying?

His voice followed me as I scooted out the door. I could hear it all the way to the edge of the store and beyond, like the last hum of a dying wind. I took the Twinkies and cupcakes out, tore the wrappers off, and stuffed them into my mouth, a bite of one, a bite of the other. Sweet and gooey. I ate them all gone and licked my fingers.

"Crazy old coot, ain't he?" said a deep voice at my shoulder.

I bent over and threw up.

"Hey hey, you shouldn't eat so fast, Fluffynuts."

"You been waiting," I said, my voice trembling.

"Yeah, I been waitin and waitin. I been stayin in that mouse hole ever since they found my truck. You sure fucked it up, Foggy; crushed the whole side in. I can't even get the door open. But you can't kill it. It still runs. Pinched the hole off in the radiator so it hardly leaks at all. It'll get us back home, buttface."

"I couldn't get it in gear. It rolled backwards. I'll pay for the damage, I promise, Mr. Beaver."

"Oh, you bet, you bet," he said. He spit a brown gob on my boot and patted my head hard. "I knew you wouldn't be far; you'd be comin round here. Fuck, I'm such a smart bastard I almost scare myself. This is the only store for miles. You had to come sometime, right?"

"Yessir, you're smart."

"Yessir, you bet. I want you to see somethin." He took off his cap and bent so I could see the top of his head. "Looka there." A lump ridged his head from front to back. It had scabs down it that formed an *x*. "How many times you hit me, Foggydoggy? Two times, three times? A hundred times?"

"Three times, Mr. Beaver."

"Three times. And you got such puny arms. How can a pair of broomsticks like yers knock out a bull like me?"

"Well, what if Mamie hit you one?"

"Now that would make some sense. But don't try to be puttin the blame on her. Mamie's trained not to hit her pa. She wouldn't raise a hand to me."

"Nosir."

"You just hit a lucky spot."

"Yessir, a lucky spot."

He put his cap back on, then ran his thumb in an *x* over my head. "Right there, *x* marks the spot. Boom!"

"Please don't kill me, Mr. Beaver," I begged.

"Don't quiver so," he said. "I wouldn't hurt yer little Fluffyass for nothin in the world, cause you gonna tell me where you stashed my Mamie, ain't you, slimecock? You gonna tell poor John that." He took a handful of my hair and yanked it.

"Oh yessir, you bet," I told him.

"Just be honest with a fella."

"I will. I'll take you there. Right now."

"Ahh, good boy. I knew you was a good boy. I said over and over that a boy like you would want to help a griefin man to get his lovin dotter. I miss that girl. She's all I got, you know?"

"Yessir," I answered, bobbing my head in time with the tugs of his hand pulling my hair. "You can have her. She's too much trouble for me. I didn't want to leave you out there with your head broke. I was all confused. I'm glad you came. I'm glad it's over."

"I know you are. Yeah, yer homesick, and I'm Mamiesick. Go on now, let's show me the way."

I had him follow and started off fast, but he caught my shoulder and told me to slow down a mite.

"Since you conked my head, I been some unsteady. I get dizzy. You might of kilt me, you know? But us Beavers are known for havin hard heads. I'd be molderin in the grave right this minute otherwise. Ain't you glad I got a Beaver head? Wouldn't you feel like a lowdown skunk if you'd kilt me?"

I promised him I'd feel like a skunk, and I told him how sorry I was, how bad I felt that he had dizzy spells on account of me and my puny arms, and that I was thankful he wasn't molderin in the grave. I told him that it had been miserable for Mamie and me, which cheered him up. He thought she would probably be ready to go home. Home probably wouldn't look so bad. Come back to her poor papa that missed her real bad. She was everything to him since her mama died. Then he talked about Mary Beaver, his wife, and bragged how she could do it all. She milked cows and cleaned the barn, cooked dinner, gave birth to four dead babies and got up and went right back to work. Except when Mamie, the fifth, was born. Mamie was too big and damn near killed her ma. Mary had to take the whole day off. He told me how she died hauling on a stuck calf that was coming back legs first to get born. Mary died trying to get it out, burst her heart, and he'd lost the cow and calf too. He'd hauled them all to the woods, skinned the cow and wrapped Mary in the hide, and buried her next to the Brule, right up in the corner of Jacob's land, buried her beneath a big birch tree, put her there in 1952.

And as he told about it, I remembered 1957, when my brothers and I found Mary Beaver. We had pulled her up with the stump of that birch tree. She was full of roots and worms – Mary Beaver reduced to a bunch of bones wrapped in a holstein hide. I remembered, too, that at the base of the stump he had carved her name and below it carved

Gud Werker. We reburied her in the same stump-hole and never put a plow near her, though we cleared the rest of the land. And soon she had stray alfalfa creeping over her grave.

In the woods he had to let go of me to follow. I took him on the east side of the tent-tree where Mamie and I lived and through some thick maples, where, within shouting distance of the pond, we had set our largest snare. It was tied to a bent maple, a wide ring of rawhide on the ground, big enough to snatch a coon or a mink or a coyote. Whatever tripped that rawhide would get to stand on its head awhile. As we got closer, my head was whirling like an unbalanced flywheel. I felt like I was going to have a John Beaver dizzy spell myself. He was so close I could feel his breath on the back of my head. As I stepped lightly around the snare I said, "Look there, John Beaver, a grouse!"

"Where?" he said, looking up. He stepped true, and out of the corner of my eye I saw him suddenly jerked hindsideto. Whoosh, the anchor stake popped in the air, and Beaver hit the ground like a big bladder singing, "Yiiiii!" as up he flew. I turned around and there he was, head tapping the earth like a yo-yo. His eyes looked like wobbling blue jello. He was caught by both legs, but the tree was straining to keep him up. I could hear it groaning, and I knew there was no time to waste. But as I started to leave, John Beaver hollered, "Wait! Wait! Foggy, yer my buddy. Come on, son, what about the poor papa come for his dotter? I got fifteen bucks, Foggy."

I squatted so I could look him almost straight in the eye. "You really think," I told him, "that I would turn Mamie over to the likes of you?"

He blinked hard, like Mamie did when she was trying to make sense of what I was saying. Then his eyes fixed on me and he spit. His face got redder than it already was. He called me a name that said I did things to my mother. I stood up and kicked him in the stomach, which was a mistake because he grabbed my ankle. I fell on my back and started kicking with my other foot and yelling, "Help! Help!" He grabbed my other foot too. We looked at each other. It seemed to me that he could eat me if he wanted, start with my toes and stuff me in his mouth until I was all gone. I screamed, while he grinned wickedly and pulled me toward him. He had me by the knees when I felt a pair of hands grab me under the armpits and start pulling the opposite way. I saw Mamie's face over me. She and John Beaver strained against each other. The tree was cracking. Beaver was swaying at the end of it, his hands locked on my legs, while Mamie dug her heels in and pulled backward an inch at a time, pulling me, pulling him, pulling the tree to its breaking point. And finally, with a loud crack it gave way, splitting and spinning at the same time as Beaver hit the ground and let go of me. Mamie and I tumbled away from him and tumbled ourselves right back on our feet and took off.

We skirted the pond and headed in the direction of the road. I looked over my shoulder and saw him coming. He took his two hands and made like he was ripping something apart. Up one hill and down another we ran, whizzing through the trees on a course we had never run before. We came to a ridge that someone had once dynamited for ore. It was a steep hillside of powdered red earth. Mamie leaped off the edge and I followed after. We were making little hops down, the fine dirt burying us up to our ankles each time we landed, and after about the third hop I couldn't get my feet out in time, so I pitched forward headfirst right into Mamie. Down we went the rest of the way in a heap. Red dust rose around us and clogged us, getting into eyes and ears and nose. I was blinded. I couldn't breathe. And I thought any minute I would fly apart like a broken wheel, bones flashing in the air like lost spokes.

When we finally did hit bottom and rolled to a stop, we heard John Beaver above us. I cleared my eyes and looked just in time to see him coming over the edge – a great, black giant with arms outstretched against the sky, legs churning like a bowlegged ape as he leaped upon us. Then he went over too, belly first, cap flying ahead of him, his face shoveling deep in the dirt, until his head looked like a plowshare making a furrow. When he hit bottom, he lay for a few seconds, still as the dead, before raising himself up, spitting and coughing and shaking his head, where blood seeped through the *x* of the scabs and dirt. He cleared his eyes on his sleeve and looked up at us.

"Mamie," he said, coughing and spitting, "whyn't you just come on home now? Ain't this awful what yer doin to me?"

Mamie didn't need to think it over. "Booshit!" she yelled.

We took off again, Mamie whooping back at him, "Booshit! Booshit!" as he was struggling to get back on his feet. When we reached the next line of trees, we stopped to check his progress. He was up and muscling his way after us. But he had slowed plenty, a hitch in his run made him look like a pegleg. His face was powdered with red ore. He had jammed the cap back on his head so hard it made his ears fold over like tiny wings. He kept rubbing his eyes with his fists and swearing at us, threatening the electric chair and life in prison and tacking our hides to the barn. He went on and on, while Mamie said, "Booshit!" and I made fun of him for being so old and slow and stupid, old pegleg can't catch nobody!

Finally he paused and threw his cap down and howled. He pulled out a knife – a pig sticker, with a long thin blade curving like the tooth of a rattlesnake – and he made gestures of gutting us and slicing morsels off and popping them into his mouth. I told Mamie we had better make tracks. We left him, still carving the air with his pig knife, and we stretched out a lead that would take him time and lots of limping effort to overcome.

Fishing up Things

We were huffing and puffing by the time we reached Plato. Then we stood in the middle of the pavement, looking right and left, up and down the road, not knowing which way was best, so we turned round in circles a few times and looked at each other for fault or idea. Then I remembered about the boats, and I told Mamie to come on because I knew what to do. She followed close, her hand on my shoulder, letting me lead her like she was blind. We came to the boats and chose one that looked like it might not sink – though they all looked pretty worn out, the way they were beached belly-up and coated with dried mud and moss and paint that looked like it had acne. We turned the chosen one over, grabbed the oars underneath it, and off we went out on the big water, Mamie rowing toward a jaw of land that would hide us from any eyes searching from Plato or the road. I watched the little town fade away bit by bit until I couldn't see it anymore. Of course, I knew John Beaver hadn't limped along fast enough, so we were safe from him anyhow.

Mamie kept the oars stroking smooth as oiled pistons as we shot out over the lake but never far from shore. There were plenty of land spits and shaggy trees to cover our way the deeper we went. I was getting calmer and calmer, and I settled back on my elbows and told Mamie we had ripped that bastard a good one this time.

"Ripped'm, Kritch'n," she agreed, grinning at me like a happy bear.

"Oh gee, that was something," I said, thinking of the way he had nosedived down the hill. "Didn't he look like a hog coming down that hill? Didn't he look like a hog rooting up a pasture?"

"A h-h-hog in a p-p-poke," she stammered, giggling as she went.

"A clay poke, burying his nasty self in a clay poke."

"Snuff snuff, achugga chugga."

"That's it! That's just what he sounded like!" I laughed so hard at the snorting I ended up in the bottom of the boat, and Mamie kept me there, going "snuff snuff, achugga chugga" till it just wore me out. Then we let ourselves drift on the water, and it was sure nice, but it didn't last too long.

A voice came hollering at us from the shore. "Hey, what the hell you doing out there?"

For just a second I thought John Beaver had caught up, but just as quick I knew it wasn't so. The voice wasn't old enough. It sounded more like Cash's or maybe Calah's voice. But, of course, it wasn't either. I looked over the rim of the boat and saw four guys about my age, standing at the edge of the water in their birthday suits and gawking at us. They looked at us. We looked at them. Seconds went by, and it was so quiet while we all decided about each other that I could hear water lapping at the side of the boat and the creaking of the oarlocks as the oars rose up and down with the waves passing by.

"Who're you?" said the same voice, finally.

"Who're you?" I asked back.

"I asked you first, kiddy," said the voice. I narrowed in on it. The face attached was dark and hard-looking, Eskimo-Indian type, with a wide chin and thin lips, high, shiny cheekbones, and black, slanty eyes. He had long black hair, the color that people would call raven. He was bigger than the rest of the boys. Everything about him was bigger: his chest and shoulders were big like Tarzan in the movies, his arms bubbled up and down with muscle, his legs looked like logs somebody had carved into the shape of thighs and calves. Next to him the other guys looked like bread dough.

"Who're you?" he said again. The tone of his voice said he meant to have an answer.

I told him who we were. "This is Beaver, and I'm Foggy," I said, trying to sound tough.

He smiled at me and nodded, which made me feel a little better. And before we could say anything else to each other, a great eagle came by, swooped down over the water, and caught itself a fish.

"Golly, see that?" cried one of the boys.

"Neat as shit," said another.

"Speared that sucker," yelled the third boy.

The hard-faced one said it gave him an idea. He said they should make spears and go spearfishing and the hell with fishing poles. "Yeah!" they all agreed. Then he called out to us, "Hey, Foggy Beaver, come on in and let us use your boat! What you say? We'll have a fish fry."

The others urged us to come on in, too, and it seemed about the best offer we were likely to get that day. I said to Mamie that maybe we should, but she was already pulling for shore. We weren't far off, and Mamie's back was to the boys, so as we came in, it wasn't until almost ten feet away that they saw she was a girl.

Someone yelled, "Hey, she's a broad!" And somebody else said, "Humping holy shit!" Then two of the boys ran toward a camp close by, where they had their tents, and the other two dove into the water.

The hard-faced boy had jumped into the water, and he surfaced and asked me why the hell I hadn't said that that big boomer was a girl. "You seen we was naked, for Christ's sake," he added.

"I thought you could tell and you didn't care," I answered. "She don't care. Shoot, we get naked all the time, right Mamie?"

Mamie jerked her head up and down fast. "Uh-huh," she answered back. "N-n-n-naaked boys. I l-like'm." She jumped out of the boat and in five seconds had her own clothes off and was in the water, diving around like a dolphin. The other two came back from camp wearing swimming trunks. They were both skinny boys like me, with twiggy kind of legs and flat stomachs and stringy muscles up and down their arms.

"Look at that, Arty," said one to the other.

"Hey," said the one called Arty, "nice bum, huh?"

"Kind of too big," the other fellow said, holding his arms out about twice the size of what Mamie's hips were. She stopped butterflying and came in close enough to shore to stand up. The boys all held real still as she showed them her front.

The little guy in the water next to the Indian said, "Oh golly, are those neat. Ain't they neat, Mike?"

"Mike, Mike," said Arty laughing. "Look out, they'll smother you!"

Mike was the Indian. He told Arty, "Fuck you, Arty."

"Fuck me? Fuck her, Mike." All the boys except Mike laughed like devils at that.

"She's a goddamn holstein," said Mike. "She's bigger'n me." He looked into Mamie's face and went, "Mooo, mooo, hey, bossy, bossy, bossy, moo."

"M-m-moo," Mamie answered, sounding just like him.

I thought I better warn him not to push his luck with her, so I told him she was solid muscle, and big as he was he wouldn't have a chance if he made her mad. He scowled deep at me. His eyes took fire. "Oh yeah? You don't know Mike Quart, kiddy." He turned to the little guy next to him. "Does he know Mike Quart, Timmy?" he asked.

"You don't know Mike Quart," said Timmy, grinning and sneering at the same time. He had crooked teeth and tiny, mousy kind of eyes.

"I don't need to; I know Mamie Beaver," I told them.

Mike laughed ugly. "Yeah, what about you? You a tough fucker too, kiddy?"

"Tough enough, but I'm not looking for trouble." John Beaver's bloody head flashed in my mind and gave me some comfort, because I was pretty sure this fellow Mike Quart couldn't have a head any harder. I glanced around and saw a heavy piece of wood behind me. I edged on over to it. The kid named Arty saw me looking at the wood. He came near me and said in a whisper not to do what I was thinking, because Mike Quart would kill me.

"He can try," I answered, but I really wasn't in the mood for what was going on. I wanted to be friends and just take it easy.

Arty winked and told me I was all right. Then he turned to Mike and he said, "Hey, I thought we was gonna spear some fish and have a fish fry, huh?"

"That's what I said," said Mike. "But that kid ain't showing respect." He had come halfway out of the water, flexing his muscles at me and scowling in such a fierce way that I felt like saying, "Umgawa, caveman, me friend; no hit friend." It's no exaggeration to say he looked like he belonged squatting in a cave eating raw meat.

"Come on," said Arty, waving him off. "He told you he ain't looking for trouble."

"He better not be. I'll break him in half."

"Break'm in half," repeated Mamie. "Break'm in half." She was looking at Mike Quart.

"Jesus, she gives me the creeps," he said. He looked closely into her face for a few seconds. Then he looked away and went off toward camp, mumbling something I couldn't make out.

When he was out of earshot Arty told me not to push my luck, that Mike Quart had a quick trigger and nobody in Iron River would even dream of getting him upset. I told him again that I wasn't looking for trouble. Mamie had come out of the water and stood next to me, cocking her head back and forth like a puppy. I thought I would impress Arty, so I said to Mamie, "Mamie, don't you stomp that fella unless I say you should, okay?"

"Yaay, Kritch'n," she answered.

"Promise me now."

"P-p-p-p-p."

"Okay, that's all right, that's a promise." Then I patted her on what Arty called her bum and told her to go catch us some fish for dinner. She reached over and swatted my own bum hard and giggled about it. Then she went off into the water and dangled for fish.

The boys, except for Arty, had gone over to the camp, and now they came back with long knives lashed to popal poles. As they saw Mamie dangling her fingers and breasts in the water, her fingers wiggling slowly, her breasts wiggling with each lick of the waves, they wanted to know what she was doing. When I explained it, I saw they didn't think much of that kind of fishing, except the one guy who turned out to be named Wes. He said he knew a fellow who could catch them now and then with his pecker. Then Wes went off to search the inlets, and Mike Quart and the little one named Timmy got in the boat and let themselves drift offshore.

I sat down to wait for Mamie's fish, and Arty sat next to me.

"We got good fishing poles," he said, "but Mike gets a hair once in a while to do stuff like this. You just got to go along, if you want to get along."

"Yeah," I said, "I got brothers like that."

"Kick your ass, do they?"

"Since I was knee-high to a heifer." I looked at Mike. He was tossing doughballs of bread on the water. Timmy was leaning back, peeling bark off his spear.

"The thing with Mike," Arty was saying, "is that we know his moods and all, but we can still get in trouble with him. We've all growed up together over in Iron River. He's always been a stinker, but he'll stick up for you too. I mean, if you're his friend, he'll fight for you. Once four guys was on me and he jumped right in the middle of them and saved my ass. Man, they wanted no more of me with him around." Arty chuckled. "He's a mean shit, let me tell you."

"Mamie isn't mean," I said. "But she could break his neck if she wanted."

Arty sized her up. She was half-bent over and the deep power of her shoulders and back was obvious. "But he's so mean," Arty answered, "that while she was reaching for his neck, he'd be cutting her throat. He'd use that knife. I know he would. Make sure she doesn't mess with him while you're here."

I told him it wasn't Mamie's way to mess with anybody. She was gentle and not too bright and never hurt a guy unless he made her.

"She's retarded, ain't she?" said Arty.

"Yeah, she's retarded all right," I said.

He wanted to know about us. Where did we live? Who were our folks?

"No place much. We're just orphans, just drifting."

"No kidding." His eyes were bright with interest, but I didn't think I should go into it. He looked like a guy you could trust all right – a clean-looking guy with bright red cheeks and clear blue eyes, honest eyes – but I didn't want to take a chance.

But he kept after me, wanting to know why we were orphans and had we really lived in an orphanage and then did we run away from it or what? He told me he had run away from home once, and it had been rough. He had gotten as far as Ashland and was starving and was cold and scared, and he slept in a church and froze the whole night long, but he didn't want to go home anyway to a stepfather who would bash him and cuss him out, who made it pretty plain that he didn't want no ten-year-old kid around. Then a cop picked Arty up and the running was over, because right when his mom came he told her how the stepfather beat him and cussed him when she wasn't around and how the black eyes weren't from fights at school but from the stepfather's fists. Arty had lied to her because the stepfather had promised him worse if he didn't. And she believed him and cried over what he had gone through. That was the end of the stepfather. And now he had a new one, and this guy was swell, not jealous at all, a quiet guy, a talker. When Arty had turned sixteen, the new stepfather bought him an old '49 Chevy.

After his being so open with me, I felt bad that I was lying to him, so I let it out about how John Beaver was to Mamie, how he beat her and screwed her and used her like a mule. I told him I was rescuing her and that there was no way I would ever go back, as long as she was alive and he was waiting for her like a wolf. Arty clapped me on the shoulder and said I was a goddamn hero. He said, too, that we could hide out with them, and if John Beaver found us we would all throw the sonofabitch into the lake and drown him.

"What about Mike?" I asked. We both looked out at him. He was standing in the boat, his spear held high and ready. He was grunting and growling and saying through his teeth, "Come on, you fuck'n fish, come on, you fuck'n fish."

"Yeah, I guess he doesn't like you," said Arty. "But I think you can get around him. Mike really isn't too bright, you want to know the truth, and he's easy to manipulate if you just give him a few strokes. Know what I mean? Just make like he's the boss of everything, and you know he's the boss. And if he's got an attitude, just back off and don't say nothing. Anything can set him off, see? You don't want to stare him in the eye. He's like a German shepherd when you stare him in the eye – take a bite out of you, it's a challenge to him. And don't mumble when you're talking cause he takes it that you're talking about him. And if you're talking about him, he takes it that you're saying something bad, which is mostly true. Don't stand in his way when he's walking somewhere; that's not showing respect. And don't smile if he ain't smiling; smiling's the same as laughing at him. You don't want to ignore him either. But then, you don't want to pay too much attention to him either. You don't want him centering on you. When he gets it in his mind to center on you, he just goes on and on until he finds some reason to nail you one. If he centers on you, sometimes it's better to humph around and fake like you're mad at whatever's making him mad, even if it's you; talk against yourself – say, yeah you sure hate it that you're so stupid, or you hate your stupid face or your stupid freckles. He'll agree with you, but he probably won't pick a fight. That's what Timmy does, the little guy in the boat. He does it all the time, makes like he and Mike are fired up about the same thing. Mike says, 'Timmy, you sure are a snot-faced little bastard.' And Timmy will say right back, 'Yeah, I know, Mike, and I hate it. I look in the mirror and I want to throw up.' You notice the strawberry on his ass? It's a birthmark. Mike makes fun of it – tells him no broad is ever gonna want to fuck him with such an ugly ass. Timmy says he knows it, and that's why he's learning to be a jerk-off artist. He's got a twin sister, Karen, and she's got a birthmark too. Hers goes from in back of her ear to down across her tits. Mike's always saying that Timmy rubbed his ass on her in the womb and ruined her tits. But she's cute. She looks a lot better than him. Real shy though."

Arty paused and watched while Mike stabbed the water but came up with nothing and screamed, "Fuck!" across the water, then turned round and kicked Timmy, who was dozing and not too interested in spearing fish. Timmy sat up quickly and said, "We need some cheese, that's what."

"Fuck you," said Mike. "Make some doughballs." Which Timmy did and threw them on the water.

Arty was very serious and he said, "Once I told Mike he was full of shit for saying that Karen wanted him to suck her pears. She's not like that. But he's never wrong. I was mad at that, though. I like Karen, and she don't deserve to have him making fun of her birthmark. I said as much to him, and then he centered on me and started chipping away. And finally he said I should know that he'd been fucking Karen since she was twelve years old. I lost my head and slugged him in the stomach, like hitting a block of wood, and that's no bullshit. But that's probably the thing to do – just smack him as hard as you can, and then when he hits you just lay down and pretend he knocked you out. It's what I did. If he sees he's knocked you out, it gets him rid of his attitude. He mellows out. He'll even pat your face to wake you up. He's not always rotten, just now and then. His old man's like that too. Now, he's a waste, let me tell you. He was a bad sonofabitch at one time, but too much beer, and man, he's got a gut like he's pregnant. He used to kick Mike's ass all the time, but now Mike kicks his. That's one thing I'm never gonna do – I'm never gonna beat my kids, never. It could make them turn out like Mike, and then what?"

We heard a splash and saw a fish flying off Mamie's hands. It was a healthy walleye, about a foot long.

"Would you look at that!" cried Arty, jumping to his feet. "That's that damndest thing I ever saw. Did you see her?"

"They'll start coming faster, now she's got them in and curious." I acted calm, but I was excited seeing him so excited.

"That's amazing. Man, I'll tell you, I'm impressed all to hell."

Mike was looking in from the boat, where his jabbing spear hadn't come up with a thing. "What's this shit?" he hollered.

"Didn't you see her?" asked Arty. "She threw this wallie right out of the water. Watch her."

I caught the walleye and put it on a string. Arty knelt close to the water and caught the fish as they came out. In a half hour or so, we had strung walleyes, trout, and perch, enough for all of us. Mike had given up trying to stab his own. He sat in the boat, drifting and looking sour at what Mamie was doing. Wes came over and sat by us. He said that Mamie was pretty good all right, but he swore there was a guy he knew over by Golden Valley in Minnesota who dangled his pecker in the water and caught the fish who came to bite it. This guy would hold a net underneath the water and swoop them up. Wes said he once heard of the guy catching a muskie better than two feet long.

"Think if that would've chomped his pecker," he said, laughing.

"Who the hell you talking about?" said Mike, calling out from the boat.

"A guy named Elmer Farr."

"Sounds like bullshit to me."

"Hey, he's famous in Golden Valley, Mike. Just go on down there. They'll all tell you – anybody knows him."

"Yeah sure, a guy's gonna take a chance like that. Yeah sure."

Wes shrugged his shoulders and went back to watching Mamie. A dozen or so fish were circling around her legs and fingers and breasts. Some were darting in, taking little nibbles out of her.

"They're biting her tits," said Arty. "Ouch, don't that hurt her?"

"She's tough," I told him. "They nick her, but she don't care."

Mike threw his spear in the bottom of the boat, picked up the oar, and started paddling in. "Yeah, well she's as fuck'n crazy as fuck'n Elmer Farr from fuck'n Golden Valley, that's what!" he yelled, and then he cut the boat close to her and pounded the oars hard so all the fish scattered. But we had enough by then, so it didn't matter. I told Mamie not to coax them back, to come on in and help clean them. Mike jumped out of the boat when it nosed into shore, and he grabbed the string and pointed to the ones he wanted.

"This one, this one, and this one," he said, claiming three of the best walleyes. "And the broad's gonna clean 'em and fry 'em for me, that's what. How you like that, kiddy?" He looked at me. I felt Arty giving me a soft nudge in the back.

"Mamie likes to do stuff like that," I told him.

"Fuck'n-A." He dropped the fish and headed to camp.

Timmy climbed out of the boat. "Fuck'n-A," he repeated. "Better do a good job too." Then off he went after Mike.

Mamie stood by, ankle-deep in the water, water dripping down her shiny skin and past the minute bites that showed up reddish purple around her breasts and bright red on her fingers and thighs. She had followed Mike Quart with her eyes as he pointed out what fish he wanted. Then, when he was through and had stomped off, she picked up the string and pointed to the same ones and said in a voice weirdly like his, "This one, this one, and this one . . . fuck'n-A."

Wes, Arty, and I laughed. Wes said if he closed his eyes he would swear it was Mike Quart talking. "Was that a trick she has?" he wanted to know.

"She's damn good," said Arty. "I mean real good. Does she do other ones? I seen a guy on TV do Burt Lancaster and Kirk Douglas. Can she do them? I'm not kidding, this guy was great."

"Yeah right, I remember that. He did Cagney too," said Wes.

"That's the guy. Can she do any of them?"

I said I didn't know, that I hadn't heard her do impressions before, except a sort of impression the time I sang Figaro, Figaro, Figaro and she sang it back to me, sounding like I was singing to myself. But otherwise I hadn't heard her. "She's supposed to be too retarded for that," I said. "Though sometimes I wonder about it."

"Maybe she's got a gift like that," said Arty. "Lots of stupid people are like that. Mostly, they can do math in their heads."

Wes was staring at her, grinning and scratching his head. "This one, this one, and this one . . . fuck'n-A," he said, trying to sound like Mike but not sounding like anything more than maybe a sick frog. Then he said, "Look at her, guys, don't she make you feel like laughing? She's so funny-looking."

"Neat funny-looking," said Arty. "I like her."

Wes said he liked her too, but she sure was funny-looking – so big, like a big plastic doll with big strong tits and eyes like marbles dipped in the sky and hair like red electricity. "She'd make a book, if I could write," he added.

"Electric hair, that's a good one, Wes," said Arty.

"Like red electricity."

He was right, and I looked at her like she was a plastic doll that was naked and had marbles for eyes and frizzled hair, and I found myself laughing right at her, and the other two joined me, pointing at her and laughing. And then she made us laugh more because she did her Mike Quart imitation again: "This one, this one, and this one . . . fuck'n-A." She laughed to see us laughing. The four of us got a little crazy, practically screaming in each other's faces, till we could hardly even draw a breath. When it was over, we slapped each other on the back like old friends should do. I was really comfortable with them then, and I think they were comfortable with us just as much.

We finally got together over knives and cleaned and scaled the fish. We built a fire and fried the fish in a big black frying pan the guys had that would take at least three fish at a time. They had butter, and salt and pepper too. It was a better way than what Mamie and I had had to do. The first ones we fried were Mike's. He was sitting away from us in front of his tent, he and Timmy. He was drinking a can of beer and now and then letting Timmy have a sip from it. "Look at that fuck'n moose," Mike said, curling his upper lip. "You fuck her you better tie a board to your ass."

"Hey, Mike, come on," said Arty. "Look what she's doing. She's cooking your food here."

"Yeah, well hurry up, moose. They don't have to be so fuck'n done, you know. Fish ain't no good when they're too fuck'n done."

"Then whyn't you fix your own?" said Arty. He was muttering.

"What's that, Artsy-fartsy?"

"What's that yourself, Mike. Fix your own, I said."

"That's brave, Artsy-fartsy. I like that. But I want her to fix my suffering fish, that's what. She thinks she's so fuck'n smart, catching 'em like that."

"Smma-art," Mamie agreed, tapping her forehead.

"Goofball cunt," said Mike.

"Smma-art, yaay, Kritch'n?"

"Very smart, Mamie. Smarter than anybody knows," I said.

"Smart as Elmer Farr," said Mike. "Get them fuck'n fish over here."

Happily, Mamie put the fish on a paper plate and started toward

Mike with them. As she walked she looked over at me, maybe to see if I was watching her – I don't know – but as she did, the fish slid right off the plate and under her feet. She crushed them, all three, almost as if she meant to. She turned and looked down, and the fish were mush. "Whoops," she said.

"Whoops?" yelled Mike. "You fuck'n moron!"

Mamie bent over from the waist and started putting the broken pieces back on the plate. As she was picking here and there and trying to clean off the dirt and pine needles, she broke wind – a huge baa-room roared out of her naked rear end. She kept on, like she didn't even notice. There was a dead silence as we stared at Mike, who was staring at Mamie's backside, his little slanty eyes wide as they could go, his mouth open, his chin quivering.

Finally Arty said very quietly and dryly, "Guess she told you, Mike."

Mamie finished picking up the fish. She stared at them a moment, as if trying to decide if they were still eatable. Then she shook her head and carried them to the water and threw them in.

"Did you see what she did to you, Mike?" said Timmy. "Did you see how she farted in your face?"

The full force of it seemed to explode inside Mike. He leaped to his feet, swearing to kill the first faggotface who laughed. He threw the beer can at Mamie, but it hit a tree and bounced away from her. She didn't appear to notice. She was bent over washing her hands. In the meantime, Mike had grabbed a trenching tool lying next to the tent. He went after Mamie with it. It happened so fast I couldn't even think to holler. Mike came up on her from behind just as she stood up, and he swung for all he was worth, but she dipped down again and did a little sidestep and managed somehow to have the shovel miss her completely. It kept going with the force of Mike's weight behind it and came round to smack him hard on the back of the head. He spun like a top and fell into the water at Mamie's feet. She came back to the fire, looking for more fish to fry.

"Jesus Christ! Jesus Christ!" Mike was saying, holding the back of his head and rocking in the water.

Timmy rushed to him and helped him up and back to the tent. He sat there with his head between his legs, moaning, while Timmy was telling us that we should see the size of the lump. "A real goose egg," he added. But none of us cared all that much; mainly, we just wanted to get the fish cooked and eaten.

"Looks like he'll live," said Arty, and that summed it up.

After Mamie ate, she got dressed and went into the woods. In a while, she came back carrying a bunch of wild onions. She took a coffee cup from the table where the guys had piled canned food and bread and other things, and she squeezed and rubbed the onions until a few drops of the juice ran into the cup. Next she added a pinch of salt, then just a dab of water and a dab of dirt. Out of this concoction she made a muddy-looking paste that she kept testing by touching her tongue to it. When it was just right, she went over to Mike and made him put his hands down so she could see the lump.

"What you gonna do to me?" said Mike weakly.

"Med'cin th-th-this," she said. "F-f-fix h-head."

Arty shook his head in disbelief. "He tried to brain her and she's gonna fix him? Damned if I'd be so nice."

Wes tapped me on the shoulder. He pointed to Mamie. "Who says she's retarded?" he asked. He looked at her like he was suspicious.

"Her pa," I answered. "Everybody."

"Well, I think they might be full of shit, that's what. I got a feeling she knows just what she's doing. That's an old woodsman's remedy she made. Salt kills bacteria and draws moisture. Mud draws too, stops the swelling and itching, and who doesn't know that onion is good for you? I think she knows just what she's doing. Elmer Farr might dangle his pecker for fish, but he caught them and so did she. I seen him and I seen her – same thing, you know. He ain't retarded and neither is she."

"Not exactly the kind you think of," said Arty. "Do you think she knew what she was doing, dropping the fish and farting in his face, Foggy? Something not right about her, that's what."

"I only know what I've heard all my life about her," I told them. "Mamie is retarded – I think there's just different degrees, that's all. But I remember I tried to teach her the ABCs and she couldn't learn them, though she can write letters if you show them to her. She wrote her name in the sand about a hundred times one day. But she can't do it if the letters aren't there to copy. I think she's retarded all right, just a different kind of retarded from what you think of when you think of retarded."

"I don't know," said Wes, eyeing her closely. "Something smarter here than maybe we can figure out. How come sometimes she talks just fine and other times she stutters all over the place?"

Of course, he was right, but I didn't have the answer for him. I held up my hands helplessly. He smacked his knee with his fist and said, "By god, she's neat – neat like an oak tree, neat like a cougar, neat like a red fox. Know what I mean?"

I told him I thought I did know. She was all of that, all right.

Mike was moaning about having the awfulest headache there ever was. When Mamie bent over to part his hair over the bump, he cried out, "Gawd, what now?" and tried to crawl away, but she straddled him and her weight pushed him down on his belly. Right away he started complaining that he couldn't breathe. Mamie didn't let him up. She parted his hair again, poured the poultice on the bump, and then started very tenderly to pat it in. "That hurts like hell!" Mike cried. "Look at this shit! She's killing me! Ow! Ouch! Fuck!" And on he went the whole time Mamie doctored him, patting here and patting there, shaping the mudpack into some plan she had in her head, until it was like a monster wart sticking out the back of his head. After it was just so, just right, she blew on it to make it dry. This took about five minutes, in which time Mike never stopped whining that he was being tortured. At last she got off, and he, whimpering, which really was kind of sickening coming from a face like his, got slowly to his feet and timidly felt the back of his head. "It feels like a watermelon," he complained.

Timmy, who had been watching the whole thing with us, went over and apologized for not doing something to Mamie. "I woulda hit her with a rock," he said. "But they wouldn't let me." He pointed at us.

"You woulda, huh?" said Mike, the fire coming back in his voice. "You little turd. You saw she was crushing my guts out." He looked at us. "You all saw it and you didn't do nothing. I ain't gonna forget it either. Next time you need somebody's ass kicked, I ain't gonna be there for you. Some friends I picked, let this fuck'n . . . this fuck'n . . . thing – ain't even human – crap on my head!" Then he grabbed Timmy by the ears and shook him hard. "And you're worse than any of 'em," he said.

"Right, Mike! Right, Mike! Owwww!" Timmy agreed.

"Let her squash my guts and stood right there doing nothing, and she's squashing me and you don't do nothing and you're the one supposed to be so tight – my buddy, my ass!" And he pushed Timmy back and slapped him, backhanded him across the mouth. Timmy fell like a stone. He curled up on the ground and was saying, "Oh gee, oh gee," over and over, holding his face like it would fall off if he let go.

I looked at Mamie. I thought she might jump in and stomp Mike. But she just stared at him like he was a bug she didn't want to touch. I had a sudden thought, and I asked her, "Mamie, who does Mike Quart remind you of?"

"M-m-mick Qwat – J-john B-b-b . . ."

"Beaver."

"Yaay, Kritch'n." She glanced at me. "You like'm?"

I didn't answer. I didn't want any more trouble. And it seemed like Mamie understood, because she came over and sat by me and draped her arm over my shoulder. Mike was nudging Timmy and telling him to go wash his face and quit bawling like a ten-year-old twerp. Timmy went with his head hanging, and Mike strutted around, flexing his muscles and saying how lucky Timmy was he didn't slug him, and that it probably would have broken the little twerp's neck. Then he started talking about all the fights he had been in and how he had damn near killed this guy and that guy and the other guy, boom boom boom, no one was as bad as Mike Quart. That got the other guys talking about how bad they could be if somebody messed with them. In the meantime Timmy came back and sat with us, but he stayed quiet as a mouse.

The night settled in and Mike fried himself some fish, while everybody talked of the drinking and the fighting they had done. This loosened me up the more exciting the stories got, so finally I chimed in with my story of clubbing John Beaver. Mike looked at me with new respect and told me the story of how he'd broken a beer bottle over his old man's head while he, the old man, was beating the old lady with a pot that went twang every time it connected with some bony part of her. The beer bottle had laid the old man low and put a wicked scar on his head. Mike said he would do it again a million times if he had to, because no one was going to beat his mom, even if she did have too much mouth for her own good. The old man, he said, kept real shy of him these days. While he was telling us the story, Arty, Wes, and Timmy stared at him as if he had turned into Hercules or something. I knew none of them had ever gone after anything with a bottle, let alone a father. I could see too, I guess, what they liked about him. Mean as he was, he was the kind of guy a boy wanted for a friend. He gave the others sort of what I got from Mamie – sort of the feeling of being on the side of the strong and mighty, who would protect you and win you respect that you wouldn't be able to win on your own.

The dark was everywhere outside our circle. There was no moon. The stars were like tons of hard white pebbles that looked good but didn't light up anything. While the boys bragged on and on, Mamie and I settled next to each other, leaning on a mossy log, our feet next to the fire, listening until they wore out their toughness and slid into their conquests of girls. Arty boasted how he had screwed his first girl when he was only seven and she was nine. He had learned plenty since then and knew what to do to get them hot. Wes said he had planked at least a dozen broads since he was twelve, and he named a couple. Mike and

Arty recognized both names. Mike said he had done it to them too. Then he claimed that the one named Gloria was a nympho and he had plugged her thirty times, and once he'd done it to her five times in one day when her parents weren't home. She was crazy about him. He'd tell her anything to do and she would do it. But that was how they all got, once he'd hauled their asses.

"A fuck'n woman," he said, acting like he knew everything there was to know about them, "has got no willpower to not fuck once she gives in the first time. That's if the guy ain't a jerk who's doing it. But if he rings her bell, she's done for from then on. Just ask Gloria what I did for her in the sack. I was her first, the first one. I got her cherry and I rang her bell. That's why she lets you guys have some. I took her willpower away. She'd kill for five minutes of my shlong."

"That's the way women are," Timmy agreed. He was looking hopefully at Mike. His bottom lip was puffed up on one side and it gave his mouth a lopsided look, like he had a marble under his lip. "If there's one thing Mike Quart knows, it's women," he added proudly.

Mike leered at Timmy. "Timmy should know that, huh, Timmy?" he said. "Whose sister is crazy for my sausage, Timmy?"

Timmy's mouth worked but nothing was coming out. He looked like he'd been slapped again. Mike's slanted eyes and high cheekbones made his face look evil in the glow from the fire. His face was tilted up just enough so that his forehead was in shadow and seemed to be just hair from his eyebrows upward. "Timmy's had some pussy too, ain't you, Timmy? Tell us who you screwed, kiddy. Don't you want to share it with your buddies? Timmy likes to share his pussy. He likes to share so he can watch."

Timmy looked like he was going to be sick. "Don't, Mike, please don't. You promised never to tell, Mike. Please," he begged.

"Hey, we're the gang here, kiddy. We don't keep secrets from the gang, that's what. Come on, she's just a cunt."

"She's not just a cunt!" Timmy's mouth was trembling, but his eyes were blazing.

"Then what is she, kiddy?"

Timmy tried once more to beg out of it. "Please, Mikey."

"He's shy, guys. He's trying to tell us he fucks his sister."

"Oh Jesus, no," moaned Timmy. He turned away from us and hid his face in his arms.

"That's a dirty deal, Mike," said Arty. "Rotten shit!"

"Aw, you're just pissed cause you're always thinking she's some fuck'n saint, Arty. You coulda done it to her any time you wanted, only you was too stupid. What the hell, we talking secrets here or not? So the little tadpole fucks his sister. What's that to us? I don't care. Do you care, Wes?"

"Naw, I guess not." Wes was looking down, his face hidden in the shadows.

Mike took him at his word. "See, Wes don't give a fuck. And the best thing is about it, Timmy shares her. Don't you, Timmy? Hey, kiddy, look at me . . . won't look, will he. I don't know what's the matter with him. It's nothing. I come over and we go in the basement and flip a coin for firsts. She leans against the wall. She likes to do it standing up. Goddamn, does she like it. She likes my shlong, hey, Timmy?"

But Timmy wasn't answering. He got up and went to the tent and pulled the flap down.

"Now what do you suppose is eating him?" said Mike, baring his teeth.

"Rotten shit," repeated Arty.

"Aw, come on, kiddy, you can do better than her. You don't want to fight about her. Didn't I teach you that once? Hey, don't we talk about pussy all the time? Huh? Well, Karen's got a pussy, a nice tight little pussy. She's fair game. You want me to tell you all the slithery things we do? Eh, Arty, eh?"

"Fuck you, Mike. She's fuck'n fourteen years old. You're going to jail, you rotten shit."

"Yeah, Arty? Who's gonna tell on me? You gonna tell on me? You a fuck'n rat, Arty?"

"I ain't a fuck'n rat, but you'll get caught, you'll see."

"You're just jealous, kiddy. What about you Wes, you gonna tell on me?"

"Hell no, Mike. That's your business."

"Damn right. I like you, Wes. You see things like they are. Arty here wants to make out like some girls are just little angels. You're an asshole, Arty. You don't know nothing. I tell you about Karen because I'm your buddy, see, and I don't want you mooning about her and making a fool of yourself."

"I never liked her so much as that," said Arty. "But what about Timmy?"

"Timmy? Timmy's a creep, you want to know the truth. He fucks his own sister, for Christ's sake. Twerp."

"Yeah, he's a twerp, but I feel sorry for him anyway. He just wants to be your friend. He wants it so bad he gives you his sister. Ugly, man – that's just fuck'n ugly."

Mike gave Arty the finger. "And I was gonna tell you everything about her too, so you'd know how to get you some. I'm the good friend here, Artsy-fartsy. But now you can go to hell. Shit, this is a fucked day, the whole thing, ever since you guys come." Mike glared at Mamie and me. "Now I got a headache again. And that's your fault too. This fuck'n mudpack is squeezing my fuck'n head." He kicked dirt and pine needles at us, then stomped off toward the lake. Next we could hear him washing and washing, washing for a long time. Mamie had put the mudpack on him to stay.

Mike Quart Meets His Match

The morning after, I woke up smelling smoke from the dead fire. In my sleep I had curled myself around the warm stones and the smoke had drifted into my face. I started coughing, and right away Mike was yelling from his tent for me to shut up. I went down to the lake to clean up and saw Mamie there, already a pile of fish flapping round in a little pool she had dug on shore. I went farther down so as not to disturb her, and I had a good, cold swim. I thought about John Beaver and convinced myself that he had gone up or down the road looking for us. I figured it was safe to leave, but to make sure I thought maybe we should hang around one more day at least.

When I got back, Arty had the fire going strong. Everybody was up and warming themselves, except Mike, who kept cussing us from inside his tent for waking him. Mamie was frying fish, and she had a pot of beans on. There was bread and Kool-Aid too. She went over to the table to get our tin plates, and as she did she passed Mike's tent. He was inside, muttering and cussing against everything living, and she suddenly tripped, or seemed to trip. Anyway, she fell sideways and caught herself on the front tent pole, which snapped like a twig under her and sent the whole tent down all over Mike Quart. Mamie recovered her balance like a cat, picked up the plates, and came back.

Inside the tent Mike sat up and screamed, "Who did that? Who did that? I'll kill the motherfucker!" He threatened blood and guts and tearing limb from limb. While he was yelling, it occurred to me that I had always thought John Beaver was sort of unique, maybe one of a kind in the world. But Mike changed my mind on that. Quarts or Beavers, it's in the blood, I guessed, and maybe coming all the way down from Cain. I watched Mike smack the tent here and there, and I heard the dull thump it made and saw its slow settling back around the shape of his head. The sight of the rolling canvas made me think of the big tom we had had once that liked to play inside of gunnysacks. He would crawl in and bat the sack this way and that, just like Mike was doing. I said out loud, "He looks like a cat in a sack, don't he?" And everybody laughed a little bit, which made Mike madder.

"Who's laughing out there?" he said. "Who's laughing at me?"

"Shit, guys, let's not get him so mad," said Timmy. "You know he'll take it out on me."

So we didn't laugh anymore, and finally Mike worked his way out of the tent. Then he grabbed it and pulled it up, stakes and all, and beat it against a tree. We cooked our breakfast and kept our mouths shut. When he got to panting hard he quit. Then he stomped over and glared at us one by one. "Which one?" he said. He looked long at Mamie. She was smiling sweetly at him, her teeth full of chewed beans. "You did it," he said. "You did it."

"Uh-huh," she agreed.

I said quickly that it was an accident, that she had tripped and tried to catch herself on one of the tent poles and it broke.

"I'll bet!" he answered.

"Hey, Mike," said Arty. "We all saw it. It was an accident."

Mike stared and stared at Mamie and she at him, smiling and chewing and taking it all in stride, looking at him like they were the best of friends.

Finally he said again, "I'll bet."

He had his hunting knife strapped to his waist and he pulled it out of the sheath. And he said in his deepest voice, "Anybody tell that pumpkinhead how good I am with this thing?" He held the knife up to the sun. It threw sparks of light. "Timmy," he said. "Tell her what I did to that toad the other day."

"You stabbed it," said Timmy.

"Yeah, but how far away was it?"

"A long ways."

"How far?"

"Ten feet."

"Bullshit, it was twenty feet."

"Yeah, twenty feet," said Timmy.

"And how did I do it, kiddy?"

"You threw your knife and got the toad in the back and killed him."

"Like this!" said Mike, throwing the knife at the ground in front of Mamie. It hit blade-first but bounced sideways instead of sticking. "Hit a rock," said Mike. "Find me another toad, and I'll show you what I can do with this thing." He pounced on the knife and threw again, only this time at a tree. He missed it completely and the knife went sailing into the undergrowth. "Fuck!" he screamed. "Goddammit!" And then he ran off after the knife. It took him a long time to find it. We were done eating by the time he got back. We had saved him some but he didn't want it, so Mamie ate it.

He got his stuff together, put on his shoes and shirt, and told us he was going over to Coffin Lake and spear fish the way they were meant to be speared. Then he took off toward a short ridge, down the other side of which was Coffin Lake, not far, not even a mile. We had nothing better to do. We grabbed a bunch of fishing poles and followed up behind him.

It was an easy trail and not very steep, so we didn't have a bad time of it. On the other side of the crest it was steeper, and we had to watch out that we didn't lose our footing and tumble down into a tree or a boulder. But we made it all right, and at the bottom was Coffin Lake waiting for us. It was a gray lake covered in mist. It was probably a hundred yards across and side to side, with lots of little pools and inlets circling it. The sun was shining at an angle through the trees and gave the mist rising up a spooky, ghostly light. The air was still and seemed thick and not too healthy at first, but a breeze came up later to kind of clean the place out.

Arty gave me and Mamie some cheese for bait. Everybody baited up and threw their lines on the water, everybody except Mike, that is. He tied his knife to a pole again and went scouring around the pools, taking stabs at the fish. First one to actually catch something was Wes. He brought in a nice, fat carp, which most people don't even like to eat, but they're not so bad. I've had trout that tasted muddier. Wes strung it proudly, baited his hook, and cast out again. Then he settled back and told us how good it felt to have a fish tugging at his line. His sleepy eyes gazed off across the water and the mist, as he told us what he thought of fishing. He said, "There's something sacred about it, that's what, about catching a fish this way. It's like you're favored by God. It's like that. Anyhow, that's how I see it, being I'm sort of a Christian and I see fishing in a Christian light. You understand what I'm saying?" He looked at Arty a few feet away. Arty was thoughtful. He told Wes what he was saying was deep.

So Wes said, "Yeah, that's what, it's a deep feeling I get because I believe in the Great Spirit. It's nothing I can prove. It's a feeling, that's what. But I've seen that people always look up to good fishermen. Take my dad; they admire him when he shows off his fishing trophies. He's a hell of a fisherman. Caught a state-record wallie out of Lake Nabagamon that stood for four years. He's always doing that. He's got trophies, that's what. But you know what he says? He says he catches fish like that because he's favored by God. If men see you're favored by God, they favor you too, because they know in their hearts that God loves good fishermen. And if you ain't one, then God's not that much on your side. That's what, if he don't favor you enough to let you catch fish, how is anybody else supposed to respect you? I mean, what is it that you feel when that fish hits your line? You feel the little tug all the way down to your asshole. It's like nothing else, something tugging at you out there, something secret there in the water. Deep, that's what. Secret. Secret water. I'll tell you – don't laugh, okay? – it's like catching a soul. It's like Jesus or Peter. Something to do with them, the whole fishers-of-men thing. Except you won't get it that way if you're not at least part Christian. You know what I mean, Arty?"

Arty nodded his head. "Yeah, that's the feeling, Wes." He glanced at me. "Wes comes up with some neat stuff, don't he? Like Elmer Farr with his pecker in the water."

I told Arty I thought Wes was great, and I meant it. He reminded me of my pa and the way he would ramble around the same kind of far-out ideas, mixing religion on his own terms because, like he said, religion was in everything a man did to try on the sense of the world. The whole idea, it seemed, was just to talk your way to the truth, and then to savor it when the feeling hit you that you were there.

Wes and all of us had really good luck that morning. We caught so many fish, in fact, that we threw back anything under twelve inches, which made us feel we were being responsible fishermen – the kind, I imagined, that the Great Spirit liked.

As for Mike, we could see him prowling around the pools, shirtless and shoeless, in his white undershorts, zinging his spear into the water and catching nothing but a hard time. But he kept at it, moving to another pool, one by one, all the way around the lake. As I watched him, he made me think about Indians coming sometime long ago before history and being quicker than the fish, never missing – not like Mike, who had lost the touch, who only looked like them now, who had civilized reflexes and was just a kid from town.

The sun got up high and hot, and the mist burned off the water. The fish quit rising to bait, so we let our lines drift and let ourselves drift too, dozing or staring off into space. It was nice and peaceful while it lasted. Then Mike quit trying to stab what wouldn't hold still (fish aren't a bit like toads) and came back to where we were. I saw him coming with his spear in hand, his shoulders wide and sharp with muscle, his Eskimo face thrust out, looking for trouble. In a way I envied how he looked – tough, burning-hard. If I looked like that nobody would want to mess with me. He looked like he might just eat you raw. As he came by me, he stopped and stared at my catch, swimming on a string at the water's edge, and he raised his spear to stab them.

"Hey," I cried out, "they're mine!"

His Mongol eyes shifted to me, and I felt my stomach get watery. I glanced at Mamie to see if she was going to do something, but she was lying back with her forearms folded under her head, staring dreamily at the sky. I wanted to nudge her, to make her pay attention, but I knew I would look pretty bad if I did that.

"I caught them," I said weakly.

"Yeah, so who gives a fuck?" he said.

I don't know what would have happened, but I lucked out just then, because Timmy started hollering that he had a big one. He ran backwards with his pole, reeling in his line at the same time, until out of the water came, fighting mad, a three-foot muskie. It was twisting and flip-flopping all over the rocks and sand, raising such hell it tore the hook out of its mouth, and before you could say "Grab it!" it was back in the water and gone.

"Jesus Murphy what a fish!" said Wes.

"Three foot or better," said Arty.

"I oughtta smack you for living," said Mike, glowering at Timmy.

Timmy's face screwed itself up into the makings of a good cry. I knew it hurt him like hell to lose such a marvelous fish. He dropped his pole and trudged off to be by himself.

Mike turned to us and said, "Did you see that? Lost the fuck'n meanest fish in the whole fuck'n lake. I oughtta smack him for living."

"I wish I'd caught that one," said Wes, sighing.

"Me too," said Arty.

Mike was growling at both of them. "See, you guys been feeling sorry for the little fart. Now what do you think, huh? The guy puts the pud to his sister, and worse yet, he loses the meanest fish in the whole fuck'n lake. Am I right about him or what? He ain't one of us. How can we like a guy like that?"

Arty and Wes looked at each other like Mike was making sense.

"Us three been friends a long time," he added.

"We won't bring him anymore, Mike," said Wes.

"I suppose you're right," Arty agreed. "But I feel sorry for him, and it ain't because I'm stuck on Karen. Christ, you know his old man shot himself, that's what, and nobody even knows why."

"And nobody even cares why. The guy was a loser, Arty; never could hold a job or nothing."

"Hey, he fainted a lot. Was that his fault?"

"He was a punk. Nobody liked him, a twerp just like Timmy." Mike shook his spear in the direction Timmy had gone. "I oughtta smack him for living," he repeated again.

While he was saying it, we could see Timmy running back toward us from the woods. When he got close, he yelled, "Look what I got, you guys!" In his hand and wrapped up his arm to his elbow was a beautiful yellow and black banded king snake.

"Hey, lemmee see that, Timmy!" said Mike, all excited.

Timmy came up to us, explaining how he'd caught it. "It tried to get away, but I grabbed it in my bare hand. It even tried to bite me, but I got its head." He showed us the snake's head in his hand, between his thumb and first two fingers. It was a small, black triangle, that head, with two pellet eyes that were full of murder. We all gathered round to admire it, while Timmy told us again how it tried to get away and tried to bite him, but he'd grabbed it with his bare hand. The snake looked sort of like a bracelet you might see on an Egyptian princess, looped round from wrist to elbow, yellow and black, and shiny. Mike stroked it and crooned to it, saying, "Neat, neat," into its stony face.

"You want it, Mike?" asked Timmy. "I want you to have it. You're my best friend, that's what."

"That's the way, kiddy," said Mike as he unwound the snake and took hold of its middle. When he reached for the head, Timmy let go too soon. The head darted out quick as lightning, and yum, it bit Mike's face, bit him on the lip, his lower one. "Eeeeee!" he screamed, and at the same time tossed the snake into the air. Up it went and over and over, like a crooked stick, and down it came right at us. We all covered our heads and ran. When I looked back, the snake was wiggling for the undergrowth as fast as it could go, and Mike was holding his lip for Arty to see and saying, "How bad am I bleeding, Arty? How bad am I bleeding?"

There was a tiny row of horseshoe dots oozing drops of blood. "It's nothing, Mike," said Arty.

"Black on yellow, kill a fellow!" cried Timmy angrily.

Mike's breath cut off short. His mouth hung open. The mahogany drained from his face. "That's right," he whispered. "Black on yellow, kill a fellow." He staggered back, squeezing his lower lip, making a noise in his throat, some kind of gurgling that was pitiful to hear.

"Horseshit," said Wes. "It's red on yellow – red on yellow, kill a fellow, you dummy."

Arty agreed. "Yeah, red on yellow, Mike, that's what."

Mike recovered quickly. The mahogany color came back into his face and exploded into purple. "Fuck! What's the matter with you? You trying to give me a heart attack? Black on yellow! By god, I'll show you black on yellow!" And he grabbed Timmy by the hair and popped him one in the stomach. Timmy's breath shot out of him and he dropped like a twig. Mike kicked him in the back, then paced around him, shouting, "Black on yellow, kill a fellow!"

When Timmy got his breath back, he gasped out at Mike, "I did-n't know, goddammit."

Mike was petting his swollen lip. "I'll probably get a disease from this. Snakes give people gang-green, that's what," he said.

Mamie went over to Mike and bumped him aside with her hip. She reached down and gathered Timmy up in her arms and carried him to the water.

"You better watch it," warned Mike, as she walked away.

She held Timmy up to his waist in the water until the pain went away, and then she brought him back and set him on his feet. He was looking at her like she was an angel. While she was gone, Mike was muttering about pounding her face, but when she came back he shut up and just gave her dirty looks. His lip had stopped bleeding. It was turning blue all around the bite. Mamie paid no attention to him. She rubbed Timmy's belly with one hand and hugged him with the other.

We decided – Arty, Wes and I – that we had had enough of Coffin Lake and it was time to start back. We gathered up our poles and fish and made our way back to the trail. Timmy and Mamie went ahead of us. She was carrying both poles and kept a hold of Timmy's hand to help him up, because it was pretty steep going back to the crest. The hill was a little bit loose, and we had to dig our toes in hard to keep from sliding back. But Mamie went up like it was nothing, towing Timmy as if he was hardly more than a balloon. She reached two-thirds of the way before the rest of us were even at the halfway mark.

It was around then that I stopped and looked up, and I saw something tiny flashing in the light, darting here and there like a silver fly. I concentrated on it, and then I could see it was a hook and line that had come loose from one of the poles Mamie was carrying. It was waving in the air and jerking up and down with each step she took. It was almost fascinating to watch it squirming and soaring and floating like it had a mind of its own. Below it was Mike Quart, crawling on all fours to get up the slope. I watched, paralyzed, as the hook darted and floated out over him, then watched it as it dropped easily and ever so lightly, gentle as a drop of rain, onto his shirt. Mamie was pounding away up the hill, and as she stepped forward with her right foot and her right hand holding the poles, the line jerked and the hook went through Mike's shirt and set itself in his back.

He shot up straight, his little eyes wide as a rabbit's. The same "Eeeeee" came out of him as when the snake bit him. The noise shot like a rocket to the sky, like he meant to tell the whole world about it. And as the "Eeeeee" came out, he tossed his spear down and tried to reach the hook in his back. He couldn't reach it, and the more he tried, the more entangled in the line he became, whirling and whirling, throwing himself this way and that, fighting the hook and line until it was like a net from his head to his knees and such a tangle that he finally tripped backward headfirst. He did a slow roll to his feet, then had a second of hesitation while he fought going over again, but it was no good – down he went in a dusty, tumbling roll, shrieking bloody murder all the way to the bottom of the hill.

The whole thing happened in less time than it takes to tell about it. Just bam bam bam, and there he was like a runaway log, and there we were, frozen with wonder and watching old Mikey roll. When he finally came to rest, he lay without moving. The only way we knew he was still alive was that he was moaning so. Finally Wes started back down, then Arty and I followed. We made such an avalanche of dirt that we almost buried him. He was in some sad condition, for sure, when we finally dug him out and could have a look.

"Check it out," said Wes. "Am I crazy or is that foot going the wrong way?"

It sure was. We quickly cut the line off him and yanked the hook out and lifted up his pantleg so we could have a good look.

"Broken," we all said at the same time.

"Oh gawd," Mike was moaning. "Oh gawd, oh gawd."

Arty tapped me on the shoulder and pointed up to the top of the hill. "Look at them, Foggy," he said. "Look at those two."

I looked, and there they were, perched like two gargoyles at the edge, back on their haunches, arms wrapped round their knees, faces peering down at us. Mamie looked wide-eyed and innocent as a baby. Timmy, on the other hand, had the look of the devil. His eyes had the fire of the sun in them.

"Hey, Mike, look up there," said Arty.

Mike uncovered his eyes and looked. His lips and his whole jaw trembled. "Fuck'n-A," he cried. "K-k-keep th-them a-way f-from m-me. K-keep th-them a-way!"

He was white from pain. It was a real bad break he had. The shin-bone was sticking through the muscle, the foot hung at a crazy angle, the wound was bleeding, his back was seeping more blood, his snake-bit lip looked like a giant grape, and he was a mess of nicks and scrapes all over. Nasty fellow or not, I had to feel sorry for him. From the time he had hit himself in the head with the shovel until his quick trip to the bottom of the hill, it seemed to me that he had gotten back a hell of a lot more than he'd given.

The next question we were asking each other was how we were going to get him out. I looked at Mamie and asked her if she thought she could carry him.

"No, no," he protested.

"Shut up, Mike," said Arty. He asked Mamie if she could do it.

"Yaay," she answered.

She bounded down the slope, picked Mike up, and threw him over her shoulder like he was a sack of potatoes. "Don't touch me!" he screamed, but it was all over. She went up the hill with us scrambling behind her, and it wasn't ten minutes before we were back in camp. In five minutes more we were at Arty's '49 Chevy.

The guys climbed in, and Mamie put Mike on the front seat. He groaned and moaned and whimpered, but he was mostly out of it, not able to talk or do anything for himself. Arty said we could go on back to camp and eat up the food if we wanted. I thanked him for that. As he turned the car around to head out to the main road, Mike, who was leaning against the door, raised his head and looked at Mamie, who was standing next to me out of the way.

She went into her act: "This one, this one, and this one . . . fuck'n-A," she said to him in his own voice.

His face went wild. "Fuck you!" he shrieked, then softer, "Fuck y-you."

They drove off, and Mamie and I went back to camp. We ate beans and bread and all the fish that night, and we slept on sleeping rolls next to the fire, under the stars.

Dragon Fire

East of Plato we were hitchhiking the next day, and finally a young fellow in a beat-up car stopped for us. He was the kind of guy to make you stop and really take a look at him. He had big, sad eyes – blue they were – with heavy lids and girlish lashes. He had a blond beard and blond hair, so blond it was nearly white. His hair fell to his shoulders like a monk's cowl. He made me think of pictures of Jesus, where Jesus is pointing to his heart. The first thing he said when he stopped the car was, "Runaways, runaways. I can spot them a mile away. What's the story, children?" His voice was deep and smooth, almost syrupy. It ran over a body and pulled it in and made the blood feel thick and calm. He had the kind of voice a person likes to listen to, not so much for the words but for the music in the words, music like a bass fiddle. I told him we weren't runaways, that we were orphans heading for Ashland, for the farms that were hiring hay buckers.

He went on singing to us, "I travel the highways of Minnesota and Wisconsin, up and down them, day in and day out, doing what little I can to get the message across. We've lost touch with the Father. We've lost touch with the love. We hate our children because we've lost touch with our souls. You poor young things, tomorrow's trash in America."

I told him again we weren't runaways, but he insisted we were, and we weren't to worry – he would die before he'd betray us. "Thirty-times-thirty pieces of silver wouldn't drag your secret from me. Armageddon is coming. I save those I can." His long-fingered hand swept the air like it was gathering the saved. Then he said in a matter-of-fact way, "Do either of you know how to drive a car?"

"Every farmer's son knows how to drive," I said.

"Yes, but can you drive this dying miracle?" He got out and pointed to his car. It was an old Nash, full of rusty holes and dents and streaks of every color in the rainbow. ROLLING GLORY was painted across the trunk, and there were two bumper stickers. One said THE END IS TOMORROW, and the other said JESUS IS COMING AND BOY IS HE

PISSED. The car was idling and little puffs of black smoke were coming out the back. I told him I was pretty sure I could drive it, that I had probably driven worse.

"Then let's go. We got work to do," he said.

We got in the car. Mamie rode shotgun, I drove, and he got in the back. The clutch was slipping pretty bad and smelling like silage. The gas gauge said empty; the temperature gauge said hot. The engine shuddered like it was hitting on only five cylinders. But the car moved, going east, going southeast.

He told us his name was Robbiė and he was on a mission to the town of Temple, where he'd been born thirty-two years ago and where he'd first heard the call. He said those who believed in his divinity were gathered there now, in Temple, waiting for him to do something dramatic. He had it all figured out. He had a plan, and he would not let them down. In two hours, at forty-five miles an hour, we would be there. I wasn't to go over forty-five.

"It's the breakup barrier for the likes of this sore-footed beasty," he said, pounding the ceiling. "After forty-five its life breath is sucked away and it starts to disintegrate; rust shatters and falls like red snowflakes, leaving us riding a bent frame, butts tanned in asphalt, terror in our hearts, and no triumph in Temple." He patted my head and asked me if I understood. I told him I wouldn't go over forty-five.

"You're a good child," he crooned in my ear.

I said I wasn't a child, I was almost sixteen, my name was Christian Foggy, and next to me was Mamie Beaver.

"Well then, Christian and Mamie, howdy!"

"How," Mamie answered.

He paused to look closely at Mamie. Then he said, "What a fine behemoth you are!"

"Yaay," Mamie said, shaking her head in agreement.

"That's the spirit. Jesus has done it again, worked a mysterious purpose this day. I can feel it. A name like Christian, and an angel-faced monster like this. It's better than Gabriel at the gates, I tell you, and it's no accident. No accidents in this life."

I told him if we didn't get some water and gas we wouldn't make it to Temple.

"Not to worry, Christian."

"Gas says empty. Water gauge says hot."

"Faith cures a nervous disposition. We ride on the breath of Jeeesus! Besides, those gauges don't work anyhow."

I glanced at Mamie, who was making funny noises. She was bent close over Robbie's golden hair, which was hanging partly over the front seat, and her lips were puckered as she blew against his neck and made the hair dance. And he was saying, "It all falls into place. My faith is rewarded with a sign – the name Christian. Keep it under forty-five. Look how close you're getting. Feel it start to vibrate? She's talking to you, Christian, saying you're getting close to the disintegration barrier. Pay attention, Christian." Then he started singing for real, "I got sun-shi-i-ine on a cl-ou-dy da-ay, ca-ause Chris-tian and Mamie ca-ame my way; tri-umph in Temple today; but go forty-five, o-o-o-o forty-orty-five, I say; old beee-easty canna take no mo-ore; we'll be fa-alling through the flo-or; yahooo, yeah yeah, ain't it so, Joe o-o?" He patted our backs and asked us if we liked his song.

"Yaay!" cheered Mamie.

"Real good," I told him.

"You know what?" he continued. "I once knew a holyman who was killed by demons. He had the gift, this guy. God told him the future and gave him the gift to heal the sick. He saw demons causing disease, and he used his power to get rid of them. But he tells me one day, he says, 'Robbie, my son, they're plotting against me. They're ganging up and they're gonna kill me. I want you to remember I told you so.' He said he wasn't afraid, he wasn't worried. That's what it means when Jesus chooses you. You never know fear. The promise of the resurrection keeps a perfect niche in heaven always in front of your eyes. Glory! I've been promised it too. Like Elijah, I'm going up on a whirlwind and never coming back, a straight shot to the orchestra seats. The holyman did die just as he said he would. It came out of the blue one day. Very mysterious, very mysterious, I say. He was out for a little ride on his motorcycle, riding along in a place he had been a thousand times and knew like the back of his hand, and the pavement as dry as Ezekiel's bones in the valley. No traffic. Nor horrible wind. Everything perfect that day, but the holyman – he crashed and burned just the same. Howdy Howdy."

"How," answered Mamie.

"Demons did it, darling. Shut his medicine down the way they do. They're like that. But they'd sure have a tough time with you. Is this girl as strong as she looks?"

"Probably stronger," I said.

"And a bit dense, maybe?"

"Just sort of."

"I don't care. Jesus loves her, yes he does, loves the likes of her – Holy Fools! Loves them, but he won't protect her from the demons."

I could see him in the rearview mirror, turning and looking behind us, then turning back again and saying close to my ear, "Wake me up if you think they're closing in." He flopped down on the seat, and it wasn't long till I could hear him snoring. I drove on toward Temple, keeping it slow, forty-five. The woods were thick going by, looking endless and heavy with the green, and shading the road and opening up in front of us like soldiers standing guard over royalty. The car kept hiccuping along and wheezing now and then and belching black smoke, but it didn't bother me. He'd said we were riding on the breath of Jesus, after all.

Mamie put her head back and went to sleep, too. Which left me all alone to let my mind wander on the things Robbie had said about the holy man and the demons. I asked myself how did they do it? Did they jump in front of the motorcycle? Did they crawl up his leg and grab the handlebars? Did they jump on his back and put their hands over his eyes? Maybe they just threw a rock at him. Maybe they wormed their way inside him and exploded his brain. How do demons do the things they do? Make pigs run over cliffs and stuff like that? How can they do anything at all if the Deity prefigures everything and decides the way it's going to be? He knows when the sparrow is going to fall and he lets it fall. He knows the plan of the demon and he lets it be. Doesn't that make him a conniver with evil? The holyman was doing his work just like Job had been, and both got abandoned to the demons. Got a friend like that, you don't need enemies.

I had talked back to Mama about it one time. She was Catholic and a believer in all sorts of devils and saints. I asked her how she could excuse God for not sticking up for Job. "Job must have had some sin in him," she said. "He was proud." That wasn't the way I read it. The way I read it, God said to Satan, "See Job? He's the best fellow I know. Sic him!" Satan kills Job's sons and daughters and takes everything away. Job is depressed about it and asks God what the hell is going on? And God thunders at him like a big bully, like it's Job's fault that Satan murdered his children and all. God let Satan break God's own law – thou shalt not kill. It's like God broke his own law himself. And then he thinks he'll be generous and give Job some new sons and daughters, better ones, huh? Seems like Job comes off looking more holy than God. Pa always called the Old Testament God a mighty warlord with the moral sense of a bumblebee in a hothouse. Pa said that the Bible is a record of man slowly making God human, making him the Deity. But still in all, I couldn't help thinking that the holyman on the motorcycle didn't get any protection, no more than Job, and neither would this fellow Robbie in the back seat, and of course neither would innocent and dumb Mamie.

The why of it bothered me. The holymen doing for God and getting a kick in the teeth – what the hell did it mean? I wondered if maybe I just hadn't been around long enough to see there was a great wisdom going on – none so blind as those who will not see, that sort of thing. Maybe it all clears up, I thought, when you get to be sixty-five. Or maybe if you read enough you don't have to wait so long – the secrets are in books that guys like Socrates wrote. Or maybe a fellow should go lose himself in the woods or on a mountain and think his way to all the answers, not eat for three days, like the Indians, and see then if the Great Spirit comes blowing in the wind. Should a fellow pray the rosary and read the Bible every living day and that's it – bingo, here it comes, revelation? Who's got the answer? Where did he get it? How does he know it's the truth? And why the hell didn't Jesus answer when Pilate asked him straight out, "What is truth?"

My thoughts were picking up steam and going a mile a minute. At first it was just thinking, being philosophical, as Pa would say. But then the thinking turned into fussing and the fussing into confusion. The confusion made me get mad and bite my lips and cuss under my breath. "Religious thinking just turns a mind in circles and gives no satisfaction," I muttered. The whole thing made me a believer in one thing – truth was that I was my father's son, and I couldn't run away from it even if I wanted to.

The miles rolled by and one hour became two, and finally we closed in on Temple. We went down a long, snaky road, down and around some sharp curves, so that I had to use the brakes a lot to keep the car below forty-five. I could smell the brakes, a sharper stink than the clutch, and I could feel them starting to slip. I pumped and pumped, but it did less each time, until finally there was nothing there and the car shot forward like it had hit a grease patch. We swooped along a thirty-mile curve doing well above disintegration forty-five, the tires yowling like sick dogs, the Nash all but standing on its side, so deep in trouble I could have reached out and petted the pavement.

The noise woke Robbie and Mamie. Mamie started pounding on

the dash, as if she meant to beat the car into behaving itself. Robbie kept crooning to me to be careful, careful, careful. We hit another curve and slid hard into the gravel, sending little rocks flying like bullets into the trees. The rear end of the Nash slipped sideways a little, but we hung in there and made it around the curve and straightened out. And then we got lucky for a minute, because the downslope gave way to a rise, just enough to slow us down to about thirty-five. Then over the top we came and saw the city itself, thousands of houses and big buildings and a water tower that said TEMPLE WISCONSIN.

We were going down again but only a little down, not enough to pick up a bad speed; in fact, we were slowly slowing. We went past the first houses, all steep-roofed, white, and boxy, picket fences in front, and so alike that if you took a picture of one you took a picture of all. Where the houses stopped, a two-story brick schoolhouse stood, with a mess of people in front of it, people who were watching us bubbling along toward them like we owned the road. They, the people, were holding picket signs, and it was easy to see they were mad about something because of the way they were shaking their signs and stomping around, and not moving out of the way, either. We floated down on them like a dying moth, and I thought to see us bumping bodies left and right, but a serious look came on the people's faces and they started scattering. At the same time, Robbie reached across my shoulder, grabbed the steering wheel, and jerked it to the right so that the car bounced over the curb and sidewalk. The marchers peeled away from the sides of it, falling like bowling pins. The car slowed going over some shrubs and came to rest in the middle of the schoolyard.

"Good one," said Robbie.

The people picked themselves up and gathered around the Nash and glared at us like we ought to be shot. Little kids stood with their mothers and fathers, clinging to their legs and looking at me with a kind of pity, solemn and pretty sure that I was going to get it, a good pounding from all the fists shaking at me. I looked over my shoulder and out the rear window, and the ones who saw me looking dove to the left and right, as if they thought I was going to back up and take another whack at them.

"Brakes," I yelled. "It was the brakes!"

A wide-mouthed woman shoved her face close to the glass and peered in. Next thing she was smashing her palm on the glass and shouting, "Robbie! Robbie!"

"Yeah, Lulu! It's me!" he shouted back.

Lulu turned away shrieking, "It's him! It's him!"

There was a cheer from the crowd. Someone yelled out, "He always knew how to make an entrance!" Then there was more cheering and more shouts of "Robbie! Robbie!" They pulled him from the car and lifted him on their shoulders. "Robbie! Robbie!" they kept saying, parading him around while he grinned and threw kisses.

"He must be a hero," I told Mamie.

She wasn't listening. Her mouth hung wide as she stared in fascination at the bouncing, shouting mob. "Easy, Mamie," I said. But it was in one ear and out the other. Next thing I knew she was out of the car and buried in the middle of the crowd, reaching out to touch Robbie like the lepers reached for Jesus.

A minute or so passed with everyone living it up, Robbie high above them holding out his arms like he was a pope blessing them, floating in the air, whirling round and round, and smiling such a sweet, gleamy smile that he looked something like a Christer's idea of the Second Coming, no doubt. I had no wonder they loved him so, and in spite of my thinking something crazy was going on, I had a big urge to join the people and jump and shout.

And jump and shout!

I got out of the car and stood on the hood so I could see better. A man in a blue uniform stepped out of the front door of the school. He was on the top step, above everyone, hands on hips, scowling; and behind him came another man in uniform and two men in gray suits, who wore glasses and had flattop haircuts. One of the men, who was a shade taller than the other, stepped forward and cupped his hands round his mouth, making a trumpet through which he started shouting at the people. The two policemen took out their whistles and blew and blew, and the shorter of the two men in gray suits started punching the air and dancing like a boxer. I couldn't figure out why he was doing it. He sure wasn't a tough-looking guy that could scare somebody.

It took a while, but at last the whistles managed to get the crowd's attention. The noise died down, and the fellow who was making a trumpet of his hands shouted, "What the hell you doing?"

Someone yelled back at him, "We're mad, Vendenberg!"

"Yeah, mad!" said others in the crowd.

"You sure are," said Vendenberg. "What kind of example you think you're setting for these little ones here? Hoodlum example, that's what you're showing them!"

"You forced this on us!" someone declared.

"We warned you!" cried another.

"Hoodlums we are," said Robbie above them. "Hoodlums for Jesus!"

The two of them faced each other, Robbie and Vendenberg, across a few rows of people in between them – Robbie leaning forward, Vendenberg cocking his head like a rooster, each checking the other out eye-to-eye. Everyone got real quiet.

"You are still a lunatic," said Vendenberg with conviction.

"And you're the devil's pawn, Vendenberg."

The people liked what Robbie said. They told him to give it to Vendenberg good. Vendenberg curled his lips at the crowd, like he was sucking a lemon. "Spare me this wonderful wit," he said.

"Booo!" they answered.

"Jeee-sus still loves you, Vendenberg," cried Robbie into Vendenberg's face.

"Hooray! Hooray!" yelled the crowd.

Vendenberg shook his head sadly and said, "Robbie Peevy, you need help. You needed help twenty years ago and you still need it today. Someone needs to get across to you that you are not the Second Coming."

"Monster of iniquity!" shouted a woman. "You had our Robbie committed!"

Vendenberg rolled his eyes in disbelief. "That's a lie," he said. "His parents had him committed. You can't just go around setting fires and expect people to think you're normal."

"I burn sin!" shrieked Robbie.

"Burning the school down is burning sin?"

"Burning the school down is burning sin, yessir, if that school produces sinfully educated children. It's a symbolic gesture ordered on me by Jesus to wake the people up. God knows I have no power to disobey the command." Robbie looked round at the people left and right, his eyes shiny with tears. "Am I a lunatic?" he asked.

"Angel, angel, angel!" the people chanted.

"Am I a lunatic?"

"Angel, angel, angel . . ."

"Was that a lunatic preaching to you every Sunday in Huckle's barn?"

"Angel, angel, angel . . ."

"Was that a lunatic who gave you the word of God when he was a mere boy? a babe?"

"Angel, angel, angel . . ."

"Where would a mere strip of child get the words to prophesy the corruption of your babies' minds from the sulphur pit of this here so-called school? Did that prophecy come from a lunatic?"

"Angel, angel, angel . . ."

And he did look like an angel, perched above them, his hair and beard bright as cornsilk flowing and sparkling in the sun. As he turned his head from side to side, his big blue eyes dripped brokenhearted tears, and "Angel, angel," rose up like a prayer around him.

As the people sang, they bounced up and down and shook their signs. The signs said things like MARCH FOR SANCTIFIED READING; DOWN WITH PORNOGRAPHY AND JOYCE; BURN FAULKNER IN HELL; *CATCHER IN THE RYE* CORRUPTS; QUEERS READ *DEATH IN VENICE;* HENRY MILLER CAME FROM HELL; DH LAWRENCE IS DOO-DOO! There were a bunch of them, all warning about some bad book or some filthy writer. Some signs had black drawings of a skull and crossbones, some had pictures of human brains being burned, and some had drawings of a library with HERE BE DRAGONS printed on the doors.

Vendenberg was holding his hands up again, trying to get the people to be quiet. The sheriffs were blowing their whistles. The gray-suited, crew-cut shadowboxer was punching the air with uppercuts and showing his teeth, like he was going to bite somebody. The crowd paid them all no mind, until finally Robbie pointed like Moses across the Red Sea and shouted, "I have returned! Vengeance is mine! Unbar the door! Stand aside!"

The people stopped singing "Angel, angel," and took up Robbie's command, "Unbar the door! Stand aside!" They surged forward like wheat in a windy field. That's when I caught sight of Mamie. She had Robbie on her shoulders. And just when it looked like the crowd was going to knock down the doors, another man joined Vendenberg and the rest on the steps. A big fellow, broad and deep like Mamie. He wore a T-shirt printed with a can of Old Style, which folded in the dips between his big belly and chest. His face was square, his neck so thick it was wider than his head. He had short, curly brown hair with sideburns that went down to his jaw. His nose was thick, like a fighter's mashed nose. His eyes looked hot.

"What you doing?" he said, looking at the people like they were naughty children. The people stopped and got quiet. The fellow scratched his head and sighed and pointed at Robbie. "Who let that dipshit back in town?" he said.

"He just showed up," answered Vendenberg.

"Howdy, Bob Thorn," said Robbie.

"Howdy yourself, Hitler. You still want to burn books?"

"Nope, don't want to, never wanted to, Thorn. But I got my orders from the Lord."

"Hearing voices are we?" Bob Thorn winked and pointed to the sky. "From on high?"

"No, not hearing voices, hearing the word of Jesus."

"And he says, 'Get thee to Temple and burn dem books, Robbie boy, my little psycho.' Is that it?"

Robbie held his arms out like he was on the cross. He raised his voice up, crying, "I am scorned of all my adversaries, a horror to my neighbors, and an object of dread. I have passed out of mind like one who is dead; I have become a broken vessel. Yea, I hear the whispering of many as they scheme together against me, as they plot to take my life. But I trust in thee, O Lord! Deliver me!"

Bob Thorn had his hand over his eyes while Robbie spoke. When it was over, Bob said, "Kiss my ass, you brain-ruptured schizo. Get back in your cloud. Get back to Camelot."

"But they laughed them to scorn and mocked them," said Robbie.

"Oh, shut up." Thorn looked at the people and he told them to take a good look at Robbie. "Look what you got here. This is Robbie Peevy. This is the boy wonder who was going to lead you to the promised land. This is the nut who used to preach in Huckle's barn and tell you he could hear the voices of angels in the rafters. This is the guy who got committed, for Christ's sake. The doctors said he was sick in the head, remember? Delusions of grandeur and stuff like that, remember? He's a nut! You got to be nuts, too, to follow a nut!"

"Each is my people," said Robbie. "The chosen ones. They called me back from Camelot. They called me! And God said to answer their call. In the name of decency and for the sake of Jesus Christ, stand aside and let us enter. We don't want to hurt you."

Thorn laughed at Robbie. "You don't want to hurt me, huh? By god, you just try it, piss-ant. I'm the one linebacker nobody got through, remember that? While you were picking your nose and preaching against the sins of football, I was stopping every fullback from here to Milwaukee. I'm the trophy wrestler, remember? While you were munching on your boogers and preaching the sins of wrestling, I was beating every heavyweight from here to Chicago. You don't want to hurt me? You're just goddamn lucky I don't jump up there and take your fuck'n head off, Peevy!"

"You always had a dirty mouth, Bob. There's women and children here. Talk decent."

"Decent? Burning the school library is decent, huh?"

"Burning filth is decent. It cleanses!"

"Bah!"

"Burning sin is decent. That's a library full of evil that you harbor there, every evil under the sun all laid out for the little ones here to train them in corruption. Sick slime and infection dribbling from sick, slimy minds, the likes of Faulkner and Hemingway and . . . and . . ."

"And Salinger!" yelled someone, helping out.

"And Salinger! Scum like that dribbling on our children. All that's ugly and crazy, putrid things that Satan's people do, and it's glorified for the children to read and call it life, and it's not life. It's perversion and slaughter! Jeee-sus save us!"

"The truth will set you free!" cried a voice.

"We're here to save our children!"

"You don't know what you're talking about," said Bob. "The books you got on your signs sit and dry-rot on the shelves. None of the kids I ever knew read them, nobody. You ever try to read them? Try Faulkner some time, I dare you. Try him. It's another language, goofy stuff, Greek or Swahili. Ain't no kid would understand a thing he's saying. Am I right, Vendenberg?"

Vendenberg nodded his head. "You never been righter in your life," he answered.

A woman raised her fist and shook it at the two of them and called them liars. "My daughter was made to read *Elmer Gantry* in Mrs. Modeen's class. When she told me what it was about I almost died! Corruption in the church, drunkenness and fornication!"

Other people shouted out names of books their kids were made to read. Filthy commie works! I heard *Grapes of Wrath* and *Brave New World* and *Anna Karenina*. In amongst the titles, I heard one I knew about pretty well. It was a book we had at home that Mama and Mary Magdalen kept called *Making It With Mademoiselle*, which was a book of patterns, dress patterns. "That's no filthy commie work," I said. But nobody was listening to me. The calling of the names had stirred the people up hot again. They were rattling their signs and starting to chant, "Unbar the door!"

Beneath Robbie, Mamie started to dance in circles to the beat of the chant. I could hear her own voice when she turned my way, singing, "Um-bar, um-bar, um-bar." Bob Thorn and the sheriffs were hollering at the people, and the shadowboxer was running down the steps and back up, hooking and jabbing the air. Vendenberg was rubbing his head like it hurt awful. Robbie took up Mamie's song and started "Um-bar, um-bar," over and over with her, and pretty soon the rest of the crowd was singing um-bar too. A great "Um-bar!" beat against my ears like an Indian war dance, and the booming of their feet sent up the sound of a huge drum.

Then I saw Robbie shouting something at Mamie and pointing toward the school like he was General Custer. She pawed the ground, backed up a few feet, and with Robbie whooping "Ummmm-baaarrr!" at the top of his lungs, she charged. Bob Thorn was knocked aside like beef on a hook. Vendenberg and the shadowboxer went scurrying over the other side. The sheriffs disappeared in the boil of people climbing over them. Robbie ducked his head, and he and Mamie galloped across the entrance, followed by the crowd come to rescue Temple from the books. And I followed hard after them, not for books but for Mamie.

When I got inside, I saw her far ahead down the hall. Robbie was off her and running in front. I kept my eyes on her head, floating above the people like a ragged bobber in a river. Through the double doors with old-fashioned frosted panes and a sign overhead saying LIBRARY, she and the rest went. And I was carried with them, past the entry and into the great den of sin itself.

I managed to get myself out of the main flow and to stand on a chair by the wall to search for Mamie. The people were pouring over the rows and rows of books, shelf after shelf of them, looking harmless enough. Dozens of hands grabbed them and carried them overhead, and dozens of voices shouted out the titles to Robbie. He was standing on a desk and giving every title he heard the thumbsdown: *From Death to Morning* – thumbsdown; *Lord Jim* – thumbsdown; *Crime and Punishment* – thumbsdown; *Studs Lonigan* – thumbsdown; *War and Peace*; *Moby Dick*; *David Copperfield*; *The Possessed*; *Nuts and Seeds* – all of them getting the thumbsdown and being chucked out the windows, where other people waited to pile them up for burning.

It wasn't long till no one bothered to look at the titles or at Robbie anymore. Everything went. And I looked out the window and saw men and women pouring kerosene over the books, then lighting matches, and the books bursting into flame, the pages curling into black ash. The smoke went straight up as the fire took off and began to roar and shoot sparks. The smell of it filled the library.

I pressed myself against the wall and watched armful after armful of all those words going to the windows. Robbie turned round and saw me. He jumped off the desk and gave me a hug.

"Christian, you hung in there," he said. "And look, we're finally doing it. Jesus said to take charge and we have. We're committed now. Wonder of wonders! I never gave up – even through the shock treatments and drugs, I knew. I knew! Christian, are you listening?" I was listening. "We are now at the center of God's will. This is the center of the universe! What can you say?"

"Help me get Mamie out of here, Robbie."

A woman shoved a book in Robbie's face. I recognized her as the same Lulu who had pulled him out of the car. Her face was pockmarked with old acne scars. Her lips were flecked with foam. A glassy look of ecstasy was in her eyes. "*Samson Agonistes,* Robbie. Is it a holy book?" she asked breathlessly.

"Naw, Lulu, chuck it!"

"And what about the Shakespeare?"

"The Shakespeare?"

"There's a whole row of it. I've heard it's really depressing stuff."

"Chuck it, Lulu, chuck it all."

"Chuck the Shakespeare!" she cried out to the others. *Samson Agonistes* went out the window, and Lulu went after the depressing Shakespeare. I was thankful Pa wasn't there to see it.

Robbie turned back to me. "You've been sent to help me, Christian. There are no accidents in my life. I'm never wrong."

I told him I would help, but I wanted him to order Mamie to come with me outside first.

"Not a chance," he said laughing. "She's worth ten men. Let her be." He bent over and picked up a paperback someone had dropped. "Here, give us a hand. Go throw this on the fire." He squeezed my shoulder and handed me the book, then turned away and leaped back on the desk.

I checked out the title in my hand. It was *Blithe Spirit*. I slipped it in my back pocket and went over to the window to watch the fire. Book after book flew toward the flames, pages open and flapping like the wings of helpless birds. The fire was getting so big it was beginning to singe the mulberry bushes that made a barrier between the grass and the building. I could feel the heat on my face, and I was pretty sure that eventually the school would catch on fire. And then through the smoke and flames, I saw a line of police cars arriving, brakes squealing, and men getting out, men with clubs in their hands.

I jumped on the desk where Robbie was yelling and thumbs-downing, and I shoved him off. He fell into a crowd, knocking some of them down. Books fell; bare legs flashed in the air. Those coming tripped over those who had fallen. They all jammed together like a pile of logs. Mamie came out from between a row of shelves, books loaded all the way to her chin. She started climbing over the people, stepping on them. They were squealing and cussing her, but she wouldn't let up, just ground her way through. When she finally got close to me, I knocked the books out of her hand and grabbed her by the shoulders.

"Cops!" I screamed into her face. "Cops coming to get us!"

Her eyes were glazed. She didn't seem to know me. I pulled her hair and slapped her. She tossed her head in a way that reminded me of a horse tossing its mane. Then she looked close at me and focused in, the human soul coming back like dawn peeping over a hill.

"Kritch'n," she said softly.

"Cops, Mamie. Gonna lock us up. Got to run."

I took her hand and yanked her toward the door. She followed, but it was like trying to swim upstream to get through all the people in the hall fighting to go both ways. Finally I put her in front and she made a path for us. When we got outside, I saw Vendenberg standing on the hood of Robbie's car, shouting orders and pointing. He was saying, "Hoodlum – get him! That one – hoodlum; that one too – get them, get them hoodlums!" The police weren't paying him much mind. They were just grabbing all the keepers of the fire and handcuffing them. Any who resisted got a quick pop on the head with a billy club to calm them down. Bob Thorn was helping out. He was tackling anybody who was trying to sneak away.

Mamie and I were working our way out between the wall and the bushes when suddenly Thorn spotted us and came running over, shouting, "Aha! Aha!" Then he got in front of us and crouched like a wrestler, his arms out, his upper body swaying.

"Come out of there," he ordered, and when we did he said to Mamie, "You're the one. You the mule who knocked me off them steps!"

"She didn't mean to, sir," I told him.

"Come on," he said to her, ignoring me. "Come on, hit me with your best shot, come on, moose."

Mamie stared at him, her eyes fascinated, her mouth hanging dopey. He was crouching lower and moving toward her, his legs bowed way out. Then Mamie was doing it too, imitating him perfectly. And round and round each other they went, with him yelling at her to take her best shot and her loving whatever it was they were doing. Finally he tried to tackle her. He rushed in, diving for her legs, but Mamie, like a bloated cat, leaped in the air, high enough that she jumped clear over him, and he came down belly-hard, holding an armful of grass. Then, before he could figure out what had happened, she grabbed him by the belt and by his neck and hoisted him off the ground. Using her knee like a catapult, she tossed him a good ten feet, just like he was nothing more than a bale of hay. He went through the air making a slow turn, his arms and legs as rigid as the blades of a windmill. When he hit the ground, he tried hard to leap back to his feet, but there was too much momentum keeping him going. He ran backward until he came up against the Nash, banging it like a cannonball with such force that Vendenberg on the hood lost his footing and disappeared with a squeal over the side.

The action had stopped all around us. Bob Thorn crawled halfway under the car. Vendenberg rose up on his knees, pulling himself up by the fender and staring cross-eyed at us. The handcuffed people were gawking. The cops and the people who were fighting back stood frozen in each other's arms. And Mamie, in her monkey crouch, waited for Thorn to come again. I was pretty sure he was through for the day. I pulled her arm and told her we had to go. It was like trying to move a tree. I pushed. I yanked. I screamed in her ear. I kicked her big butt. But she wanted Bob Thorn again. When she finally figured out he wasn't coming, she went over to the car and pulled him out from under, grabbing him by the ankles and hauling him across the grass.

"Whoa!" he kept saying. "Whoa! Whoa!"

I don't know what she was going to do with him, but his hollering "Whoa!" gave me an idea. I ran at her and leaped onto her back. Grabbing a handful of hair, I shouted, "Haw, Mamie! Giddup now, you! Scudda-hoo! Scudda-hay! Haw! Haw!"

It worked. She dropped Bob Thorn and snorted. She turned round in a circle, then leaped in the air and took off across the grass and across the street, her stride so smooth it seemed she hardly touched the ground. We galloped away from the school at eye-watering speed, and when I looked back, everybody was still watching us like they were watching an upside-down dream. We came to the end of the street and galloped across a vacant lot toward a stand of trees in the distance.

"Into the woods!" I yelled. "Haw! Haw!"

And Mamie answered, "Hippa-weee!"

Man of the Trains

On the other side of the trees was a road. To the left was Temple. We could see cross-streets and stop signs, buildings and people. To the right were some railroad tracks and a train station. That's where we went. I had an idea that we would hop a train and get a free ride going somewhere south where the big farms were, where a guy could get a job. And a train would take us far away – too far for John Beaver. We crawled under the platform, way in the back where it was nice and cool and the dirt was as fine as powder to lie on. The station house was above us. We could see up and down the tracks and down the road too, all the way to town, but we were in the dark where no one passing by could see us.

We weren't there five minutes when a car roared to a stop near the platform steps and a policeman got out and yelled, "Hey you! Get out here!"

"Shit, we're dead in the water," I whispered to Mamie. "Somebody must have seen us and told."

"D-d-dead?" she asked. "In da wada?"

Then I heard someone shuffling his feet above us. A door slammed and a voice said, "Who you think you're talking to like a dog?"

"I'm in a hurry, mister!" said the cop in a command kind of voice.

"I don't give a good gaddamn if you're a doctor on a 'mergency call," sassed the man. It was an old man's voice, kind of high-pitched and gargly. "Doctor on a 'mergency call," he repeated, giving special emphasis to 'mergency. "You don't say to me 'Hey you, get out here.' I don't know any man or beast walking on two, four, or flying that's got nuff lead in his ass to give Amoss Potter orders to 'get out here.' You don't give me no orders, you punk cop. I'll tell you right now, I been a man of the trains forty-four years, and I been the last fifteen years right here as the stationmaster. And I tell you what, I throwed paying customers out the gaddamn door for getting smart with me. I held up the gaddamn U.S. of A. mail itself cause some punkass engineer thought he had nuff lead in his ass to yell at Amoss Potter. I even told my two-bit, beak-nosed boss to put it where the hand of man don't belong when he got uppity with me. Nosir, I brook no brass and take no sass from man, woman, child, or morphodite. Don't give a damn if you're rich or poor, old or young, a fat slob or so bony you have to stand up twice to make a shadow. This is my station, *my station*! And nobody tells me a gaddamn thing, not nothing, see? And specially nobody tells me to gaddamn get out here on my own platform, and it don't matter none at all if he's a shiny-faced, sassy-assed cop or the gaddamn president of the whole gaddamn country. And let me tell you one more thing, youngster –"

But the cop wasn't in the mood for one more thing. He interrupted the stationmaster, screaming at him, "Listen here, Amoss Potter, if you don't shut up this minute, I'm going to arrest you for obstruction of a peace officer in the line of duty!"

There was silence for a few seconds. Then the old man shuffled his feet back over us and we heard the door closing.

"Come back here!" the cop ordered. It was quiet. "Damn, damn, damn, damn," he cussed. Then he climbed the stairs and crossed the platform, and we heard the door opening. "Look here, Amoss," he said in a more respectful tone. "We just want you to be on the lookout for any strangers trying to hop a ride out of town. Some outside agitators have been sent here to cause a riot. They've already tried to burn down the school, but we stopped them and we caught the ringleader. If you see anything, give us a call, okay?" There was no answer. "Amoss, will you give us a call?"

"I might," said Amoss. "If I see something."

"Fine, that's fine," said the cop. Then the door closed and he hurried to his car and roared off the same way he had come.

When the car was out of sight, the old man said, "Might not, either. Most likely won't, you sonofabitch. Just try to arrest me for ubstruction. I'll ubstruck your gaddamn nose from your gaddamn face, you sorry, sassy, punk sonofabitch. I'll shove that gun of yours down your sissy throat, you butt-sucking blue-belly bastard, and you'll be shittin little toy pistols, you upstart, lowlife, morphodite heathen. Little Ronnie runny-nose. Knew you since you were sucking titty, and you gonna tell me 'Hey you, get out here'? Nobody says 'Hey you, get out here!' to this stationmaster. Not talking to me like I'm a dog, you sonofabitch!"

For a long time we could hear him grumbling. After a while he talked so low it was hard to make out what he was saying, but every few minutes he would yell, "Sonofabitch!" Then his voice would trail off and we could hear a growling sound, like a dog might make with its mouth closed, until the next "Sonofabitch!" would burst out of him. This went on for probably a half-hour. Then the sonofabitching and the growling faded into what was definitely a loud snore.

I crawled out and went to look in the window to see if the old man was really sleeping. And sure enough, he was, leaning back in his chair, feet up on his desk, his chin resting on his chest. He wore a striped engineer's cap, a blue shirt, and overalls. Sewn on the cap was a red patch that said AMOSS. He had a worn-out face full of deep wrinkles and brown splotches and moles. He looked kind of yellowish too, a sicky kind of yellow, like watery mustard. As he slept, his hands twitched a little, and each time they did he would scratch them – first one, then the other. Then he would fold them together across his belly. There were scabs all across the backs of his hands from all the scratching.

I went back to the edge of the platform and sat down. Mamie came out and started playing on the tracks, picking up rocks and throwing them at trees across the way. After a bit I remembered about the book in my back pocket, *Blithe Spirit*. I pulled it out and read some of it, but it was kind of boring, so I flipped through it fast and came to a place I liked. Someone named Madame Arcati was saying, "Ghostly spectre – ghoul or fiend / Never more be thou convened / Shepherd's Wort and Holy Rite / Banish thee into the night." I said it out loud a couple of times until I had it memorized. Then I stood up and tried to act it out, like I figured Madame Arcati was doing in the play, with wild gestures, shaking fists at the ghosts and ghouls and fiends. Mamie watched me, and I felt like an actor on a real stage almost. She was really interested in what I was doing. She came close and took it all in, staring at me like I was a marvel and a wonder.

When I was done, I asked her if she thought I was a good actor. She threw out her hands, just like I had done, and she said in a high voice like I had put on, "Ghostly spectre – ghoul or fiend." She shook her fists at the ghouls and fiends same as I had.

I clapped for her. It was great the way she did it. "You're the damndest," I said. "I wish I knew how the hell you did some things."

"Ghostly spectre – ghoul or fiend," she repeated, gestures and all, and waited for me to clap.

"I got to know, Mamie," I said. "How do you do it? How do you make a voice like mine, and like you did Mike Quart's?"

"Smma-art," she said, tapping her head with her finger.

"Yeah, smart," I agreed. But it had me up a stump, the Figaro thing, the Mike Quart thing, and the ghostly spectre, ghoul or fiend; these were parts to Mamie that didn't fit. It was neat what she could do, but it was freaky, chilly, a willies kind of thing. She was retarded; she stammered; she hardly ever put more than three or four words together at the same time. And yet, every once in a while she would pull off a perfect imitation of something someone did or said, like a little button in her brain would get pushed and bingo – she was someone else, an actor. Then she was herself again, the dumb Mamie going, "Uh-huh, yaay, smma-art," and all that.

"Mamie," I said, "you tell me how you do that now. What happens in your head that makes it so you can be somebody else's voice?"

Her eyes narrowed as she thought about it. Then she shrugged her shoulders and went back to throwing rocks, and I was left to ponder about it and get nowhere. Just like the question of the holyman and the demons, I finally decided that the answer was probably in getting older and reading a few tons of books.

My thoughts were interrupted by the sound of moaning. The sound was coming from inside the station. I tiptoed over and looked in the window. The old man was leaning forward in his chair, holding his belly and moaning. He looked like he was in some pain and needed help, so I took a chance and went inside.

"Who are you?" he said. "What you want?"

"I heard you in here. You sounded sick," I told him.

"Christ, yes, I'm sick. If I don't get some milk in me my ulcer is gonna bust wide open. It's happened before. Got me all upset today, punk cops picking on an old man."

Mamie came in and stood behind me. Amoss paused and gave her a look of awe. "Holy humpin leviathan, who's that?"

"It's my buddy, Mamie," I answered. I was beginning to be proud of her, the way people reacted to the Mighty Kong look of her. To her I said, "He's got ulcers, says he needs milk."

Amoss searched in his pants pockets and brought out some change and asked me to take it and buy him some milk. Half and half was best for coating, he told me. I took the money and went outside. The road to town was in front of me, but I didn't want to take it. Yet I didn't want the old man to suffer either. I thought, why can't he go himself? It was dangerous for me to go. That cop might come by and catch me, and then what would Mamie do? She was more important than him. When you don't know what to do, arrange your values in the order you hold them, Pa always said. It was at that moment I realized I valued Mamie more than I ever thought I could. I wasn't going to do anything that would jeopardize her. But I didn't really have to make a decision between Amoss's sickness and Mamie, because next thing she came out the door with him cradled in her arms. He was blinking and smiling like a little boy who couldn't believe his luck. I told her to put him down.

"Leave her be," he said. "Don't you know who's sick around here?"

She held him easily, like he was hardly more than a sack of feathers. I tried to explain to him that we couldn't be going into town. We had our troubles too. "Can't you make it on your own?" I asked him.

He shook his head. "I'd be burping blood before I got halfway. But let me tell you, son, ours is the first house you see on the right of the road, past the woods there, next to the movie house. It ain't far. I'll vouch for you if we get stopped. Trust old Amoss. I'm a man of the trains forty-four years." He snorted and stuck out his lower lip, as if saying there was no more honorable man in the world than a man of the trains forty-four years.

"All right," I said. "The Samaritan thing to do is take you on home, so we will, and we trust you'll help us if need be." We set off toward the house he said was his.

"Was a cop here looking for agitators who burned down the school," he said, as we walked along. "You and this one, huh?" He glanced at Mamie, then back at me. "Don't you worry none, sonny. I wouldn't turn you in, not to the likes of them gaddamn Philistines. Forty-four years a man of the trains, and if you help me out that's what I go on, not what some wet-behind-the-ears punk sonofabitch says. Are you my friend? If you are, that's all my judgment cares. First house there, this side of the movies. What a gal this is here. I'd like to marry her. Feel safe as God Almighty with her arms wrapped round me. But oh, this ulcer – uhhh, uhhh – gaddamn it's a killer, guts just a-churning. I tell you what they say – they say I should retire. They find out this happened, they'll boot me out the door for sure."

Mamie carried him home to a shabby house with chipped yellowy paint and rusty screens and a wooden porch that looked to be full of dry rot and ants. In the driveway was an ancient Ford, something from Herbert Hoover's time. A big, half-dead elm tree took up most of the front yard; it shaded part of the house and porch, running humpy roots up under the sidewalk so the sidewalk tipped and cracked in half a dozen places.

"Let's go right in," Amoss told us. "Right in. I got a share of this joint. I can invite who I want."

I opened the door and Mamie carried him in and put him in a big chair, but he got up and shuffled off to the kitchen and grabbed himself a quart of milk from the refrigerator. He drank it down without stopping. Then he burped – four huge, gut-bubbling burps that rolled like tiny thunder from his mouth. "I'll like living a bit longer now," he said. He was looking in the refrigerator and he called out what there was to eat. "Weenies and cheese and beer. Ugh. Kill a fellow." He came back to the chair and sat down carefully. "Better," he said. "Much better, but can't handle no weenies and beer just yet. Gimmee my money back." He held out his hand and I dropped the change in it.

I also pulled out the leftover candy bars all melted in lumps that I had stolen from Plato. I offered them to him and Mamie. "You're a gaddamn good kid," he said, "but I can't eat no candy either." Mamie could. She tore the wrappers off with her teeth and gnashed the chocolate into mush and smiled at us.

Amoss giggled. "Ain't she something?" he said. "Looks like she's been eating mud. What a mess. Who the hell are you folks anyway? You sure as hell ain't from round here."

"We're orphans on our own. Just passing through on our way to get jobs down south."

"Orphans, huh?" He winked at me like he didn't believe it. "Life is tough on orphans."

"We milk cows. We know farming."

"Farmers, huh? Hard work, farming. Break your back. Mudface here looks like she could handle it." Mamie was busy running her tongue round and round her lips, searching for any stray chocolate she might have missed. "But you," said Amoss, pointing to me. "You look like you'd be about as much help as me, which is no help at all." He pulled the sleeve up on his shirt and held his arm next to mine. Our arms looked nearly alike, both without much hair, both thin and veiny. I had more tan and a string or two more muscle, but nothing worth bragging about. Our hands looked alike, too, wrinkled and rough. He noticed it.

"You got an old man's hand there," he said. "Now that's a farmer's hand all right. If you want to say you're a farmer, I'll believe you. I don't care much one way or the other. If you say you're orphans and farmers, it ain't Amoss's business to pry. You helped him; that's all he needs to know. Except maybe what's your names."

When I told him our names, he said they were good names and that if we couldn't be friends nobody could. And he told us that if we wanted to hang around for a few days and sleep on the floor, why, sure we could, because he said so. And then he told us about Don Shepard. "Shepard will welcome you too. He don't care. He's my partner. We bought that movie house next door, and we're gonna renovate it and show this town what classy movies is all about. Shepard is an expert on them. You'll like him. He's a big, overgrown baby, a big goof. He reads the dictionary from cover to cover and says it makes him a genius. But he's not a genius. He's just a slob, a big old slob who bawls like a baby if you look cross-eyed at him. What you say, you want to stick around and meet him, stick around and sleep on the floor? You're welcome to. Maybe Shepard'll hire you to help fix the movie place up. If you come cheap nuff."

I shrugged. I had no idea if I wanted to stick around. It wasn't much of a place, but it was probably better than being bare in the woods. There was a couch a fellow could sleep on, and there was a big chair with its arms split and tufts of cotton spilling out. In front of the couch was a dusty coffee table with folded beer cans on it and sheets of paper with words written on them. I looked closer and saw hundreds of words with the meanings written in a thick scrawl next to them.

"That's Shepard's stuff," said Amoss. "He thinks he's a genius. He's gonna bring culture to Temple, he says. See all them books? All his. Wouldn't catch me reading so many books. Boils the brain. Thomas Paine is plenty for me. A man with horse sense. Shepard, he likes to read things about the movies. Thinks he's an expert. Ever see so many books?"

I had seen more in the library, but what Shepard had was impressive all right, a whole wall covered with books stacked tight on knotty-pine shelves. In front of the shelves were more books crammed into crates, one after the other like little train cars.

"Go ahead and look around," said Amoss. "My room is on the right back there, Shepard's is on the left, and the bathroom's in the middle, if you have to go. Don't mind the mess. We're just batching it. I keep saying I'm gonna clean it up tomorrow, haw haw."

I peeked in Amoss's room. The bed was a mess and the floor was full of junk – socks and shorts and dirty shirts everywhere. They made me think of little stuffed animals lying around for some kid to play with. On the wall was a picture of Hedy Lamarr as Delilah and Victor Mature as Samson. The picture was curling at the corners and ready to fall off. On a stand next to the bed was a book called *The Age of Reason* open with a pencil in the middle. Underlined was the sentence, "My own mind is my own church."

Shepard's room was just as messy. It had a big desk in it piled high with books. I saw titles like *Great Movies of the Past, Movie Classics from the Past Twenty Years, The Great Money-making Films of All Time*, and so on – a dozen of them, with covers wrinkled and torn and with slips of paper here and there marking pages he wanted to read again. I opened one book at a marker and saw a picture of a blond man in a black outfit. His name was Laurence Olivier. Beside the picture in the margin was written a note – "Open Artlife with this!" The movie was *Hamlet*, my pa's favorite Shakespeare play. Now that would be something he would go a long way to see, I thought. Somebody had made a movie of *Hamlet*. I wondered if he knew.

I went back to the living room. Amoss was keeping watch on Mamie. He was looking at her like she was nuts. "Look what's she's doing," he said.

She was holding a book upside down in her hands and moving her lips like she was reading the words. "She can't read," I said.

"Not upside down," he replied.

Then out loud we heard her chant the words, "Ghostly spectre – ghoul or fiend," as if she saw it there on the page. And she kept repeating it, "Ghostly spectre – ghoul or fiend." It was like watching a movie that kept sticking and backing up at the same spot.

"She's doing that because she saw me doing it," I told Amoss. "'Monkey see, monkey do' is her. She pretends to be smart." I tapped the book she held and told her it was not *Blithe Spirit*. I said she had it upside down and she should quit pretending to read; holding a book upside down just made her seem a fool. I took the book away, but she just picked up another one.

"It's okay," said Amoss. "She ain't hurting nothing. Sounds just a bit like you when she says it. She's a mimic is what she is." He sighed and scrunched down in the chair. "Boy, I sure feel lousy." He started complaining about how bad he felt. Then he made me promise not to tell anybody what had happened to him at the station, not even Shepard because Shepard might blab, he's such a talker, and then the powers that be would want forty-four years to be the end of it. "Retiring is dying," he explained. "They do that to old people, you know, catch them on a bad day and make them retire. It means it's time to go die, that's what it means, and any old fart knows it. What you got left when you can't work? This country hates its old folks; everybody knows that. They let them die in hospitals every chance they get, just so it looks natural. Get the old carcasses out of the way. Whew, my guts are turning still. There's some Tums on the kitchen table. Would you get them for me? I feel like I'm bloating." Another huge burp roared from him. I got the Tums and he popped a handful in his mouth and chewed them. "Gag a maggot, this stuff," he said, making a sour face.

Mamie went on playing book, picking one up, looking inside, making her little speech. Amoss sat up straight and burped more, then leaned back and said he felt better. "Just bear with me. I'd get really sick if I didn't let it go. Worn-out guts. It's what happens when you get old. You turn into a gas bag." He ate more Tums, burped more, and bitched more about being old and full of gas. Then he changed the subject and asked me did I know anything about who set fire to the school.

"A guy name of Robbie Peevy," I told him. "We were there, but we didn't do nothing. He wanted to burn the books. Mamie and I had hitched a ride from him, that's all."

"Haw haw! Robbie Peevy. What do you know? I thought that brain-dead varmint was still in Camelot. Wait'll Shepard hears this. Little Peevy's come back to haunt Vendenberg and Temple. You probably don't know that Vendenberg and some others got that nut committed some years back. He was always setting fire to things. He wanted to burn all the libraries of the world, all the putrefaction, and now he's come back to haunt them. That'll stir things up. He was something when he was little. I think he was maybe five or six when he started preaching. The little miracle. The little bullshitter. 'You're all hanging over the pits of hell, hanging by the spider-thread of life,' is what he liked to say. Pretty good, huh, for a tyke?" Amoss had chalky lips from the Tums. They made me think of ghost lips, the way they were white and the only things moving on his old yellow face. Bad sickness was written all over him.

"You know," he continued, "that Robbie took over Huckle's barn, that's right, and made some real money preaching there. I seen him myself and paid a dollar to the plate. I was curious. And I admit I got a kick out of him. He was so little and saying all these big things about Jesus coming and the raising of the dead, and hellfire, Satan, and all that stuff. Could almost make a fellow believe there was something to it, coming out of such a little one that shouldn't know nothing. But it wore off as he grew up and lost his cuteness. He turned into a long-haired, gawky nuisance, just a pain in the ass, full of Bible talk about the Lord. That's how the Christers get, all of them. Blah blah blah, heard one you heard them all, like a bunch of robots, bunch of clones. They get touched is what happens, and I mean touched in the Camelot way." Amoss twirled his finger near his temple.

"Am I right?" he asked. "Jesus this and Jesus that, and never a thimbleful of proof about anything they say except they *feel* it. If feelings is proof, then my feelings is as good as theirs, right? Well, I feel that the God of the Christers is a pretty ornery fellow that don't have an ounce of pity in his bleeding heart. What'd I do to deserve ulcers like this, I'd like to know. You know, it's mighty strange if you think about it that this here *loving father* and all has to have a human sacrifice because he can't find any kinder way of forgiving these dumb bastards that he created than to kill his own son. Ferocious, ain't he? He can do anything he wants about his little creation, and what does he want? Blood. Got to have blood. If that's loving kindness, those knee-bending bastards can have it. Amoss Potter wants no part of such baloney. Am I right? But they know how you should think and how you should live. Truth is tucked away in their hip pockets. Bah! Hey, what's she doing with them books? She's throwing them away!"

Mamie was throwing books out the door.

"That's what the Christers were doing," I explained.

"Well, you better stop her before Shepard gets here. He ain't gonna like that."

I stood in front of Mamie and shook my head no at her and asked her why she was doing it. She frowned at me. "Kritch'n," she said, opening a book and pointing at the words. "Say it dis."

I didn't understand at first. "Say it dis what, Mamie?"

Her finger went down the book as she repeated, "Ghostly spectre – ghoul or fiend. Say it dis, Kritch'n." Mamie looked frustrated. It was like she had figured out that there had to be more words than ghostly spectre, ghoul or fiend in all the books she was going through, and it made her mad to not know the words so she was going to throw them out. I took hold of the book in her hands. It was *Great Expectations*, by Charles Dickens. It was too thick to read to her. I tried to explain how many words were there, but she didn't understand. She kept tapping the book, wanting me to read it. I opened to a page and read the first thing I saw: "Pumblechook sat staring at me, and shaking his head and saying, 'Take warning, boy, take warning!'"

Mamie waited for me to go on, but I turned from her and started picking up the books that she had thrown out. When I had them back on the shelves, she was still standing there, giving me the eye.

"Mamie," I said. "I can't read it all. It would take days. Now, I tried to teach you how to read. I tried to teach you the ABCs, remember? If you want to learn what's in these books, you'll have to learn the ABCs. There's no other way, so don't give me dirty looks. I can't read it all and that's that." I walked outside and stood on the porch with my arms crossed.

I heard her picking up the book behind me and repeating back what I had read, "Pumblechook sat staring at me, and shaking his head and saying, 'Take warning, boy, take warning!'"

"Yeah yeah," I said, over my shoulder. "You can do that trick, but that don't mean you can read."

"No accounting what a nut thinks, eh?" yelled Amoss. "But she's a hell of a mimic, son. She's got something going for her."

I went back inside. "But it's not her, Amoss," I told him. "What good is it, if it's not her? Just makes her more freaky."

"That ain't freaky, son. What's so freaky? Hey, Mamie, bring your book here. I'll read it to you."

Mamie handed the book to Amoss and sat on the coffee table next to him while he read to her. He was a good enough reader, but it was stop and go Dickens between burps, until finally he snapped the book shut and said it was making him nervous and getting him bloated. He rocked forward and belched, a long, rolling, wet one.

Mamie swallowed air and imitated him. He burst out laughing so hard he nearly fell out of the chair. He kept pointing at Mamie and crying, "Look at her! Look at her face! What a frog! Gaddamn, I like that face!"

She just looked like Mamie to me, except her mouth was still ringed with a smear of chocolate and her teeth were stained. The rest of her was the same open-eyed, freckle-faced, round-headed moon-glowing Mamie I was used to. She grinned and entertained Amoss with her endless burps and he did the same to her, and they both acted like it was hilarious beyond belief. I stayed by the front door in the fresh air. I sat down on the floor and leaned my back on some books. Mamie and Amoss kept booming at each other and laughing, but I didn't get what was so funny.

Bleeding Ulcers

Singing woke me. I was curled around a pillow on the floor. The door was closed and the lights were on. Amoss and a huge man were sitting on the couch facing Mamie, who was still sitting on the coffee table. The two men were singing to Mamie. They were singing, "May-mee, May-mee, give us your answer do, we're half cra-zee, all for the love of youuu." Mamie was howling as the men sang; she went, "Oooo . . . oooo."

When they were finished, Amoss said, "Do Shepard, Mamoo. Let me hear him. Come on. Don't make a liar out of me."

Mamie had a can of beer in her hand. She drank from it and watched Amoss at the same time, as he tried to get her to do an imitation of Shepard. All three of them were drinking. Crushed cans were scattered on the floor. The place was full of the smell of it, of booze.

I sat up and Amoss waved his arm to me. "Come here, sleepyhead," he said. "Come here and tell this ton of blubber that Mamie ain't a faker. He says she is. But I heard it with my own lips; she can sound just like this boy here, perfect, perfect. Annnd she can do you too. Assk the boy, assk him. She a faker, boy?"

"I believe you, Amoss," said Shepard. "You don't have to prove her to me."

"You said she waas a faker."

"A teasing tautology, Amoss, yum yum. A face like this could never fake a thing. So pret-ty, so pretty pretty."

"Say hello to my partner Shepard," said Amoss. "Shepard, thisss iss Christian, a good boy."

Shepard stood and held out his hand. Best way I can think of to describe Shepard is to say he looked like a toothless walrus – big mustache and no front teeth, just the dogteeth grinning out of an otherwise pink hole; heavy cheeks and double chins; eyebrows wiry and long, like the mustache; eyes in a nest of wrinkles; forehead like a washboard; tangled hair, mostly brown with streaks of gray. Best thing about him, though, was his nose. It was tremendous. It had the size and nearly the shape of a plum smashed onto his face. It had a plummish color too, but it had pits and ripples that gave it a kind of cauliflower bumpiness. It was a wonder, that nose, a real beauty. I stood up and held out my hand to shake. His belly was showing beneath his T-shirt, and when he walked to me his belly shook and bulged and trembled. When he stood in front of me his navel was about the level of my chin. It looked like a pale eye goggling at me, a hairy, pale eye. But the nose I liked the best. I could see right up into his nostrils. They were tiny compared to his nose, almost hidden, in fact, by the ball-shaped end and the bush of the mustache underneath.

"Annnd you thought Mamie was big, hey?" said Amoss. "Iss he a monster or what?"

Shepard waved a hand at Amoss and told me to never mind him but to "disengage the puttering of a mind so futile as the mind of Amoss Potter." And he added, "I, on the other hand, am a bona fide genius, yum yum, spouting pearls of Socratic flavor for the fomentation of your tender mind."

He grabbed my hand and gave it a quick shake and said that we had come to the final depot of culture in a vast valley of bone-bare intelligence – this Temple of ignorance. "And thank you for saving Amoss," he said. "He is playing the last sorrows of time."

"You can stay long as you want," Amoss put in. "Long as you want as you've a mind to."

Shepard tipped my head back and looked into my face. "Ah," he said, "shiny luminescence of such tender years in your clear eyes. Luster, lush, and luscious, yum yum. I once had eyes like that." He spoke slowly, with a darting of his tongue around the words, like he was tasting them before letting them go.

"Cut the crap" said Amoss. "You never had eyes like that, not in a million years. Hey, let's get some gaddamn booze out here. Thiss sis empty." He crushed the can and threw it on the floor.

"No more for you, Amoss," said Shepard.

"Hump a duckfuck!"

Shepard ignored him and asked me what was the name again. "Ah, Christian, yes . . . no." He backed away and looked me up and down. "Nomenclature on the fragile side," he said. "A crystal Christian. A crystal! I like it. Crystal Christian. And you may say that I am Shepard, conductor of the whole river of soul, the *anima mundi*, the collected river of art." He patted me gently on the shoulder and crooned my new name to me, "Crys-tal Chris-tian. How well it fits on you, so fragile, fragile as a long-stemmed glass, yum yum."

"You sound like a gaddamn Martian!" Amoss shouted. "You're gonna scare the kid outta here. Now get the gaddamn splow."

"Poof poof," Shepard answered. "Genius has power and magic that callow youth can't understand. It's not for the rat-a-tat likes of you, Amoss." He turned away and went into the kitchen. He bumped his belly first into the table, then into the stove, and then bounced it off the refrigerator and grabbed the door at the same time. He gathered beers, three in each hand, and brought them back to the couch and dumped them there.

Amoss waded in, and Shepard said, "My dear old dipsodear likes his beer, doesn't he? He runs from sun to sun, like a savage. Drink your heart into contentment, Amoss. What else has he got? Poor boy, poor poor boy." Real tears were running down Shepard's face. He took out his hanky and gave his nosc a good blow.

Amoss looked sideways up at him and cackled. "Ain't he a big baby? He bawls over everything, it's no shit. Tweak him on the ass, he'll wail like you shot him. Sssit down, jellybelly."

Shepard sat and the couch dipped under him, the sides pulling in and the frame creaking like a rusty hinge. He handed Mamie and me each a beer and opened a can for himself. "To our new friends, Mamie and Crystal," he said.

"You don't have to ask me twice," said Amoss, and he drank off a whole can at once. Then he burped like a machine gun and laughed like no one had ever done anything so funny.

"He's determined to disgust us," said Shepard. "Ignore him."

"Sstick your rear in your ear annnd your rear in your beer. Put a nose up your rose till it glows, hee hee hee." Amoss grabbed another beer and opened it.

Shepard asked me if I liked movies. I said I did. He said he and Amoss had bought the theater next door and were going to make it the art center of Temple. He was renovating it now, inside and out. "A labor of love for art the precious. It'll take six or seven months, hand-woven. And then I'll choose only the great movies. It will be relevance and purity or nothing at all. Like books," he said, pointing to his books. "And who is your favorite writer?"

"I like Jack London's *The Call of the Wild.* I like that dog."

He made a face like he had drunk poison. Then he stabbed his finger in the air and said, "Trash! Trash! The dregs of opposition to the intellectual life. Oh, Crystal, dear dcar, an underculture author. Portentous philosopher of Darwin and savagery, ugh. No refinement, no delicacy, no subtle persuasion. He hits you over the head with a whip of intestine. You can't really like him, Crystal. Tell Shepard it's a lie."

"It's not a lie," I said. "I like him. I'd like to be able to write like him. Lots of people read his books, I think."

Shepard stroked his nose and looked down it at me. "So, poof poof on me, huh? Caught me in the coils of a child's wisdom. What can I say? Jack London does have an incandescence, yum yum. And I, the Shepard, am merely mortal. The immortal London; the mortal Shepard. Writer versus critic – nasty, ephemeral critic, yum yum. I love the pomposity of it. I am a genius, after all, a genius abandoned on the frontier of backwoods understanding. Fortune meant me to be rich, yum, so I could defray the cost of mental whimsy. But somehow I've managed to baffle fortune, to baffle my destiny – till now! With the Artlife, I will fulfill my early promise. Is that right, Amoss?"

"Gaddamn sure, buddy, ole bubbybub," he answered. "Ask Mamie. She's made of magic, right, Mamie?"

Mamie whistled at him, a wolf whistle loud and shrill enough to hurt our ears. "She's drunk," said Amoss. "Drunk as a bedbug in June."

"Barbarian profundity that." Shepard jerked his thumb at Amoss. "In the annals of Oxfordian inclination are listed the famous utterances of Amoss Potter, man of trains forty and four years, whose immortal aphorism shines forth – 'drunk as a bedbug in June.' Amoss, you have a god's plethora of vocabulary and a mind as tenacious as a cobweb."

"Kiss this bumbomb, mushmouth," said Amoss, raising his leg and letting his rear end roar.

"Ugh, disgusting," said Shepard.

"It's coming to get you, moosenose!"

Shepard stroked his nose again, as if soothing it. "Neanderthal. Homo erectal pithecine, throwback to dark and dreary caves, genetic survivor of the omophagists, plague of my twoscore years, you've proved your head is as full of air as your cacophonous behind."

"Hee hee hee, what do I care whatcha call me, banananose. You never make no gaddamn sense nohow. You understand any of hiss two-bit lingo, Christian?"

"Some," I answered.

"See, nobody unnerstands you, shiphead. You're speaking voodoo."

"Poof poof."

Amoss burped at him. "Thass your language, makes ass much sense."

Shepard twirled his mustache and said to me, "It just won't take cultivation. It is chromosomally damaged. Don't let it influence you, Crystal. Your broad brow is meant for Johnsonian enlightenment, not for the dribblings this dipsodunce can produce."

"Want to see me ssstand on my head and drink beer?" cried Amoss.

"Oh yes!" said Shepard, suddenly interested. "Do it, Amoss. Stand on your head and show them how you drink beer. You'll like this, kids."

Amoss shouted happily, "All right! Hardly a man on the fist of the earth can do what I can. Not wartnose here, thass for sure." He sneered at Shepard once more. Then he turned himself upside down on the couch, throwing his legs over his head, his heels booming into the wall. He held himself like that and sucked beer into his mouth, working his throat muscles, his Adam's apple bobbing, until somehow he drank the entire can of beer. When he was done, he threw the can at Shepard, who let it bounce off his shoulder.

"Isn't he a talent?" said Shepard. "You know any seventy-year-old men who can do that? Nobody. I've tried to get him to entertain on streetcorners downtown, but he's too shy – right, Amoss?"

"Shy as that plum on your face."

Shepard touched his nose again and stroked it like he was petting a mouse. "Don't make fun of this noble biscuit," he said. "Durante should be so lucky to have one. Tis a badge of great character."

While he was talking, Mamie went over to the couch and joined Amoss upside down. She smiled hugely at us, her face getting bright red from the blood sinking down, and reached out her hand for a beer.

"Let her try, juss let her try," said Amoss.

I gave her a beer, and she stuck it to her lips and tried to pour it in. The beer ran up her nose instead, and she was snorting and coughing so bad she had to stand up again. I pounded her on the back. Amoss was cackling and saying, "Tell me it ain't a gift, tell me it ain't a talent. Ain't a man I know can do it, hee hee hee, and damn sure not a man my age. Iss a special gift from God."

Mamie coughed and coughed, and Amoss told her not to go and die on us now, but it was a while before she could quit. Then she was back upside down on the couch, reaching for her beer. Amoss coached her this time, saying, "Suck it, Mamoo. Don't let no air in your mouth. Suck it like iss a hose you siphon with. Thass the secret." She did what he said, gluing her lips to the opening and siphoning the beer out. It worked. And when the can was empty, she wanted another, but I told her to quit showing off. It was Amoss's trick she was stealing, and I could tell by the look on his face he wasn't sure he liked it.

"I give her the secret and gaddammit she does it," he said. "But I can drink more!" He reached out his hand for us to give him more.

"No more. Your face is as red as a firecracker," said Shepard. "Now get down before you have a stroke."

"You too, Mamie," I said.

Amoss flipped back over on his feet and Mamie did too. She rolled over on her fanny and sat next to Shepard. "Mamie listens to you," he said.

"Nope," I told him. "I think it depends on her mood."

She picked up another beer and guzzled it down. She crushed the can and threw it with the others on the floor, then burped like fire was in her belly. Her face was glowing like a light was on inside. Shepard liked the way she looked. He patted her thigh and squeezed it. "This is a magnificent creature," he said. "Yum yum yum."

"Yum yum yourself," said Amoss. "I'm hongry and my ulcer hurts me. I wanna weeny. Fix a weeny, Shepard."

"Don't you have more sense than that to put hot dogs and beer on top of an ulcer? It's barbaric, antediluvian, no more sense than Noah, who drank himself to death. Hot dogs on top of beer. It refuses to listen. It refuses to learn."

Amoss stuck his tongue out. "My ulcer, fatnose, my fuggin ulcer, and it wanns a weeny!" And he stomped off to the kitchen to make himself one.

Shepard showed his dogteeth and laughed. "Profound Oxfordian, you know, the Mr. Bones of science labs, yum yum, isn't he?"

We shared the hot dogs, all of us, with Amoss, putting cheese on them and rolling them in slices of bread and washing them down with beer. Afterward I felt sleepy and wished we could go to bed. But sleeping seemed pretty far from their minds. They blabbed on and on, especially Shepard, who said geniuses like him needed to talk in order to make room in their heads for all the ideas coming in. He said he wanted to tell us about the history of wisdom and integrations catastrophically learned by him before he was ten years old, and about certain unsuspected connections between politicians, who spoke the purest cant imaginable but were digestibly believed by the ilk of the earth, and philosophers, whose written tongue-twistings were held up by college-cloistered scholars as examples of unparalleled insights into the puzzlements of modern man, yum yum. All the while he talked, he sat with his fingers drumming on his belly and his mouth chewing all the flavor it could get out of his words. And at one point he paused and said, "Of course, this is too far advanced for you to understand. But listen anyway, fill the brain with words."

I tried hard, but I couldn't keep listening. I knew he was saying something I should want to know. But I was too dull to get more than bits of it here and there. And besides, I was sleepy.

It got more interesting when he got off the subject of politicians and philosophers and started talking about himself. He said again how he was a genius, that he was one of the chosen few of the earth and was meant for a special destiny. But he was twoscore years now and still didn't know for absolute what it was he was supposed to do that was so special, except he hoped it was to bring great art to Temple, which was better than working as a janitor at the college, which is what he had been doing. The art movement in Temple might be the bringer of better things, maybe even the start of a movement that would find disciples in all parts of the world. He would wait and work to see it happen, and he would be patient, because patience was the most important attribute of geniuses. He would be patient and apply his brilliance to the discernment of his destiny, and it would come to him one day full-blown, as if from the head of Zeus. Then he would know what the ultimate connection was between his genius and the *anima mundi* flowing throughout the world.

Up to now, he said, he had managed to figure out how to manifest his eccentricities – by dropping out of school when he was ten because it was a haven of reactionary thought creating mental robots to unfeelingly perpetuate the monstrosity of the capitalist system, with its disgusting pride in survival of the fittest; by dropping out of the army when he was drafted, twisting the intricacies of his thought around the ineptitude of an army psychiatrist until that psychiatrist recommended a medical discharge for the mentally unfit; by dropping all contact with women who refused to have anything to do with him, who judged him by exteriors rather than interiors, where he shined like the most handsome of movie stars, a Gable or a Cooper or even John Wayne; by dropping in on his father, who had disowned him, and convincing the old fellow to leave all his money to the growth of sensibility and culture. The old fellow died and did leave money, and it was in use right now in the rehabilitation of the theater next door, so aptly named Artlife. Though *all* the money wasn't there – some of it was going to doctors and medicines for old Amoss Potter, a minion crawling like sore water beneath the blind eye of heaven, who took the money but still wouldn't take care of his ulcers.

Shepard got upset at the idea; he took out his hanky and wiped his eyes and blew his nose. He said he was the only genius he knew who had such depth of soul, such bad teeth, and such a bad back, and whose heart was too big for his own good. Then he broke down and really cried. It was hard to resist. I had to blow my nose a couple of times. Amoss was weeping too and declaring himself the only true friend of the truest of friends, that greatest genius of all time. Amoss stood and shook his fists at me and told me not to forget it either. Then he threw himself over Shepard and hugged him and hugged him. They both sobbed over their wonderful friendship. I patted them both on the back. Mamie went over to the empty beer cans on the floor and raised them one by one to see if she could squeeze out any more drops on her tongue.

"Mmm-ore," she said, looking at the three of us.

"It's all gone," I told her.

"Kritch'n!" she shouted, stamping her foot. "Mmm-ore!"

I got up to see if there was one more hidden in the refrigerator, but there wasn't. On top, though, I saw two quart-jars of something that looked like tea. The label was kind of vague. It was handwritten in ink and said SPLOW 150 pruf. I opened one and sniffed. The stink made my eyes water. It was definitely some kind of whiskey. I took it to Mamie and told her to try it. She loved it. She had it half-gone before Amoss could grab a drink for himself. Next Shepard took it from Amoss and drank, and then Mamie stood up and wrestled the jar from Shepard. He tried to take it back but lost his grip and fell over backward, hitting the floor like an anvil. Mamie sat on his belly while she finished the splow. When it was gone she jumped up and kicked her boots off, sending them crashing into the shelf of books.

Shepard grabbed one of her feet and kissed it. "I love you!" he cried. "I've been waiting for you all my life."

"What a woman!" said Amos. "Marry me!"

"Mmm-ore," demanded Mamie, shaking the empty jar.

"Get her more, Amoss. Help me up, Mamie."

She grabbed hold and pulled him to his feet. He turned on the radio to a polka station. The sounds of a polka filled the room.

Shepard took Mamie's hand and coaxed her to dance. He yelled at Amoss to get the splow before she lost the mood. He reached down and gave Mamie's bottom a squeeze. But Amoss wasn't moving. He stared at them, both of them bouncing like huge balls around the room, making the floor beneath our feet roll and sway like an earthquake was happening.

"Waa-hoo!" Amoss yelled suddenly, leaping to his feet and taking one of Mamie's hands, then one of Shepard's too, and dancing around with them, bobbing his head up and down and crying out, "Yip yip yip!" The three of them whirled like in ring-around-the-rosies, and to keep from getting stomped on I hopped up on the couch. The couch itself was doing its own dance; all the furniture was. Mamie and Shepard were following Amoss's lead and bobbing their heads and hollering, "Yip yip yip!" with him, moving clockwise and kicking their legs toward the center of the circle. Faster and faster they went, round and round, not stopping even when the music stopped and some announcer was trying to sell Doctor Moth's Witch Hazel. They kept yipping and twisting themselves in circles, while the man finished his spiel and put on another polka.

But by that time Amoss was looking pretty sick and had lost the steam in his kicks and his yips. A few seconds later, he let go of their hands and fell with a bang on the floor. He lay there doubled-up, holding his stomach. Shepard went down too, huffing and puffing as he lay looking up at Mamie, who was pretty fresh yet as she banged round the room, kicking beer cans, knocking books over, and making the floor boom like a drum beneath her feet. She was having a hell of a time, so when the music quit again she made her own, singing the hiya norain – "Hiya no-rain! Hiya no-rain!" – her eyes going from Amoss to Shepard like she was calling them, but they lay there gasping like dying fish. She even bent over and yelled into their faces – "Hiya no-rain!" – but they couldn't live up to it. Shepard tried. You could see it in his face he knew this was his chance. But he could only get to his knees and say, "Magnificent," before he fell over on his side.

Amoss was trying to do something too. His legs and arms were jerking like somebody was sticking needles in him. Suddenly he sat up and said, "Oooo, I'm sick." Then he burped, huge and wet and long. "Ughhh, something tastes funny," he said, making a bitter face.

Mamie stopped singing and dancing. Shepard looked over to Amoss. Amoss looked from me to Mamie, and his eyes held there. His mouth was open wide, and a pure wonder and a pure fear were in his eyes.

"Tastes like salt," he said. "Somebody poured salt in my mouth, sticky salt. I know that taste. I know what it is. Here it comes! Here it comes!"

From deep in his belly came another ugly burp, and with it flew a clot of blood that hit the floor and splashed over Mamie's bare feet. Her eyes fixed on the blood, like it was a strange puzzle. More blood came out of Amoss's mouth, lots of it. It poured into his lap, foaming with pink bubbles and bits of weiner and other junk.

"I'm dying," he whispered.

I looked at Shepard. His eyes were open but he was out cold.

"Hobbidal," choked Amoss. "Gid me to da hobbidal."

I glanced at Mamie. She was still fascinated with the blood on her foot. She bent down and ran her finger through it, shaping it so it looked like it had wings, like it was a moth or a butterfly.

I lost my head. I ran across the floor and kicked her. Then I kicked Shepard. "Do something!" I kept saying. Mamie did. She grabbed Amoss, and held him in her arms and rocked him. Kicking Shepard didn't do any good, so I ran into the kitchen and got a glass of water and threw it in his face. It woke him up.

"Amoss is dead," he said, first thing. Then, "Don't show me his blood!"

The blood had quit pouring from Amoss's mouth and clogging up the way he talked. He said to Shepard, "Ain't dead yet, Don, but I'm gonna be if you don't get me to the hospital."

Shepard made a mighty effort and got to his feet. He stood with one hand against the wall, swaying and looking away from us. "Cover the blood," he said. "I'll faint if you don't cover the blood."

I covered the blood with dish towels. Then I led Shepard out the door and to the car. Mamie came behind us, carrying Amoss. As we started to get in the car, he said, "Paine, Paine, I want my Paine." I ran back in and got the book off the nightstand and hurried back. When we got in the car and had started off, Shepard asked Amoss what he wanted Thomas Paine for, and Amoss said, "To remind me who I am, that's why." He was sitting in Mamie's lap, looking over her shoulder at me. He told me to read the part where the pencil was. "My own mind is my own church." I read, and then he had me back up some. He put his bloody finger on "I believe in one God and no more; and I hope for happiness beyond this life." When I had finished he said, "I'm sure glad I'm drunk. It ain't so scary when you're drunk. I ain't scared. Save me! I ain't scared. I ain't scared at all."

"Beer and hot dogs on an ulcer," said Shepard. He kept wiping his eyes and wiping his mustache. Little sobs kept breaking out of him. "Beer and hot dogs on an ulcer, you harlequin, you fool."

"Dribe da gaddamn car and shud up," answered Amoss, his voice clogging again with blood.

"Beer and hot dogs on an ulcer. Never listens to me, *never*."

The rest of the way we were quiet. I sat in the back holding *The Age of Reason*. Mamie hummed a song and rocked Amoss. Shepard couldn't quit wiping tears off his face. By the time we got to the hospital, Amoss was soaked deep in blood. Mamie carried him through the doors. A nurse ran up with a gurney and Mamie laid him on it. Someone came with papers on a clipboard and started asking questions. Shepard was trembling and blowing his nose and saying he was rich and would pay. But the guy with the clipboard kept asking, "What insurance, sir? What is the name of your insurance?" Amoss made a noise that was a sort of "huck huck huck," and more blood boiled out of him. Shepard's eyes rolled and down he went.

"Get going, nurse!" yelled the man with the clipboard.

The nurse and another man in white took off with Amoss down the hall and disappeared with him through some double doors. At the same time, a doctor stuck something under Shepard's nose and woke him up. "Save him, save him," he said weakly. Everybody helped to get him on his feet. Then he was led to where he could sit and fill out the hospital papers. Mamie and I went outside and leaned against the car and waited. Pretty soon Shepard came out too.

It wasn't even an hour before a doctor came out and told us that Amoss hadn't made it. "He lost too much blood. He didn't suffer. He didn't know what was happening." Shepard was sobbing the whole time, so the doctor patted him on the back and kept repeating how Amoss didn't suffer. Finally the doctor said he had to go back in, so I took over patting Shepard on the back. No matter how I patted, though, he wouldn't quit crying. I had never seen someone who could blubber so much, and it got a bit on my nerves. I had an impulse to slap him and say, "Be a man!" But I didn't do that. It wouldn't have been very sympathetic, seeing how Amoss was dead.

At last we got Shepard into the car, and I drove us home. As we pulled into the driveway, he said, "You're staying, aren't you? You're not leaving me alone?"

"We can stay awhile," I said.

"I can't believe he's dead. It's just awful, awful. Why does this have to happen to me now? Everything was going so well. Beer and hot dogs - I tried to tell him. Stubborn. Stubborn old nitwit."

When we got him inside, he went right to the second jar of splow and took it with him into his room and closed the door. Mamie and I looked at each other. "What now?" I said.

"Kritch'n, Amoth drowd'n man," said Mamie.

"Just like that," I answered, snapping my fingers. The quickness of it was hard to get a hold of. He was alive, then he was dead. A man having a dance, then a man heaving blood and saying "I ain't scared. Save me!" Where did he go? I wondered. Where was he now?

"Kritch'n, look dis." Mamie pointed to the blood all over her farmeralls and her feet. Then she started taking her clothes off.

"Take them off. Go take a shower," I said. Naked, she went into the bathroom.

I decided to take a shower with her. We soaped each other down over and over, and in the soaping I managed to get Amoss out of my mind for a while. It felt wonderful to have Mamie's hands on me, cleaning me all over, especially when she went round and round my stomach and chest. And when I did her, the picture of Amoss dying all but disappeared. I soaped her back first, all the way down to her feet, then soaped the blood off her feet and soaped back up her legs and up to her neck. She felt so nice as my hands slipped over her skin, over the broadness of her, the solid broadness of her. I even washed her bottom, right into the crack up and down, and never felt it was wrong, not a bit wrong. When she turned round I soaped her front, spending a long time on her breasts, feeling through the slickness of the soap the firmness of them, the hardness of the nipples, the valley running down to her belly, which pooched out some but was as muscled as the rest of her. I washed her legs and in between her legs. I made a mound of soap there on the wiry, red hairs and felt with the tips of my fingers a different kind of wetness from the wetness of water.

We rinsed off and soaped each other again, and while I was doing Mamie she pulled me into her arms and rubbed her body on mine until we had lather that nearly hid us, except for parts of her breasts and most of the boner I couldn't help but have. We rinsed off again. We were so clean we squeaked, and we couldn't wait any longer to do the no-rain dance.

It was different this time, though. Mamie was soft about it. She didn't throw me on the bed and jump on me. She put herself there first, on her back, and held out her arms. I don't know if it was seeing her like that – with her arms out, her white body with its pure skin, its shiny hair, the tiny freckles, the sleepy eyes – that made me choke up a little, or if it was the memory of dying Amoss – who I saw just a flash of, held in Mamie's arms and saying, "Save me!" and he wasn't scared. The two things together, I suppose, got to me and I started to choke. Then I started to sob, started crying every bit as bad as Shepard had. I cried and I got on top of Mamie at the same time. It made me feel stupid at first, the crying on top of her when we were supposed to be doing the no-rain. But she put my head on her breasts until I got a better hold of myself; and then it was natural to kiss her breasts, they smelled so soapy good, and I sucked on them too, like a baby would. It was wonderful and sad at the same time. I kissed her on the lips next, on her big, soft mouth. For a long time I kissed her mouth, and in the kissing of it my tears went away and I thought only about what I was feeling. I felt her legs part, felt her hand grab me and put me inside, felt the warm wetness close all around, her arms around me, her body rocking back and forth, up and down with mine, her mouth sucking mine. And then the letting go inside her.

In the calm that came after, I stayed on top of her, loving her so much I had to say it or burst. "I love you more than the whole world," I told her. "More than anybody; more than anything."

"Yaay, Kritch'n," she said in a whisper so soft I almost missed it.

After a time I dozed off, for I don't know how long, but she woke me saying, "Mmm-ore, Kritch'n . . . more," and pulling on my bottom and pushing her hips up. I was still inside her and the movement got me up again, so we did it more and more and more, like she wanted. But the second one wasn't as good. It just wasn't as full of thunder as the first. But it was worth doing all right, and I was sorry when I finally couldn't go on because she was still saying more. Then she felt me going soft and she quit. She held me for a while and patted my back, like she was saying she knew I had done the best I could.

Finally I got up and turned out the light and got back in bed. It was really too narrow a bed for both of us, even on our sides. So narrow, in fact, that when Mamie fell asleep and turned over, she pushed me out. So I took one of the blankets and went to the living room, where the streetlight outside was shining in the window and I could see the towels soaked with blood dark on the floor. I stepped round them and went to the couch, and there on the wall above I could see Amoss's heel marks, where he had banged into the wall doing his upside-down beer-drinking trick. It came to me that only hours ago the marks and the blood had happened, and now Amoss was dead. And Mamie and I had come home and done the no-rain dance. Sometimes, when people die, the best thing you can do is the no-rain dance.

Being Hollow

Shepard had Amoss buried in a graveyard at the edge of town, between Temple and the country. The graveyard overlooked some nice farmland, gentle hills where corn would get harvested in October and cows would be let out to pick at the leftovers. There was plenty of shade, and there were lots of tombstones with dead people under them to keep Amoss company.

There weren't many of us at the funeral, just Mamie and me and Shepard, Charlie Friendly from the bar next door, and two guys named Jim and Cody. Shepard wouldn't allow a preacher to give a sermon because, he said, it would be an insult to the spirit of Amoss, who loved God but despised all religions. Instead, Shepard talked to Amoss at the graveside and told him how much he would be missed after fifteen years of their being together and sharing the same roof and the same table. He told Amoss not to be lonely but to look up Maurice Shepard and introduce himself, to tell Maurice that his son, Don, had sent along the best friend he'd ever had to keep his father from being lonely. Time would tell another tale one day, and there would be three of them to talk it over before long. Shepard said he was feeling his mortality, a cold shadow rested on his feet. He hoped when the time came to mingle souls that Amoss would have learned a lesson about mule-headedness and that Maurice would have learned to appreciate the unique gift of a son's genius. As soon as Shepard had finished, we all took a hand with some ropes and lowered the coffin into the hole. Then we shoveled dirt on top. And that was it. Amoss was down there in the dark.

When we got back to the house, Shepard and Mamie went with the others over to Charlie Friendly's bar. I didn't want to go with them. I knew they would sit around and get drunk and carry on, which I didn't feel like doing. I went into the house and picked out a book to read. I tried my best to forget about Amoss and all the blood and how quick and easy people die, and how quick and easy I might die some day and not have a thing to say about it.

It was that way with me for a lot of days after the funeral. I couldn't help thinking about Amoss and death and "I ain't afraid. Save me!" I kept wondering what my last words would be and whether I'd be scared or not when my turn came. I tried hard to imagine it – me, Christian Peter Foggy, dead. But I could only get so far, to some brave words, Mama and Pa crying, and everybody carrying on about how wonderful I was; I couldn't make myself stay down there, sealed in a coffin, self being spoken over, self going down down down, self inside while the dirt fell and made no noise, self inside the dark, under the dark. That I couldn't do. It couldn't happen to me – I would be the one chosen to never really die. During that time I memorized a poem by Keats that starts, "When I have fears that I may cease to be." He talked about how desolate it would be to die before he got to write all he wanted to write and before he got to love the "fair creature of an hour" that he looked on, and so he stood on the edge of the wide world and love and fame meant nothing to him. Nothing means nothing if you're not alive – all the looking down from afar is cold comfort, fairy talk. I didn't want to go the way of Amoss or Keats, not ever ever ever.

Shepard and Mamie spent their days either sleeping or eating or drinking, mostly drinking. Shepard brought home a case of splow, and he and Mamie went at it. Shepard got so he was telling her she was a better drinking partner than Amoss, that she didn't talk as much and she listened better and she never argued. He liked that. Then he would stare at the ceiling and apologize to Amoss if it hurt his feelings. Shepard talked a lot those days about how hard it was to be him – a bona fide genius. Normal people couldn't understand the misery of seeing the world so clearly as he did. He had a poet's vision into things, he said, and it hurt him to tears. All his nerves were out to register the pain of the world. He talked and talked about his misery. It was endless. And Mamie never said much of anything back to him except to ask for more splow. She sat in the big chair across from him, wearing her stained farmeralls – she had washed them but you could still tell that the stains were Amoss's leftover blood – her feet on the coffee table on top of all the papers covered with Shepard's words. She held a jar of splow in her hand, out of which she would take a nip now and then, and nodded cheerfully to Shepard as he droned on and on; everything was "Yaay" and "Mmm-orc."

One week passed, then another, and finally I woke up at dawn one morning thinking I had heard Pa calling me to get up and get my lazy ass down to the barn. I got dressed and went outside. A warm wind was coming from the south, making the leaves rustle on the big, half-dead elm and bringing the smell of fresh-cut hay from some field far away and the faint sound of a tractor from somewhere where a farmer was already up and doing. Then, as I watched, the air began to fill with black and yellow butterflies, hundreds of them, or thousands, riding the south wind, dipping and fluttering round each other, like flower petals in an eddy. Then, as quick as they had come, they left, heading north to the big forests by the big lake. It struck me that for the first time in a long time I was feeling pretty good and that I wanted to walk about and see something besides the insides of Shepard's house. I took off toward the center of town.

In the early morning like it was, the streets were quiet, just a car or two passing by now and then and nobody but me out walking yet. None of the stores was open, not Charlie Friendly's, or the Red and White Grocery, or Smithson's Barber Shop, not even the Sunshine Cafe, though when I looked in the window I could see folks getting things ready inside. Walking further down I came across the Cunningham yard. They owned the Allis Chalmers place where you could get tractors and implements and parts. I climbed all over the tractors, wishing I could take off on one and go help that farmer I had heard far off. I missed the farm, which was kind of funny because I never thought I would miss such a nasty thing as chores.

I had gone a few blocks and was going up an alley when suddenly I heard someone calling my name. I thought I was hearing things, maybe Amoss's ghost. But it wasn't Amoss calling me; it was Robbie Peevy. I looked at the building next to me, a big, red-brick building, and there he was, staring at me from behind bars. There was a small vacant lot between us, full of weeds. The sun was up and shining full from the east on the building, showing up the old age of its brick and the rust on the bars covering the window out of which Robbie squinted at me and called my name. I went up close and asked him what he was doing in there.

"I'm in jail," he said. "I been here more than two weeks. You didn't hear about it?"

I told him I hadn't heard a thing. "I've been staying kind of shut in," I said.

"It was in the paper and on the news. 'Robbie Peevy returns. Followers riot.' And there was a wonderful story about me, how I was a prodigy and how I hypnotized people and how some said I was the Second Coming and others said I was the devil. 'The worst are full of passionate intensity,' it said. They gave my whole life history, and they wrote about whether or not some books should be burned. I'm not the only one who thinks there is evil in a lot of books, you know?"

"Yeah, but you were burning everything, Robbie, not just some. I kept one. There was nothing wrong with it."

Robbie thought about what I had said. He stroked his beard, tugged at his chin whiskers. "You know what it is?" he said. "To make your point, you sometimes got to exaggerate."

"Yep, but that kind of exaggeration got you arrested."

"What, for burning books? You think it was for burning books? No no. They arrested me for telling them the truth. Just like they did to Jesus, yes. And like him I've been persecuted and now I'm waiting for my death and resurrection. I'm so glad to see you, Christian. Deeply moved that you have come, that Providence has seen fit to move at last." His voice was almost like a song as he spoke to me. "Christian, don't you see how it fits? Robbie in prison, full of faith that the power of Jesus will move for him. And with the sun in the east a boy called Christian comes. Do you think it could just happen? Nothing in my life is an accident, nothing. I've been given a destiny. You have been sent here to help me fulfill it."

"How so?" I wanted to know. "What can I do? You're in jail, and I'm out here. I can't do much about that, Robbie."

"Christian – you can free me," he whispered. "Jesus will give you the power. Believe, Christian, believe."

"Oh no, I can't. I can't free anybody. Don't even think it, Robbie. I got enough troubles in my life. You got yourself into this, and you got to get yourself out. I'm sorry, but it's what a fellow has to expect if he goes around burning books. A friend of mine named Amoss – he's dead now – said you were a bullshitter and a pain in the ass, and you shouldn't go around thinking you got the truth in your hip pocket. He knew you when you were a kid."

Robbie shook his head. "Never *knew* me," he said. "Never ever *knew* me. Those who know me have their eyes made clear by Jesus, yes, and they see that I'm a child of destiny. You say he's dead? That should tell you something. Speaks evil of me and dies. God struck him down." Robbie's face was beaming in the morning sun. I saw there was no way to convince him of anything but that God had struck Amoss.

"I got to go," I said.

"Jesus will clear your eyes," he told me. "Jesus will make you see what I am. Jesus will not – *will not*! – allow you to abandon me! Listen to me, Christian. You are one of the elect! Where's Mamie?"

"She gets drunk every day with Don Shepard," I told him. "We live with him now. You know him?"

Robbie shook his head no. "I don't like that Mamie is drinking," he replied.

"I don't like it either, but there's nothing I can do. Amoss died. That's what started it. We met him right after the book-burning. Mamie carried him home because his ulcer was hurting. Then he felt better and Shepard came and we had a party. He was having a good time, and then he died. I knew him for half a day, and then he died. He was seventy, so I guess it's what you have to expect."

"Jeee-sus called him back!"

"You just said he died because he spoke evil against you."

Robbie closed his eyes and raised his face toward heaven. "'Father, forgive them, for they know not what they do,'" he said. He looked at me with a large sadness in his eyes. "Your friend spoke evil but it was out of ignorance, not malice. Shouldn't I imitate Christ and ask for forgiveness for Amoss? It is not a mystery, Christian. Man is corrupt from the blood of Adam. Man is steamed in the decay of the devil's heart. I bleed for man, for he is lost if I do not bleed. Blood washes. Blood cleanses. Jeee-sus is the way, oh yes. Take him, heavenly Father, this man Amoss, and forgive what he bespake against thy servant. Jesus, let him come into your magnificent court and lay himself at your feet. Place thy feet on his head in forgiveness, for thou art great, Lord. In your infinitely merciful name I pray, Jesus Christ, amen."

Robbie looked at me with a self-pleased expression on his face. "Now you see what kind of guy I am, Christian. One who prays for his enemies, as the Lord told us to do. Am I still so bad in your eyes? Am I a bullshitter and a pain in the ass?"

I thought it over and decided I didn't know. "I'm not smart enough to figure you out, Robbie," I told him.

He held his hand through the bars to me. "Come closer," he coaxed. I took his hand. It was warm and hard and thin. "What we need to understand between us," he told me, "is that Amoss is just fine in the bosom of Christ now, just as fine and perfect as he can be; I took care of it. But what we got left is a *living man*, a living man, a breathing man, a living, breathing Robbie-man, and a living Christian and a living Mamie. We got to understand, honey, that Mamie is in danger, deee-eep in danger, oh yes, drinking the hootch every day, eating out the magnificent soul with the worm of alcohol. Jesus save her! A crooked path is in front of her, full of sawdust hiding bad blood and lacerated livers. That way lays death and darkness and the maw of

Satan! The hungry hungry maw, I say, and the teeth gnashing for the Mamie-girl. Satan wants to suck the marrow of her soul. Don't let it happen, honey. All she's got is you. It's your duty to save her. It's what you were put on earth to do. Don't argue. I know these things. Listen to Robbie. Get Mamie away from this Gomorrah. If you don't, it will be the end of her, mark my words – the seraph of Camelot speaks!"

He leaned his head on the bars and stared at me without blinking, his big wonderful eyes holding me in a spell, his hypnotic voice still tingling in my ears. It was hard to think straight.

"I can help you," he said softly. "And Mamie."

"How can you help?" I asked. "You're all locked up."

"First I got to get out of here, of course. And it has to happen soon. They're sending me back to Camelot soon, and this time they'll make sure I never get out. I've been called incorrigible and a menace. They'll lock me in the criminally insane section, worse than where I was before – much worse, woe, woe. My light will shine in the darkness, but the darkness will know me not. Christian, baby-one, don't abandon Robbie. Camelot will kill me. Pills and shots – I'll be hollow again. Save me. Save Mamie. Hollow is the future without your tender mercy."

I pulled back from him. I was confused. I didn't know what to do. "I got to think about this," I said. "What you're asking is for me to break you out of jail. As if I don't have enough trouble. I got to think, Robbie. I got to think!"

"Not too long," he told me. "Remember, it's important beyond imperative. Life or death, Mamie and her drinking. Mamie wallowing in the filth of hootch, and Satan filing his teeth. She's in trouble. We got to save her."

"I can save her myself," I said, and then I turned on my heel and walked away. I could hear him making little weeping noises behind me. At the end of the block, I stopped and thought about what he had said about the pills and the shots waiting for him in Camelot. He didn't deserve that, no matter how many books he had burned. I knew it was bullshit about Mamie. I didn't need him to save her, but I was sure he had told the truth about Camelot. It had a bad reputation. It had always been talked of as the house of the boogyman when I was little; be good or the boogyman will take you to Camelot. Shots and pills and being hollow for sure, no doubt about it.

So I went back to him. "How could I get you out anyway?" I asked.

He giggled and told me to come closer and put my hands on the bars. I did, and as soon as I grabbed them I knew how to save him. The bars were loose. They turned in their sockets.

"They're all that way," he whispered. "Old and loose as a Jew's version of the truth. Jeee-sus is the way, amen. The brick and mortar are crumbling all around. Look." He shook the bars, and bits of grainy cement rained down on us.

"A few good wallops with a two-pound would break these bricks to smithereens," I said, excited.

"You got it, baby-one. And especially if Mamie swings the hammer."

He was right, but I still didn't know if we should do it. I told him how I was in the middle of it. I told him how Mamie and I had a lot of troubles, how if we got caught and they sent for John Beaver he would chop us into little pieces, or worse.

"We won't get caught. The guards are up front of the building. They play shit-kicking music all day long and come back here only twice to feed me. If you come after dinner, we'd have a whole night's head start. We'll disappear. We'll go to California. No winter in California. Think of that!

"Bring a hammer and a crowbar. We'll use my blanket to muffle the noise. Pry up a corner, that's all. I'm skinny as a rail – can squeeze through any place I can get my head through. I'll be out of here so fast – like the wind! We won't get caught. Gone with the wind, my son."

I shook my head. "We'd get caught. I know we'd get caught. Then John Beaver, Jesus Joseph Mary, what he'd do to us."

"We won't get caught, I tell you. Jesus will protect us. I know these things. You came from the east with the sun. Your name is Christian. It's not just an accident; nothing is an accident. You'll do it. The Lord will move you. Believe, believe – come to Robbie, my precious one!"

"Got to think," I said. "Got to think."

I walked away again and he called out after me, telling me I'd be back, that I wouldn't abandon poor Robbie to shots and pills and the hollow world of Camelot. I'd be back. Jeee-sus would move me.

I walked out of town to the graveyard where Amoss was buried. I sat on the mound and stared at the trees and the cornfield where the south wind was making the tassels dance. I told myself that I owed that Robbie nothing, not a damn thing. He made his own trouble and almost got Mamie and me caught too. I said I shouldn't have anything more to do with him. Maybe Camelot wasn't such a bad place. If it was as bad as everyone said, the government would close it down, wouldn't they? People who thought they had cornered the truth probably belonged there. Anyone like that was crazy. And who wanted to go to California? Talk about crazy. I'd heard about that place – land of the loonies! Full of Robbies and probably Mamies and Shepards too.

Worse than Wisconsin, which was plenty bad enough. Naw, I told myself, the last thing we needed was to have anything more to do with Robbie Peevy.

I forced myself not to think about him being hollow, and after some time passed, my mind grew quiet, and I relaxed. The air was so nice, so warm, making all the smells steam – the grass and the dirt and the corn and the trees. I said this was too nice a day to be messing up my mind with the likes of Robbie. I closed my eyes and let him drift on out. I refused to think about Amoss either, or that Mamie might become a gutter drunk, or that John Beaver was out there somewhere waiting to pounce, waiting like a giant spider to sting us. I said, don't think about that. Sleep.

When I got back to the house, it was dark. The lamp was on inside and I could see through the window. Mamie and Shepard were sitting on the couch, sharing a jar of splow. They were leaning on each other, slapping each other on the legs and laughing. Shepard said something to her that made her howl. Then he was holding the jar to her lips and pouring the splow in like she was the kitchen sink. When he tried to stop, she grabbed his arm and brought it back so she could drink more. He tried to pull away, but she wouldn't let him. Then he was getting mad and pulling really hard. He started screaming at her, calling her a no-good lushy fat bitch. He stood up and slugged her on the chin. She let go of the jar.

"Aha, you see what happens when you mess with me?" he cried. "You frozzle-headed freaker, you titmouse moron, you frippin jibber-jubber dunciad!" He sucked off the last of the splow and stood in front of Mamie, swaying.

Rubbing her jaw, she stood up, a dopey look on her face, like she wasn't sure what had happened. Shepard leaned over and patted her bottom, then pointed to the kitchen. "G'wan, g'wan, Meemee," he said, trying to push her. "Get mmm-ore." He did a little half turn and fell back onto the couch.

Mamie quit rubbing her jaw and was standing over him. He was kicking at her legs and telling her to get more splow, and in a sort of slow motion she raised her fist and brought it down, fump! on top of his head. He went over like a dead ox. I hurried in, hoping she hadn't killed him. He was on his side, eyes closed, snoring through his plum nose and making an awful racket, something like the honk of a mad goose. Mamie tottered off to the kitchen.

"That's enough of that," I told her.

She glanced back at me, curious.

"This splow's no good," I said. "It's gonna ruin you."

"Nup nup nup," she said.

"And I say yes. I say we got to get out of here before it's too late."

"Nup nup."

"It could be you and me again, Mamie – Mamie and Kritch'n. Wouldn't you like that?"

She thought it over. "Yaay, but bring it sssplow." And she tottered over to the cupboard and grabbed herself another jar. She offered it to me.

"Ugh, that stuff is shit," I said.

"Shhhee-it," she answered and took a big swallow. She set the jar down on the table and put her arms around me. "Kritch'n, mmm-yum, Kritch'n, Kritch'n, mmmmm." My feet were off the floor, and she was holding me so tight I couldn't breathe. Then she gave me a shake that made my legs flip loose right and left, like I was a Raggedy Andy doll. I whacked her on the sides with my fists, but it was like a fly trying to swat an elephant. Holding me against her, she waddled to the bedroom and dropped me on the bed. I was gasping for air, and she was kissing my face and crooning to me, "Ko down, ko down, Kritch'n, do da no-rain in me."

But I was in no mood. She took her clothes off and then mine, and I let her rub on me and use my fingers for a while. But it wasn't like when Amoss died, feeling the need to be alive, to feel full of life, and feeling like there was a lot of love there too. I didn't feel any loving. Or maybe it was just that she was drunk and stinking like splow and pushing me around. Finally she realized I wasn't going to no-rain her, so she got up and went back to her splow. I lay a long time thinking that Robbie was sure right, that Mamie was getting ruined and I had to do something about it.

The next morning I came out and Shepard and Mamie were at the table already, drinking coffee and eating toast with bacon. Shepard looked okay, except his nose was darker plum than normal, and he turned toward me like he had a stiff neck. I asked him was he all right, and he said he had a headache and his back hurt. He told me to sit and eat, that he wanted to talk to me. When I sat next to Mamie, she pinched my cheek and heaped food on my plate. She looked into my eyes cowish, like she knew she had done wrong.

"Look what she did this morning, Crystal," said Shepard, waving his hand at the living room behind us.

It was cleaned up. The cans and jars were gone. The dictionary was closed and Shepard's lists of words were stacked neatly on the coffee table. The floor looked mopped, the windows looked sparkly, the couch pillows were fluffed. Sun poured in the windows, and some nice country music was playing on the radio. It looked like the grieving was over.

"She cleaned the house," I said. "Real good."

"And while she was doing that," said Shepard, "I went to the store and bought food. A coincidence occurred of which I must relate the particulars, Crystal. You see, I ran into Teddy Snowdy. He has a dairy farm just twenty miles south, off of Road 6. He's putting up his second crop of hay and needs help. I told him you were just the man. In short, I got you a job.

"All right! Good one!" I said. "We got jobs, Mamie!"

"Oh no, oh no, Crystal, no no, not Mamie. You. I procured you employment." He put his hand on my arm and looked at me solemnly. "I am saturated with hopeful certainty that you want what is best for Mamie. Am I right, Crystal? Sure I am. You have tender feelings for her. Shepard can tell these things." He tapped his forehead. "No mere mortal can fool me, not this genius. I have psychic powers as well. It is my blessing and my curse to be able to look into the hearts of men. I am a very sapient and tender-minded sage. This I cannot help, no more than you can help being a mere farmboy or Mamie a mental defective. Such are the salient features and burdens of our lives, oh my." Shepard sighed profoundly and stroked his nose.

"You remember Amoss?" he asked.

"Doubt I'll forget him. First man I ever saw die."

"I miss him, Crystal. Miss him so very very much." He took out his hanky and wiped his eyes and blew his nose. It tooted like a toy trumpet. Mamie had quit dunking toast in her coffee and was listening to him. She laughed at his nose noise.

"That's not nice," I told her.

"Poof poof, pay no mind, Crystal. She can't help what she is, and in fact, she is probably a better behaved idiot than most. Now as to Amoss – ahem, excuse me a minute." Again he wiped his eyes and blew his nose. "Just the mention of his name, oh dear, oh dear, just the mention of his name – a tried and true friend of long and enduring comprehension and stability, yum yum. I miss the old angel with all the tender inclination of my poor, tortured soul and all the immense sensitivity of genius, which hates the injustice of certified death, yum yum. You understand me, Crystal? I think so, even though the loneliness of my intellectual level creates an unspanable abyss between us – genius and pastoral offspring. What's to be done? Heavy, heavy burthen. For had Amoss understood me at some more penetrating level, he would be alive today, sitting here with us for toast and tea, he and me and thee."

"Coffee," I said. "This is coffee."

"Trifles," said he, waving me away. "I talked to the doctor who told us of Amoss's horrible death that night. An intelligent man. I told him of my solicitous care for Amoss, how I had succored him for fifteen years – a burthen and a bother to some, but not to me. 'He ain't heavy.' My incredible sensitivity would have not allowed me to act otherwise. The doctor told me that without my efforts Amoss would no doubt have died long ago. He told me this looking me straight in the eye. A wonderful man. He knows I failed in my ultimate intentions but that even in failure there was a grand capability. After all, I am not God. I can bewilder but not ultimately defeat the spirit of death." Again, Shepard took his hanky and honked into it. He groaned and sighed several times, and his chin quivered until he finally got himself controlled.

"Well, there is only so much any mortal can do," he continued. "Only so much, no matter who he is and what his gifts. Let Jeremiah himself judge the purity of my intentions and that my abilities are too impressive to ever allow me to do anything that is lowdown, rotten, dirty. Did I not tell the cretin, no hot dogs and beer on an ulcer? Of course I did. And I was proved right. He died. He paid for the backwardness of his mental chemistry. Time taketh away from all the paucity of its gift, yum yum."

Hound-dog sorrow was all over his face. It seemed to just overwhelm him for a second. He hung his head low and bent forward, but the bending must have hurt because he cried out, "Ooooch," and straightened up. He rubbed the back of his neck and whined, "Why me? What did I do? Why does everything happen to me? Oh, heavy, heavy burthen."

I patted his arm. Mamie patted his cheek.

"What would a man be without his friends?" he murmured, smiling his dogteeth at us. "Few can understand the suffering I've endured. Even you, my dear ones, cannot feel it as deeply as I do. So be it. A bitter blow, stereotypical of my life. None can feel as deeply as I. And so, the bounty of my heart quite overwhelms me, you see. And yet that same bounty seeks its reflection in your own callow but caring heart, Crystal, and gives me hope to sway your generous nature to understand the agitation it would cause me to send Mamie with you to

Teddy Snowdy's. It would, my dear Crystal, it would, I think, nearly kill me dead."

"Huh? You want me to leave Mamie here with you?"

"With me, my child, with someone who loves her dearly beyond life itself and will endeavor to teach her a trade and make her independent in life."

"You'd teach her a trade?"

"Exactly, a trade that would give her a future."

"What trade is that?"

"I will teach her to run Powers. Powers is my movie projector, a Powers projector from Chicago. I'll teach her to master it."

"Movie projector? Mamie? I don't know, Mr. Shepard."

"I do. I know. With me behind her, she can do anything. If you love her as I do, you will give her this chance."

He was staring down his nose at me, giving me cocked eyebrows and stern eyes. It wasn't that Mamie couldn't do it. For sure I knew she could. She could run tractors and implements, all kinds of machinery. She could take care of cows. She knew how to live in the woods and how to use herself as fish bait. She could run Powers, sure. But was it right to leave her, *my* Mamie, with a guy like Don Shepard? I answered myself with a list of Shepard's selling points. He was a genius. He owned a house and a movie palace and a car. He would teach her a trade. He was a genius. He probably even knew ways to teach her to read, and God knew she wanted to learn. She was hungry for learning; the way she looked through books proved she knew something important was missing from her life. And the *Blithe Spirit* thing – it seemed to prove she could learn. She couldn't read, but she had a memory like nothing I'd ever imagined. And yes, he was a genius.

"Do you think you could teach her to read?" I asked.

He snapped his fingers. "Like that, oh absolutely. I promise. Give me six months and I'll have her quoting *War and Peace*!"

"And what about all the drinking? Is that over now?"

"I pledge my sacred honor, no more. Except maybe a toot on the weekends at Charlie's."

I looked long at Mamie. What would she want, I wondered. "Mamie, you like it here, right?"

"I like it," she said.

"Do you want to stay and work for Shepard? He'll teach you to run a movie projector."

She thought it over and shrugged.

"Stay here and learn to read books?"

Her head turned to the shelves of books. "Yaay!" she cried.

"Wonderful," said Shepard. "Then it's all settled."

I felt sick in the belly. Shepard held out his hand and we shook on it. Mamie was his.

Escape

Later in the day Shepard said he had to go over to the college and collect his final check. They had fired him finally for not showing up. According to him it was all in his plan – now he would have all his time to devote to the Artlife and to Mamie. He said when he got back he would drive me out to Teddy Snowdy's farm. When he left, Mamie went with me over to the jail. I wanted to explain it to Robbie, why I couldn't help him, that it was too big a risk, especially now that Mamie and I had jobs. I thought probably he wouldn't want me to put all that on the line for him, especially when jail was his own doing and it would be awfully unfair. Still, as we walked over there, I was feeling bad about not helping him. It reminded me of what I did to Mamie, taking John Beaver to her, and sure, look how that turned out. But I had to think of the future. I had to remember that Robbie was a nut and not to be let loose on the world.

Close to the jail there was a street crew working on a section of sidewalk that had frost-heaved over winter. They were banging away with a jackhammer, but they stopped and watched us when we walked up to the back window and called for Robbie.

He rushed over and threw the window up. "God be praised," he said. "I knew you kiddies would come for me. Mamie, Mamie, you look just glorious. You shine bright as an archangel. Come close and let me touch you."

Mamie grabbed the bars and put her head against them, and Robbie ran his fingers through her hair. Her curls shot up like little flames as his hand passed over them.

"I got a job," I told him. "At Teddy Snowdy's farm."

"Teddy Snowdy! He's a demon, a vicious killer," said Robbie. "You don't want to work for him, Christian. He's a walking slaughter-machine."

"I've seen cows put down before," I answered.

"That's not what I mean. Teddy Snowdy is a killer. He kills anything that moves and he stuffs it. Everybody knows about him. He built an addition on his house, just to fill with dead animals. I'll tell you what, nobody of sane mind round here would work for him. There's a guy should be in Camelot, believe me. I don't wish it on no one – but that guy . . . don't go there, honey. Ask anybody."

"But I need a job and that's that."

"Nobody needs a job that bad. Don't do it, baby-one."

"I'm just going to milk cows and help with second crop. I won't have nothing to do with stuffing animals." Robbie was getting me sore. I didn't want to hear the bad about Teddy Snowdy.

But he wouldn't let up. "He'll stuff all the birds you flush out when you mow. He follows behind like a cat and pounces on the ones you cripple with the mower. Oh, the stories I've heard about this guy, Christian, would give you white hair. I went down to save him once. I'm telling you, he took his gun to me. I ran like a deer, and I heard him blasting away, and I could see the puffs of dirt kicking up round me. Only the hand of Jesus kept me from getting my head blowed off. You listen to me, honey. I wouldn't put it past him to stuff *you*."

No one's that bad, I said to myself. Robbie's judgment was pretty suspect, as far as I was concerned. "Look," I said to him. "I'm going and that's that. I need the job, and I won't be far from Mamie. She's gonna stay with Shepard and learn the projector business. He's teaching her a trade. It's an opportunity for a future."

"Naw, you're not falling for that," he said.

"It's a good deal, Robbie."

"Jeee-sus, clear this boy's eyes so he can see the truth! You and Mamie are getting used. A trade, poo. Running a projector ain't a trade. You think your Shepard's gonna pay her? Use her, that's what. And Teddy Snowdy sure will do that to you, too. It ain't a good deal, Christian – think."

"Everything is sour grapes to you except what you want to do, go to California and all that. I've heard about that place, full of the craziest people in the world, and it's falling into the ocean. We're not going there with you. We can't help you."

Robbie took a deep breath and stroked Mamie's hair again. "You didn't come here to tell me you're coming tonight?"

"Nope, got a job."

"Tomorrow they take me to Camelot. You gonna let them put me away, honey, stick me in the hollow sock?"

"Got to think of us, Robbie. You're the one put yourself there."

"Justice, righteousness, move the boy," he cried out to the sky. He shook the bars and made them wiggle some, but they were solid enough. I glanced at the workmen. They were still watching us. When I looked back, Robbie had his big eyes on me, his eyes begging me, big tears welling up in them and dropping down his cheeks. "I'll die in that fairyland, honey," he said. "Give me a chance."

I couldn't let go of the look in his eyes. It came over me, the sick, hollow feeling I had when I realized I done Mamie wrong in showing John Beaver where she was. The thought came to me that this was another one of those moments of truth and that I had to act with what my feelings were saying and not my head. Robbie didn't deserve what was coming to him – not that bad, not Camelot and the killing of his mind. It wouldn't be right, even if the law said it was. Or it might be right but it wasn't truth. I thought it out in five seconds, with him staring at me and me at him, the thoughts seeming to come out of him and into my mind so that they were there so solid I couldn't run away from them. It was borrowing more trouble, but I knew I wouldn't be able to live with myself knowing that Robbie was dying in Camelot. I looked again at the workmen and thought about asking to borrow their jackhammer, but I knew that was stupid. Then I thought maybe I could go back to Cunningham Chevrolet and ask to test-drive a pickup, and get a chain, sure, and pull the bars off. We'd have a getaway car like that. While I was planning it, Robbie was shaking the bars and Mamie was watching them move. Suddenly, she grabbed them too and gave them a hell of a shake. Chips of cement and brick fell all over her.

Robbie caught her wrists and said, "O Jeee-sus, Mamie, yes – pull them out, honey. Free Robbie from this place."

She looked over her shoulder at me. "Can you, Mamie?" I asked.

"Yaay, Kritch'n," she answered.

I knew that no one in the world could pull those bars out by hand, not even Mamie. I knew it in my head. But I believed her anyway. She had said "yaay," and that meant she thought she could, because Mamie didn't know how to bullshit anybody. She was gripping the bars, and her hands were so tight on them that the muscles in her shoulders and back began to swell and take on a bowed look, like a bull when he lowers his head and gets ready to charge. I looked at the workmen. They were quiet, just watching, watching Mamie. And Robbie was watching her too. It was all building up in her hands, coming from the ground, up her legs and back. I knew I wanted to see it. I wanted her to do it.

"Rip 'em out," I whispered in her ear.

She rattled the bars again, and more cement and brick crumbled. Then she climbed up them to the upper right corner. She caught one bar with both hands and held it as she placed her legs against the wall, so that she squatted crablike, with her feet on the wall but her hands on the bars, her hands reaching down between her thighs. She took a breath and gave a hard pull, but nothing moved and it seemed right away that she had met her match. One of the workmen laughed. Another one said she looked like a monkey. The one with the jackhammer told them to just watch, and he said a couple of times, "Do it, baby."

Mamie was increasing the pressure, pulling so hard her neck and face turned red as a warning flag. Her arms bulged tight up against the sleeves of her shirt, and her thighs stretched the seams of her pants so you could see white thread at the point of snapping. She grunted and growled like a frustrated bear. And nothing was happening. I got scared for her. I was sure that if she kept it up something would break inside her.

"She'll kill herself, Robbie," I said.

"No no, honey, not with Jesus' hands on her. She can do it. Listen – listen to the breaking away!"

I listened but couldn't hear it.

"You don't hear? It's cracking," he said. "Cracking deep inside. Jeee-sus, burn the power into her flesh and make her Samson, give her Samson's power against the pillars of the Philistines!"

Then I could hear it too, a deep cracking, like a house settling at night, only this was longer and getting louder.

"Jesus Murphy, she's doing it!" said one of the workmen.

"She sure as hell is," said another.

Then all three started cheering her, telling her, "Go, baby, go!"

Some people passing by stopped to watch, and they got excited and started yelling. I heard car doors slamming and more people joining in. It was getting so loud, the cheering, that I couldn't hear the cracking. But I could see it – long, thin cracks running from the corner and away in all directions, like spider threads. The people and their yelling were getting awful loud. I looked at the man with the jackhammer, cupped my ears, and pointed toward the jail. He nodded at me and started hammering away, trying to drown out the people. And Mamie, stuck on the side of the building like she had nothing to do with gravity, pulled all her big body together into what seemed like the faith of a mustard seed that could move a mountain. And there was no brick and no steel that could pit its might against hers. The sight of her was breathtaking – light blazed in her hair and seemed to set her whole head on fire, making it a little sun that was nearly blinding, and she was the light herself, fiery with the power swelling up in her and making her glow like a halo.

"Jeee-sus is in her! Jeee-sus is in her!" cried Robbie, above the roar of the jackhammer.

And the cracks grew larger, widened, and began to rain down dusty cement and brick all around. Then the corner began to give way. Mamie ground the bar through until it suddenly snapped out of the rest of the brick and started bending toward her chest. Her legs were beginning to straighten. The bar next to the one she had through started bending backward. Then the crossbar broke from its anchor and half of the top row popped through. There it was, the whole corner out from the wall and wide enough for Robbie to just squeeze by. Which he did, sliding beneath Mamie's right leg as she pulled and falling into my arms, a free man heading the opposite of Camelot.

The cheering behind us overwhelmed the jackhammer. The faces of the people shone like they had seen a miracle. They clapped and whistled. They hugged one another. Some stood like they were in shock, but most carried on like it was a carnival. None of them seemed to think what we were doing was wrong. It was like it was too tremendous to be wrong.

Robbie was hugging me. Mamie jumped down from the bars and he fell all over her, squeezing her and kissing her. She shuddered like an earthquake in his arms, like her muscles were protesting what she had done. The people came over to us. The jackhammer man slapped Mamie on the shoulder and called her Queen Kong. The rest of them reached out for her too, slapping her in a friendly way, or just touching her. She took it all in and was happy about it, I could tell. The people couldn't get enough of her, it seemed, sort of like a bunch of kids who had cornered Santa Claus. They wanted to touch her, stroke her, pet her, pat her. Like a goddess, she held out her arms to them and let herself be worshiped.

"Queen Kong," said the jackhammer man over and over.

A girl pulled at my arm and asked, "Who is she?"

"I don't know who she is," I answered.

"Feel her," said someone. "Ain't she wonderful?"

"Oooo," the people said.

"Ahhhh," the people said.

"Who? Who is she?" they wanted to know.

"Did you see? Did you see?" Robbie kept asking everyone.

Then through the broken bars came the voice of a man who was mad as hell. "What done this!" he shouted. The bars had sprung back a little. He shook them and glared at us and kept asking, "What done this?" After a pause, he said, "You all done it?"

"Only one of us," answered a voice from the crowd.

"Yeah sure," he said. Then his eyes narrowed with thought. "You the goddamn book-burners, huh? So that's what's going on. Don't nobody move!"

Hollering back over his shoulder, he told a guy named Putnam to get round back and arrest us all. But Putnam's face appeared at the window, saying, "Huh? What you talkin bout, Harper?" He grabbed the bars and shook them. "Who done this?" he asked.

"Putnam," said Harper with impatient patience, "Putnam, would you mind going round back and arresting them people? They're the ones set the school on fire, and now they broke the jail to get Peevy out. I'll keep an eye on them, if you just go arrest them, Putnam."

"No shit? How'd they do it?" He looked at us. "How'd you folks rip them bars out like that?"

"I'm gonna kill you, Putnam, if you don't get your ass out there right now and arrest every damn one of them. Now sic 'em, boy!"

"Don't nobody move!" Putnam ordered. Then he looked at Harper and whined, "I tole you to see what all the hollerin was about, didn't I? How we gonna explain this?"

"You're all under arrest!" yelled Harper.

"Like hell! I was just watching," said someone.

"Me too. I got nothing to do with this," said another.

"I didn't do nothing!"

"None of us did nothing."

"We were just driving by, that's all."

"And I'm driving on, bye-bye."

All the people, even the three workmen, took off running in every direction. Mamie, Robbie, and I tore across the street and down an alley. In back of us we could hear Putnam and Harper screaming to halt in the name of the law. Guns went off into the air.

"Holy shit, they're crazy!" said a man, as he ran by us for all he was worth.

We went between some houses and across another street. We passed the Cunningham place and ducked down another alley. I was in the lead, and all I could think about was getting back to Shepard's and hiding inside until it got dark, and then Robbie could do what he wanted, and Shepard could drive Mamie and me to Teddy Snowdy's. She wouldn't be safe from arrest if I left her behind, and besides, I hadn't wanted her to stay anyway. Inside I was glad things were going the way they were.

Next thing we got to Shepard's, but he wasn't back and the door was locked. I checked out one of the bedroom windows and it was open. I took out John Beaver's knife and was going to cut the screen when somebody started hollering from across the street, "Teef! Teef! I see you. Teef!"

I saw a tiny woman, fifty or sixty years old, standing on her porch across from Shepard's and shaking a broom at us. "Teef! Teef! I see you!" I remembered seeing her before. She had a little dog that barked a lot and a husband in a wheelchair.

"We live here, ma'am," I said. "We got locked out."

She looked at me like I was a liar. "I not see you ewer before dis time. You look a teef to me, I tink so."

"Honest, we live here with Shepard. We've been here more than two weeks. We went to Amoss's funeral."

Her face was softening. I thought things were going to be all right, but then I heard the sound of sirens heading in our direction. "Ya, my hoosban call dem," said the woman.

"That's it," said Robbie. "Can't stay here."

"Something wrong you, you shoo! Get avay, shoo shoo!" She waved her broom at us and took a step off the porch.

There was no time to argue, with the sirens getting closer, so we let the lady have her way. We headed to the woods at the end of the block and made our way through them toward the railroad tracks not far off. The woods were thick, but we could hear the sirens coming closer. I knew when they got to Shepard's the lady would tell the police where to look for us, but at least we were in the trees again, in the wild, and on the other side of the tracks were miles and miles of forest and creeks. We could lose them all right.

On the other side of the tracks, Mamie took over the lead and led us at a good pace but not so fast that we'd get winded. Trees were thick the whole way and grabbing at our clothes, and a branch would snake one of us now and then, making us bob around like boxers. We had to jump a couple of creeks and wade through a knee-deep pool, but the sound of sirens was gone, and it would be hell for anyone trying to track us down. It was twenty or thirty minutes before I finally sang out to take a rest. We walked just a little farther till we came to another creek, and then we had a wash to cool us down.

Robbie sat next to me, and when he'd got his puff back he said, "It was a wonderful thing you done, Christian, a farsighted thing. I can't thank you enough. All I can say is, Jesus will be with you from this day forth to the end of time. He told me you are special, and he loves you for listening to your heart."

I listened for sirens or voices, but there weren't any, only the sound of wind rustling the tops of the trees and the gurgle of the water next to us. I was sweating and my heart was pounding so hard it made it hard to talk, but I told Robbie that I had done what seemed the true thing to do.

"And you did the good thing by that," he said. "And it would be a fine world if everybody would listen to the voice of truth when it talks to them. That voice is Jesus trying to show you the way."

"Maybe so, Robbie. I wish he'd come show us the way right now."

"The way is California, Christian. The golden land. We just keep heading west, straight that away." He pointed to California.

But I wasn't going for it. I shook my head against the idea. "California is no place for me and Mamie," I said. "We don't have nothing to do with California. What we know are cows and farming, right here in Wisconsin. I think it's best we stick to what we know."

"And that's true too," he said, shaking his head slowly. "It might be the worse thing to haul you and her off to a foreign land like that. But I'd sure like you to go. I'd like it, but I can see in your face that you won't. Well, that's all right too. Maybe this one I'm supposed to go alone, and Christ has another mission for you."

"I guess we'll miss you too," I told him. "Even though you got us in a mess of trouble. But still, I don't feel guilty. Hell no, in fact, I feel pretty good."

Robbie came even closer, and he took one of my hands and took one of Mamie's hands. He leaned toward us, his face still shiny with the water, eyes fixed on a point just above our heads, as he talked. "We'll be missing each other, but we won't be. Jeee-sus says, 'Listen to the songs of the wind, because I am the wind and the song and you are a part of me,' so listen. And you will see me when the clouds drop their tears on the earth and wash the sins away, and in the smile of a baby you will see the innocent love of Christ. You will see me, because I am a piece of Christ and so are you. Yes, Jeee-sus is in you, praise God."

He paused a minute, looking higher above us, like he was listening to the words to tell us. "And you say what you did was done for truth, Christian. Truth is, what Robbie did was done for truth. Truth is, there are books that should be burned, evil teachings. Evil, like good, is taught through the word – and evil teachings should be burned. Remember this, Christian, if a book can make you yearn for loving kindness and can teach you what is wise, then by the grace of God, it can also do the opposite. It can make you evil and stupid and mean as a cannibal. Yessir, honey, if a book can inspire and improve, it can also depress and corrupt. Burn ye out the corruption; vomit ye the evil word and burn it. Truth is, we only need one book for our pleasure. Jeee-sus is the way.

"And even if you never see me again, honeys, it don't matter. Naw. We've done what we were supposed to do for each other, and now we've got to get on. But I'm sure gonna be with you, because I'm part of Jesus and Jesus is part of you from now on, everywhere. Everywhere, you are a piece of Jesus Christ. Mamie is a bigger piece, a special piece of Jesus Christ, and her special mystery will soon unfold before you. She's not an accident. There are no accidents. And look here, I'm gonna be everywhere with you, guarding you and Mamie. Yes, Lord, wherever you go and each time you are true, that's the piece of Jesus and me moving inside of you. If you see a man hungry and dirty and you wash that man and you feed him, there is the piece of Jesus and me moving in you, praise God. And if you hear the people talking dirt, talking corruption, and you tell them in the name of Christ don't do it because they are pieces of Jesus, then there you are with Jesus and me moving in you. And if you come on men fighting and you say to them that they are punching the face of Jesus, then heaven sings your praises and Jesus and me are moving in you. And if you know a man who ain't crazy but is getting sent to Camelot and you get that man free because he's a piece of Jesus, then Jesus and me are moving in you. You help the sick, you give shelter to the homeless, you stand up for the coward, you carry the weak, you love the unlovable, and you forgive the unforgivable – because they are all pieces of Jesus. And you are a piece of Jesus, which makes them all a piece of you, praise God!

"And don't go falling for the lie of the American Dream either, honeys, the dream of give me this and that and I'll be happy. That dream ain't got nothing to do with Jesus. That dream is a piece of the devil and leads you straight to hell. Don't get caught up by that dream. Say, 'Get behind me, Satan,' and get on with being a piece of Jesus. One man caring for another, neighbors caring for neighbors, those are pieces of Jesus. That's all – got that? It's simple. Just act like Jesus would, because that's all he wants you to do. If you find evil – burn that evil. Jesus would."

He let go of our hands and stood up, and without another word, he walked off, heading west, long and skinny and fair-haired as a ghost. That was Robbie Peevy, mad about Jesus Christ. But maybe not mad.

Mamie and I sat and watched him disappear in the trees, and then it was time for us to go too. We turned southeast on a route I figured would bring us back to the railroad track, eventually. Then twenty miles more or less south was Teddy Snowdy's place. Robbie had said Teddy was a killer, a walking slaughter machine, but I told myself that some farmers are just that way when it comes to animals. It didn't mean they had to be insane, did it?

Teddy and His Mommy

Mostly it was just a lot of walking to get to Teddy Snowdy's. Mamie and I had to spend one night outdoors, and except for the dew settling over us and making us wet, I enjoyed sleeping with her once more beneath a tree, with piled leaves and grass for a bed. In the morning when we got up, the sun was already putting out enough heat to make our clothes steam as we walked along a country road. Hay and cornfields were all around us, and big barns and silos and big white houses rising up every so often in the distance. Farmers were in the fields making second crop. The clatter-siss-click of the haybines, the deep roar of the tractors, the hiss of the hydraulic pistons as the knives were raised and lowered at each turn was wonderful music to me, though I had never thought of any of it as music when living at home. But out on my own it was different, something I missed and wanted back, a surprise to my old, complaining self. I smelled the fresh alfalfa mixing with the odor of diesel and hot oil and the traces of far-off cows and pasture, and I breathed deep and said, "Ah, Mamie, don't it smell good?" And she bobbed her head in agreement with me and said, "Ahhh, ahhh." I noticed all the clean lines of the farms where nature didn't get to have its way, and the windbreaking trees around all the houses and along the driveways, and the woods at the edges of all the fields, and all the restful shades of green, and it made me want to go and tell every farmer there that he had done himself proud. Oh, I was missing home, missing the land, and I could hardly wait to get to Snowdy's and get my hands on a tractor and start milking some cows.

Twice we had to bother somebody for directions. The first fellow knew of Snowdy but didn't know quite where he lived, somewhere east on County Road 6, he thought. But farther on, the second fellow we asked knew exactly where Snowdy lived, and he asked us if we were sure we wanted to go there. I told the man we were going to help Teddy make second crop.

"It's none of my business," said the man, shrugging his shoulders. Then he gave us directions and walked away.

I watched him go back to his tractor and climb aboard, and I wanted to go after him and make him tell me what he meant. But I knew better than to do that. He was like most farmers I had met in my life – none of them really wanted to talk bad about another farmer, but they would find little ways of letting you know if something was wrong with the fellow down the road. We had been warned, and that was all we were going to get. But I didn't know what else to do but keep going.

We came on Snowdy's around noon. It was a bit different from most of the farms we had passed, a bit more hilly, and the house was small, a one-story shingled house painted dark gray. Attached to it was a cinder-block addition, long and low, only two feet high, the rest all underground. The house stood on top of the highest point around, so you looked up at it from the road or from the fields. About a dozen big elms surrounded it, keeping it in shade even with the sun almost straight overhead. Down the hill fifty yards west were a barn and a silo. The silo was one of those shiny tile types, cinnamon colored, with an open top. The barn was painted white, and it was set low on the side of a slope, where it had good drainage. There was a shabby machine shed straight up from the road in front of us, a wire corncrib beside it, and a chicken coop beside the crib. Next to the coop was a garage that leaned to the east and looked like a heavy snow could bring it down. The fields ran east and west and south of the buildings, rolling away like rumpled blankets needing a good, hard pull. Black-and-white holsteins grazed on a pasture out back of the barn. I counted forty-two of them and four calves. The field west of the barn was all alfalfa. It was more than knee-high and overripe, purple flowers blooming so thick the field had the look of a giant bouquet. I wondered aloud why no one had cut it yet. The stems would be getting tough, the leaves would be giving up protein every minute, and they would probably shatter once the hay was dried. A good farmer would have had the field down at least a week before. Mamie heard me talking. She nodded. Then she pointed to the machine shed where the haybine and a tractor were parked.

"Want to cut some hay, Mamie?" I asked.

"Yaay, Kritch'n," she answered happily.

She ran to the tractor, climbed aboard, and started it up. She worked the throttle up and down and played with the brakes and clutch. It was all familiar to her. The tractor hummed like it had a lot of business to take care of. I walked up and hollered at Mamie that she should shut it down for now. Snowdy hadn't hired either of us yet. She turned it off, and as the noise died away I heard a door slam behind me.

"If you're gonna steal it, I'll give you a running start. Go head, go head," said a man with a voice that jarred on my ears like a squeaky brake. I turned and saw him smiling hugely, showing all his teeth, top and bottom rows. The rest of his face was tiny compared to his teeth – a small, upturned nose, little eyes behind round, steel-rimmed glasses, a bullet-shaped head with tiny spikes of hair on top and shaved down to the skin above his ears, which were also small and had a waxy shine. In his hand was a rifle, with which he motioned for us to make a run for it down the road.

"Go head, go head," he kept saying through the gleam of his teeth.

"We're not stealing," I said. "Don Shepard sent us down from Temple. We came for second crop."

"You Crystal?" he asked. When I told him I was he said, "Shit, I didn't know you were so skinny. You ain't gonna be much help."

"I was raised on a farm. Everything you see is muscle," I bragged.

His teeth clicked as he laughed at me. "And who's the Clydesdale setting up there?" he asked, pointing his gun at Mamie.

I told him who she was and that Shepard had sent her along too.

"She can stay. You gotta go."

"We're a team. I go, she goes," I told him firmly.

"A team? Shittin Shepard didn't say nothing about a team." He rubbed his cheek with the barrel of his rifle while he looked us over some more. Not once the whole time did he quit smiling, but it wasn't a nice smile; it was one that made a fellow nervous.

"You're all muscle, you say?" He said to me finally.

"Wiry," I replied. "I've put up lots of hay."

"And what about cows? You know anything about cows?"

"I know 'em like I know my own hands."

He laughed again, his teeth clicking along in time to what sounded as much like a chattering wolverine as anything. I noticed his eyes at the same time, like pinpoints behind his glasses, like two beads of lead. "We'll see what you can do," he said.

A gray-haired woman appeared at the backdoor. "Teddy," she called. "Who is that, Teddy?"

"They're a team, Mommy," he said. "Shepard sent them to help us with the hay and the cows."

"Oh good," she said.

Teddy looked at me, his teeth sparkling as he talked. "You ever listen to Shepard talk? Is that another language or what? I never can understand anything that tub of blubber says. I tell him he uses words that aren't in the dictionary. He doesn't like me to say that. He thinks he's a genius. He's a genius like I'm the Green Hornet. I put pins in his balloon. I call him Baby Huey, the funny-book goose. I think you'll find out pretty soon that I'm a lot more clever than Shepard is. You like him, Slim?"

"He's okay," I answered.

"Oko loco okay. I get the creeps around him. You never know what a guy like that might do."

"Ted-dy, Ted-dy," called the woman at the backdoor, who had been staring at us as we talked "Ted-dy, are they hungry? Would they like some lunch?"

"You're not hungry, are you?" he asked.

"We didn't get any breakfast."

"They're kind of hungry, Mommy," he told her.

"Well, come on then. There's plenty," she said sweetly.

Teddy motioned for us to follow him into the house. As we crossed the yard, a pair of crows flew overhead, cawing noisily. Quick as a gunslinger, Teddy raised his rifle and fired twice. Both birds fluttered down out of the sky, hitting the elms in front of the house and bounding through branches and leaves all the way to the ground.

"What a shot!" cried Teddy, doing his wolverine chatter again. He patted the butt of his rifle and called it his good boy. While he praised his rifle, two blond tabby cats came running from beneath the machine shed, pounced on the birds, and dashed with them back under the shed. Teddy noticed it too late to do anything.

"Okay," he said, glaring in the direction the cats had disappeared. "I saw that." Then he looked at me and said that he was going to make hats of those cats.

We all went inside, and Mrs. Snowdy fed us cold venison with milk and homemade bread and butter. We sat at a table made out of oak by Teddy's father. His name and the date were carved in one corner: BEN SNOWDY 1940. Mrs. Snowdy pointed it out to us as soon as we sat down.

"That's my husband," she said, putting her finger on the name. "He made all the furniture in this house. He's an artist and too sensitive to live around Teddy."

"He's a jerk," Teddy whispered in my ear.

Mrs. Snowdy heard him. "But he can make furniture and you can't, Teddy."

"I can do other things, Mommy. Hey, who runs the farm? I keep it going, not Daddy. He sits in his stupid cabin in the woods and makes stupid furniture for stupid people who never pay him." Teddy looked at me, his lower lip curled out in a pout. "You can't trust a guy like that. You never know what a guy like that is going to do."

"The deal was," Mrs. Snowdy explained, "that Teddy could stay and run the farm and fill the house with his little animals, so long as he was nice to his mommy and didn't tell nasty stories about his daddy. Teddy, what are you doing?"

"I'm not telling nasty stories about him. I'm just telling the truth, Mommy." Teddy whined like a little boy, but he wasn't a little boy. He was somewhere around forty years old. There were gray patches in his crew cut and wrinkles around his eyes and a sagginess in the skin beneath his chin.

Mrs. Snowdy had a set of teeth and a grin that was a smaller version of her son's. She grinned at him as he whined, and when he was finished she said sweetly, "You can be such a snot."

"But who's your favorite Teddy, huh?" he replied, smiling back at her, though whining still.

"Oh go on," she said. "What a child." Then she sat down in a rocking chair that sat on a little round rug next to a small table and lamp. She rocked back and forth as fast as she could go, filling the house with the creak of dried wood. Teddy sat down too, only at the table with us. He put his rifle across his lap and eyed us as we ate. Mrs. Snowdy watched us too, as she zoomed along. And both of them grinned. It was hard to eat with so many teeth bared on each side of me. But Mamie didn't notice it at all. She ate her share and then ate mine too.

"What's her name?" said Mrs. Snowdy, as Mamie wiped her mouth on her sleeve and looked around the table.

"She's Mamie, ma'am," I said. "And I'm Christian."

"I thought you was Crystal," said Teddy. "Well, see there what I mean bout Shepard? Can't even get a name straight."

"Mamie," said Mrs. Snowdy, clicking her teeth as if trying to get a bite on the name. "Oh yes," she went on finally, "President Eisenhower's wife has that name. The sweetest thing. She likes to help." Mrs. Snowdy rocked her chair and smiled, rocked and smiled, and said at last, "Mamie, Mamie – Teddy, Teddy. Mamie, Mamie – Teddy, Teddy." Click-click went her teeth. She stopped rocking and looked at Mamie.

"Can you cook, honey?" she asked.

Mamie thought about the question for a while. Her eyes rolled toward the ceiling as if the answer was printed up there. I could see her tongue working away at her cheek on one side, then the other. The quiet lasted for at least a minute before Mrs. Snowdy said, "That's nice," and started rocking again.

Teddy tapped my hand so I would look at him. "I've shot fifty-four deer in my life," he bragged. "How many you got?"

"None," I answered.

"None? Mommy, you hear him? None? By the time I was his age I bet I'd killed a dozen. None. Poo."

"Teddy has always been a go-getter," Mrs. Snowdy told us. Then she looked at Mamie again. "Can you keep a clean house?" she asked.

Mamie rolled her eyes and thought about it.

"And I've shot thirty coyotes, four wolves, ten bald eagles, a blue heron, fifty goldfinches, seventy-two ducks, sixty-seven geese, forty red-tail hawks, and two hundred and two crows. How many you shot?"

"I've trapped mink and rabbit and gophers," I said.

"That's pitiful."

Mamie started to say something, but Mrs. Snowdy spoke first. "That's nice," she said, and went on to ask Mamie was she good at scrubbing floors, doing dishes, dusting furniture, making jam, washing clothes, baking bread, sewing, and could she do all that and milk cows too. Mamie thought hard about each thing Mrs. Snowdy asked her. But before she could answer, Mrs. Snowdy always said, "That's nice."

All the while she was asking questions, her son ran down endless lists and numbers of animals he had killed and stared at me with contempt that I had no list of my own.

He stood up at last, took my hand, and told me there was something I had to see. He took me down the hall. Mrs. Snowdy stood and took Mamie's hand. "Did I ask if you sew?" she said, as she pulled Mamie along behind Teddy and me. We came to a door at the end of the hall. Teddy opened it and motioned for me to go inside. He turned on a light, and I saw steps leading down to a basement. I went down into a room full of animals frozen in a last second of flight or leap or run or crawl or bite or claw. All had their mouths open on the edge of making some kind of noise. From the high ceiling hung hawks and eagles and crows, a blue heron, even a seagull, and four goldfinches set in formation – two in front, two behind – flying nowhere. Sparrows and swallows, woodpeckers, hummingbirds, robins, and blue jays dipped and darted from corner to corner. A king snake flew after a titmouse, a hawk closed in on the king snake. Rabbits ran from eagles. Badgers chased mice. Cats pounced on sparrows. Gophers fought each other. And along every wall from floor to ceiling were shelves covered with the heads of deer, wolf, coyote, fox, badger, mink, skunk, muskrat, raccoon, dog, and cat. Teddy pointed his rifle at each animal, named it, and told what kind of shot had brought it down. An hour passed before he was finished. Then he took us into a back room, where there was a long, high bench full of tools and wire models with skins draped over them. Papier-mâché heads of all sizes with wire ears and necks were lying everywhere. There was a gun rack on the wall above the bench. A dozen rifles hung there. Teddy named each one for us. All of them were his "boys."

We went back into the main room, and Teddy spread his arms and declared, "You get to sleep with them. I'll give you a mattress for the floor, and you can lay right in the middle and watch them chase each other. I've done it. It's wonderful, Slim." He clicked his teeth and turned his head from side to side, staring at his animals.

Mrs. Snowdy patted Mamie's stomach and told her, "And you can sleep with me. Do you . . . ?" Then she paused, her eyes suddenly puzzled, as if she forgot what she wanted to say.

That afternoon, Mamie and I and Teddy worked in the fields. Mamie drove the tractor, pulled the haybine, and cut alfalfa. Teddy followed behind her, holding one of his "boys" at the ready and shooting all the birds and mice that got spooked out as the tractor passed. I came behind Teddy with a gunnysack. It was my job to bag all he shot. Before the afternoon was over and it was time for chores, the sack was better than half full.

After milking cows and eating supper, I was pooped out and wanted to go right to bed. I told Mrs. Snowdy that if it was all the same to her I would just as soon sleep out in the loft, it being such a warm night. But she and Teddy wouldn't hear of it. They said it was cool in the basement. I'd sleep much better down there. Mrs. Snowdy had already put a mattress on the floor and covered it with quilts. No ifs, ands, or buts, I would sleep in the basement.

I was too tired to argue. I took a shower, and Teddy gave me one of his nightshirts to wear, which hung on me like a tent and might almost have fit Mamie, though Teddy was nowhere near the size of her. Mrs. Snowdy called me the cutest skeleton in a ghost sheet she had ever seen. She and Teddy had a good laugh over it. I didn't care. I went down to the basement and flopped on the mattress. My head was buzzing with the aftereffects of Teddy's rifle going off constantly all afternoon.

Then I heard Mrs. Snowdy yelling, "No no, Mamie! No no!" And the next thing, there came Mamie down the steps with Mrs. Snowdy after her.

"You sleep with me," said Mrs. Snowdy.

"Nup nup," Mamie told her. She grabbed my hair and pulled me into a sitting position. "Sleep Kritch'n," she said firmly.

"She's used to us sleeping together," I explained.

"Well, I never," declared Mrs. Snowdy, throwing her hand over her mouth.

Mamie let go of me and climbed onto the mattress. She pushed my head back down and rolled me up in her arms. "Kritch'n, Kritch'n," she murmured.

I looked up at Mrs. Snowdy across Mamie's shoulder and tried to smile. "Teddy!" she cried out. "Ted-dy!" her voice rising shrilly on the last syllable. "Come down here!"

Teddy came downstairs and asked what was going on. His mother pointed at Mamie and me all cuddled up on the mattress.

"Well, he said they're a team, Mommy." Teddy clacked his teeth, giving us his wolverine laugh.

"But this, Teddy. This . . ."

"She'd sure make some fine big babies," he said, stroking his chin.

Mrs. Snowdy's face changed from the look of shock to the look of curiosity. "Then you like her, Teddy?" she asked.

Teddy bent down and looked Mamie over carefully. He stroked the tips of his fingers with his thumbs, slowly, as if he had pieces of Mamie there. It was hard to tell what he was thinking. His eyes were no bigger than beebees behind his glasses. At last he straightened up and said, "She'd look fantastic stuffed, standing in the corner on a bit of pasture, next to a stuffed cow. I'd call it 'Super-milkmaid with Cow.' Oh, think of that!" Teddy rubbed his hands. "Mamie the milkmaid. 'Super-milkmaid with Cow.' It would make the *Taxidermist Quarterly*. I'd win a prize."

"That's not what I had in mind when I asked you if you liked her, Teddy. Now will you quit fooling around?" She looked at me and shook her head. "He's such a teaser," she said.

"But think of it!" he told her.

"Now, you stop it. I don't think you're being funny." Her voice was very stern. Teddy hung his head, but he continued to stare at Mamie, until finally his mother, with a sniff and a snort, grabbed him and went back up the stairs.

After the door closed, I whispered to Mamie, "Super-milkmaid with Cow. One wants to marry you off, and the other wants to stuff you." We thought the whole thing unbelievably funny and laughed about it until we were hurting for air. I lay on Mamie's arm, looking at the animals shining a pale blue in the light from a small, ground-level window, their mouths open, full of silent laughter joined with ours. I grinned back at them until the minutes passed and the joke faded away, and I realized I wasn't looking at laughing. I was looking at silent screams frozen for all time.

Immaculate Reception

We stayed on with the Snowdys for the rest of the summer and fall. We filled the barn with hay and the silo with silage and turned the corn stalks under to get the land ready for the disk and the harrow and planting come spring. We took over all the chores in the barn – milked the cows twice a day, cleaned the milkers, shoveled out the gutters, took care of the calves, kept things repaired and painted and running – did everything.

Once Teddy saw we didn't need him to boss us, he stayed out of the way and spent his days either hunting up and down the woods or stuffing what he killed. He didn't care about nothing but to shoot it and stuff it and bring it to his ma so she could praise it. She would always tell him that some squirrel or crow or beaver or toad looked so lively, like it would run away. She said Teddy was an artist, just like his father, except that his father was an artist in wood instead of animals. But they were alike as two peas in a pod, she insisted, so it was no wonder they couldn't get along.

Ben Snowdy did come by once or twice a week and visited his wife. Sometimes he would stay to dinner, if Teddy was off running in the woods, and now and then he would stay all night and sneak off early in the morning, doing his best not to let his son see him. Whenever Teddy was around and Ben was there, Teddy would stay as close to Mrs. Snowdy as he could and yet not be sitting in her lap. It looked a bit strange to see her trying to talk to her husband all the time around Teddy's shoulder, her face popping out one side or the other to say something to Ben. It was like that every time Teddy was home, so Ben didn't stay long. His cabin and workshop were just a mile down the road, and now and then he would bring up a piece of furniture, a small table or chair, one time a hall tree, to show Mrs. Snowdy. She would always praise him as much as she did Teddy, making a fuss over what wonderful artists she had.

I liked it when Ben was there. He always asked about the cows and made compliments to me and Mamie about how much better they looked and milked since we had taken over. He wasn't quite as tall as Teddy, nor as thick in the chest and shoulders. His eyes were small, like Teddy's, only they seemed larger; there was such a lot of light in them, a quiet light that made him seem to walk in a calm air. And he didn't have those big, hungry teeth and wasn't forever smiling at nothing; nor did he have Teddy's high-pitched voice, which could set your teeth on edge. Ben's voice was smooth and gentle; it fit the rest of him. In all, he seemed a straightforward, no-nonsense farmer, who wasn't farming – who, for some reason all his own, let his son have the farm and have his way. Only thing I could figure is that maybe Mrs. Snowdy, who doted on Teddy like he was a treasure, had arranged all three of their lives so she could have the best of her men and they could each have a share of her. Whatever the reason, Ben went along with it and didn't seem to mind too much that he didn't live in his own house.

¶ Once, for a few days in October, I was sick. Mrs. Snowdy took care of me, while Mamie did all the work. When Teddy saw I was sick, he made faces at me and said he couldn't stand sick people. He claimed he was never sick a day in his life, and he couldn't understand why anyone would let it happen. It was a weakness for which I should be shot. After he made sure I knew his opinion, he took his rifle and said he would be gone a couple days, and I better get well or else.

Actually, I wasn't so sick. I had a fever and a sore throat, but I had been worse off many times before. Once I even had pneumonia and once the German measles. But it was nice to get babied by Mrs. Snowdy, who made me hot soup to eat and put cold cloths on my forehead and read me stories out of the *Saturday Evening Post*.

The third day I was recovering. Teddy was still out hunting, and Ben came by and sat in the basement with me and Mrs. Snowdy. She asked him if I reminded him of anyone.

He thought a second and said, "Oh, you mean Teddy, when he was little. Yes, he was a sickly boy, you know? Many was the time I stayed up nights with him, putting cold cloths on his head."

"So many times," she said.

"He told me he was never sick in his life," I said.

Ben shook his head. "You know, Teddy wants to believe he's a special person. And if you're sick, then to him you're not special. Truth is, he was the sickest boy there could have been short of death. Every child's disease seemed to own him. It's a wonder he didn't die. He forgets things like that. You can't be very special if you're sickly, you see. He's a mighty hunter now. He's God out there."

"So far as he's concerned, he's never been sick," I said.

"That's it. That's Teddy. He always sees things the way he wants them to be. Nothing changes him. Not the truth anyway."

"He's healthy as a horse now!" said Mrs. Snowdy.

"Yep, he's made himself a real speciman," Ben agreed. "He started when he was about ten, I think. He took one of my rifles to the woods one day, and believe it or not, he shot a bear. First thing he had ever killed, and it was a bear, half-growed, like him. He gutted it and lugged it home and wanted me to tell him how to stuff it. He was that proud. But I had no idea how to stuff an animal. It made him mad at me. He's been mad ever since. Remember, Lily?"

"He has a terrible temper. He can be a little monster."

"To say the least, my dear."

"But Teddy loves us, I'm sure, Ben. He loves you, and in time he'll grow to know it. Just give the boy time." Mrs. Snowdy smiled confidently, her big teeth shining like piano keys.

Ben looked at me and winked. "But you know," he said, "I would have thought by the time a fellow was thirty he would come to realize his father wasn't the real enemy of life. Teddy passed thirty ten years ago, and he still ain't looking back."

"He doesn't hate you, Ben," Mrs. Snowdy insisted. Her voice was impatient with him.

He looked at the animals crowding in on us. "Since he was ten, he's stuffed everything in sight. And when it wears out or starts looking shabby, he burns it and stuffs another like it. I wonder what possesses a fellow? What do you think, Christian? Ain't it odd? Look at this."

I was looking. I told Ben it was hard to get a hold of, because I knew plenty of hunters who thought nothing of killing. Killing was natural, a man thing same as a lion or tiger thing, and I had trapped for years without a bad conscience. But something about Teddy's way wasn't quite right; it reminded me of the cold way I had seen John Beaver skin a mink alive. It struck the wrong note. It had the kind of viciousness I'd heard about that lived inside men in big cities, the kind that takes a pleasure in suffering, so long as it isn't their own. I'd seen Teddy not finish an animal off because he didn't want to mess up its pelt, though a little tap on the head wouldn't have hurt the fur. He didn't mind to watch and wait for something to die, which wasn't a trait I could admire. All my thoughts on Teddy's oddness I explained straight out to Ben, pulling no punches. Ben kept nodding over and over, like I was taking the words out of his mouth.

But Mrs. Snowdy didn't like it. She sat mostly looking down at her hands and rolling and unrolling a magazine in her lap. When I finished my opinion, she gave me hers, "A man who skins a mink alive is a maniac, a vicious man worse than a viper, and not at all to be compared with Teddy, do you hear? The very idea that he enjoys watching something suffer! He's not like a normal person, I know that. He's an artist like Ben. He has to think about his art. Would a savage beast dedicate himself to the creations you see in here? Would he? Certainly not. Teddy is a creator – a creator! Look how lively these animals seem. They're beautiful, that's what. They're as much a work of art as . . . as . . . who's an artist, Ben?"

"Rembrandt."

"As Rembrandt. Isn't it so, Ben?"

"It's true they have a beauty in them, Lily."

Mrs. Snowdy's lips trembled. She gave Ben a tender look. "Do you remember when our little Teddy used to climb in bed with us on those cold winter mornings?"

"Yes, and we would warm him up."

"And treat him like he was the only boy on earth. And he was to us. And could that darling be compared to someone who would skin a mink alive?" She shook her finger at me. "And shame on you, Christian. You're just a regular boy, just an ordinary one making judgments about something far above you. You're no Rembrandt, and you might do harm to a person's reputation. What do you know about art or artists like Teddy? Not a thing. I've lived with him for forty years. I know the inside-out of him. Don't tell me!"

Mrs. Snowdy harrumphed at me. Then she looked over at a lynx licking its paw. She pointed to it. "I remember that one. It was sitting in the front yard under the elms, cleaning itself like that. Tell me it isn't lovely. Teddy made it immortal."

That day I wrote my parents for the first time and told them where I was and what had happened to Mamie and me. In my letter I asked for their advice and asked what the situation was with John Beaver and the situation with the law. I apologized for all the worry I'd caused and tried to explain the difference, as I saw it, between right and truth, and how what I had done seemed like the true thing to do at the time, though according to the law it wasn't right. I told how so much had happened since then that it seemed I had already lived a lifetime. Yet there was tomorrow, and I didn't know what to do about it, or any of the tomorrows coming up. I needed advice.

A day after my letter was sent off, Shepard came to get Mamie. I heard the steps groaning, creaking, cracking, and there he came, his nose leading him into the room, where I was still in bed but feeling much better. First thing he said was, "No wonder you're sick, Crystal. Look at this place. Ugh and yuk! Neanderthal lives. What a disgusting means of inducing catharsis. Is he gone? Is he off to make havoc on the poor beasties, like Mrs. Snowdy says?"

"As far as I know," I said. "So how are you, Mr. Shepard?"

"Miserable, of course, miserable, miserable. I'd have come sooner, but Teddy made me wait until winter was upon us, which it is now, impending on the ebb tide of autumn, yum yum."

He kept staring from one animal to another as he talked. "These," he said, pointing to them, "are indications of a mental aberration of vast and potentially dangerous proportions. Hmmm. I always heard Teddy had arranged a Great White Hunter's delight, but this is beyond even my superior imagination. There is a flagellation here. This is a microcosm of how he sees the world. Cat chasing rat, snake fanging mouse, hawk clawing snake, lynx pouncing on calf – kill kill kill, everything in the cosmos living by killing. Even the cat licking his paws looks like he's just had a bloody meal. Look at the wicked eyes of the birds, the beaks like fishhooks. Can the deadly creator be far behind with his thunderbolts? Hmmm? Jung should get a hold of Teddy, a Jungian delight, yum yum. Where's my Mamie?"

"She's in the barn," I told him. "She might not want to go with you though. She likes the cows here plenty."

He stuck his fists in his eyes and groaned, "Ohhh, I knew it, I knew it. I shouldn't have listened to the little blighter. He was manipulating me! I have the worst luck."

"Well, it's been a good deal for him. We do all the work. Mamie is wonderful with the cows. They milk heavy for her."

"Ohhh, the pee-eyed perpetrator, eyes yellow as pee, you ever notice? 'Wait until winter,' he says to me, 'until the harvest is through.' And all the while he's working his charms on her, his bovine charmers. It's true, isn't it? Teddy wants Mamie for himself."

"I don't think so," I answered. "Teddy just wants his mommy."

Shepard sat in the chair next to me and leaned over to say in my ear, "You are aware, Crystal, aren't you, that Ben and Lily are in the middle of . . . are the progenitors of . . . a salient Oedipal complex the size of a whale's member? Yum yum. Little Teddy agitated them asunder. He has gonadal heat for his mama. Classic Freudian freak. I should write a book and get famous, yum yum."

"Mrs. Snowdy thinks Teddy is a god. Ben wonders where he went wrong. He keeps hoping Teddy will come round."

"The follies of parental permissiveness. Poof poof, Teddy is a perverted Hippolytus to his mama Phaedra. Ben is a poor, blind Theseus. But none noble enough for *tragedy*! Perverts are never noble. Nothing to be done about it."

"I suppose not. But I feel sorry for Ben. I see it in his eyes sometimes, like he knows it's hopeless. He stares at me a lot, like I'm sort of the son he wanted."

"Noble Crystal."

"We're going hunting in November. He knows a place with lots of deer."

Shepard leaned back and gazed down his nose at me. He needed to clip the hairs in it. And he needed to wash his hair too. It was tangled up on his forehead, and there was dandruff over the shoulders of his blue jacket. He rubbed his belly and said that hunting was fine for me, but what about the future of Mamie? He said the Artlife would be ready to open by the first of the year. The projector had been completely overhauled and would be back in the booth by Christmas, ready for Mamie to start training. She was slow-witted, so it might take weeks for her to learn. Didn't I want her to have a chance to be something other than a manure-flavored farmer?

"You got it all wrong," I told him. "It's up to Mamie, not to me. You got to ask her about it. She knows her own mind better than you think. But listen, before you go to the barn, tell me what happened to Robbie Peevy after we left. You know we broke him out of jail, right?"

"Of course I know. I know everything. Ahem, let me see, Robbie: they chased him, dogs and state police, tracked him for four days through the woods, over the farms thereabout, but could they tree the wily fox? He vanished like a ghost, as if he flapped his wings and flew away. Robbie the phantom. He had the dogs chasing their tails – baffled, all baffled. And don't you know that in the repositories of those inky-dinky minds belonging to his followers, those true believers have dubbed it Robbie's Immaculate Reception, yum yum. They say he promised to go like Elijah, and so he did. There's a movement afoot to have the dissembler canonized and name after him his own church. The Church of Robbie Peevy of the Immaculate Reception, tee hee hee. Elijah, my bunghole."

I was happy to hear he'd got away. "He said he would go like Elijah in a whirlwind," I said.

"The Robbinites say God pulled him from harm's way, took him from our midst, since we have not the courage of his convictions and we are too baffled by the propaganda of freedom of speech to recognize we are destroying our children. Hoopteehoo! They would destroy the books. They would destroy my right to think and your right too. Take it away from one, take all, and give it to the pusillanimous ilk. I'll tell you what – it's ignorance and fear, ignorance and fear, and the abysmal standards of puritanism and terror clogging the free flow of the freedom-mongering blood. Humph! They say that the fact of one girl pulling the bars off the jail is proof without peer that Robbie stands at the right hand of Jesus. Poof poof, they don't know the Mamie you and I know. I knew it was Mamie as soon as I heard the story."

"Do the people know?" I asked.

"None in a million. They think she was an angel. Such asininity depresses me, Crystal." He stroked his nose for comfort. "An angel, poof poof, they don't know our Mamie. What say you, Crystal, did our precious one really rip those bars out all by herself?"

"You should have seen it," I told him. "She did seem like an angel, a monster, warrior angel. She shined with power, no kidding, lit up from the inside. And she pulled and pulled until the brick cracked and broke up. She pulled a corner out just enough for Robbie to slip through. I was there. It wasn't human."

"The article in the paper called her Queen Kong, haw haw!"

I asked him about the woman next door, who had called the cops on us.

"That's just old Anna," he said. "A Scandihoovian busybody, full of the nose for everybody's business. She has phobic visions of murderers looking up her dress. But not a bad sort, once you know her eccentricities."

"She sure would have liked to take her broom to us."

"She said you looked like beatniks. 'No truck vit dat scoom,' she said. She's been assisting me in the renovation of the Artlife."

I changed the subject back to Robbie. "Isn't he something," I said, "to disappear the way he said he would?"

Shepard pondered the mystery of Robbie. "I don't know, Crystal," he said in his superior way. "It's really nothing for me to interpret Robbie's peripeteia, yum yum. I have psychic powers, you know? I see it as clearly as if I were there. Robbie walked across only half of a fresh-cut field of hay, and then the devil rode the other half behind a tractor out cutting hay. The farmer let him off at the end of the field, where there's a stream running north to south. Robbie walked the stream clear to the next county. It's that simple. I see it here." He tapped his head. "No Immaculate Reception."

"But are you sure, or just guessing?"

"I wasn't there, Crystal. But when you're a genius you get flashes of insight beyond the ordinary. A genius doesn't need to behold miracles to understand how they work. The application of his brilliant powers, plus second sight brought to bear, and yum yum, he knows all, sees all, sees even miracles clearly as humbug." Shepard sighed over the burden of his genius. He took out his hanky and blew his nose, then patted it sympathetically.

"Did you tell the cops what your psychic powers showed?" I asked.

"I did indeed. I assisted in the later stages of the investigation, even drove to the scene of the Immaculate Reception and told the authorities my suspicions. Their own investigations bore me out. Of course, they took credit for everything – pretenders! But I solved the case."

"Good for you," I said. "You showed them."

At the top of the stairs, the door opened and Mamie leaped down into the basement. Shepard stood up and held out his arms to her. "Look who has come for you!" he cried.

But she went right past him and knelt down to put her cheek on my forehead. "Fever g-gone," she said. "Yaay, Kritch'n?"

"I'm fine," I told her. "Just being lazy. Here's Shepard. You remember him?"

She waved him away and pointed in the direction of the barn. "Down cow, Kritch'n. Come see."

We had been waiting for one of the cows to calf. "Is it Jewel?" I asked.

"Yaay," she answered. "Mmm-ilk fever. Stick her vein." Mamie put her finger on my neck on the jugular vein.

Shepard's voice sounded close to tears. "Doesn't she remember me?" he asked.

"There's a cow in the barn that might die," I explained. "We got to do something."

"I can't see how she could forget me like that," he continued. "Maybe she's just too dumb. Maybe she has the memory span of a dog."

Mamie caught him by the shoulders and said close into his face. "Shep, shut up now." She turned him around and pushed him toward the stairs.

"Did you hear that?" he cried out. "She told me to shut up!" He was grinning back at me, showing his wet gap and his dogteeth, as she bulled him up the stairway.

Down Cow

I got dressed and followed Mamie and Shepard to the barn, where I found them bent over Jewel, petting her and crooning to her. The cow fit her name. She was mostly white, with black legs and black brisket and a black blaze that ran like a diamond from her forehead to her muzzle. The rest of her, from horn ridge to tail, was white, a creamy, bluish white like a cloudy opal. She was a friendly cow, one of those that love to have their tails rubbed and under their necks scratched. She would come to us in the pasture and slip her head under our arms and rub on us, which made us feel pretty tender toward her, especially since she was almost one of a kind in the Snowdy barn. Most the cows were a bit skittish and always looking over their shoulders, showing the whites of their eyes, as if they were expecting us to beat them, or worse. But in the three months that Mamie and I had cared for them, they had settled down some. A good rub on the tail and some quiet conversation can do wonders with most any cow.

Jewel was down and hurting. On the walkway behind her was a fresh-born calf wobbling about, not at all sure what it was doing there. It was a heifer, white like her mama. She had eyes as big as golf balls and black as coal, eyes that had amazement in them as she stared round about. I took her to the front of the stanchion to see if Jewel would try to get up to lick and feed her baby. And Jewel did give it a try, but only one of her hindlegs seemed to work. The other one was curled near her stomach and wouldn't do its share.

"This isn't milk fever," I said. "That leg is paralyzed."

"The poor bovinity," wailed Shepard, petting her back. "Will she die? Don't let her die in front of me. Another witness would kill me. O fate, why did I have to come here, today?"

I thought probably she would die, but we could try a few things first. I opened the stanchion so Jewel could get her head out. Then the three of us pushed and pulled and jerked her out into the aisle, where she had more room to rock herself and maybe get up. With us to help, she tried it, but mostly she just thrashed around and kept flopping back onto her side. After a while she got too depressed to try anymore. She tucked her head over her shoulder and closed her eyes. It was her way of saying, "Go away, I die now." In fact, the way she had positioned herself was exactly like cows do when they've got milk fever, which made me think it was that *and* a paralyzed leg. I took her temperature and found it low.

"She's got milk fever too," I told Mamie.

As soon as she heard me, she went to the medicine cupboard and got a bottle of calcium and the tube and needle. I put a noseclip on Jewel and tied it to one of her back legs, so that her neck bulged out and I could see the artery. It took only a couple of tries till I hit the jugular inside and the blood came spurting out, like a little red fountain arcing over my hands.

"Aghh," groaned Shepard. "Blood, blood, ohhhh." He stumbled away from us, hit the wall, and slid down it with his eyes closed. I told Mamie it was a good place for him to be; we could wake him later. She turned the calcium bottle upside down and let the air out of the tube, and I fitted the tube to the needle in Jewel's neck. We let it go in slowly, twenty minutes before the bottle was empty. Any faster might have given her a heart attack. Her big body shook like she was freezing to death. The life was coming back. I untied her nose and she came around, head up, eyes alert. Amazing stuff – calcium. We tried again to get her up, and she was willing, tried her hardest; but the leg stayed dead, and the cow stayed down.

While we were standing over her wondering what to do next, Shepard woke up on his own and stood up. Steadying himself by keeping one hand on the wall, he asked, "Is there going to be any more blood? My sensitive nature can't help how it reacts."

Just then Teddy came in from the hunt, his rifle in one hand and a dead woodchuck in the other. He threw it down and said angrily, "That for three days of freezing my ass off! It's like a ghost land out there – there's nothing! Where the hell have all the specimens gone?" He walked up to Jewel and poked her with his rifle. "So what's her problem?" he said.

I explained about the milk fever and the bum leg.

"She looks all right to me," he said. "She looks fine enough. You guys are just too namby-pamby with these cows. Get up there, Jewel!" And he goosed her with the rifle barrel. She rocked and thrashed but it did no good.

"So that's the way you want to be!" Teddy hollered. "Huh? Okay then, okay for you. I got a trick to put some mustard in a lazy cow."

"I don't think she's being lazy," I said.

"Lazy! Just ornery and lazy! I seen it before."

As we watched what he was up to, we saw him run to the back cupboard and get the extension cord. He shoved a piece of bare copper wire into the female end of it, then plugged the outlet in and zapped the wire on Jewel's spine. A tiny blue light crackled in the white hair and the cow threw herself, legs flashing like mower blades, all over the cement floor. Zap! he hit her again, zap zap zap! The blue light arced and sizzled, and Jewel tried to get up but was unable to get her dead leg under her. It finally wore her out completely, and she couldn't move. All she could do was moo; and she mooed long and hard, more a moan than a moo. Zap! Zap zap zap! The blue arc flashed; a wisp of smoke rose from the bare spot on her back. Zap zap! Until finally she couldn't even moo, just could only stick her tongue way out and twist her head the way cows do when they're terrified and in pain.

We were all stunned. We just stood there gawking in disbelief, until finally Mamie went over and unplugged the cord. Teddy looked at her like she had committed mortal sin. Then he screamed at her to put the plug back in.

"This is my fucking farm and my fucking cow, and I'm the one in charge here, not you!" he shrieked. "You plug that in or you're fired, Mamie!" His lips were pulled back as far as they would go, showing mean teeth snapping as he yelled, snapping like he was going to go for her throat.

But Mamie didn't even blink. She just gave him a stare and dared him to try it. She wrapped the cord round and round her hands and tore it apart and threw the two ends down in front of him.

Jewel was eyeballing Teddy; Shepard was sobbing and begging in a whisper for Teddy to be good; I was barely recovering my wits. All I could think of to say was, "Don't mess with her, Teddy." I meant Mamie, but he might have thought I meant the cow. He looked from one to the other. Then he turned his attention on Shepard.

"What you crying for, you big baby? What you doing here, anyway, you big blubberpuss. Guys like you make me sick."

Shepard tried to control himself. He took out his hanky and blew his nose, wiped his eyes, and told Teddy, "I've, ub ub, come for Mamie, you bucolic cretin!"

"Come for Mamie? You can have her, Baby Huey. She's fired. She's fired! Don't take that crap from nobody, nosir, no way, not this old boy. My farm. Kill that goddamn cow if I want. I will. I'll stuff it, that's what!" He squinted through his glasses at Shepard. "Look at your face! Snotty nose, boo hoo hoo, crying over a dumb cow. Can't believe you, Baby Huey. Millions just like her go to Packerland every day, get their throats cut, get made into hamburger and steak and you eat 'em. We all eat 'em. Meat! That's meat, you dumb shit – living, breathing meat. You cry every time you eat a roast? Haw haw! If you don't look silly, big bozo like you bawling over a stupid cow, haw haw haw!"

Teddy chucked me with his elbow. "Ain't he silly, Slim, crying over a stupid cow? Big sissy. He ought to see them moaning and coughing and rolling their eyes at the slaughterhouse, huh?"

"He's just got a soft heart," I said.

"Well, what's he doing round here then? Soft hearts don't belong on no farm!" His voice was so shrill it hurt my ears.

"I've come for Mamie Beaver. I had no intention of witnessing your despicable infamy," said Shepard, staring contemptuously down his nose at Teddy.

Teddy glanced at Mamie, who still hadn't taken her eyes off him. "What you want her for anyway?" he asked Shepard. "She's got less brains than this cow here."

"She has more brains in her earlobes than you've got in that entire bullet head of yours," Shepard answered. "You have the intelligence of an inebriated bully with the conscience of a Nazi. This display of cowardice fills me with loathing. In my estimation, you are the first man I've ever met who I would call imminently clubbable. Humph!"

Teddy stuck his tongue out. "Who cares what you think?" he said. And he looked again at Mamie, who was still looking at him. He walked past her and picked up his rifle from where it leaned on the wall.

"You staring at me?" he said to her. "Here, stare down the barrel of this." Pointing the rifle at her, he told me I better make her stop staring or he'd blow her head off. "Then I'll stuff her and stuff this shittin cow. How'd you all like that, huh?"

"The fellow's mad, mad as tyranny," cried Shepard.

"I'd have my Milkmaid with Cow. That's a thought hard to resist! And if she don't quit giving me the eye, I'm gonna have to do it – I swear! Mamie! I swear!" The rifle trembled.

Mamie wouldn't quit, so he kept raving about what a temptation she was providing and how he was going to have to stuff her for sure. He would do her that favor, make her immortal mummy, give her and the cow to the arts. As Teddy described all he would do, Shepard listened and moaned and wiped his eyes and cursed "the frothing dog's excess loquacity" and warned him of "protracted consequences" if he didn't lower the gun. But Teddy ignored Shepard, until Shepard lost heart and tottered over to Mamie and pleaded with her to quit staring at Teddy.

"Just come away with me," he said, his voice trembling, "from all this sordid, smelly, primitive ick, where cows are beaten by the likes of this devil's minion. Come away from all this saponaceous shit and this Teutonic terror with blood in his beady eyes. Come come, Mamie, from this inspissated gloom, come." He tugged at her arm, but she stayed solid as stone, staring.

Teddy suddenly screamed at her to get out. "You and Baby Huey, out! Get! Get! You're tempting me and that ain't cute no more, fatso! You're fired! Get it? *F-i-u-r-d,* fired! I'm the boss and I say you're fired!"

The door opened and Ben and Mrs. Snowdy came in. "Who's fired, Teddy?" said Ben.

As soon as he saw his parents, Teddy puffed out his lower lip and pointed with his rifle at the broken extension cord. "Look, Daddy, look what Mamie done," he said.

"He was electrocuting this cow!" said Shepard.

"I wasn't either. I was trying to make it get up. Lazy bitch."

Mrs. Snowdy clicked her tongue at Teddy. "Why, Teddy," she said, "wherever did you learn such a cruel thing?"

"What's cruel about it, Mommy? If I don't get that cow up, it's gonna die. That's what's cruel. Sometimes a farmer's got to be harsh and all for the cow's own good."

Ben pulled the piece of copper from the cord and held it out. "This ain't anything I ever taught you, Teddy. This isn't just a kick in the ass or a jab with a pitchfork. This is a hundred and twenty volts of fire. You've stuck your finger in a light socket. You know what it feels like."

"All I know is it works good. When I tell a cow to get up, by gum she gets up. I'm the farmer here. I'm the boss. Am I the boss?"

Mrs. Snowdy nodded yes. "You're the boss, honey. No one disputes that. You've made us proud."

"Yeah, and I've kept things going without them." He pointed the rifle at us and his pa. "I'm the farmer now, better farmer than Daddy ever was."

"Too bad it ain't true," said Ben. "This plan of Mommy's letting you run things has only made you worse, far as I can tell."

"Worse than what? You're the one causing all the trouble. You never liked me. You always wanted her for yourself, and you hated her paying any attention to me." He pointed a rigid finger at Ben. "You never know what a guy like that might do!"

Jewel started trying to get up again. We jumped back to give her room, as she rocked and threw her head forward and kicked her one good leg out behind. But the other one stayed useless, and all she did was throw herself a few feet farther down the aisle.

"That's nerve damage," said Ben, watching her. "That can be real bad. That's the sciatic nerve runs right down over her hip, down her leg. It gets pinched from calving. I don't remember any cow I've had ever get over it. Though I know some do."

"So there!" Teddy cried. "Daddy says so hisself! Best to save the critter from pain, I say." He turned the rifle onto Jewel's head, putting the point of it just between her eyes.

"Hold on there!" yelled Ben.

All of us yelled except for Mamie. She reached over and caught his wrist with one hand and snatched the rifle away with the other.

"Oww, you goddamn buffalo," he hollered. "Lemmee go!"

Mamie let him go. He rubbed his wrist and showed it to his mommy. "I'm paralyzed," he whined.

Mrs. Snowdy wasn't very sympathetic about it. She gave his ear a twist. "You scared hell out me doing that, Teddy!"

Teddy made an "Eeeeeee!" sound and petted his mommy's arm.

"No reason to shoot that cow yet," Ben told us. The tone of his voice was pure exasperation. "I said some do come out of it."

Teddy got away from his mommy and sneered at us. "You all can be against me," he said, baring his teeth and making a tight face so you could see all the bones beneath and see the grinning skull he would be someday. "I don't care a damn. I'm still gonna be carving steaks off this cow. You'll let her die slow, that's all. And in the end you'll be the mean ones, not me. I know animals from nostril to asshole, and I know when they're gonna die, and this one is gonna die. Gonna die slow and hard. Just wait and see."

"Maybe Teddy's right," said Mrs. Snowdy. "He does know animals."

"I am right. And I'm sorry I had to hurt her, but I had to see if there was a chance she could get up. I hope I didn't scare you too much, Mommy."

"Oh, Teddy, come here." She hugged him up hard and kissed his grinning mouth. "You precious boy. You come to the house now. I've got cherry pie, just warm from the oven."

They grinned hugely at each other, two forests of teeth in love.

"Can I have my rifle back?" he asked meekly.

"Of course you can," said Mrs. Snowdy. She took the rifle from Mamie and handed it to him. He picked up his woodchuck and followed after his mommy, complaining to her on the way out about Mamie, how you never knew what a guy like her might do.

We all sighed with relief when the door closed. Shepard said, "That fellow is a menace to sanity. I suppose we should pity him, but primarily, I think, someone should take a stick to him and pity him later."

Ben looked from Mamie to me. "You two ain't leaving, are you?" he asked. "That was just a little Teddy-fit, you know. No harm done."

Shepard disagreed. "No harm, my foot. It's dangerous here. That man is a threat, a walking bomb, stupid and depraved and evil. You can't stay here. Both of you must come with me. Of all the anfractuosities of the human mind, none is so blunt as its love of killing, none so primitive and sure, driven into our antediluvian blood, yum yum, by the demands of hunger, basic as instinct, basic as lion tooth and tiger claw. He is nature with a veneer of civilization. He is will and appetite uncoupled from reason. Doom is in those bitty pee-eyes of his. I beg you to listen to me, sapient sage that I am; Teddy Snowdy is a fractious monster!"

"Oh now, listen," said Ben. "Come on. Teddy's got his problems, but he's no Lizzy Borden there, Don."

Shepard's eyes pinned Ben with a stare of contempt. "Even with my uncanny gift of lexicography, yum yum, I cannot *exaggerate* the perversions I've seen here today, Benjamin Snowdy. I'm sorry that you've forced me to say this to your face."

"Whyn't you just go, Don. I'm not in the mood, okay?"

"Well! So 'truth's a dog, must to kennel.' I'll leave, if that's the way you feel. Yes, my Promethean insight goes unappreciated here, I see. Mamie plays with a cow's leg. You tell me I exaggerate. Christian bites his lower lip and says nothing, doesn't defend me, even though he knows I'm right. One word more: you have a butcher in your midst. Beware. His mind is a carving block, Benjamin Snowdy, and remember this, that 'worms eat men, but not for love.'"

Shepard tossed his head, petted his nose, stroked his mustache, and with great dignity waddled past us and out the door.

I knew he was right. I knew it in my bones. And had it been just me, I would have gone with him. But I couldn't leave Mamie behind, and she wasn't going anywhere. She knew Jewel was a goner if she left. Jewel was just a cow, and Teddy wouldn't give her much chance to recover. Few farmers would. It was the nature of the business to be cold when you had to – to kill a cow when she couldn't earn her way. Soft-hearted farmers had it the toughest. They would hang on and nurse a cow to the end, and if it died, the soft-hearted farmer looked like a fool. But more often than not, a down cow will live, if given half a chance. I had seen it happen plenty of times, cows coming back from death's door. My pa was a soft-hearted farmer. He hated to give up on a sick cow, always felt he owed it to her to try everything he knew to make her well. He said she was the supporter of a farmer's dreams and gave more than she got, and there was a union in nature between man and beast, a union that too many farmers forgot in the name of running a business. Pa insisted farming wasn't a business; it was a way of life and more – it was a religion.

Mamie, Ben, and I pinched a cowlift over Jewel's hipbones. Then we took a chainfall and hooked it to an overhead beam and then to the cowlift. Mamie cranked the chainfall and got Jewel's hindend off the floor, but Jewel must have thought we were going to torture her more, because she hung loose, with her head down, her butt in the air, and she wouldn't make an effort to stand. We petted her and loved her up, talking soft and trying to convince her we meant well. But she wasn't having any of it after the shock treatments Teddy had given her. Forelegs folded under, head down to the floor, hindend jacked up four feet high, she hung like a rumply old rug waiting to be beaten.

Ben said the thing to do was get her front end up and even with her back and see if she would let her legs down. He went out back and got a four-by-six long enough to go under the cow. Ben and I got on one side of the board and Mamie the other. We heaved together and got Jewel's forelegs up all right, but she stayed limp and looked very depressed about the whole thing. So we let her back down again.

The next idea was to get the heifer back around and put her to Jewel's udder. Mamie got the heifer and showed her the teats, squirting some milk on her face to get her interested. It was just the coaxing Jewel needed. She looked at her calf and came alive again, rose up on her front legs and mooed over her shoulder, mooed softly to the baby, telling her to suck. The calf reached in and caught hold of a teat and gave a tug.

We were pretty pleased with ourselves. Jewel was up, leaning a bit goofy to the left, where her leg dangled useless, but the rest of her seemed to be working all right. I tightened the cowlift enough so she'd be straighter, and then the three of us stepped back and left Jewel and her baby alone. We talked it over and figured we would have to keep lifting her up and down several times a day for a while, and we'd have to massage the bad leg to see if the nerve would come alive. Ben said if Jewel wasn't standing on her own in ten days, then it was permanent damage and he would have to let Teddy shoot her.

Mamie's Obsession

Time went fast. And Jewel was not getting well, no matter that Mamie took over completely and stayed with the cow around the clock, raising her five times a day and massaging the bad leg and the hip, kneading them, trying to find that magic spot that would bring the nerve back alive and put Jewel on all fours. Each time Mamie massaged up and down the muscles, she would grab the leg and force it to stretch out, pulling it back as far as it would go, then letting it spring up again. She did this a dozen times. Then she went back to digging her fingers into the muscle and working at it like it was a mound of bread dough. I tried it myself once, kneading the muscle, but my hands started cramping after five minutes. So I stayed out of the way, just doing most of the chores and milking and letting Mamie give all her time to the cow.

The days numbered ten before we knew it, and it looked to me like we would have to do what Ben had said and put Jewel down. Not only was the leg still shriveled but the cow's hips were being chewed up by the cowlift and had become raw and bloody. To help this problem, Mamie wrapped the cowlift rings with rags to make them softer, but it didn't do any good. Still, Jewel milked all right, and she ate and drank good, so it didn't make sense right then to just shoot her, tenth day or not. Bleeding hips and all, she had a lot of life in her. Teddy was insisting that ten days was enough. Ben said he was afraid Teddy was right. I argued that the cow was giving milk enough to earn her keep and should be let to live until she started costing the farm money.

"But look," said Ben, in a kindly way. "You go down there and what do you see? You see that cow's hips turning into hamburger. She's in pain, Christian, and it's just going to go on till she has to be shot. So what's the point? We're not much if we let our animals suffer that way. I'm afraid I have to insist now."

Teddy already had his rifle, so we marched down to the barn with him. On the way, he pointed out to us how stupid we were for not listening to him the first day. The cow would be dead now and not have had ten days of Mamie pestering her.

"I suppose so," I said, just sort of agreeing with him.

He clicked his teeth at me. "You're all right, Slim," he said. "Most people don't want to admit when they been wrong."

When we got into the barn, Mamie was standing in front of the cow, giving us a warning look.

"Now, Mamie," said Teddy. "I'm gonna shoot that cow. So you step out the way, Mamie."

"Booshit," she answered.

"See there, Daddy? See why I fired her? She won't take orders. That's my cow and I'm gonna shoot it, by God."

"Booshit," said Mamie again. She took a step towards Teddy, and he backed off.

"Talk to her, Christian," said Ben. "Make her understand."

So I did. I went through the whole thing about it being ten days and about Jewel being in pain and going to die anyway, so it was cruel to keep her going. If Teddy shot her, she would never know what happened. It would be over with. It was the right thing to do. After I finished, Mamie cocked her head to one side and looked me up and down in a way that made me think I wasn't much.

And to me she said, "Booshit, Kritch'n."

"Well, Mamie, dammit, she's not your cow."

She didn't reply. She put her hands up and set her feet, ready to battle all of us if she had to.

"Let's not fight over this," said Ben. "Give her more time. Mamie doesn't want the cow to suffer. She wants to do the right thing."

"I could wing a shot in there before she knows what's happening," said Teddy in a whisper.

Ben shook his head no. "That's too dangerous," he said. "And you'd probably have to shoot Mamie too."

"Then I'll come down here when she's asleep and do it." Teddy turned on his heel and left the barn.

Ben and I left too. I was feeling pretty rotten for taking the side against Mamie, and I wanted to make it up to her. Not that I thought she was right. Ben and Teddy had right on their side. But she wasn't wrong either. It was the thing about truth again. They had right, but she had truth.

When I got to the house, I asked Mrs. Snowdy if she would make some lunch for Mamie for me to take to her. Mrs. Snowdy fixed me a basket of cold rabbit and buttered bread, which I brought to Mamie as a peace offering. She sat and ate with me and acted like nothing had happened. But when we finished and I started to leave, she caught my hand and said, "Kritch'n, you no know w-what I do?"

I thought about it. Did I know what she was doing? I thought I did. "Yaay, Mamie, I know," I told her. "But the cow, she's suffering, and it's bad if you let an animal suffer, you see?"

Jewel was resting on her side, her head in the stanchion, chewing her cud, pretty much the picture of the contented cow, except for the gashes around her hip bones. Mamie nodded towards Jewel.

"S-s-suf-fer?" she said. "Nup nup, Kritch'n. W-why you s-say?"

"Nothing, Mamie," I answered. "I'm for whatever you want." But I lied; I wanted bad for the down cow to be a dead cow.

The days went by, one after the other, and nothing changed with Jewel. Mamie stayed always in the barn, and some nights I stayed with her. I would sleep and wake and offer to stand watch while she slept, but she would turn me down. She didn't want Teddy to catch her off-guard. When she slept was a mystery. The days went by. She stayed awake and kept after the cow's leg.

Most nights I would leave her about ten o'clock and go back to the house. Teddy would be there, sitting at the table, having his cold cereal before bedtime, and he would growl at me about how the stupidest farmers he ever met were those who made pets of their cows and then couldn't shoot them when it was necessary. I'd tell him that according to my pa, catering to a cow when it was sick wasn't stupid; it was the least you could do considering what the cow had done for you, giving you a milk check every month. Teddy would holler at me that what I was talking about wasn't the same thing as what was going on with Jewel. But it was. He just didn't see it. He would say, too, to let Mamie starve, not to feed her down there, and she would eventually get hungry and come to the house. He could sneak down then and quick as a bullet get it over with. Mrs. Snowdy always said to get that thought out of his head. She wasn't about to let that brave girl starve.

Mamie went on and on with Jewel, lifting her, feeding her, milking her, putting her back down, and rubbing the sores on her hips with lanolin and sulphur. And of course, she exercised Jewel's leg tirelessly. A whole month went by. We had a nice spell of Indian summer just before November took over and made a mess out of everything. Rain came and knocked the leftover leaves to the ground, and the trees became a ghostly gray, and the hay stubble went from gold to brown to black. And even after the rain stopped, the clouds stayed on and let loose a shroud of mist that hung in the air and made it twice as gloomy.

And what was worse than the weather was the decline of Jewel. She was losing weight and her milk was down to little more than a half-gallon a day, and the sores on her hips had turned into the hamburger

Ben had said they would. I was all on Teddy's side for shooting her. I even thought about doing it myself, and I told Mamie she was being as mean and cruel as John Beaver himself not to let Jewel die. But what I said made no difference to her, and I couldn't get up the gumption to transfer my opinion into action.

By that time it wasn't five times a day that Mamie massaged Jewel's leg – it was almost constantly. Whether the cow was up on the chainfall or down, Mamie pushed and pulled and kneaded and stretched. I had never seen anything make her tired before, but I saw her tired now, and getting more and more tired each day. Her skin turned white as ash and there were deep circles under her eyes. Her clothes got baggy from her losing so much weight. The cow was dying, and I began to fear that Mamie was dying too. I tried to help, but just a few minutes of doing what she was doing wore me out. I didn't see how she could go on. I yelled at her that she was going to kill herself over a stupid cow, and wouldn't that be the dumbest thing ever? I said she wasn't brave and kind, just stubborn and stupid, and she reminded me of her pa. I got mad at Jewel for not getting well. "Stand up or die!" I screamed at her. And I said, "There's nothing stupider than a stupid cow, unless it's a stupid Mamie Beaver!" I said a lot of things like that. I wasn't being the kind of friend Mamie needed.

But she didn't seem to mind. All her single-mindedness was focused on the cow, and nothing else got to her. It got so bad, I just couldn't stand to stick around and watch, so I started staying away from the barn. I still brought food to Mamie, but I didn't stay to eat with her. I milked and did my chores, and then I got out and tried my best to not think about her down there, digging her hands into that leg, feeling for the nerve that had died. But trying not to think about her made me think about her more than ever. I spent a lot of hours wondering if she had gone fully crazy. I thought of all the forms of craziness I had seen since running off with her, from John Beaver to Mike Quart to Robbie Peevy to Shepard and Amoss and Teddy – not one really normal mind in the bunch, as far as I could tell. But then I tried to think of what was normal, and decided that *I* was the only one. No one else, just Christian Peter Foggy. And that kind of thinking made me laugh and tell myself that *I* was crazy. So I said crazy is normal and everybody belongs in Camelot where things are normal, just like in Madison and Minneapolis and Maple and . . . everywhere. The thoughts piled in till I couldn't sort them and could only see in my mind the way Mamie was fading away, getting thinner, her eyes looking like two gray spots of ash and her hair hanging like wilted leaves. She smelled of manure and damp cow and spoiled milk. Only her hands stayed the same, long-boned and muscled, with freckled backs and tiny golden hairs standing up like they were full of electricity.

Every night in bed I made the sign of the cross to get God's attention, and I prayed for Mamie, prayed that he would snap her out of it. I even prayed to Robbie, just in case what he said was true about being a piece of Jesus. I prayed myself to sleep, and in my sleep I had nightmares of cops chasing me and Mamie, and I was always riding her and saying she had to run faster and faster. She always did, and she leaped over boulders and logs and ponds and went higher and higher with each leap, until we were going over whole barns and trees. I would feel the sickening sensation of being so high and knowing we were bound to come down in a crash – but we never did. We'd hit the ground, and it was like rubber that would bounce us higher than ever, boing . . . boing . . . boing, up and down, up and down, until somewhere in the dream we would come to Teddy Snowdy's farm. He would be there with his rifle. His teeth would come at us, clicking as they came, and they would catch my foot. My foot would disappear, and then my ankle and then my knee, and down we'd go, both of us, swallowed by Teddy's teeth. He would take us to the basement and make us into papier-mâché.

Night after night I had the same dream, until I didn't think I could stand to sleep anymore. But I couldn't stand to not sleep either. I wanted Mamie to come back. I wanted Jewel to die. I wanted to go to California. I wanted to be a piece of Jesus.

One day a letter came from home. Mrs. Snowdy brought it to me.

"You got kin in Maple?" she asked, turning the envelope round and round in her hands. "It's thick," she said.

I took it from her and went downstairs to read it. Teddy was there working at his bench, rubbing the inside of some skin with borax. He had been working hard for days, preparing balsa-wood and papier-mâché bodies for a mess of animals he had ready to stuff. I had to admit that Teddy was talented when it came to carving balsa. To me the figures he made looked like pieces of art he could have sold. Sewing the skins and fur over them only made them ugly, in my opinion. He thought I was nuts. He said he turned straw into gold, and only an idiot would want to leave it straw. It was an eye-of-the-beholder kind of thing, only I was dead sure I had the better eye.

When I came in with my letter, he said, "Hey, that goddamn cow dead yet? No? Well, it's gotta be soon now. That cow is on my mind all the time. I see her standing over there in the corner with her head down and those two wolves at her hindquarters, trying to hamstring her. Or maybe put them in front, going for her throat. There's a picture for you! Don't you think I've got magic in my fingers, Slim?"

"Yeah, magic," I said. I saw I wouldn't be let to read my letter in peace, so I went back up the stairs and out to the loft, settled myself into the hay, and read my letter.

Dear Christian Peter,

This is your sister Mary Magdalen writing for me and Mama. We get to go first, Papa says. First I got to say something myself that I wish I could say it to your face. Christian, brother, I am so proud of you I could just cry. God will bless you, I know, and keep you safe from harm. Your letter explained so many things that John Beaver left out, like he didn't mention a word about you hitting him because he was set to scalp Mamie. Not a word, the skunk. He said you hit him because there was a plan for the two of you to rob him and steal the truck and run off. Don't think for a second we believed what he said. We know you better than that. We have faith in you that you did what you had to do, and your letter just confirmed what we had guessed but didn't know the details. You saved Mamie, Christian. What a wonderful Samaritan you are. What a brave thing for little skinny you to do. Our little Christian just like a knight in shiny armor. I pray Rosary for you every night before bed.

And now Mama wants me to write this. That when you left she just cried and cried. She misses you, her baby boy. When your letter came she just sat down and cried and cried. She prays to Saint Jude for you. She says Rosary for you every night. She thinks this is a good time for you to think of being a Catholic instead of following in Pa's footsteps. Because nobody should make up his own religion. Except Pa. (He said to say that.) He is giving Mama a lecture now, so I want to say that your letter sounded real depressed. We know things have been hard for you. We wish there was some way of making it better. Please have faith in God, Christian, and remember that He loves you like we do. Be thankful for what you have right this minute. At least you are safe and you have a roof over your head and food. You can see. You can hear. You can touch. You can smell. You can think. And you can write us letters. Which you better do a lot more.

Mama wants to say that it is all right if you want to have a religion like Pa. Just so you believe in God is the important thing. They both agree on that. Mama says she has been so tired lately but cannot sleep for worry of you. Her bladder has hurt a lot too. She thinks it is from worrying about you. And from her heart aching because she misses you so much. She says to be good and work hard for those good people who gave you and Mamie a job. She is glad they are such nice farming folks. She is thankful to God that you and Mamie are healthy. She wishes you would write more often because she worries about you and can't keep from crying all the time. (Not all the time.) She wants to know if Mrs. Snowdy is a good cook and does she sew your clothes when you tear them? That is all from us. Now Calvin thinks he is a big shot because he gets to write for the boys. So get ready for two cents worth of nothing. Bye. Write soon! XOXOXOXO

Mary Magdalen and Mama

Christian, this is your big brother Calvin. Don't lisen to Mary Magdalen, she is as much a brat as ever. So Christian, you hit old Beaver on the head with a club he told us. Good for you. All your brothers say good for you, we ain't gong to pick on you no more when you come home. So Christian, you stoled his truck and recked it. Was he mad! He come here and yelled about how bad you was but pa stuck up for you. And he come at pa to hit him and pa picked up a rock and said he would send him to hell with no lunch. Cush and Cutham and me come running to beat up Beaver but pa said we should not unless Beaver didnt get off our land. Beaver swared at us like a devil. We itch to poke him bad. Cash and Calah come in from the fields on the 350 with the loder on front. You know Calah can be meen. He saw Beaver and us with our fists up and he put the 350 in 4 geer and put the bucket down and lit out after Beaver with it. He chased him up and down the yard. Beaver shaked his fists and cussed and run in circels. His face got red as fire. We laughed so hard we fell down. Even pa could not help hisself. Beaver jumped in his truck that you recked but it runs still and Calah put the bucket on his bumper and pushed him out the yard. We seen no more of him for a time. So Christian, we stuck up for you. Teached that mongrul not to mess with the Foggys. You should be proud of us. All the brothers says hi. Sugar had a heifer just last week, she is milking heavy.

Your brothers, Calvin Cutham
Cush Calah Cash

Christian, my son,

Well, son, I have mixed feelings about it all. We cannot live in this grate contry of ours without being lawful. But when the law is on John Beaver's side there is something rotten in Denmark and no two ways about it. He told us his side and now we got your side. We always knew that your side was the beter one. John Beaver says he has the law and will put you in jail and throw away the key forever. So you better lay low for now, son. The Deity's anger will come on John Beaver one day I predikt. He is a evil man and I admit I was wrong as rain to tell you to give up Mamie to him. Now I tell you to not give up Mamie to that low living son of a cloven hoof. Your conscious can be clear, my son. Remember what Hamlet said, Let the doors be shut on him, that he may play the fool nowhere but in his own house. Not that I really believe he is a fool, he is crafty as a weasel. But he won't learn anything from us and neither will anybody. The doors are closed to him. I know in my heart that the Deity is on your side. And John Beaver has not dreamed what Horatio knows. I seen him drive up and down in his beat up truck that you smashed the side in. I know he wants to stop and see if we heard from you. He don't stop tho, not yet anyway. You know Calah. He sees John Beaver go by and he runs to the tractor and gets it ready to run him down. All the boys want to beat him up. I have to get on them hard not to chase his truck when he drives up and down. You know how they are. They like to punch each other round and roll in the mud. We have had lots of mud this fall. I bet you have too. But it is one thing to play grab ass with your brothers and quite another thing to take on a man the size and meanness of John Beaver who would cut your gizzard out like he would pluck a chicken. Then I would have to shoot him to save the boys and I would go to jail and rot. I can not say what will come of it. All I can say is you stay put and lets see if this don't blow over and John Beaver gets tired of acting like the second coming of Job. No one believes him anyway. I talked to my old friend Ken Maydwell the other day. He says no one believes Beaver but that don't mater, since you did hit him and steal his truck the law would have to punish you for it. So he agrees that you should just stay low for now. He said you sure outsmarted him the day he met you and you had just laid Beaver low. I told him you were the smartest of all my boys. You didn't get your mother's side in you from all her wierd brothers and pa, and it didn't surpize me that you outsmarted him. He didn't get mad about it, he's a good guy I think. He says he hopes you can just keep outsmarting John Beaver. He thinks Beaver has a lot of killer in him. I am not worried about it. Any son of mine who could not outsmart that bastard I would have to send back to his maker for a new transmission. Calvin told you about Sugar. She is fine. Triggerroom had a heifer too the other day and she is already milking 60 pounds. She might look like a horse but she milks like the queen of cows. We put up 8000 bales this year. The Massy Harris 44 snapped an axle when pee-brain Cush popped the clutch too hard. Calvin saw him do it but Cush tried to lie and say he didn't do it. Then Cutham said he saw Cush do it too. You know those two, they can't keep away from fighting. They had to wrestle for it for an hour before Cutham won and made Cush fess up. Anyway we had to pull the whole hind end off the 44 to fix it. I guess you know Cush has had to give his soul to God since then because I've had his ass for a week or more and might keep it for a month. Be careful and write some more. We will let you know what Beaver does.

Your Pa, Jacob Foggy

It was a big relief to me to know that my family was all on my side. I was sorry about Mama worrying and crying so much, but there wasn't anything I could do about it, so I hoped Saint Jude would help her. I walked around outside and then went into the barn and watched Mamie working over Jewel's leg. All of a sudden I hated her. Hated Mamie. She was the cause of all my family's trouble with John Beaver. If it weren't for her I would have been home instead of running around the country with John Beaver and the law after me. And here she was, obsessed with a stupid cow, not eating or sleeping or caring about me and letting herself go to the dogs. She stank worse than a civet cat and she looked like a worn-out ghost. And I didn't exist for her, yet I had given up everything for her, my whole life gone to save her. Some kind of thanks I was getting. I told myself that for two cents I would tell her to go to hell, and I would go back to my family.

That same night I went to bed alone again, and I started having the same nightmare about Teddy getting us between his teeth and making us into papier-mâché. But the dream was interrupted by someone shaking my shoulders. The first thing that came to me was the smell of cow, old cow, long unwashed by the rains. I looked up to see what a cow was doing shaking me, but there was only Mamie standing over me, a dark silhouette with a pumpkin head. She threw the covers off and pulled me into her arms. Though she was thinner, she was as strong as ever. She cradled me like a baby, went up the stairs two at a time, and ran with me out the back door. The shock of the November night air on my skin made me gasp like a chub out of water. I clung hard to her neck and tried to burrow into her. She galloped at full speed to the barn.

Once inside, she set me down and pointed to Jewel. And there was that big, old white cow staring me face to face, standing in the aisle on her own. She raised her head and gave a long mooooo. I could smell the green cud on her breath. I grabbed her neck and gave her a hug. "You old bossy," I said. "You're standing on your own." Jewel raised her neck up for me to give it a scratch. We fussed over her. We brushed her down and got all the old hair off, then washed her with wet rags and dried her. We made her shine like fresh snow, except for the sores on her hips, which would take a while to heal.

"What you've done here," I told Mamie, "is made yourself a miracle. This cow should be dog meat by now and its hide inside Teddy's dampbox. But you wouldn't give up. You knew what you were doing, even though all of us thought you were wrong. It's just a miracle. I'll never doubt you again, Mamie. You are magic. Mamie is magic."

I kissed her stinky face. "Yaay, Kritch'n, I kn-now," she said.

We put Jewel back in the stanchion and gave her and the rest of the cows fresh hay. Then we ran back to the house and down to bed. I jumped under the covers and held them for Mamie, but she took her clothes off and started to leave.

"No no," I said. "Where you going? I want you here with me."

Turning round she sniffed at her arms and shoulders, then held her nose. "Woo woo," she said, waving the smell away.

"Who cares?" I answered. "You just smell like a farm. I'm used to it. Get in this bed with me. Shower tomorrow. I'm missing you."

She looked down at me, a thoughtful look on her face, her face a hundred years old. She came under the quilts with me and wrapped me up till we were like rubber bands round each other. I hugged her like I was hugging life itself. She smelled of cow and hay and manure and herself, which was the smell of damp earth and green fields and the morning air straight from the breath of God. I was ashamed of hating her for a while, but of course, I never really did.

Ambush

The first storm came on the fifteenth of November. It was a big one, with high winds that knocked over trees already loose from having so much rain all autumn long. Snow blew across the land and covered it so well that not even the stubble of corn stalks could be seen. The wind made drifts better than four feet deep on the north and west sides of the buildings. The temperature dropped to nearly zero and stayed there day after day.

There wasn't a jacket on the place Mamie could wear, nor a hat. So Mrs. Snowdy took one of her quilts and made Mamie a coat with a coyote collar. Teddy gave me one of his old barn jackets, and he gave Mamie and me each a fur cap that pulled down over our ears. He called them tabby caps. They were blond and orange striped with limp tails hanging in the back. I recognized them as the two cats that had stolen Teddy's crows the day Mamie and I arrived. They were warm enough, which is what we needed, some little bit of warmth against the cold that had come to stay.

The morning of the first day of deer-hunting season, Teddy woke us up two hours early to do chores. Ben Snowdy even came over to help out. He and Teddy were getting along pretty well, chattering like a couple of old pals about the great hunting weather and how they would be the first on South Range and would probably bag their bucks before noon and be home in time for a hot dinner. They talked about their old hunting trips together, the six-pointer Teddy had shot some years ago, the clean shot from Ben that had brought instant, painless death to a four-pointer one year, and so on. They complimented each other and patted each other on the back. It was weird, such a change, especially from Teddy, who had been almost soft to Mamie since she brought Jewel back from the door of death. Teddy could be likable, if he put his mind to it.

After milking, we went to the house for breakfast. Mrs. Snowdy gave us eggs and fried chicken with bread and coffee. While we ate, she bustled about offering us more of everything. We weren't to leave the table unless we were ready to bust. As she went back and forth with her coffee pot in hand, she would touch Ben on the shoulder and then touch Teddy on the shoulder; she would play with Ben's hair, then play with Teddy's; she would whisper something to one, then whisper something to the other. Her face was pink with excitement and happiness about her two men talking and laughing together, all set to go out and hunt like men should, bringing home meat for the table like men should, the way nature meant it all along. I had never seen her so full of energy and good humor. She laughed at everything, her own thoughts, it seemed, and laughed hardest of all whenever Teddy or Ben made a little joke. It was a very unusual sight – the three of them laughing together – and I thought what an amazing family they were. It even fooled me into thinking that deep down Teddy loved his daddy. I was happy to watch them being close, and it seemed to me a good beginning for a lucky day.

It was still dark when we left. Mamie and I huddled in the back of the pickup, while Ben drove and Teddy kept his carbine automatic at the ready, in case he saw something on the way. Now and then he would roll down his window and blast a stop sign or some farmer's no-hunting sign. Then he would roll the window back up and reload. A lot of metal was turned into scrap by his enthusiasm before we got to where we were going.

It was an area of forests and back roads and clearings, only forty to fifty minutes from the Snowdy farm. We turned off the main road and followed a snow-covered trail for a mile or so, until we couldn't go anymore without getting stuck. On our left was a twenty-acre meadow surrounded on three sides by trees. Straight ahead and to our right was all snowy forest, and the wind was blowing the snow so that it whirled like dancing ghosts around the trees. It pelted our hats and coats and took nips at our faces. Even bundled up in my chore jacket and tabby cap, I was already freezing, my feet especially. I kept kicking one of the tires to warm my toes. Mamie stood still and looked longingly at the forest. Ben was like me, kicking the tires to warm his toes. Teddy seemed to think we were weaklings. He didn't even wear his hat or gloves. He was kidding us about being pussies, saying how when you lived the great outdoors the way he did, you could go bare-chested at twenty below. Then he told us his plan for flushing out the enemy.

Ben and Mamie and I were to go in on foot for a hundred yards west and then circle back until we were coming east toward the meadow, where he would be waiting in ambush for whatever came out. Ben complained that if anyone should wait in ambush it should be him because Teddy was younger and stronger, so he should go in and circle back. Teddy lost all his good humor. He glared at Ben and said he was damned if he would. It was his plan to come to this spot and have us drive the prey to him. He made the plan. He told the plan. He had had the plan in mind for weeks and weeks. And why was Ben always trying to be the boss and make people think that Teddy didn't know eggs from buttercups? Teddy was shaking his finger in Ben's face, almost hitting his nose with it, and suddenly Ben grabbed the finger and held it. It shocked Teddy into silence. The two men stared at each other, Ben still squeezing Teddy's finger. Finally Teddy blinked and said, "Daddy, ouch." Ben let go. He turned to us and waved.

"Let's go get Teddy-boy a deer," he said.

"I won't miss," Teddy called out as we walked away.

It was hard going at first, with better than a foot of snow to get through, but once we were inside the forest the snow wasn't too bad. Still, I was breathing hard and so was Ben. But of course it didn't bother Mamie. She ran ahead of us, tracking left and right, leaping over little drifts and shrubs, then circling back behind us and running on ahead again, looking like a big bear puffing and waddling in and out of the trees.

"She's such a happy one," said Ben, pointing at her. "Wish I had that kind of energy."

"She's got more energy than ten of us," I told him.

"She's like nobody I ever saw or heard of in my life. I can't make up my mind about her. Is she touched or not?"

I shrugged. "I don't know. I thought I knew once, but I don't know anymore. All my life I'd heard she had molasses for brains, that she was retarded and hopeless. She couldn't learn anything, couldn't read, couldn't talk without it taking an hour to make up a three-word sentence. But I'll tell you, Ben, she's not as simple as people think. She's a mystery that I can't figure. You know, when she really wants to, she can talk perfectly. She once learned a little poem from me. I had said it to her maybe two times is all, and she repeated it back to me word for word, not a stutter in her. She does stuff like that every once in a while. It keeps me guessing. I never know what she's gonna come up with next."

"I know what you're saying," he told me. "That thing with the cow now, would a retarded person know to do what she did? Not likely, I think. I can't make up my mind if she knew more than the rest of us or was just too stupid to quit. It seems she understands cows like she's one herself. They've never been healthier or milked better, not even when I had them, and I'm good with cows. I know how to take care of them. But Mamie's got a special touch. She's like a genius with them. Is there such a thing as a retarded genius?"

"I've never heard of that, but there's a lot I've never heard of," I answered.

"Actually, I suppose I could be talking about Teddy in some ways," he went on. His breath was coming hard and so was mine, so we slowed down, while Mamie kept coming in and out of sight. "Teddy is good at only one thing – his taxidermy. In every other way I can think of, he acts a wee bit retarded. Take the cows now. He was raised with them. He should know better by now how to handle them. But he won't learn. Since I left, just ten years ago, he's hired better than a score of herdsmen, better than twenty. They just don't last long with him around. I've spent a thousand hours driving back and forth from my place to the barn to milk cows because the hired help quit and Teddy was off shooting up the forest. I'm glad you and Mamie are here. I've managed to relax a bit. I trust you."

I wanted to ask him why he didn't just stay home and kick Teddy's ass once in a while, take over like my pa would, but I didn't want to spoil what a good talk we were having.

"Yeah," he said, gazing with pride at Mamie, "I'd take her, retarded or not, whatever faults she's got. Any farmer would. She fascinates me. She gives me a feeling like I used to get when we had Morgans to pull the plow – sweet, gentle, real power. I'd like to bring those days back again. Things were tough, but it all seemed worth the trouble. Nowadays, I don't know. It's all a grind and you wonder what for. If I'd had a gal like her instead of Teddy, well, who knows?" Mamie streaked to our right and disappeared behind a stand of evergreens.

Ben looked down at me and said, "They tell parents these days it's their fault the way a kid turns out. If that's true then it's a good thing Mamie wasn't our kid, huh? We probably would've ruined her for sure, made a female Teddy out of her."

I was on the verge of telling him about John Beaver and that if such a father as that couldn't ruin Mamie, no one could. God only knew what she might have been with Ben Snowdy as her pa – maybe a saint. But before I could say anything, Mamie came back into view and stopped suddenly. She got down on all fours, her face close to the ground as she looked at something. We caught up with her and she was kneeling next to a frozen creek. She held what looked like a yellow flake of ice up for us to see.

"Hey, that's a tooth," said Ben. "How do you like that? Broke it right off, didn't he. Must've wanted a drink pretty bad, poor fella."

"A wolf, do you think?" I asked.

"Big enough to be. Yeah, I'd say it was a wolf, though not many left these days. All of 'em gone to Canada. Look at the bite marks he left. Frustrated old lobo, tired of eating snow and so he knocks out a tooth on the ice. Probably diseased, poor old martyr. We got something in common." Ben tapped his own teeth. "Nature takes the bite out of all of us eventually. Mine get any more tender I'm gonna have to start eating pabulum." In the hard gray light of morning, Ben looked every minute of his age. Long creases made his forehead like a washboard, and a nest of wrinkles webbed his cheeks and lips. Silver hairs bristled on his jaws and chin. Mamie gave the tooth to him. He dropped it in his pocket and said he would polish it up and put it on a chain for Lily to wear.

We went another twenty yards, then turned left and walked until we thought we were pretty nearly opposite the meadow where Teddy had set up his ambush. We spread out, just a few yards from each other, and walked toward him. I didn't hear or see any deer as we made our way, but as we got near the clearing, just ahead of us stood a small doe, which was no good since we were allowed only bucks. We kept moving toward her. Mamie was a few feet to my right and Ben a few feet to the right of her. He hollered for Teddy not to shoot – a doe was coming out. As soon as the doe hit the edge of the trees, she broke into a run. Teddy bounced up from behind a drift and started firing.

"Doe! Doe!" yelled Ben.

But the machine-gun spray of the carbine was too loud for Teddy to hear. As the first bullets whizzed by, the doe spun round and headed back for the trees. Teddy spun with her, raining a storm of bullets as he turned. I could hear bullets slapping the trees and I could see twigs shattering and falling like a plague of centipedes. Everything happened so fast I never even thought to take cover. Teddy held the carbine at his hip and kept the trigger down, firing in the same zig-zag pattern the deer was making. Out of the corner of my eye, I saw Ben's rifle fly from his hand and saw him going over backward, clutching at his chest. The doe was hit too, and she staggered in the snow but didn't fall. Teddy ran out of bullets and changed clips and gave the doe another burst. Her hindend exploded. She kept trying to crawl away, using her front legs to inch her body along. She went down twice and got back up, her hooves flailing at the snow as she tried to dig her way to the safety of the trees.

The firing had stopped. Teddy was cussing and banging his fist on the side of his rifle. "Jammed!" he shrieked. "Jammed!"

The doe quit struggling and just stood there in front of us, her legs stiff at the knees and quivering, her head up, her tongue out, her eyes huge with terror, her bloody bottom steaming in the snow. I wanted Teddy to hurry up and clear his gun and finish her. When it seemed like he never would, I started towards Ben's rifle lying near him. Mamie went to the doe, and as I stopped and watched, she caught the doe by the neck and stroked it a few times, then took the head to one side and gave a twist. Something popped and the doe went limp. Mamie lay the doe down gently and closed her eyes. Next she went up to Teddy and snatched the rifle from him.

"What?" he cried. "Again? Again you take my gun? You two-ton turd, gimmee that!" He kicked her in the shins and punched her face, but it was like he was hitting her with foam rubber. She tossed the rifle behind her so that it spun through the sky up, up, and up, like a twiggy, dark spear out of control. Teddy screamed in her face, his huge teeth snapping, threatening Mamie's chin. She took hold of him by the crotch and the neck, turned him upside down, and rammed him in the snowdrift so hard he went out of sight, except for his fat boots and red socks flailing the air, like he was having a tantrum.

Mamie didn't stop to watch him. She hurried over to Ben, lying all bloodied and dead-looking. She picked him up and lumbered with him to the pickup. Somehow I got my numbed brain to move my numbed feet and went out after her. As I climbed in behind the wheel, I looked back across the meadow. I saw the body of the doe and slashes of blood soaking up the snow, and a few yards away were Teddy's booted feet, still pounding the sky. I wondered if he would suffocate. Mamie nudged me and jerked her thumb toward the main road. I looked at Ben draped across her lap, washed in his own blood just the way Amoss had been.

"Shades of Amoss," I said. "Good God, what's happening?"

"Kritch'n, go!" she ordered, jerking her thumb again in the direction of the road.

It took us thirty minutes to get to the hospital in Park Falls. At the emergency room it was a replay of what had happened with Amoss. Ben was put on a stretcher and wheeled away from us, down a hall and through some double doors. A man in a white coat shoved a paper on a clipboard at us and asked about insurance. I backed away from him and held up my hands. "I don't know nothing," I said.

"Well, who is he?" said the man. I told him to get a hold of Lily

Snowdy. Mamie and I left with the man hollering at us to stay because there had to be an investigation. He followed us out to the parking lot. "I've got your license number!" he yelled, as we pulled away.

We drove straight back to the Snowdy farm. It took us an hour to get there, and just as we pulled up Teddy himself came out the back door, carbine in hand. Mrs. Snowdy came with him.

"Get off! Get off!" Teddy hollered.

"How could you leave my boy like that!" Mrs. Snowdy cried.

"Hold on! Hold on!" I screamed. "How the hell did he get here?"

"No thanks to you," said Mrs. Snowdy. "A bunch of hunters rescued him and brought him home. The poor boy was dying. Don't you understand what you've done?"

"Get off!" screeched Teddy.

"Hold on, Mrs. Snowdy," I cried, pointing at Teddy. "He shot Ben! Shot him in the chest!"

"What? What's that?"

"I never did!" said Teddy.

"Shot him bad. We took him to Park Falls. They need you to sign papers."

"Ben? Shot?"

"Shot him in the chest."

She looked at her son. "You shot your father? You shot my husband? My Ben?"

"He shot your Ben, Mrs. Snowdy."

"Mommy, it was a accident. I was shooting at a deer. I was gonna tell you about it. This deer –"

"Shut up! How bad is he, Christian?"

"Real, real bad. Lots of blood. Look at Mamie's coat that you made. She carried him."

When Mrs. Snowdy saw the blood, she went nuts. She turned on Teddy and started pounding him with her fists, punching him so hard his glasses flew off and blood spurted from his nose. "You you you!" she screamed at him, smacking him with all she had, driving him back to the pickup, where he turned away from her and leaned across the fender, letting her pound on his back until she was exhausted.

When she finally stepped back, he peeked under his arm and said, "It was a accident. I was gonna tell you. It was a accident."

"Shut up," she ordered. "Just shut your stupid face! Get in that goddamn pickup and get me to that hospital. Ben needs me." Her voice was harsh as the hiss of a snake. Teddy looked at her, flabbergasted.

"But Mmmm-ommy," he stammered.

She kicked his rump. "Move!" she ordered.

He did. He scrambled in the snow and found his glasses and put them on and then jumped into the pickup and hit the starter. Mrs. Snowdy got in, took another whack at him, and pointed towards the road. They shot away from us, the back end of the pickup fishtailing, the engine roaring, and Mrs. Snowdy smacking Teddy.

After they disappeared, I told Mamie it was time to move on. I was sad to leave Ben and the cows, but there wasn't any choice as far as I could see. Anything was better than living with a homicidal nut. You never know what a guy like that might do.

In front of us was a gravel road with a couple inches of hard-packed snow on top of it, which made walking treacherous but not impossible. On both sides were ditches banked with more snow. Long, slow-rolling fields met lines of trees farther out. Here and there was some barbed-wire fencing, most of it strung along plots of pasture or holding pens. I knew that inside the barns we passed were tons and tons of hay. The silos were packed with silage, and the machinery was greased and put away for spring. Chickens rested in straw inside their coops; and outside the cows stood in line, wanting to get back in the barn where they could eat and be warm. And I knew that it all seemed to be quiet and calm everywhere – everyone and everything settled in for a long winter's nap. Time to rest. And I knew also that what I looked at was a lie. The cold would come in and cause pipes to freeze and break, milk-house drains to plug, water cups to ice up and overflow, frozen manure to break barn cleaners. The cold would make batteries die and tractors not start and hydraulic lines freeze. The cold would give heifers frostbite and even kill some of them. And the fires would roar up the chimneys and cause fires, and some farmers would watch helplessly as their houses burned to the ground. Or worse, some fan or exhaust motor or overloaded fuse in a barn wouldn't be able to take the strain of twenty-four-hours-a-day running, and there would be a spark, a cobweb would flare up and catch a bit of hay, and in an hour the barn would be black boards and ashes, and the cows, calves, and heifers would be dead. Winter was always a fooler. It never was a farmer's favorite time of year.

My thoughts went back to Ben and how it must have hurt to get smacked by a bullet. In my mind I saw him falling and saw the deer's rump explode, saw the twigs and bark shower all down. Could have been me all bloody and dying down. Could have been Mamie. Snow like a raspberry cone. And did Teddy mean for it to happen? Teddy had said he would wait in ambush, but had he meant ambush for the deer or for Ben? Could a son, even a Teddy, kill his father, who had never lifted a finger to hurt him? Was I learning things I didn't want to know? Yeah, I was.

Good Country People

Mamie and I made about twelve miles before it started getting dark. The clouds had cleared off, but the air was so cold that the sun was useless. It just glittered there on the horizon, like a jewel in an icebox. A narrow road ran off to our right. Bare trees lined the north side of the road – tall, thin poplars in columns all the way back to a long white building that looked like it was a machine shed. Mamie and I headed for it to get out of the air, which was making our noses feel like they were going to snap off. Far off to the east we could see the closest farmhouse, just a white dot with a barn nearby. In every other direction there wasn't anything but snowy fields and barren trees. It was a lonely spot and just right for us.

The building we found had some steps out front leading to a platform and a big sliding door that wasn't locked. We slid it back far enough to get inside, and there we came upon a huge room stacked with gunnysacks wall to wall, stacked six or seven feet high, with narrow walkways crisscrossing and winding in and out like a maze. We walked from the front to the back. There was a small window, and a door opened out on a yard, where an ancient iron-cleat tractor sat on a heap of rusted harrows, useless stock tanks, barbed wire and broken pieces of tin sheeting, old gears, and crumbling bits of wood.

We rummaged through the junkpile and found an old frying pan made of cast iron, but there wasn't anything else we could use. Farther back, in a ring of trees, we found an old outhouse. The door was gone and the roof had caved in. On the floor were the remains of a Montgomery Ward catalogue, which I took back to the warehouse.

Inside, Mamie and I made ourselves a gunnysack bed next to the window, covered ourselves with gunnysack blankets, and laid our heads on gunnysack pillows. Snuggled up together, trying to ignore the growling of our stomachs and the memories of the day, we looked at the pictures in the catalogue, old pictures of old times, like the forties. We turned the pages and pointed at the things we wanted. I was surprised to see that Mamie wanted all the dresses. "That one, that one, and that one, yaay." I had never thought of her in a dress. But I promised I would buy her one someday, and some shoes, and a hat with a feather, and a pair of gloves that went up to the elbows. She tore out all the pages of things she wanted and stared at them longingly, while I went on, looking for my own kinds of wishes, until it got too dark to see anymore.

I woke in the middle of the night, so hungry I could hardly stand it. I went outside and ate some snow, which helped me not at all. The air was freezing, the sky clear and loaded with stars. A full moon gave a bluish glow to the snow, and all the trees pointed black fingers in every direction. In the distance I could see a yard light, a tiny, bright point, like a star that had fallen to the ground. I wondered if the farm underneath that light had a milk house and a bulk tank full of milk. It seemed like it would be an easy thing to sneak over there and fill my belly, and maybe steal a pail of milk to bring back to Mamie. I decided it was the thing to do, and I started off down the road. But I didn't get far before Mamie showed up. She had a gunnysack in her hand.

As we got close to the farm, we could see that the barn was old and small and had no signs of life – no trampled snow, no manure pile nearby, and no fenced-off cowyard. It was not a dairy. There would be nothing to eat or drink inside. I told Mamie we might as well go back to the warehouse. There wasn't even a chicken coop for eggs. Everything was bare and looked poor. I started back, but Mamie went the other way, toward the house.

"Hey, hey," I whispered, catching up with her. "We can't go in there. We been shot at enough today, don't you think?"

Mamie pulled away from me and kept going. I saw that she had already decided and that I might as well talk to the wind. I shrugged my shoulders and followed her. We tiptoed along the outside of the house and came upon a pair of cellar doors that weren't locked. We opened one door and slid inside down some cement stairs that led into pitch darkness. I held onto Mamie's collar as we went inside. The air was cool but warmer by far than it was outside. I felt a cement wall and then a shelf of some kind with jugs on it. I let go of Mamie and stood still. In front of me I heard a tinkling noise; then the room filled with light. Mamie stood there, her finger still wrapped up in a string from an overhead bulb. She was looking the place over. It was loaded with food. Hundreds of potatoes sat in an open bin, onions filled a burlap bag, meats of all kinds hung from the ceiling, and shelves of canned tomatoes, corn, green beans, peas, beets, carrots, pickles, and watermelon rind lined the walls. Gallon jugs of wine and vinegar and apple cider made a column across the floor beneath the shelves. I felt like I was Ali Baba.

Mamie went to work plucking a smoked ham and a big sausage from the ceiling. She took a jar of watermelon rinds, then some potatoes and onions. She stuffed everything into her gunnysack. I grabbed a jug of apple cider. Then I told her we had enough and probably what we took wouldn't even be missed. We turned out the light and went back outside, closing the cellar door softly behind us. Home free, I thought, and it was so easy. We slid back along the house. I was about to tiptoe on across the yard when I felt a quick rap on the top of my head. Then Mamie suddenly picked me up and held me to a window so I could see inside. The moon shone through behind me and lit up a big table in the middle of a dining room. On the table was what looked to be a chocolate cake sitting on a platter. Mamie smacked her lips in my ear and said, "Yum yum, Kritch'n."

I whispered back to her that it wasn't worth the risk.

"Poof poof," she said, her voice sounding just like Shepard's.

She put me down and snuck over to the back door. It wasn't locked, and the next thing I knew she had gone inside. I put my jug of apple cider down next to her gunnysack and followed. It was warm as toast inside, real cozy, and smelled of such good things as bread and fried pork chops. There was a cloakroom just to the right of me and a refrigerator and stove straight ahead. Next to the stove was the entrance to the little dining room we had seen. In the silence I could hear a clock ticking somewhere. I opened the refrigerator and found a bottle of milk and took it to the table, where Mamie was already devouring the chocolate cake. She smiled at me, and for a moment I remembered the time with Amoss and the candy bars. She looked the same, mouth ringed in chocolate, teeth black, eyes full of the delight she was feeling. It made me start giggling, and I had to stuff my tabby-cap tail into my mouth to muffle the noise.

Then, as I managed to get myself under control, lights flashed across the window and a car pulled up outside. Mamie and I jumped up and ran into the living room. I was looking for the front way out, but before I could find it, a bedroom door opened and a woman walked in, tying her bathrobe and yawning. We looked at each other. She was in mid-yawn, her mouth frozen open. She wore paper curls in her hair, which made it stand up like a hundred little horns poking out all over her head. Her hands had gone up to her cheeks and so made a frame for her face, out of which her eyes bulged. Her nostrils jumped like she had a sneeze coming. Behind her came a dog, yawning and wagging its tail. It was a golden labrador, with dark, sleepy eyes and a pet-me disposition. I reached down and stroked its back, while it stretched and yawned some more. The woman still hadn't managed to scream or to do anything. And then a man walked in the back door and turned on the kitchen light. He stepped into the coat room. I could hear him unlacing and taking off his boots.

He said, "What a night, Marge. Both Norm and Hubbard stayed home sick, and I had to mill all by myself. I'm starving, I'll tell you. Boy, that cake smells good. I can smell it and . . . hey, what's going on?" There he was, standing in the doorway of the dining room, looking through it at us frozen in place. "Who are you guys?" he asked. Then he looked at the table and what was left of the cake. His eyes fastened on Mamie. She was licking her lips and grinning.

Suddenly the woman came to. "They're robbers, Jed!" she cried.

The man jumped back into the kitchen like she had bit him. Mamie and I bolted for the back door, the woman screaming behind us, the dog suddenly come to life and barking at our heels. As we tore through the kitchen, the man, Jed, was standing there with a pot in his hand. He reached out and smacked Mamie first as she went by – boing! Then he got me too. I hardly even felt it. We made it outside and headed for an open field in the direction of the warehouse. Behind us, I could hear Jed yelling, "Sic 'em, Emma! Sic 'em, girl! Sic 'em, sic 'em, sic 'em!"

And Emma did sic us. Sort of. She came after us, barking joyfully, as we ran across the field. At about twenty yards, she caught up with us and went right on by, yap-yap-yapping at God knows what, the moon maybe, and zigzagging and leaping along like she was getting ready to fly. She ran so far in front of us that she became little more than an inkblot bouncing across the snow. Then we lost sight of her, but we could still hear her barking far far away. Somehow she must have remembered that she had been told to sic us, because she finally did turn round and come back. I saw her come out of the darkness like a little bat, flitting here and there, chasing stars, until she saw me and sobered up. She stopped and shook her head and barked in a serious way, then came for my legs, diving in at them and tripping me up. I went tumbling over into the snow with her. She was yelping like I had shot her.

I lay there a few seconds with everything quiet, and when I finally raised my head, I saw Emma raising hers and looking sheepish. Then her eyes fastened on my tabby cap lying a few feet away. She growled at it, then jumped up and pounced on it like a lion. She sank her teeth in and fought that tabby cap as if her life was at stake – shaking it wonderfully, rolling over on her back as it got the upper hand for the moment, then on her feet again, more fierce than ever, stomping the tabby cap, tossing it in the air, leaping after it as it tried to get away, snatching it not a moment too late and pulverizing it with a tremendous biting and tearing of her teeth. When she was finally finished, little remained of the cap but a few strips of hide and fur. Satisfied that it was dead, Emma backed off and barked a few times, jumped in and gave it another bite and a shake, then flipped it over her shoulder and snorted. At last, the battle won, she came to me, wagging her tail.

"Good girl, Emma," I told her.

She whined and put her head under my arm. I gave her a big hug and scratched her chest. Mamie came over and picked up the remains of my cap and stuck it on my head. It felt like a scalp might feel off a dead man, all wet and slimy. Mamie was laughing at me and clapping her hands.

"Oh yeah," I said. "Real funny, Mamie. My cap's ruined, so my head and ears are gonna freeze. I got a bump right here from that stupid pot he hit us with. My knee hurts from falling over this stupid dog here. And I'm still hungry. And dammit, you ate that chocolate cake! We could have been back by now, eating ham and drinking apple cider instead of being chased all over creation by this brainless, frigging dog. You and that bloody cake!"

Mamie pulled me up and squished me in her arms.

"Oh, let me go!" I said, and shook myself loose. I started limping off toward the warehouse. Mamie and Emma followed me. I turned on the dog and told her to go home. I tried to kick at her, but it made my knee hurt more, so I made snowballs and threw them at her. She liked it. She tried to catch them in her teeth. "Stupid dog," I told her, and trudged away.

It was a relief to get into bed and pull the gunnysacks over me. Mamie got in too, and Emma went round and round between us until she had the place to her liking. Then she settled down with her chin resting on my stomach. She whined softly and wouldn't quit until I petted her head. I told Mamie that we didn't dare sleep too long, in case Jed came looking for his dog in the morning.

She felt me over, patting the gunnysacks close to my sides, tucking me in. Then she put her arm across my chest and pressed her head against my shoulder. She smelled of chocolate.

It was Emma's leaving the bed that woke me in the morning. I opened my eyes and blinked, not wanting to believe that I saw Jed standing over me. Emma yawned and stretched and reached her head up to him for a pat. He scratched her nose, all the while looking at me and Mamie, his eyes all sad. He was a worn-out looking fellow, with a face full of deep lines. He was thin and not very tall. His hands had the look of burnt cowhide, cracked and dark. He stood above us for a good two or three minutes. Then he took Emma and went out. I could hear them walk away, and then I heard a car door slam. Next thing, I heard footsteps coming back. Jed opened the door and held it so his wife could enter first. Her hair was still in curlers. In her hand was the apple cider I had stolen. In his hand was Mamie's gunnysack full of food.

"See?" he said softly to his wife.

She nodded and set the cider down. He dropped the gunnysack on the bed between Mamie and me. Neither of them said another word. They left, closing the door quietly, and soon I heard the car pulling away. I looked over at Mamie. Her eyes were full of wonder.

"We got food," I told her. "They gave it to us."

"Yaay," she said, patting the sack. The chocolate had dried on her mouth and it cracked as she spoke. I scraped it off with my fingers and gave her a kiss. "Aren't some folks great?" I said.

She leaped out of bed and ran the length of the warehouse and back again. I got up and we danced in a circle around the gunnysack. Then she had me get on her back and she galloped me all over, weaving in and out of the burlap walls, both of us hippa-weeing for all we were worth.

Finally we settled down to make ourselves a nice breakfast of ham and sausage, potatoes, and onions fried in our rusty junk-pan over an open fire. We ate with our fingers, stuffing each other's mouths like newlyweds do with wedding cake. We ate the watermelon rinds too and washed everything down with apple cider. After we finished, we sat back and rubbed our bellies and brought up huge burps to entertain each other.

By the time we were ready to leave, the sun was a handspace above the horizon. But just like the day before, there was no warmth in it. I wouldn't have been surprised to see our breath freeze and fall at our feet. And we had such a long way to go. In our sack there was still enough food for a lunch. After that we would be right back where we had started, and I didn't want to have to steal anymore. I was sure there was no way we could have such wonderful luck again. I told Mamie there was no stopping until we reached Shepard's. We got back out on the road and headed north. Looking back from a rise, I could see where the white house sat, all but invisible at the top of the hill, so far away and so much white all around it, and I felt that maybe my mother's and sister's prayers had led us to such good-hearted people. Or maybe it was the piece of Robbie attached to Jesus that was attached to us and throwing little miracles our way, making Teddy's bullets pass by, making Jed give us food. The road stretched out in front of us like a frozen snake, white and wavy and long, a far walk to Temple. But our bellies were warm, and our memories of the people and the dog named Emma, living in the white house on the white hill, were warm memories too.

Anna Gulbrenson

We ate on the walk, not daring to stop for a minute, it being so cold that anything not moving was bound to freeze, and we finally made Temple about an hour after dark. We got to Shepard's soon after, but he wasn't home. The window I had tried on the day we left still wasn't locked, so I cut a tiny hole in the screen and flipped the latch, and we crawled inside. It was fine to feel the warmth of the place and to see the familiar mess in Shepard's room. But when we went into the living room and turned on the light, something was missing. There weren't any books. No crates of books stacked up, no books on the shelves – no shelves even – no books on the coffee table, and none on the couch or chair or floor. In the kitchen, on the table, was the unabridged dictionary and sheets of paper covered with words and "yum yum" written beside them, but everywhere else I looked – no books. Mamie and I looked at each other with puzzlement. "Maybe the Christers raided his house," I said.

We would have to wait for an answer, so we fixed ourselves some fried ham and potatoes and ate. Then we took a hot shower together, scrubbed each other raw from top to bottom, and came out squeaky clean. I borrowed a pair of Amoss's old overalls that had the name tag on them, which I tore off. But Mamie wanted it and pinned it to a pair of Shepard's overalls that she wore, a bit baggy in the belly but otherwise fitting all right.

It wasn't long after that Shepard came home. We heard a pounding on the porch – boom boom boom! – and Shepard's voice calling, "What incubus is within wasting Edison's glory? Speak out, housebreaker, lest I unleash my wrath!" The porch boomed more before I could get the door opened.

"Crystal!" he cried. "Tis you! Did you bring Mamie?"

"Yep. We've come to wear out our welcome."

Mamie peered over my shoulder. "Yaay, Shep," she greeted him.

"You've come back to me, my precious, my metronome of love, oh yum yum!" He tore open the screen door, pushed me aside, and clutched Mamie to him, kissing and cooing, "Sooo happy, sooo happy, sooo . . . soooo and soooo." Then he broke into tears and sobs all over

Mamie's shoulder. He bawled so hard his belly was shaking them both, and it went on for at least a minute, the two of them doing a kind of hiccup-dance in place. Finally he backed away, wiping his eyes, a great happy sigh whistling through the gap in his teeth, and he said, "This must be celebrated! My heavens, child, I thought I had lost you forever. My greatest love, my only from the first. 'Whoever loved that loved not at first sight?' Oh yes! Oh my! Oh me!"

He lumbered to the kitchen and came back with a jar of splow. We each took a sip in celebration. It was god-awful stuff. We sat around the coffee table, and I told Shepard all about Teddy and what he had done to Ben.

"It seems inevitable now," said Shepard wisely. "You know, looking back at the events of their lives, a man of my gifts should have predicted such a show, and if you'll recall I did say something to the effect that Teddy's mind was a carving block, beware! The mad little bastard. And yet it was – ahem, I say – perhaps it was a lavation for them both, a washing to cleanse – to make clean. If Ben lived through it, he will be purified. No more meretricious show for the sake of Lily, who has had the man long-chained to her pubic hairs from the beginning. Take note, Christian."

"But you should have seen how Mrs. Snowdy smacked Teddy," I said. "She hit him so hard his nose bled."

"When you told her about Ben?"

"Yeah. She went nuts. I bet she'd never hit him in her life. He was stunned, you could tell."

"Good for her. I'd have sanitized that film-flam clot of garget long ago. Why, I'd have pinched his head off when he was birthed. My clairvoyance would have reached out and made a morsel of his potential curse, yum yum. When my blood is up, I am capable of terrifying acts of physical desecration. You have never seen me with my blood up. He's lucky it was Lily punching him and not yours truly." Shepard's eyes narrowed with the toughness of his talk, and his dogteeth poked viciously from under his lip and mustache.

"Well," said I, "lucky for him you weren't there."

"Indeed, the luck of the devil."

"He's no good."

"Son of a cloven hoof. Lower than snakeshit. Less than the most contemptuous hoi polloi. Hoi polloi – the masses, the common humph."

We spent a few minutes dragging Teddy Snowdy up and down the gutter, and then Shepard switched the subject to the Artlife and what he was doing there. On schedule, he said, and ready to open in January or February at the latest. He had bought paintings by Wisconsin artists, which he was hanging on the walls for customers to buy. And he was going to sell books too. All of his own books were there now, and he was buying more. We had come at a perfect time to help. We would work together and together watch the dream unfold itself. We would sell books and paintings and tickets, tickets to see the best movies ever made – true art. Movies that the ilk could imitate with no shame. No *Billy Buck Does Dodge City* or crap like that. Olivier! Richardson! Barrymore! Garbo! Bogart! Gable! Cooper! Vivian Leigh, yum yum, and more! Pure strokes of genius. Not only fortune but fame as well would descend upon Don Shepard. And Temple would become the cultural center of America for the recovery of true art. Don Shepard would be revered. And so on and so forth.

Mamie killed the last of the splow and licked the rim. Shepard got her another and then told us how Anna Gulbrenson, vigilant lady, the astronomer of our fair street, was helping him at the Artlife and giving him daily reports about every transgressor who walked by, all of them wanting to look up her dress, all of them thieves and murderers. "You have to meet her, a Sargasso Sea of unfathomed motives, yum yum – unfathomed motives, I say – unfathomed motives lying in that suspicious bosom. But she can be a dear little thing." He glanced at me, blinking his eyes and rubbing his nose with pleasure and giving me a gummy, gap-toothed grin. "It's time you two met the nemesistic Anna Gulbrenson. A tart, she is, and a hag, and a bit of a pixie harridan, and a sweetheart too. You'll love her! I'll be right back, kiddies."

He left. I watched him hurrying and trying not to slip as he crossed the street to her house. Then a minute later the two of them together arm in arm skated back across the street. She came in rubbing her hands and arms and saying, "My oh my, fweezing off my toot-toot."

He introduced her. She shook her finger at us and said she remembered us and how we scared her half to death one day. She looked the same as on the day Robbie escaped. She even wore the same dress, a brown one with a bright red apron. A short lady she was, less than five feet tall, and a bit chunky but not fat; maybe on the verge of fat but tucked together pretty well for her age, which was somewhere in the fifties, I guessed. She had thick brown hair with waves of gray running through it. She had quarter-moon eyes, high cheekbones, and thick eyebrows that made her look almost Chinese, except her skin was too pale and her nose was too narrow and button-blunt. She had a thin mouth loaded with bright red lipstick. Her teeth were too perfect to be her own. She had a high voice, like a choir soprano.

She chucked my chin and said, "Vhut a mama's boy you are. So pwetty a boy. I take you home vit me."

"You see why I named him Crystal?" said Shepard laughing. "Tee hee hee, Anna understands. Anna knows. Sit your little toot-toot down, Anna. Let me get you a glass of splow."

She stared at him suspiciously as he poured her a glass. "A dwop a dat vould kill me, mister," she said. "Vhut it is?"

"Nectar of the gods, Anna. One-hundred-fifty-proof splow, smooth as Halley's Comet. Just a tad, my dear."

"You vant to get Anna dwunk. I know you. Vant to see vhut Anna's got up dis dwess. Gimme dat. I dwink it. Oh, vhut a bad boy." She took the splow, sipped it, made a face. "Oh ho ho, dat's not so goot as aquavit, but I like it! Oh ho ho. Sit down, let's dwink it some mo."

Shepard sat next to her. She turned her attention to Mamie and me. She wanted to know if we were brother and sister. I told her we were cousins. She said I looked like an unfed version of Mamie, which was a surprise to me, as I never thought Mamie looked a bit like me.

"Sometimes people grow to look like each other," said Shepard. He agreed I had some of Mamie in me, especially the open blue of my eyes and the wide shine of my forehead.

Mamie smiled at Anna and Anna smiled back. "Hey, pwetty one, you got wa gap in you toof. Vunce I had a gap like dat. Da men, it dwives dem crazy. Sexy vooman vit a gap like dat. Den dey pull my teef out all gone. You vant to see?" She took her thumb and forefinger and popped her top row of teeth out. "Thexy, huh?" she said, batting her eyelids at us. The teeth went back in. She took another sip of splow and went "Oh ho ho" again.

"So! Tell to Anna, tell me vhut you be. Novegian, I tink."

I shrugged. "Heinz fifty-seven, I guess."

"Nope. Novegian. Maybe Iwish is Mamie, and Novegian." She raised her glass to us. "Skoal," she said and polished it off and held the glass out for more. A midget version of Mamie, I thought.

Shepard poured her another, while she accused him of wanting to get her drunk and to look up her dress. He put an arm round her and sang, "Oh Anna, oh Anna, oh Anna oh!" and broke off laughing. She laughed too and called him a "dewil" and slapped his knee over and over. They roared in each other's faces like two braying donkies. Finally she turned away, wiping her eyes with her red apron and saying "Oh, my oh my, sooch a time we hawing."

There was a scratching at the door then, and Anna jumped up and opened it. "Vhat you doink, Chee Chee?" she said. "You bad dog you." She shook her finger at a little brown dog with a pug nose and big black eyes, eyes that looked dipped in syrup. "Dat gotdam Sowen let you out. You naughty vun, I spankee you." She picked the dog up and pretended to spank it. The dog squirmed in Anna's arms and licked her face happily.

"Dis my Chee Chee," she told us, holding the dog out for us to see. "Is she pwetty?" Chee Chee looked back and forth from me to Mamie to Shepard. She seemed happy to see us, and we all agreed she was very pretty.

Anna sat the dog in her lap and gave it a lecture. "So you make it too much noise for Sowen, ya? And he can't vatch dat telewision, ya? And he kick it you out, gotdammit him, into the snow. Po baby-vun, you come to mommy. Naughty vun. Comes a auto smash you like pancakes, ya. And den all gone Chee Chee, poof like dat. Vhut a bad papa you got. Some day I bweak it dat telewision."

Shepard smoothed his mustache and put on a wise look, his nose raised like a monument, his eyes half-closed in disdain. "Television," he said. "Television is a painless lobotomy for the masses. It turns their minds to cabbage. Television is the opium of the people."

"Opeeeum, ya. I tell it to Sowen he a wegtable!" Anna finished her second glass of splow and told Shepard she had changed her mind, ya, splow was better than aquavit. She would have some more.

He poured her glass full. "The genius who makes this," he said, "is a local boy, born and raised right here in Temple. You wouldn't think such a backward setting could produce a chemist's dream named splow, smooth as the smoothest Russian vodka with the slow sting of German beer." He raised his glass high. "To Bob Thorn," he said, "inventor of splow!"

We toasted Bob Thorn.

Shepard shifted his attention to Mamie. "By the way, he knows our valkyrian Mamie here, says she is on his shit list for good. Apparently she wounded his pride."

I told Shepard what had happened the day Bob Thorn tried to tackle Mamie during the book-burning, how she had tossed him under the car, dragged him round by the ankle, and generally made him look like a fool.

Anna pinched Mamie's leg and told her she didn't sound like much of a lady. Mamie pinched Anna back. "Ooch, oh my, Bwunhilde, dat make it bwuse on Anna. Don't be a naughty vun." She patted Mamie's hand carefully. "My my oh my, it varm in dis woom, ya?" And down went the splow in a gulp.

"More splow, my dear?" asked Shepard, holding the jar out.

"Oh my oh my. Vell, vhy not? I'll hawe anudder." He filled her glass again. Some of it went over the edge onto the couch, where Chee Chee tried to lick it.

"No no, dat's not fo you," Anna told her. The dog yipped, like she was telling Anna she wanted splow too. Anna stuck her finger in the splow and let Chee Chee lick it off. "Shame on you," she said. "Vant dis foo-foo get you dwunk? Shame a shame. Oops, look out, my teef." She jammed her thumb against her teeth. "Sometimes dey fall out, my teef. Den I talk funny some. Oh my."

"Den I talk funny some. Oh my," said Mamie in Anna's voice.

Anna's eyebrows shot up. "Hey, dat's pwetty goot. Can you do udders?"

"Mamie can do just about anybody," I said.

Anna thought about it for a second. Then she asked, "Ya, so vhut dat do fo you?"

"Well, it's just kind of neat, that's all," I answered, "because otherwise she doesn't talk so good. Just when she's imitating."

Patting Mamie on the cheek, Anna said, "You know vhut I say? Vagner vould pet dis vun. Such a Bwunhilde."

"A treasure, indeed, a magnificent creature," added Shepard, his mustache trembling as he stroked Mamie's leg. "I'm going to teach her to run the projector. I'm going to give this precious one a trade, a future. I'm going to teach her to read and write. I'm going to rescue her from her abyss of ignorance, yum yum. I'm going to give her knowledge that is inextinguishable. I'm going to release her from those dark caverns of unenlightenment retarding her mind. I'm going to give her words – words! – which are the daughters of the earth, the contours of the soul, the power of creation, the manipulators of tomorrow. I'm going to –"

"Ya ya, Don, okey-dokey, vee get it," interrupted Anna. She jerked her thumb at him and said to me, "You unnerstand dis man?"

"A bit," I answered.

"Den I put you in dis pocket." She held out her arms. "I giwe you sooch a sqveez, you pwetty boy, so polite." She grabbed me suddenly and gave me a wet kiss on the cheek. The movement threw Chee Chee to the floor and made her mad. She scrambled up on her short legs and gave my ankle a nip. I kicked her under the chin, which made her yelp and back off.

"Don't be a naughty vun," said Anna, picking up Chee Chee. "Anna can kiss dis pwetty boy if she vant. I spankee you, you don't be nice to him." She squeezed the dog till its tongue stuck out and it moaned. "Oh my," said Anna, "vhut a time vee hawing. Sowen should come. I tell to him, 'Sowen, life is too tough, but nutting happen so bad dat vee can't vait for someting to get better. Dat vheel come up to fowtune again fo us, and den vee be happy.' I say dat to him ven he cwies he is a wictim. See now, vhut a time vee hawing? Instead of vatching telewision, he shoot come and dwink a sploo."

"Have another," said Shepard.

"Okey-dokey, big boy, I vill." Anna tilted her glass and let the last few drops fall on Chee Chee's tongue. "A sveety, my Chee Chee. Ven I dead I vant her buweed vit me. Put Chee Chee in da box. Hic! Hic! Oh my!"

I remembered seeing Soren in his wheelchair. I asked Anna what had happened to him.

"Bwoke it his back, sveety. In dat shipyahd in Duloot. Bwoke it his back, and not a penny dey giwe him. Dem gotdam lawyas vait fo Sowen to die. Dey make paper fo dis and dat, and dem gotdam lawyas make da money. Not Sowen. I tell Sowen he dies I feed him to Chee Chee. Wight, Chee Chee?" The dog twisted her head to look at Anna with puzzlement. "She vants mo sploo. Naughty naughty, shame on you. You can't hold you liquoo. Shepard, you get me some sploo fo Sowen? Make him happy. You buy it fwum you fwiend, ya?"

"Okey-dokey," Shepard replied.

Anna waved her hand in front of her face. "Oh my my, vhut a time. Vee should sing a song. Gott bless Amewica. Sing vit me, Bwunhilde."

Mamie chimed in, "Fig-aaa-row! Fig-a-row! Fig-a –"

"Not dat song. I pick da song. You sing too, pwetty boy."

"I'll hum," I told her.

"Gott bl-ess Ahhhh-mew-ica . . ." she sang in her high, clear voice. Mamie watched closely. I hummed and Shepard whistled. Chee Chee closed her wobbly eyes and rested her head on her paws. Anna sang with real feeling. When she was done, we clapped.

"Okey-dokey," she said. "I not so vondaful I vunce vas. Oh ya, I vas a singer. I dance too. I vas on da stage. I vas a beauty. Boys call me baby and dey twy look up my dwess on da stage. Sowen too. He vun me. A nice Novegian boy, vit a nice job in dat shipyahd. He fights all dem boys twying to look up my dwess. Oh my my, vhut a time. I tell to him, 'Sowen, dey don't haum to see Anna's legs. Let dem look up me dey vant to.' 'You be mine,' he says. My little hawt go boom boom. But dat vas long time ago. Now I can go naked in dat stweet, and he don't giwe a gotdam. In dat vheel machine he get old. Dat gotdam shipyahd.

Gotdam lawyas." She paused and rubbed her forehead, like she was trying to rub out the memories of shipyards, lawyers, and Soren in a wheel-machine. "So!" she said suddenly. "Do you belew I vas a beauty vunce?"

Shepard told Anna she was still a beauty. His eyes were sad for her, and his nose was getting redder. I thought he would probably cry all over her.

"Oh ya ya ya, vhut a flattah-face, you. I know vhut I look like – auld lady now, gway hay. Fat vaist." She ran her hands up and down her stomach and breasts. "Stwaight as a twee. Dat's vhut happens to all of us." She laughed and kicked out her legs. "But look at dem legs! You bet. Not bad fo an auld lady, ya?" She pulled her skirt up over Chee Chee's head and stuck her calves out, rolling her tiny feet to show us what nice legs she still had. They were stark white, so white the veins showed through like blue lines on a map. They were thinner than what I expected but looked strong enough.

"Very, hmmm, ah, prime!" said Shepard.

"Real nice," I said.

"Vhut a polite boy. Put you in my pocket." She turned her feet from one side to the other. "I look at dem and I say, 'Okey-dokey, you sexy bwoad, vunce da boys dweam to look up you, but no mo. Ven you get auld no vun looks. Eweytink falls, skin gets dwy, winkles come. No vun vant fight fo you.'" She put her legs down and threw her skirt over them, grabbed her glass, and finished off the splow in three apple-bobbing gulps. Then she stood up and tucked Chee Chee upside down under one arm. The dog, butt up and head down, opened its eyes and glared at me, like I was to blame. Anna stumbled to the door, hiccuping and saying, "Oh my!"

Shepard followed her, and bowing like Sir Raleigh, he said, "May I escort you home, O vision of pulchritude, yum yum? Pulchritude – from the Latin *pulcher*, beautiful, yum yum."

Anna took his arm. "If you veren't so gotdam big, vit sooch a big guts, and you talk English to me, I twade Sowen fo you."

"My heart goes boom boom," he said, pounding his chest.

They bumped against each other as they went through the doorway. Then they walked with a weaving sort of dignity down the steps and across the street, careful on the hard snow not to fall.

Secrets

November and December went by. We stayed busy getting the Artlife ready for the grand opening. Painting the walls inside took the longest, up and down ladders day after day with paint bucket and brush. It was really boring. Shepard had sent the seats out to be upholstered, and as they came back, we bolted them down, about a hundred of them or more. We varnished the stairs that led to the projection booth. We cleaned all the carpets. We put in a popcorn machine and a refrigerator for apple juice. In all, we transformed the place, made it from a dingy, water-spotted, paint-peeling junkyard into a pretty respectable house of art – what Shepard called "an auditorium of inspiration."

All the while we were working to get it ready, Anna kept coming over to give a hand. She had no problem with grabbing a paintbrush or a hammer or wrench and going to work on whatever was doing. She could stay with it all day and keep up a constant rain of chatter too. Chee Chee was usually there, ready to yip and nip and sink her teeth into our pantlegs and shake them, as if they had caused her some serious insult. And finally even Soren came over in his wheelchair and helped out. He wasn't the talker Anna was, nor did he have an accent like hers. When he spoke, he spoke slow and to the point, like he only wanted to say it once and not waste words while he was at it. He had a tired voice with always a bit of grump in it. His shoulders were what caught my attention first. They were so broad and out of proportion to the rest of him, his little bitty skinny legs and his almost-nothing belly. To go with his shoulders, he had long arms and big, rawboned hands. His face was long too, and pale like milk, and his eyes were sunken so deep they looked like hot, black holes. He had deep lines in his face and puffy blue patches under his eyes.

It seemed every time he would come, Anna would try to pick a fight with him, and she wouldn't let up until he got red in the face and yelled at her. Sometimes even then she wouldn't quit. She'd always turn away and smile when he yelled. There wasn't much for her to pick on, but she made the best of it, saying to him what a slob he was because he dripped paint on his pants, and how he never held the brush right, and how he cleared his throat like that just to make her sick, picked his nose in front of her to make her sick, and wouldn't talk back just to make her mad. Stuff like that, almost always the same every day, like she needed to make him mad to see if he was still alive.

One day I coaxed him into telling me how he broke his back. He started to talk, but Anna kept interrupting, trying to tell the story herself. He let it go on for a while. Then he started grumbling and snorting at her, and she said he sounded like a goat.

"You damn woman," he said. "Shut up and let me talk. My goddamn story."

"You don't know fo shit!" she said.

"I don't know for shit? Was I there? Was my back broken or yours?"

"You tell it ewery time a new vay," she said, kicking his wheelchair. "I know the twuth."

"You weren't there. I was there. It happened to me, old lady. You think because you heard the story from Harold and the others that you know it all. You don't know it all. Now shut up."

"You shut up, you auld goat!"

"I'm gonna smack you, Anna."

"So, who cwy vhen you make a thweat? Phooey on you. You vant to tell dat stowy, go head. So tell you gotdam stowy. But it vas my tuhn." Anna had a brush full of varnish in her hand, which she suddenly flipped at Soren, spattering his face.

"You want to blind me?" he cried, taking out a hanky and wiping his face.

"Now you got fweckles," she said, laughing.

He shook both fists at her. "You think it's funny to pick on a cripple."

"Ah phooey, you big baby. Tell you stowy."

Soren looked at me, his long face longer, his skin spanked with hard, white wrinkles and varnish dots. "What do you think of a woman like her?" he asked. "What do you think of a woman who gets her kicks out of making fun of her husband in a wheelchair?"

I didn't want to get in the middle of it. I looked at Shepard to help me out. He held his hands up like a referee holding two boxers apart. "These epithalamiums must cease. I say, these nuptial songs must end, must give pause for more serious endeavors; like, say painting the shelves or varnishing the rails or –"

"He's sooch a big baby!" said Anna.

"And you're a nitwit. Now shut up!" His face turned a harsh pink. He wheeled his chair around so his back was to Anna. She smiled and rolled her eyes at us. She had riled him good, made him show there was life in the old carcass yet.

Soren said, "I'll tell you how my back was broken, if that dumbhead will keep her mouth shut now. I worked twenty-nine years as a crane rigger. See these hands? Hard-working hands. And I didn't miss a day but maybe two or three in twenty-nine years. And one day I was working with my friend Neil to hook up a scaffold and take it away from the side of a ship in dry dock. But we didn't know the pipes that held the scaffold onto the side had been cut away and it was standing there on its own, ready to go over. That scaffold weighed a ton, and it was just standing there by itself, forty feet up, ready to fall over and kill us. One good puff of wind and look out. So, the gantry was coming. Neil was climbing up the scaffold to hook up the chokers. I was coming behind Neil. We didn't get there. Halfway up I could feel the rumbling of the gantry as it got close, and then I felt the scaffold sway. I jumped and down it came – boom! Neil was under it. He didn't jump." Soren paused to look us over. "You understand?" he asked. "Probably you don't. That scaffold wasn't supposed to be cut away until after we had hooked up to it. But bosses are always in a hurry. They don't want to wait till things are safe. Time is more important to them than you are. Neil died for hurry-up money. Broke his liver, smashed his lungs for hurry-up money. I crawled to him on my hands. He was under a tangle of pipes, all bloody as hell. 'Neil!' I said. He opened his eyes and looked at me one time and he said, 'Oh, shit.' Very quiet like that. 'Oh, shit,' and he dies. Twenty-eight years old. I curse them, those bosses. Neil was a victim of hurry-up money. Can't take two minutes for a crane to hook up and make it safe. Hurry, hurry. Grind up Neil. Grind up Soren. Grind up you too, and throw you away if you let them. You understand me?" He wheeled away from us, across the entrance and out the door.

"Immutable web of history," said Shepard. "Everywhere."

"I could hawe told it as goot," said Anna.

I had written my folks just before Christmas and told them about our bad luck with Teddy Snowdy, our good luck with the potato farmer, Jed, and about living again with Shepard. I said how we were getting the movie house ready for a grand opening and Mamie was going to learn the projector. I told about Anna and Soren and Chee Chee too. In January I got a letter back.

Dear Christian,

This is Mama. Thank you for writing for Christmas. It wasn't the same without you. I sat and cried of a broken heart. The Lord above has a reason for all this I am sure but it breaks my heart. I wish you could come home now but Papa says you better not. As John Beaver is crazy and is scaring us half to death. The boys take turns watching for him with the gun. He comes two or three times a week and stands in the snow at the bottom of the hill and cusses us and cries out for his Mamie. Papa says things will get better with time. I pray he is right. I pray on my knees three times a day that you are safe. I say Rosary every night. I pray on my knees on the hard floor and it hurts. Which is good because God and the Saints listen better if they know you are willing to pray to them in pain. You should pray too Christian. Pray to Saint Jude. He is the one. Ask him for the faith to make you a Catholic. I always thought you might be the one of my boys to come to the True Faith like Mary Magdalen did. I pray all the time that Papa will convert but after all these years it would be a miracle which the Holy Mother can make if she wants to. But you are perfect for it Christian. You are the smart one. I am always proud of you in school. I always hoped you would convert and then became a priest. This would win us a place in Heaven. Mothers of priests go to Heaven. They are special above the other mothers in Gods eyes. Mary the Mother of God would welcome me at the gates. It is a dream I have. It makes me feel my suffering less. So you think about it. Pray on your bare knees for guiding from Saint Jude. Pray till you are in pain. He will listen then.

Love, Mama

Hi Christian,

So what do you think? John Beaver cant get up the hill to get nobody. We watch him and shoot over his head if he tried to get up the hill. Cutham shot close enuff to kick snow in Beavers face one day but Pa says not to do it no more. If Beaver comes with a gun then we get to shoot his legs, otherwize we dont get to shoot him. We hope he comes with a gun. He yells Mamie Mamie like crazy down there. You should see him with his arms out like a big tree yelling for her. Where is my Mamie? he says. What did you do with my Mamie? he says. Give me back my Mamie. And we tell him she is not here so he rolls in the snow and cusses at us. It looks so funny Christian. We throw snowballs at him but he dont care. He throws snowballs back at us and says words that are not fit for cows. They should take him to camlot and throw away the key like they do for crazy peopel. What a loon. But dont be scard, you are the little brother and your big brothers are looking out for you. We have a suprize for Beaver. We cant tell you what it is yet but boy will he be surprized.

Calvin Cutham Cush
Calah Cash

Brother Christian,

We miss you bad. You are our hero. At Christmas we sang the Battle Hymn of the Republic just for you. And we read again the part in your letter about that man named Jed and his dog Emma who chased you and tore up your hat that you said Teddy made out of a cat who stole his crow. What a nice man Jed was to see you weren't a crook really, and give you and Mamie all that food. Mama and I said three Hail Marys in his honor that God may bless him for his charity to you. There are some good people in this world aren't there, Christian? You've had some bad luck in meeting some of the worst but you've met some of the best too, thank God, and that I am sure has kept you from becoming one of the tough guys who hates everything. Isn't that right? This great adventure of yours has a purpose beyond what any of us can see right now. Of this, there is no doubt in my heart. Take care of Mamie. Aren't you sick of all the snow? I sure am. Happy Birthday, sweet sixteen pretty soon. Have you been kissed yet?

Love, Mary Magdalen XOXOXO

Dear son,

Well, Christian its tough times all around. I know what Beaver wants to do. He wants to plague us into making you give back Mamie. But this we will never do. The Deity is on our side. He has told me in a dream that He has His eye on us. So I don't want you to worry. You have made us special and we will be worthy of it. We will keep that bastard Beaver at bay until he gets tired of his silly game or freezes to death. The boys sure want to beat him up bad but I don't think so. He would cut some one. He is crazy but not so crazy to bring a gun. Then we would be in the right to shoot him in self defence. I think he is playing for our hearts when he cries out for Mamie so sad and rolls in the snow so we will feel sorry for him. It sure don't work on me and the boys. All we want to do is boot his ass to kingdom come. He gets to Mama tho, and a bit to Mary Magdalen. They feel sorry for him some days but they would never tell him even the time of day, so don't worry. A female might have a soft heart for a man's troubles, but if they are protecting some one they love then their souls are tougher than a cast iron pot.

Beaver lets the boys hit him with snowballs and he stands there with his head down like he is a martyr. But you know the boys. When Beaver just stands there they get bored and start throwing at each other. Beaver hears them squeeling and having such a good time he can't help but quit being the martyr. He always gets excited watching them he starts yelling for Calvin to watch out for Cush sneaking up behind, or telling Cutham to rub Cash's face in the snow, or telling Calah he don't throw no harder than a frigging girl. As the war goes on and on they all forget who they are and who John Beaver is. And he forgets hisself too and he starts throwing snowballs at them, and they start throwing snowballs at him and each other. Sometimes, Christian, they even make up teams with John Beaver on one of the teams! Can you believe it? And they build snow forts and throw at each other. This has happened two or three times now and it is something to see. I just shake my head and go about my business. What can you say to something like that? But you can see why I don't believe him when he wails for Mamie. It's hard to take some one like that serius. When they get all tired out from their snow wars then the boys get nasty and ask Beaver what does he think he is doing on their hill? He cusses them good and goes back down the hill to stand in the road and wail for Mamie.

He can be a clown, Christian, but I am not fooled by it. I know he is still a dangerus fellow and he is not to be taken with a grain of salt. I wish I could tell you when it will be over but only the Deity knows that. I do know that it will be over some day. Everything ends some day. In the meantime you are safe and making a living with Mr. Shepard there, who seems to be a funny kind of man but also a good one. I would like to sit and talk to someone who knows so many words as you say he knows. Did he really read the dictionary? You said he likes to say yum yum when he uses big words. I would like to see that. It is a feeling I have had myself some times when I talk about Horatio

> and Emerson and use their words. The words seem to have a taste that makes my mouth glad to say them. "Oh, that this too solid flesh would melt into a dew!" yum yum. Yes. Try it in your mouth and I think you will understand Mr. Shepard better. Does he know quotes like that? Does he know any from Emerson? "Belief accepts the afirmations of the soul, unbelief denys them." I think that's how it goes. Can he whip the Bible on you? "All the horns of the wicked he will cut off, but the horns of the righteous shall be exalted." I walk round the farm with pieces of paper in my pockets and I memorize this and that all day. Keeps the dust off my mind now that you are gone. Miss you sorely, someone to talk to. Until we meet again, my son, lay low.
>
> Your Pa

It made me feel terrible to know that John Beaver was plaguing my family like he was. But I had no idea what to do about it. What Pa advised seemed to be right – just to lay low and see if time would settle him down. I had my doubts that it would though. He wasn't a normal human being, who would get tired of the game eventually. I knew one thing in my heart for sure – he would never get Mamie back, not because of anything I could do about it but because of what she could do. I had learned that others might think of Mamie as retarded, but in her own mind she wasn't. Mamie's mind had no connection with John Beaver's. She was a million light years above him, beyond him, like they were two separate planets. If he only knew how wide the gap was between them, I was sure he would give up trying to get her back. But I also knew that there was no way to make him understand it. Even I, who knew her better than anybody, could not understand her, not what she was really, or how she could do what she could do, which was anything she wanted to do. Retarded girls weren't like that, I had heard. But where Mamie fit – if she wasn't retarded – in the up and down scale of human beings was as much a mystery as ever.

¶ A few days before the Artlife was set to open, Shepard started teaching Mamie to run the projector. It was an old machine, but it looked pretty good because he had sent it to Chicago to have it fixed up. He called it Powers after the name plate on its side: Powers Electrical Chicago. It stood on a flat base with four little wheels that could be locked in place. A solid column stood on the base, like a fat leg on a swollen foot. Then came the body, large as a fifty-pound bale of hay and shaped the same, if you set the bale on its side and jammed a two-inch pipe in one end so that it stuck out a few inches. On top of the bale a guy would have to put a pair of twenty-inch clutch disks standing up on end and he would have a fair resemblance of Powers – bale of hay for the body, pipe for an eye, clutch disks for ears. And inside Powers, under a metal cover, were a hundred little wheels and gears that the film wound around, like a thin, gray tapeworm.

Mamie learned the mechanics of Powers the first time Shepard showed her. He ran the film through and wrapped it round the back reel. He released the lock on the wheels, slid the projector forward to a little window, turned it on, and adjusted the focus as the name *HAMLET* hit the screen. He adjusted the sound so the music smoothed out. Then he turned it off and ran the film backward until it flapped round and round the front reel. Mamie didn't have to be asked to put it all back together. She grabbed Powers, unlocked his feet, and rolled him back; then she threaded the film, rolled him forward into position, and fine-tuned the focus and sound after she had turned him on. She did it perfect, first time. It made Shepard happy.

"Isn't she incredible?" he said. "What potency. What effulgence, ahem, effulgence – to shine with brilliance. And in my own brilliance I recognize and predict she is the *sine qua non* of any further intellectual evolution, yum yum. Who says retarded? Who dares say retarded? Not applicable to our Mamie, not to my Mamie." He pinched her cheek. She petted his nose. I got bored and went back downstairs.

An hour passed. I was going through the shelves, pulling out a book here and a book there that were slightly out of alphabetical order, when Shepard came down from the booth. He was very pale and he was trembling. I asked him if he was sick.

"Mamie," he answered, his voice hardly more than a whisper. "You won't credit what I saw her do, what I heard her say. No no, I must think about this. It is a new form, a new species. A wonder worth, perhaps, millions. Mamie is a mock moon. I can't tell you, Crystal, not yet. Portentous implications. The ideas are flooding in."

"Huh?" I said.

He waved me off and went out the door. I saw him heading for the house, his fingers playing a little tune in the air, his mouth steaming with words. And so I ran upstairs to see what was going on, and it was nothing. Mamie had an oil rag in her hand and was cleaning all of Powers's little wheels and gears. I asked her what she had done to Shepard.

She said, "Nutt'n."

"You must have done something," I said. "Did you do the no-rain with him?"

"Nup."

"You know, Mamie," I said, "if a guy was sober, you could scare him to death with the no-rain. You got to be careful. Most won't understand like me." She looked at me like she wished I would make sense, as she kept on rubbing Powers all over. I watched her work on him, and I knew the no-rain idea was way off.

"You like Powers?" I asked her.

"Yaay, Kritch'n," she answered. And she picked him up. She hugged him, kissed him, and grinned at me from between his ears. Then she put him down and came over to me, took me by the shoulders, and looked into my eyes.

"Pow-ers, he teached me, Kritch'n," she said. "I luf him now."

Then she went back to Powers, rag in her hand, cleaning him from top to bottom. She was humming too, a happy made-up tune that reminded me of bright mornings at home, listening to Mama and Mary Magdalen sing as they cleaned house. Mamie had a clear, almost childlike voice, humming along, then singing out, "Hey non nonny, nonny, hey nonny," just as crisp as the winter air. And she glanced at me like she had secrets, smiling with her lips pressed together, her eyes full of mischief.

"What are you up to, Mamie?" I said, grinning back at her.

"Hey non nonny, nonny, hey nonny . . . hmmm . . ."

And that was all I could get out of her.

We finally had our grand opening on Valentine's Day in February. It wasn't much of a success. I sold only eleven tickets in all for both the showings of *Hamlet*. Anna came over to help at the book counter and with selling popcorn and apple juice. A sign on the wall in back of her said SELLING YOU INTELLECTUAL AND PHYSICAL GOOD HEALTH, signed, Donald Samuel Shepard. No one bought any books, and they made faces at the idea of drinking apple juice with popcorn. "Don't you have Coke?" they kept asking. One guy said he had always heard Shakespeare was great, but he didn't know what was so great about him. "It was a stupid movie," he said, "Just blah blah blah, and then they all die at the end." Another one said the actors were a bunch of fairies. No one had anything good to say, and the dirty looks they gave us made me feel like I was from Mars or the moon.

And Shepard wasn't any help. He stayed upstairs in the booth with

Mamie and didn't come down until long after the last customer had left. I told him the customers grumbled about the movie being no good, and they didn't like apple juice. He didn't seem to care.

"Poof poof," he said.

Anna scolded him. "Vhut's da madder you? You vant to make it money or not? You got to help. You do someting. Vhut's da madder you?" She stamped her foot at him, like she always did to Soren.

"Dear Anna and Crystal," he said, looking sort of bored with us. "All I can say now is that these are trifles and mean nothing in comparison with what is to come. You will understand very soon, I promise you." He rubbed his hands together. He hugged himself. "Oh, when this bursts upon the world, it will be gigantic, mercurial, sprinkled with godly inspiration, yum yum. You'll see. Be patient, please, my good friends. A few days more to work it out, then – magic! glory!"

"Magic, glory what?" I said. I was pretty miffed.

Shepard put his finger to his lips. "Shush, shush, we must not spoil it by giving birth too soon. It's a fine secret, ha ha, worth keeping it so."

He left Anna and me staring at each other like we had seen a crazy man. "Vhut's he gone coocoo?" she said.

¶ *Hamlet* just wasn't what the people of Temple wanted, so after a few days, Shepard sent it back and started showing *A Streetcar Named Desire.* About twice as many people came to see it but not enough to make us think we were a success. The next week Shepard got an old film he claimed was a classic, *Major Barbara.* And practically no one came to that one, so we were back where we started. Then he got *On The Waterfront*, and that was a real movie. Our best crowd ever came – sixty customers on one night – but after that they dropped off again. I could understand not coming for the other movies; I didn't like them much either – talk talk talk. But I thought *On The Waterfront* was terrific and better than any movie I had ever seen. When the people didn't keep coming to it, I lost heart and figured that Temple wasn't the place for what Shepard had in mind. The people didn't care for his choice of movies. They didn't buy his choice of books or paintings. They made faces at the apple juice with popcorn.

But Shepard sure didn't care either. Anna and I were running the place by ourselves. All he did was get the movies and have Mamie show them. I was beginning to wonder if all he wanted was to be lazy and take advantage of us. He spent all his time with Mamie and kept putting us off about the big secret he had. And Mamie herself was no help. She kept all her time for Powers, and if I wanted to see her I had to go upstairs and sit in the booth, where she was with him, running the movies over and over again and working on his gears and wheels. It reminded me of the obsession with Jewel, the same kind of thing. I didn't like being around it much, so for days on end I hardly ever saw her. She came in late at night too, after I was already in bed, and she slept on the couch. And not once from the time she had fallen in love with Powers did we do the no-rain. She just didn't want me touching her that way. I would try, and she would give me a funny-looking smile – made me think of pictures I had seen of the *Mona Lisa* – and then she would turn away. It was depressing for me, seeing as how I had gotten used to the no-rain and felt like I needed it.

Instead, I spent most of my days lying around reading or going over to watch television with Soren. At night Anna and I would take care of customers, but our hearts weren't in it. We even got to complaining right along with them that the movies we were showing were lousy. And then, after everyone would leave and Anna and I went home, Shepard would lock up and turn off the outside lights. He and Mamie would stay and do whatever it was they were doing every night. It got pretty aggravating.

At the end of three weeks, I decided I had had enough. I wrote my folks to tell them what was happening between Shepard and Mamie and to ask if they thought I could come home now.

Pa Surprises Me

I woke one morning and looked out the front window, and there was our pickup with the old man in it, parked behind Shepard's Hoover-time hunk. Pa was wearing his winter hat. He had the earflaps up and the ties hanging loose and the brim pushed down to shade his eyes from the rising sun. In his mouth was one of his curving pipes that hung down past his chin and had a mahogany bowl big enough to fill the palm of his hand. Smoke poured out of his pipe like from a chimney, and it clouded his face so that all his wrinkles disappeared. It gave me a notion of what he must have looked like when he was young – long face full of cheekbones, sharp nose curving left, no-nonsense mouth biting hard on the pipe stem. I was happy to see him. I stood for a minute and took him in.

Then I banged the door open and yelled, "Pa!" I ran down the steps. "What you doing here, Pa?"

He grinned at me and got out of the pickup. "What you think I'm doing here, prodigal? Come to see you."

"I'm glad you did," I told him. We shook hands. His grip was rough and strong, filling me with pride that he was my pa.

"Well, you best be glad to see me," he said. "It was a pain in the ass to get up at two this morning so I could have a day here and not have to worry Beaver was following me. I bet you wouldn't want that."

My heart sank at the thought. "So he hasn't calmed down," I said. "Still got scalping dreams about me and Mamie."

"Seems so. In fact, I'd say he's enjoying himself too much to calm down. He's like some spoiled brat, just eating up all the attention. He's an entertainer though, I'll give him that. Roaring and raving like a big ole bear. Gets me to giggling something awful, I swear."

My heart was sinking more and more. I knew Pa hadn't come to collect me. He was looking at the houses up and down the street. The sun was high enough to see them clearly. No one inside was stirring. "City types always sleep too much," he said softly, pulling on his pipe, the smell of it taking me back to the kitchen and sitting at the table while Pa smoked and talked and talked.

"City types stay up late and honky-tonk," I told him. "I stay up late too, but I can't sleep like them. I'm still a farmer, I guess, Pa."

He gave me a sly grin. "Well, I don't know. That's a switch from what I recall you being. You always slept in pretty good at home and come dragging ass for chores."

"I'm different now. You wouldn't have to holler so much to get me up. I'd be more help now."

"No kidding?" he said, pausing to look me over. "Well, maybe so. You do look more grown up. You got an older face. Shows there are some hard things you've seen or have been done to you. I bet you got some stories to tell. Your letters sure are entertaining. We kept them all. So farming ain't so bad now?"

"Farming is heaven."

"Haw haw haw, let's not go too far now. Farming is a living, but it ain't ever heaven." He looked again at the houses and the crossroads edged with stores. "But neither is this," he added. "But hey, is that the picture show you wrote about? Sure looks old. But you say you got it looking pretty good inside. And you're almost making a living of it?" I was nodding my head. He stroked his cheek with the stem of his pipe. "Must be something to see all them movies. I bet you learn a lot from them."

"I saw your favorite one, Pa, with Horatio in it. I saw *Hamlet*!"

"No shit? You shittin me, Christian? They made a movie of it? The whole thing?"

"I guess the whole thing. He says 'To be or not to be' and all kinds of stuff I remember hearing from you – about Yorick, and to thy own self be true, and if you do you can't be false to any man, the conscience of the king, the play's the thing. The end! You should see the end. Swords flying, people dying, getting stabbed, drinking poison. Neatest thing you'd ever see."

"All cause a fella couldn't make up his mind," said Pa, scratching his chin, the whiskers rasping. "You know what I'm wondering though? It's who the hell is smart enough in this backwater to care for Shakespeare?"

"Nobody, Pa, except Shepard and me. It closed fast. People thought it was stupid and that Hamlet was a fairy."

"That's cause you got to use your noggin for Shakespeare. He won't let you slip your clutch. Most people can't take making them think. It hurts. Feels like an insult." Pa spit into the snow. "Bah! They don't know nothing. And it's all right there for the taking – Shakespeare and the Bible got all the foolishness and the wisdom of the world worth knowing. But you got to use your noggin. So who played Hamlet? What'd he look like?"

"He was a blond guy named Oliver. He wore a black outfit. You could see it was a symbol."

"His inky cloak."

"Yeah. And sometimes he talked so fast I couldn't get it. It was like a foreign language."

"Oliver?" said Pa. "Like an Oliver tractor? Never heard of no Oliver the actor. I'd pick Errol Flynn. You can understand what he says."

"Half the time I couldn't make it out. Some guys said he moved like a queer, kind of swishy."

"That's why you need a good actor. Shakespeare can be tough if you don't have someone who knows what he's doing. It's too bad they didn't get Flynn. So what other movies you see?"

I told him what else, and he wished he could have seen them all.

"Boy, that makes me jealous," he said. "Next time you write, you write about the movies you see. Makes me want to go home right now so you can start writing. You write real good, son. We sure like getting letters from you. Even the boys like it. Goddamn, can you imagine what a mess they'd have made if they'd been in your shoes? Any one of them. Can you see them selling tickets at the window? Shit, they'd scare everybody away, that's what."

"Hardly anybody comes anyway," I answered. "They don't like Shepard's choices. One of them asked me why we don't show good movies, like cowboy movies, or gangster movies. Another one said, 'What's all this cultural crap, anyway? Whose dumb idea was that?' Not much I could say to that."

Pa cleared his nose, first one nostril and then the other, a commentary on what I'd told him. "I'll tell you what I think. It came to me when I was your age and just trying to figure out Shakespeare because Mrs. Cima, my teacher, made such a fuss over him, and I wanted to know why. The kids in my class had a fit that they had to read Shakespeare. They talked like the people you're talking about. It's this here – people are naturally dumb, just dumb as cows, when it comes to cultured stuff and what's good for the mind. People make a virtue of being stupid about it. They make fun of you if you know something. Stupid people make fun of smart people cause that's all they got to offer – stupidity – and they know it. You have to teach them what is good and what ain't, what isn't, I mean. They don't have it naturally in them to do much more than put one foot in front of the other. Thank the Creator for creating teachers, I say.

"Now, most these potatoheads will take a stab at the Bible and get a phrase or two and stop there, pretending they got all the knowledge they need. And they'll listen to a preacher, and the more ignorant he is the better they like him. I've told plenty of the walking wrathful that they don't know bullshit from mashed beets, and they train their children to be the same way. I tell them there's more in heaven and earth than is dreamed of in their goddamn Northwoods philosophy. And they tell me if it ain't – if it isn't – in the Bible, then it's not worth knowing. And so that's what you and Mr. Shepard are dealing with here. You're going to have to be patient as Job if you want to teach an ox to be an eagle." He had worked himself up, puffing a fine cloud of smoke that curled and fell in the cold air. His eyes were bright and happy. His face glowed with the love of telling.

"I sure have missed you, Pa," I told him.

"And haven't I missed you, you think? Nobody to talk to since you been gone. You're the only one who listens. Them other boys put on a face like I'm cussing them out. All they can do is pick their noses and flick boogers at each other." Pa flicked his finger to show me what he meant.

"It always made me feel important that you talked to me," I told him. "Made me feel special."

"That's the way it is with all the philosophy that comes into a person's head. It's like a special book, something in Greek, and you ain't Greek. But if you got any sense at all, you know that it's *special* and the most important thing you got to do – thinking about what's Greek and making it English. Deep stuff. Horatio-kind of stuff. That's what makes you bigger, makes you special. And when you get my age and have read what I've read, deep thinking gets easier and not so Greeky. You got more words to draw on and process to make what's wispy more solid. Soak yourself in the words – a slow digestion. You got to go slow digesting experiences cause they come too fast when you're a young buck ruled by your balls and you don't realize that the brain is taking in all kinds of other things important to it. The brain's a glutton, son. It can't get enough of the world. But damn if we don't damp it down and bank it like a hot fire. Ninety percent of the time it's us that makes ourselves stupid. Ten percent got wrecked in the hamper or some accident later on, sort of like the way your brothers were put together with too much of your mama's inbred side. But that's not most. Most is to blame themselves, making themselves stupid just to fit in round here." Pa gestured in a circle to indicate the town of Temple, but I knew he meant the world.

He caressed his jaw and smiled. The talking was what he came for, I could tell. He had stored it up for me. "Yesss, yes, takes time to make a philosophy you can live by. Takes time to make it you, to fill your soul with it. But someday, someday it's there for you and it is what you are. Mark what I say. I'm not just a farmer with cowshit on his boots, like the idea in folks' heads. Not me. Nope. I read Shakespeare and can quote some of it. I'm a philosopher who knows about Emerson and the Deity. I did that. I created that. Nobody else was that way exactly, though Grandpa sure had the Bible down chapter and verse. But I switched to Shakespeare. I created a Foggy growing beyond Grandpa's Old Testament fierceness. It is natural for a Foggy to grow in the direction of the spirit, and I saw that direction as the direction of philosophy. I know some Bible too, but it don't dictate to me; I just handy quote it when I need to. And I don't need someone else's personal vision of religion or a church. Nobody does. Nor all that groveling prayer stuff that just proves you got a disease of the will in the same way that politics proves you got a disease of the intellect. The proper study of mankind is man, someone said, can't remember who, but he spoke the truth, and there's no better way to study mankind than studying Shakespeare. That and taking the Bible for what it's worth for telling us how men used to think about themselves and their god, who was created in the image of their brutal, nasty selves and then did a little evolution thing by becoming all-loving all of a sudden when men thought they'd had enough of being Job-sport for Satan. Someday maybe your mama and sister are going to realize it too and stop rolling those silly beads to convert me. What I got is more than they can dream of, or Horatio either – a powerful combination of heaven and earth. Wouldn't give that up for a string of beads from here to Africa." Pa punctuated his idea by clasping his hands together, like one was heaven and the other earth. He looked pretty satisfied with the way his thoughts had come together.

Taking the pipe from his mouth, he tapped the ashes from it and said his feet were getting cold. He wanted to go into the house. I held him up, telling him how I had lied to Shepard and the Gulbrensons about me and Mamie, saying we were cousins and orphans. Pa said not to worry about it, that anyone with an ounce of brains would understand why, once they learned the truth of that goddamn Grendel chasing us all over creation. So we went in, and there was Shepard at the table, eating his breakfast.

He looked at us, his eyes full of questions.

"This is Jacob Foggy," I said. "He's my pa."

"Your pa! You've got a living daddy? You prevaricator, you. Haw haw, the orphaned Crystal caught in the signature of a lie." Shepard stood up and swept his arm across his waist and bowed. "Welcome, Pa of Crystal Foggy," he said.

Pa looked him up and down. "You said he was big, Christian. But this is big; this is bigger than John Beaver, maybe."

"I told you he was monstrous."

"It's what you said all right. But Beaver is monstrous. You, Mr. Shepard, pardon me, sir, could see eyeball to eyeball with Goliath himself. Any relation?"

Shepard's chin went up and he showed off his gums. "I am," he said, "a most recalcitrant philistinian optimist, yum yum, but otherwise unrelated."

Pa laughed hard at that. "Okay! A regular cartoon! Yum-yumming and everything. What's that you say – a philistinian optimist? What might that be?"

"Philistinian optimist – one who embodies the character of our country; one who lives by the god of materialism and greed. Recalcitrant – refusing to obey custom; stubbornly defiant!"

"I like it," said Pa. "The word. Got a nice philosophical ring to it, a nice feel in the mouth. Philistinian optimist. But the recalcitrant kind. He's everything you said he was, Christian. I'm gonna like talking to him. 'A most recalcitrant philistinian optimist, yum yum.'"

"It has the flavor of truth," said Shepard, holding out his arms like he wanted someone to hug him for what a brilliant thing he had said.

He had Pa sit down and the two of them had coffee. Shepard said how he was never fooled by the orphan thing, his gift of second sight allowing him to pick out lies as soon as they were told. Not much could get by a man with that kind of brilliance, he insisted, and he hoped I would trust him enough always to tell him the truth from now on. "And what about Mamie?" he asked. "What's her story?"

"Too dumb to lie," said Pa.

Shepard bellowed laughter into Pa's face and cried, "That's what you think! You'd be flabbergasted beyond recovery to know what that hunk of walking motion picture can do. Hawww hawwww hawwww!"

Pa leaned away and grinned at me, then gazed at Shepard like he was the one-hundredth wonder of the world. "I suppose you know more than me about it," he said. "She's not an orphan, it's true. Though she'd be better off if she was."

Shepard got serious, furrowed his eyebrows at Pa. "Better off an orphan? My infinite wisdom is picking up your thought waves. She was born retarded, and so her parents despise and treat her abominably. They beat her, don't they?"

"Close enough. There's just her old man. Vicious fellow; got fists like a pair of hams."

"A tyrant, yes, I see. And has he done *things* to her? You know what I mean . . . intimate things."

"He's a varmint, a liar, and a mongrel dog," said Pa up into Shepard's face.

"So!" cried Shepard. "Now it makes sense to me. She's a victim of trauma. The stammer, the stutter – all the symptoms of trauma. Her gifts were always there, stifled, buried under the vulgarity of her father's wrath. I knew I could clear this up!"

Pa leaned back and lit his pipe. He told Shepard, "Yeah, you better hope her old man never finds out she's here. He's a dangerous desperado. Half man, half grizzly. Mind of a rabid wolf. He finds out she's here, I wouldn't give two cents for your chances."

"*My* chances? What did I do? I took her in, a poor orphan, as far as I knew. And I fed her and housed her. And now I'm teaching her a trade. He should thank me."

"He'll as soon put a knife in your ribs. Hope you're as tough as you are tall. Guy your size might make him work for it."

Shepard bared his gums and dogteeth menacingly. "If my wrath is provoked," he growled in a husky voice, "I can be a torrent of devastation, a reincarnation of Tyrannosaurus rex! A nightmare!"

"Well, it would be a match I'd pay to see," said Pa, tugging happy puffs of smoke from his pipe. "Yep, I wouldn't mind seeing it at all, not if you could make him work for it. Some tough old shits have tried, but none of them made him work. He's hardly human, I tell you, more like a myth of the days when monsters roamed the earth. You as strong as you are big?"

"Strong as Hercules when I'm aroused. Be he the Minotaur himself, I'll grind his bones to make my bread. Look out."

"Yeah, well, that's what it'll take," said Pa.

Shepard puffed his chest out, but it was no match for his belly. "Bring the noodle on. He'll know he's messed with Don Shepard before I'm through with him."

"I like your attitude," said Pa.

Mamie came in and stood there at the edge of the kitchen, yawning and rubbing her sleepy face and looking at Pa. "You know me?" he asked.

"Yaay, F-f-oggy," she answered. She patted him on the shoulder. "I know you."

"Well, you're lookin good, Mamie. Better'n I've seen ever. You lost some weight, huh? You let your hair grow long. You know, dammit, you're damn near pretty, I'd say. Ain't it so, Christian?" I agreed she was.

Mamie liked what he said. She pulled him up and gave him a hug and a pat on the butt. It made him laugh and get all red. "She likes me, I think," he said, half-choking.

"Today she likes the world," Shepard told us. Then he said he had an announcement to make. At noon we would see Mamie display her wondrous art. It was a secret. He couldn't say more, "But! This day, this day an apotheosis, a glorification of my own and Mamie's genius. I discovered the hidden springs of genius inside her, and I have developed them, brought them gushing forth, yumity yum, from the largess of her *anima mundi*, her world soul. Once it was traumatized to stammering silence, and I – Oh, I! – brought it back from the abyss of extinction to astound the world. This great soul 'yearning in desire to follow knowledge like a sinking star, beyond the utmost bounds of human thought.' And I – Oh I! – found it."

Mamie reached over and petted his nose, which made him beam with pleasure.

"Did you make that up?" asked Pa. "It was good, 'follow knowledge like a sinking star.' It's good."

"Everything I say is original. Now append this coda. At noon today, we shall gather in the Artlife. Crystal, dear one, will you tell Anna and Soren to come? I say no more." He fluttered his fingers mysteriously, like a magician over a crystal ball.

I told him I would tell Anna and Soren. He shook hands with Pa and blessed him for coming and clearing the cobwebs of the past away. Then he told Mamie to come to the Artlife for rehearsals as soon as she ate. Another mysterious flourish of his hands, and he lumbered out of the room, on his way to make preparations.

As soon as the door closed, Pa said, "A talking gargantua wonder, like you said, son."

"He's a genius," I explained.

"Got to be to talk that way."

"He's had something going with Mamie. A secret."

"I think he's struck with her. Stares at her like she's wearing seven veils he wants to peel off. I think that would be a fair match, don't you? At least he's bigger than her." Pa took his cap off and said it was warmish.

I felt a little pang in my belly at his thinking Mamie was for Shepard. I thought to myself, wouldn't it be something if he knew what she and I had done, all the no-raining? "I don't know if he's for her, Pa," I said. "He's big, but he's all blubber and bluster."

"Yeah, I figured so. Belly like a pregnant cow." He glanced at Mamie, who was eating a loaf of pumpernickel. "You like him, Mamie? You think he might marry you?"

"Nup," she said quickly, her cheeks bulging with bread, reminding me of a gathering squirrel.

"I bet he wants to," said Pa. "I bet he's got it in his head that that's the way it should be." Pa bit on his pipe stem, like he had said the last word on it.

"Nup nup," Mamie disagreed. "Powers for me. He luffs me so."

Pa looked like he had smelled something bad. "Who's this Powers?" he asked.

"Powers is a movie projector," I told him. "Mamie thinks he loves her. She kisses him and gets graphite all over her face."

"He luffs me so," she said softly.

Pa's eyes were tangled up in wrinkles. "Huh? What's that? A movie projector in love? What you loving that for?"

Mamie studied it a minute. Then she said, "He teached me." She tapped her forehead. "Married me here."

"What's that mean?" Pa asked me.

I told him I didn't know; that I had given up trying to figure her out. All I knew was she wasn't crazy exactly. There was more to her thing with Powers than bats in the belfry. She was changing almost minute by minute.

"In a state of becoming," said Pa. "Yeah, she's creating herself, like I told you before what people do. She's creating herself. 'Married me here,' she says and taps her head. Hmmmm, yeah. That's a goddamn concept, that's what that is. She's attached herself to that machine cause it's teaching her something nobody else can. Watch a movie, you learn. Goddamn, I'm glad I came today! This is getting more and more promising."

He was having such a good time. I was happy for him, chewing his pipe, blowing smoke, stabbing the air – *talking*, talking and warm with the Horatio part of him that loved to speculate. "Oh, look at her, stuffing her face with pumpernickel. Not a damnation bone in her whole pretty body. Never knew her to be evil. Never gave her credit for enough brains to sin. Now what do we think, hey? There's a darkness on the earth causes all our troubles. Is what we see happening here the darkness or the light? The darkness is made of Will, the force that makes the flower grow and makes a man grow and also makes him restless and makes him throw out tentacles of evil when he gets bored. Creating yourself, eh Mamie? Mamie and Powers. Mamie and evil. Mamie and the darkness. Mamie and the light. The light is reason shining in the darkness and the darkness sometimes knows it not. Maybe so. And what a shame that each of us is such a whole world packed in such a small sack and can't see the other worlds round us – that they're made up of the same dust as our own and we all have to fight our own selves to come up with the least tidbit of truth. It's a crying shame all right. It's the reason for finding comfort in philosophy, which lets you know the thickness of your skull to make you humble. And it tells you that the worst human perversion is the way some people cling to the lies that drown out any horse sense they got. The widest river in any part of creating yourself is the big lie, the easy way. The widest river pouring into the Will, choking an unfolding flower so it can't swim the river of truth, can't go so far as Washington's silver dollar. And so the sack of soul gets smaller. And the mind gets darker. But the ember burns, all the time a white dot of hope.

"Creating yourself in what direction, Mamie? What was it Shepard said the people were? Philistine optimists. Is that the blood come down from Goliath that planted its seed in a whole nation? Is that what he meant? Should it be the mark of a decent man in this century to feel shame for it? Rotten in Denmark. A nation turning into a pillar of salt. Hmmm, yes, a pillar of salt. And the darkness says if man is the best nature can do, best she can create with the will of a wolverine, then she deserves the darkness coming. And Mamie is having a love affair with a movie projector. Creating her in what direction, Powers? In what direction? Hmmm?"

And on and on he went, the dam bursting in words he couldn't help, a sort of river I couldn't rhyme.

"Are you listening, son?"

The Wonder of the Mystery

I At noon I got Soren and Anna, and together with Pa we went over to the Artlife. Pa admired the way we had set up the books and paintings to sell. He told Soren it was diversification that kept most businesses from going belly-up when times got tough. It was especially true of farming, he said, which was why it was good to have some extra acres for a cash crop and not depend on milk, which was too attached to the whim of a government that never understood and never would understand what it meant to be a farmer.

"Nor a man in a wheelchair crippled for hurry-up money," Soren added.

When we went in, Pa sat on an aisle seat so he could be next to Soren in the wheelchair and they could talk. Soren wanted to know more about farming, which was one of Pa's favorite subjects. All Soren had to do was listen. Anna sat next to me. She could not make heads or tails of what Shepard was doing. She hated the mystery. She hoped he wasn't going to embarrass us with something stupid.

Finally the lights went down and on came the lamp from the projector, shining its light on the stage. We waited while Shepard came down from the booth and climbed into the light. And he told us it was his privilege to present the wonder of the mystery.

Mamie came onstage into the beam of Powers's eye. She was wearing a black robe. Her hair was pulled back tight in a braid down her back, but its hundreds of curls on top and the sides still stuck out, like little thorns shining all over her head. Her face was dusted with a white powder that made her lips and eyes seem dark and not real, like lips and eyes on a puppet. She stared into the hard light without blinking, and her mouth hung like it had loose hinges.

Shepard, standing back out of the light, said to her, "Now, Mamie, ahem: 'If it be, why seems it so particular with thee?'"

In the next breath Mamie became someone else. All that was blank and stupid in her face disappeared. She took on the moves of Olivier, his voice as her voice: "'Seems, madam? Nay, it is; I know not "seems." 'Tis not alone my inky cloak, good mother, nor customary suits of solemn black, nor windy suspiration of forced breath, no, nor the fruitful river in the eye –'"

"Now, Mamie," interrupted Shepard.

She quit to listen to him. Stood as before, eyes and mouth black in the light.

"'Mark me,'" he said.

"'I will,'" she answered, face alive again.

"'My hour is almost come, when I to sulphurous and tormenting flame must render up my self.'"

"'Alas, poor ghost!'"

"'Pity me not, but lend thy serious hearing to what I shall unfold.'"

"'Speak. I am bound to hear.'"

Shepard stopped and came to the edge of the stage to look out at us. He was trembling. "Can you hear all right?" he asked.

"We can hear," Pa answered. "Can she do any more? It's pretty good stuff so far."

"Mr. Foggy, she plays all parts. She is the greatest actress in the world. Listen." His face was twisted with excitement, and his voice seemed at the edge of tears. It shook when he spoke again.

"Now, Mamie, ahem: 'Propose the oath, my lord.'"

Straight and fast, she answered him, "'Never to speak of this that you have seen, swear by my sword!'"

Then to show us how great she could do, he prompted her into one of Ophelia's speeches, and she became Ophelia and said the lines in the sweet voice of the actress in the movie. He led her into the king, then the queen, and on to be Polonius, then Laertes, and finished up with Horatio saying, "'His purse is empty already; all 's golden words are spent.'" For each of them Mamie was no more Mamie.

Shepard came out again, wiping his eyes on his sleeve, saying, "You've seen, you've seen – what I've created." He cleared his throat and told us that she could do more than just *Hamlet.* Any movie was her movie.

"They stick to her glue," he said. "Total recall at will!"

To show us what he meant he had her do some lines from other shows: from *A Streetcar Named Desire* – "Whoever you are, I have always depended on the kindness of strangers"; from *Major Barbara* – "Yes, through the raising of hell to heaven and of man to God, through the unveiling of an eternal light in the Valley of The Shadow"; from *On The Waterfront* – "You should have looked out for me a little bit, Charlie."

We sat listening to her, none of us saying a word. I could hear Anna beside me, gasping at the lines, holding her breath, muttering things I couldn't make out. And when it was over, she spoke up first, "Vhut twick is dat, Mista?"

"You like it, Anna?" he asked.

"Pwetty goot, I do. How you make Mamie do dat?"

He pointed to Mamie. She was standing in the light, her mouth unhinged again. "It's just Mamie, Anna. It's been in her all along, buried in her since birth. I exhumed it and created her thus. Think what people will pay to see this! She's worth a fortune!"

"I don't get it," said Soren. "This ain't natural."

"Natural? Of course it's natural," said Shepard, his voice rising some. "It's her chemistry. It's . . . it's . . . never mind. It's too complicated to explain. Uneducated men! Such a savant called idiot is criminal. But she is comprehensible only in the distillery of a superior mind, such as my own. I can't expect any of you to see. Do you see?"

"This ain't too overwhelming. This isn't too overwhelming," said Pa. "I saw her do something like it a long time ago, when she was little, real little – if you can ever believe she was that."

We all turned to Pa, who was nodding his head like he had the answer to the whole mystery. He had put his winter cap on again, with the earflaps up and curling out like half-lifted dog ears. The tie-strings whipped his cheeks as he nodded and told us in the best prophet he owned, "'I hear a voice I had not known. I am the Lord . . . Open your mouth wide, and I will fill it.' What I'm saying is there are more things in heaven and earth than are dreamed of in your philosophy. This here is just the completion of what Mamie promised and none of us understood long ago."

I couldn't keep still. I thought he might go off on a roll of proverbs and philosophy cause he felt so good, and I wanted to know what he was talking about. I interrupted him. "What you talking about, Pa?"

"Ya, vhut da dewil you talking about?" said Anna.

Pa had his audience. He took it slow. "Well, it's this way. You see, Mamie's got a gift. People get gifts. I know of a fellow played piano like Beethoven, and he never took a lesson in his life. What's more, this fellow couldn't hardly talk or walk. He couldn't do much at all for himself, in fact. Sit round and drool. They called him an idiot, but those who called him that couldn't play piano like him. It was a gift from the Deity. Just got up one night and sat down at the piano and played a piece he'd heard on a record. He woke them all up, scared them half to death. There was the idiot playing the piano like an angel. He *was* an angel, sort of."

"A piece of Jesus," I burst in, thinking of what Robbie had told me.

"That's a way of putting it," said Pa. "It's like a miracle but not a miracle, though it sure does have a feel of something holy. A slobbering idiot playing like Beethoven. A Mamie Beaver playing like Katharine Hepburn."

"*And* Laurence Olivier!" Shepard shouted.

"And him too. It's a gift, and she's always had it. Tell you how I know. Listen here – Mamie, come out of that light now and listen here! She looks like a Halloween monster up there."

Mamie obeyed Pa and came down next to Shepard sitting on the edge of the stage. She looked better out of the light than in it. In it, she looked like a ghost. Too much white powder.

"Tell you how I know," Pa repeated. "Listen here – Beaver didn't used to be so standoffish. This is years ago now. You could go borrow something from him, and he'd borrow from you. He was young then, but you could see he had a lot a meanness boiling inside him. He kept it down some, and he farmed like the rest of us. Those were the days before he got lazy and started working Mary – Mary was his wife – started working her to death.

"Well, I come by one day to borrow a field rake from him. Mine had busted. You know that gear that makes the tines go round, makes them stop and start?"

"Pa!" I cried. "Come on. We don't care about that rake."

He gave me a sly smile and winked. "Got ants in your pants. It's the city living does that to you. Makes you impatient about everything. Can't sit back and enjoy a good story. Now, where was I? Oh yeah. That gear broke, and Beaver had borrowed mine once, so I thought I'd let him repay me. So I drive over in the pickup and ask him, and he says he has to fetch it in the field and he'll be right back. He goes out on his tractor – was a gas Massey-Harris twenty-two, as I recall – those were good tractors. And I sit down on the porch to wait.

"Mamie, she was playing something in the yard. I watched her. All by herself she was, and she's got on an old pork-pie hat with the brim turned up. She's wearing baggy trousers and an old secondhand coat that hung to her knees, and she's got a pair of her pa's shoes on. In her hand she's got a stick that looks like a cane. Now, get me right on this – she's no more'n four years old at this time. Of course, when she was four she looked big as an eight-year-old. Mary told me she was fourteen pounds at birth. Now, if you could have seen what a tiny little thing Mary was, you'd call it a miracle she lived through birthing Mamie. I bet Mary wasn't more'n five feet tall, five one at most. She had that red hair like Mamie's got. She was a pretty little woman, sweet and pretty, like a little girl. Beaver sure didn't deserve her. But there's one thing I've learned about men and women – there's no accounting for how they pair up. Everybody is kind of odd that way."

"Paaa!" I cried again. He was driving me crazy.

"What? What's the matter?"

"What did Mamie do when she was four years old?"

"I'm coming to it, son. Hold your horses." While we waited, Pa lit his pipe again. We stared at him. "Pipe helps draw the words out," he told us.

"All right, listen here then, this is what she was doing. She was walking round like a duck. Yep, walking round like a duck and twirling her cane. And I thought to myself, boy if that don't look silly. It didn't dawn on me, you know, that she meant something by it. I remember their dog was sleeping under a tree, and she goes over by it and picks up one of its bones and starts gnawing it. 'Poor thing,' I says to myself. Thing, you know, it's a symptom of being retarded.

"Let's see – she dropped the bone and she started sliding her feet back and forth in place, like walking on ice and going nowhere. And what else did she do? Oh yeah, she acted like she was drinking something. That was after sliding in place a while. Now get this – Mary come on the porch and was watching her with me. 'What's she doing?' she says. I says she's playing something. Then I recall that Mamie takes a piece of twine she found, piece of baling twine, and ties it round her waist and ties it to the dog round his neck. And she starts acting like she's dancing. Yeah, going round in circles with her arms out, like she had a partner. That dog is getting jerked this way and that. He don't know what's going on. He just follows her where she jerks him to. She's dancing and tugging, dancing and tugging. It dawns on me that I'm seeing something pretty strange here. Then I say to Mary, 'What *is* she doing?'

"Mary's got her hand over her mouth. She looks like she might want to cry. I say, 'What's the matter now?' And she says, 'It's Charlie Chaplin, Jacob. It's Charlie Chaplin.' You can imagine how lost I was. But she explained what she meant. What happened was that she took Mamie into Superior to a movie. And it was an old silent one, *The Gold Rush* with Charlie Chaplin. And Mamie was acting out some of the things that Chaplin did in the movie. 'How can she do that?' I says. Mary shakes her head, cause she don't know. Doctors say Mamie's retarded, and retarded kids can't do that. Something like that is what she said to me. 'Well, maybe she ain't retarded,' is what I said. It was a mystery we couldn't figure out.

"Now, I might have not have told it to you exactly, but pretty close. It made an impression on me. And I know now she *was* being Charlie Chaplin that day. I just wonder how many other clues she put out over the years that no one picked up on. You see, I think you're right, Mr. Shepard – that thing you said about trauma. Beaver was hard on her. Hard hard. Everybody knows how he treated her. Mamie was his mule, and God knows what else. I remember him coming back with the rake and seeing her acting Charlie Chaplin. He knocked her down and told her to leave his hat and shoes alone. You see the look on her face right now? The way she can just stare like there's nothing but midnight in her head? That's the same look she gave Beaver that day. That's all I got to say. That's all that happened. But that put together with what we just saw makes a lot of sense to me."

Mamie slid her eyes over and looked at Pa for a while. "You taking it all in?" he asked. "Or is it just midnight to you?"

Real soft she said, "Yaay, J-Jacob."

And just as soft, Pa said, "'And He has sent out His maid to call from the highest places in the town.' What will you do now, Mamie, now that you got your gift back?"

"She'll get rich and famous," said Shepard. "There is a well of wealth here, and I'm the entrepreneur who can make it flow. Trust me."

"A well of wealth," said Pa. "That's seeing things like a true philistine optimist, all right."

Shepard thought a second. Then he answered, "No, this is different, different as wealth is from poverty. It is for her that I bring my genius to bear in that particular direction, not myself. I have already given her a trade. Now I give her a profession!"

"Oh, then that's okay, I guess," said Pa. It was hard to tell if he was serious.

"If she's so smart," I said, "why can't she learn to read? Or have you taught her to read?"

"She cannot read, Crystal. Apparently, she is incapable of learning her letters," said Shepard. "I've tried, but it doesn't happen for her. The words won't come together in her brain. As best as I can tell from what she has written for me, she sees everything backward, or she jumbles the combination of letters into a word that is meaningless. But there is something to be learned here – that we may pause awhile from words and still be wise or gifted or brilliant in elocution, though we cannot learn our ABCs. She certainly has compensated for the inferiority of those crooked letters with not only Johnsonian memory but a triumphant gift of mimicry – 'With these celestial Wisdom calms the mind, And makes the happiness she does not find.' And, I might add, her fortune and our fame. Who could resist this, an idiot who speaks purest prose in ghostly voices from the Silver Screen? Humph, would you quibble about small deformities when her general power is so colossal, yum yum?"

"Vee should poot her on telewision," said Anna.

Shepard put his hands on the armrests in front of Anna's seat, bending way over into her face, and with excited, trembling lips he said he had a plan, had it all worked out. The Artlife would be our base. The people would come to her, and the television too. "The world will see *us*," he said, "not we the world. And you know what that does? It puts us in control! yum yum!"

Pa stood up and stretched and scratched under his hat. "That's all well and good," he said. "But I've got to head back 'for long, and I ain't even had breakfast yet. What say we get something to eat, sonny?"

"My treat!" said Shepard. "I'll take you to Charlie's next door."

We went next door to Charlie Friendly's bar, except Anna and Soren had things to do at home, so they didn't come. Inside Friendly's place it was warm and quiet. Charlie was all alone, standing behind the bar and reading a paper. We took a table near the back, next to the pool table, while Shepard ordered hamburgers and beer for us. Charlie was bald and had a red face and baggy eyes and moles on his forehead. He wore a white shirt with grease spots all over the front. As he flipped the hamburgers, more grease flew up on him, and he'd wipe it with his hand and not care. He said to Shepard that he heard the Artlife was already going under.

"Pure fabrication and sour grapes," Shepard told him. "Those who practice such calumny will be flogged with their own words. We are about to break out, Charlie. We are about to soar on the wings of eagles into the rarefied atmosphere of fortune and fame. Look at my Valkyrie, Charlie. Look at her, yum yum. Tomorrow's headlines: 'Mamie Beaver Soars Among the Stars!' Going under? Charlie, wait until I unveil my protégée here."

"Uh-huh," said Charlie, pouring a pitcher of beer for us. "So I guess that means you're doing all right. You doing all right, Mamie?"

"Yaay, Ch-Charlie."

"Glad to hear it. Take these glasses over will you?"

She brought the glasses to us and he set the pitcher down. We drank beer and ate the hamburgers. Shepard kept his mouth full of food and chatter, telling Charlie what a wonder he was going to see pretty soon and how the whole town would wake up and find itself no longer just a spot on the map.

Pa and I pulled our chairs up close so we could talk with each other. He said I had to know about my cow, Sugar. She had taken over Minna's place as supercow in the barn. She was doing seventy-five pounds of milk a day and a 4.8 butterfat test.

"That's my Sugar," I said. I had raised her from a calf, and I was as proud as if she was my own child.

"You were sure right about her," said Pa. "You're a good judge of heifers, maybe even better than me now. When you come back, after this thing is settled, I'm going to turn more of the breeding over to you. Send you to breeders school. Now there's a future for you, son."

"Artificial breeding is the way of the future, Pa." The word *future* sounded real good to me right then.

"We'll do it right and get to be big farmers, I'm thinking. Nobody'll have to go off to the city for a job. Can't imagine those boys in the city, can you?"

"Can't imagine, Pa."

"Cash got his toes frostbit. Lost all his toenails on his right foot. Said he just didn't feel that cold, haw haw. I was gonna tell you something else. Let me light my pipe." He lit it, and the smell of cedar filled the room.

"Your brothers need a keeper, I tell you. Haw haw. The shenanigan they pulled the other day was a beaut. They got this big idea that they were gonna trap John Beaver – in a bear trap, mind you. They couldn't tell me what they were gonna do with him once they caught him, but they were gonna catch him, trap him like an ole bear. Thank God, they didn't use the one with the sawteeth. They used that smooth one, the old one your grandpa had. They set it up between those two big poplars at the edge of the driveway. It got buried in the snow there. But you see, they didn't put a marker on it. They didn't even have it chained to one of the trees – just put it near where Beaver likes to pace up and down.

"Only, guess what? The day they set it up, Beaver didn't show. I seen them sneaking round all morning, hiding behind the house and the shed, staring at the road and snickering and pinching each other. I said to myself, 'What in the hell is going on now? What're them shitheads up to?' Finally I called them over and asked them what they were up to. 'Oh, nuthin, Pa,' they said, 'oh, nuthin. We're juss spyin for Beaver if he comes.' I told them they had better things to do down the barn. And I ran them down there and had them start cleaning out the vents and washing the cows and combing them. Oh, did they whine about it. Then, of course, they had to fight each other over who's pulling the chips off the cow's behinds, as if a little cowshit ever hurt anybody. I finally had to give each a job to do and stand there and stare at them to make sure it got done.

"Then Duane came to pick up the milk, so I went out to talk to him. He didn't look so good. Too much bending the elbow, hey? Gotten bloated. I told him he was getting fat from bending the elbow. He said, 'Half the county is drunk, so why shouldn't I be? What else is there to do when you live at the edge of the shittin world?' I told him it ain't the edge. He twisted his mouth like he does and laughed at me. 'It might not be the edge of the world, but you can damn sure see it from here,' he said. You know, that guy was born bitching about everything, that's what I think. Might as well shoot yourself if all you're gonna do is grump your way through life. Well, what the hell, I like him though. Nothing he won't do for you. Anyway, I was teasing him when I heard the boys screaming like they do when somebody's fighting. I ran back inside and there was two of them wrestling round in the cowshit at the back door. Can you guess who?"

"Cush and Cutham," I answered.

"You know those twins all right. Cush and Cutham it was. I could've killed them. I made them go to the milkhouse and hose down, and you should've heard them squeal. It was cold, you know? Squealing like pigs getting castrated, and I told them I ought to run them down the Brule and break the ice with their heads and drown them. They kept blaming each other. 'He started it, Pa!' 'No I didn't, he started it, Pa!' I had to kick them both in the ass to make them shut up.

"When I got the shit off them, I sent them to the house to get changed. So of course, the other three had to start whining that Cush and Cutham were getting out of chores. My patience was wore out. They try me every day, you know? I suppose you've gotten whacked a few times just cause I was wore out cause of them. Though most of the time I suppose you earn your own."

"You never really hit hard," I told him. Pa never put his heart into a beating, not like John Beaver would.

"Yeah, haw haw haw, but you'd think I was kicking holy hell out of you guys, the way you yell. Then your mama's got to get in the act,

'Now, Jacob, remember about your vein.' She can drive me nuts, you know? I guess I wouldn't trade her though." Pa suddenly slapped the table hard with his fist, so hard the beer slopped over the edge of our glasses, which we had just refilled. "Whoa horse," he said, with a little snicker. "I gotta watch I don't get a snootful. Promised Mama I'd be back tonight. I ain't used to drinking much, you know?"

He looked at me and winked. "Sure have missed you, son. Did I tell you that?"

"Yeah, Pa. And I've missed you too."

"Mama misses you. She turns on the waterworks whenever you send a letter. She's an old sweety. Loves her boys."

"I miss her like crazy," I said. And in my mind I saw her, with her thick hair in a bun, almost all gray but with blond still showing through, and her kind eyes and all the fine wrinkles on her cheeks and round her mouth, my mama.

"I know you do," said Pa. "You're all good boys, even though I've needed the patience of Job raising you. I bet I wouldn't trade you if I could – well, might trade the twins. Did you know your sister thinks you're some kind of hero? She brags you up one side and down the other. Did I tell you Ram Brown came over and tried to date her again? He did. The fool. She told him what she thought of him, but he didn't want to take no for an answer. You know, your sister is getting to be like honey to the bees. Another year and I'll have to get a stick to beat off the boys. Ram Brown just kept trying to paw her when she had already told him no, so she sicced Calah on him. Calah is a tough little sucker, you know? He got Ram down in the snow and rubbed his face, and when the others seen that they got excited and all five of them damn near snowballed poor Ram Brown half to death. Haw haw haw! You know, he should've never two-timed Mary Magdalen. You get on her bad side, she don't forget. She's got a mean streak, for all her looking like something out of fairyland. I think it comes from having some ornery brothers, hey? Get tough or die, hey? Haw haw haw!"

Pa puffed his pipe hard, till he had it going like a steam engine. He settled back on the chair and crossed his legs. "You know," he said. "I'm having a good time sitting here talking. Yeah, we've had some good talks before, but none as good as this, hey?"

"All our other talks were when you were telling me about Shakespeare and the Bible, Pa," I told him. "Philosophical stuff. This is better."

"Well, we'll do it lots more. But let me tell you about the boys and that bear trap. You see, the night after they'd set it, it snowed and covered up where it was, so you couldn't tell by the mess they'd made where to look for it. Not a trace of it. So the next day I seen them standing down by the trees, arguing like gophers. I asked what they were fighting about. 'Oh, nuthin, Pa' they told me. I'd had enough of that. I told them if I didn't get the truth I was gonna send their souls to God and make sausages of their asses. I looked at Cash, cause he's the little one now that you've gone. And I pointed my crooked finger at him. That finger always scares him." Pa held it up, his index finger on his right hand, a thick finger gnarled up and curving to the left. It had a look like he might shoot lightning out of it.

"And I pointed my finger at him and that was it. 'Calvin's the one!' he yelled. 'Calvin did it, Pa!' Calvin called him a turd and then tried to lie. But all the boys started pointing at him and saying it was all his fault, he thought up the idea and talked them into doing it – blah blah blah. And I still didn't know what they were talking about. I put a ear-lock on Cash and made him talk straight. 'Gonna trap John Beaver,' he said. 'You gonna trap John Beaver and do what with him?' I said. They looked at each other with faces blank as mud. 'Where'd you set your trap?' I said. They pointed to a place between the poplars. I told them to dig it up. 'Oh, yes, Pa, yes, Pa,' they said, bobbing their pointy heads up and down like they do, like chickens pecking at the same spot. Drives me crazy. I gave each of them a whack.

"Then I went up the hill. But before I could get to the house, I heard this here blood-curdling yowl – worse than the time that cat got caught in the baler, remember that? I ran back to see what happened, and there was your big brother Calvin with his arm in the trap. If he'd used the sawtooth it would've bit his arm clean off. The rest of the boys were just staring down at him with their fingers up their noses, and he was screeching like a rabbit. I jumped in there and grabbed the jaws and pulled them apart. He pulled his arm out, and you could see it was broke pretty good right above the elbow. I had to take him to Superior and get a cast put on.

"But I'll tell you, on the way to the doc's, I asked Calvin what kind of shit for brains stuck his arm into a trap he had set his own self? So Calvin told me that he didn't know exactly where the trap was. None of them knew. So he thought he'd feel round under the snow and find it. Jesus, haw haw haw, can you believe it? So I asked him why didn't he take a stick and poke round till he set it off? And he says, 'Gee, Pa, that's a good idea. That's what I should've done.' I'll tell you, haw haw haw, it's a miracle that boy's lived this long. I said to him, 'You're twenty going on two.' He pouted about it until he got home and everybody wanted to make a fuss over his cast. They all wanted to sign it. He even got John Beaver to sign it one day, in between hollering and throwing snowballs at him. I swear, those boys will be the death of me some day."

Pa drank his beer off and set it down with a sigh. We looked at each other and burst out laughing so hard the others came over to see what was so funny.

"Haw haw haw! Shepard, my friend," said Pa. "You think Mamie is a wonder and a mystery, do you? Haw haw hawwww! I'll tell you, I got some boys at home – Oh, haw haw haw – some boys at home – Oh, shit, haw haw haw. Talk about a wonder, talk about a mystery – Oh, Christ, haw haw! They're the wonder of the mystery, not her. Ain't I right, Christian?"

I had to admit he was.

P*hoebe* B*umpus*

Pa left that night, and I missed him right away. But as long as John Beaver wanted to scalp me, I knew I had to sit tight where I was and make the best of things. And besides, I wasn't sure I could really leave Mamie. Days here and there it seemed like leaving her wouldn't be hard. Then other days I'd get to thinking about all we'd been through together, from thumping John Beaver's head to learning the no-rain, to settling Mike Quart's hash, to burning books; we'd learned death from Amoss, religion from Robbie, mean-spiritedness from Teddy, and wild ambition from Shepard – all of it crammed into not even a year. And then I'd think "Christian Peter, you can't leave Mamie ever in this life." And I'd know she was in my blood and brain and giving me life same as air. She was a hot spot in my soul that nothing could cool, no matter what happened.

Her getting so close to Shepard and Powers bothered me and made me restless – and made me realize how much I wanted to be the center of her attention. She spent practically all her time in the booth, scarcely knowing I was alive. And whenever I asked her if she was happy, she would say she was. And if I said I wasn't happy, she would squish me and whine in my ear, which wasn't what I wanted at all. Too much like pity. I wanted to take hot showers with her and do some no-rain.

A few days after Pa left, Shepard was ready to hold Mamie's grand debut in front of a real live audience. He had been advertising her all over the city as a miracle and a phenomenon. He had a hundred handbills made and tacked up on telephone poles and stuffed in mailboxes. The handbills said: Mamie Beaver Opening Saturday March 9 – See the Idiot Phenomenon of the Century – A Moron Quoting Shakespeare – How Does She Do It? Nobody Knows! Doctors Are Baffled! She Is Called a Miracle! Come to Don Shepard's Artlife Theater – 3 Arbor Street – Witness a Phenomenon Extraordinaire! Mamie Beaver Playing ALL the Roles from HAMLET – It Will Boggle Your Mind!

By the time of opening night, we were all pretty excited. Which was a waste of energy, because Mamie bombed. Twelve people showed up and sat through about forty minutes of Mamie's act. Then one by one and two by two, they started leaving.

"What's the big deal?" I heard one of them say.

"It's a gyp," said another.

A nice lady said it was certainly something the way Mamie could change her voice and make it sound like a man's.

"It's a gimmick," said the man beside her.

A stoop-shouldered fellow with a red face and angry eyes stopped me and said, "You sure got nerve charging a dollar for this!" I pulled a dollar from my pocket and gave it to him. "Hah!" he laughed, as he snatched it away.

So the whole thing went bust. Anna blamed it on *Hamlet*. Shepard said it was the wrong time and the wrong place – "A city of abysmal and appalling ignorance, humph!" He wondered if he shouldn't order cheaper movies and show double features and forget the books and paintings and give them what they wanted, give them Coke and candy and action films, shoot-'em-up stuff. We were all pretty glum, especially after thinking we were on the road to something big.

That night Mamie went upstairs in the booth and didn't come down even for beer and burgers at Charlie's. I didn't know if her feelings were hurt or what, but she hauled up some blankets and a pillow, and from then on she slept with Powers. All the time she was with him – night and day – except she would come down to eat, because I wasn't going to have it like the thing with the sick cow; I wasn't bringing her food, so she had to come down. And when she did, she had the graphite on her hands and face. It got worse and worse, like it was forever. When I asked her why she was changing so much, she said because she loved Powers. I felt like stomping that damn machine to death.

A couple of weeks went by with very little talking between any of us. Shepard spent most of his time at Charlie's. I mostly read and walked around town and visited Amoss's grave. And Mamie spent her time with the goddamn wheels and gears.

One day I was sitting on the porch taking in the sun. The snow had melted, except for patches here and there in shady spots, and bits of green were shooting up and tiny buds were forming on the half of the elm still alive. As I sat there with my eyes closed, I heard someone coming up the walk, and a woman's voice said to me, "Is this where I can find Don Shepard, who has the phenomenon extraordinaire?"

I shaded my eyes and saw a woman about twenty-five or so years old, not bad-looking except for ears that stuck out through her hair. She had dark eyes and nice, straight teeth smiling at me. Her mouse-brown hair hung down across her cheeks and curled under her chin. She was tall and skinny, with breasts the size of oranges pushing against her sweater, and she wore tight pants that showed her hips were bony.

"I'm Phoebe Bumpus from the *Temple Daily Star*," she said, showing me some sort of card. "Is this Don Shepard's place?"

I nodded that it was. She held out one of our advertisements for Mamie and said she had found it blowing in the wind. She thought it sounded like it might make a story.

"The show was a couple of weeks ago," I said.

"Yes, I know. Is she still here?"

"Why do you want to know?" I asked, not mean. I kept my voice friendly, but I was curious.

She looked the house over, glanced at the Artlife, and made a quick pout with her bottom lip, like she was shrugging it. "I might want to help, I don't know, stir things up round here, if this is true." She waved the handbill.

"That doesn't say the half of it," I told her. "Mamie is like nothing you've ever seen. I couldn't even begin to explain her. You'd probably think I was lying."

"Who are you?" she wanted to know.

"I'm Christian, Don Shepard's assistant in charge of tickets."

"Well, Christian, why don't you tell me about Mamie? And let me see if she sounds extraordinaire."

"Nope, Phoebe Bumpus. You've got to meet her. I don't have the right words to make you see."

"Well, I'm willing. Where is she?" She looked past me, like Mamie was in the house.

"Nope, she's not in there," I said. "About this time she comes out of the booth and goes to that bar there and gets a snootful and then goes back to the booth."

"A snootful?"

"Mamie likes her splow. She likes it like you like water."

"Oh, I see. She's a drinker." Phoebe Bumpus looked doubtful.

"Yeah, she can drink gallons of the stuff, and you'd never know it to watch her."

"Splow? Gallons? Nobody drinks gallons of splow. I think you're trying to do a number on me."

"Not me. I'm not trying to do a number."

"Sure. And how come you're not in school?" She was sizing me up. "Playing hooky?"

"I'm an orphan," I told her, trying my best to look sad about it. "I'm all alone in the world and need to earn a living. Mr. Shepard gave me a job, God bless him."

"You're really an orphan? How long've you been an orphan?" She looked at me like I was more interesting. Her voice even sounded sympathetic.

"Oh, not long," I answered. "Just a few months back my pa got shot dead."

Her hand flew to her mouth. "Oh, how awful!" she said. "And your mother's dead, too?"

"No, Ma's alive. A poor widow."

"I thought you said you were all alone in the world."

"I meant that I feel all alone in the world, here away from my mother and five little brothers."

"Five brothers? She's widowed and has five mouths to feed? That's a story in itself. Who shot your father?"

"Hunters," I said. "Never caught 'em."

"Hunters," she repeated, her tone full of disgust for the breed. "I swear I can't understand why men think they have to hunt. Every year they go out and shoot helpless animals and end up killing someone like your dad. It's just a crying shame."

"Yeah, he was shot nine times," I said.

"Oh come on!"

"Yeah, nine in the gut and chest. Practically made hamburger of poor Pa. The last words he told me was to take care of Ma and the little ones. He coughed up blood and died." Inside of me a little voice was saying, Why're you talking like this, Christian? And I didn't know. Just felt like it.

She was eyeing me close, like she wasn't sure what to make of me, but she was pretty sure the truth was getting stretched.

"It's affected my mind, I think."

"Well, I don't wonder."

I thought maybe I should add some more stuff, like telling her how the pieces of flesh flew from Pa when the bullets hit him, and how the snow turned into slashes of red. The pictures of it were crowding my mind, and I realized I was seeing Ben and the dead doe, and I was talking because I needed to see what those pictures looked like on Phoebe Bumpus's face. I wondered if I could make her cry. I wondered if I could make her like me. She had a pretty face, and I liked her for that and wanted to see her sad for me and for what I had seen in my young years, wanted her to pity me for all that pain. But before I could decide whether to keep lying or not, Anna, who had been peeking at us out her window for some time, couldn't take it anymore. She came out on the porch and yelled across the street, "Who you got dare, Cwistal?" I told her it was a reporter from the *Temple Daily Star*, come to write about the idiot phenomenon.

Anna turned round and shouted at Soren, "A witer, a witer!"

Soren yelled at her, "What do I care? Close the damn door, woman. I can't see the screen with all that light on it."

Chee Chee started barking. Soren yelled at her, "Shut up, you damn mouse!"

"You don't know fo shit!" said Anna. She took off for Charlie's place, flitting along on her little legs like a spooked quail.

"And who is that?" asked Phoebe.

I explained about Anna and Soren, that Soren had broken his back for hurry-up money and was in a wheelchair and pretty grumpy about it. And that his friend Neil had died.

Phoebe shook her head sadly. "Such tragic lives," she said.

The way she said it was so sincere I felt bad about lying to her so much.

Shepard came banging out of Charlie's, thundering up the walk with Anna right behind, taking four steps to his one. He came at Phoebe with his hand out, introducing himself three or four times before he got to her – "Don Shepard of Artlife fame, Don Shepard of Artlife fame." He was a bit unsteady, weaving some, like a man standing in a boat. Phoebe took his hand and he sneezed, blowing strands of her hair backward.

"Aghh, the sun," he said, hanging onto her hand and wiping his nose on his sleeve.

Phoebe looked over her shoulder at me, her eyes full of astonishment. I knew she'd never seen anything like him.

"Happy to accommodate the press," he said. "One minute, forgive me, sensitive olfactories. Aaa-choooo! Eeee-aaaa-chooooo! – gaaddammee for this horrid depuration of the nose." He patted his nose in sympathy, then took out his hanky and honked into it a couple of times, keeping hold of Phoebe all the while, like he was afraid she might run away. When he finally finished taking care of his noble biscuit, it looked like a purple cauliflower.

"Ahh, that should purify this envy of Arabia," he said. "Now, what can I do for the press?" He gave her hand some more shakes, like he was jerking on a bellrope. Then at last he let her go.

Phoebe immediately backed up onto the steps with me, flexing her hand and shaking the blood back into it. "I came because of this," she said, holding the handbill out.

"Ahh, my advertisement, of course. And not the least bit exaggerated, miss, miss, ah?"

"Bumpus, Phoebe Bumpus."

"Bumpus? Onomatopoeic, bump, bump – a good omen."

"I'm from the *Temple Daily Star*. You see, I read the handbill, and I thought it might make a good story, if it's all true, of course."

"All true?" said Shepard, smacking his lips and showing Phoebe his gums and fangs. "Why, she's only a walking miracle, Miss Bumpus. A story about Mamie Beaver could make you famous!"

"You newer saw sooch a stowy," said Anna, stamping her feet with excitement.

Once again Phoebe looked at me, half-scared, half-amazed. I tried to let her know with a wink that everything was okay.

Shepard was telling her that he had at his command, for her delectation, "a phenomenon extraordinaire, a phenomenon that defies all expert hypocrites and scientific quacks to explain. Mamie Beaver cannot be defined or categorized by any sense other than the great Platonic ideal of forms."

"I beg your pardon," said Phoebe. "Platonic ideal?"

"Of forms," he answered, raising his hand like he was going to swear an oath or give Phoebe a judo chop. She took hold of my arm. Shepard continued, "My Mamie is the incarnation of the universal thing in itself, the absolute, the eternal form first imagined by the mind of creation when it gave birth to the idea of woman full-blown in perfection!" His voice rose to a roar. "Earth-goddess woman!"

"Oh," said Phoebe shyly.

"She is – ub ub – what else is she, Crystal?" He was rubbing his temples to try and bring up what else Mamie was.

"Strong as a horse?" I offered.

"Immense power! Truly legendary. A female Hercules. All the noble qualities of heroism reside in her. She is, as well, she is – evolution accelerated, yum yum!"

Phoebe trembled beside me. I patted her bum to calm her down. She looked at the handbill again, holding it close to her eyes as it rattled. I stroked her bum some more, as I had done with many a heifer to sooth them. "Evolution accelerated," she said meekly. "It says here she's an idiot and a moron who quotes Shakespeare."

"And that's true too." Shepard thought a second, petting his biscuit and swaying in place, like his shoes were nailed down but the rest of him wanted to get going. And he said, "Judged by our common standards, we could call her a moron or an idiot; yes, no denying. But we might say the same of a Martian were we unable to comprehend his level. Mamie is like that. On an ordinary level, few but geniuses like myself can absorb what she is – evolution accelerated. Does she contradict herself? Of course she contradicts herself! She contains multitudes! It is her cross to bear that she must lower herself to communicate with us in the idiom of Shakespeare, or Shaw, or a sweaty snot like Tennessee Williams, humph!"

"Lower herself to Shakespeare?" Phoebe laughed suddenly, and at the same time pushed my hand off her bum. "I'm sorry," she said. "Forgive my laughing, but this is such startling information, I feel a little giddy. Hard to take it all in at once, you know? It's – hee hee hee – oh, excuse me. Hee hee, I think I'm getting hysterical. Oh no, heee heee heee – haw haw haw! . . . Stop it now, Phoebe. So unprofessional. Ah, shit, haw haw haw haw!"

Phoebe's laugh was catching. Shepard, Anna, and I joined her, which made it harder for her to stop. "Lower herself to Shakespeare – idiot phenomenon – moron! Shit! Haw haw haw! I'm gonna choke! I'm gonna wet my pants!"

Anna was doing a little dance. Shepard had his hands on his knees and was bellowing like a happy cow. Phoebe's legs were as wobbly as noodles. She plunked herself down on the step, pointed at Shepard, who looked like something out of a cartoon, and she roared some more. Finally she put her hands over her ears and lowered her head so she couldn't see him, and after a little bit she settled down and so did we.

"Oh," she said, "I can't tell you how embarrassed I am. So sorry, but oh, haw haw! Stop it now, Phoebe! I don't know what's come over me. I haven't been drinking, honest. It was just what you said! Well, it's not just what you said, but the way you looked saying it, so serious but so funny. Your little teeth sticking out, pink gums, that nose, hee hee. And this kid with his hand feeling up my ass. Haw haw! Ooops, there I go again. Where am I? Did I fall down a rabbit hole? I'm sorry. I don't mean to insult you. I'm sure that you're all normal, and you, Mr. Shepard, are an intelligent man. But oh gee, I can't explain it. I'm just getting myself in deeper. Please forgive me, so unprofessional." Phoebe sighed and covered her eyes with her hand.

"I am a genius," said Shepard carefully, like he didn't want to set her off again. "And I understand the ironic humor implicit in Mamie's situation. I laugh about it myself, so don't feel badly, Miss Bumpus. A lesser man than I might take offense, but never one who sees the comic levels of all life's caprices, such as I."

"You are very nice," said Phoebe. "In fact, there's something rather refreshing about you. I'm glad I came. When can I meet your phenomenon?" She straightened herself up, ready to go.

Shepard's cheeks trembled with excitement. "Yes, you must meet Mamie. She's with Powers in the booth. Will you come?" He swept his hand in the direction of the Artlife.

So we all tromped over there and up the stairs to the booth, where Mamie was with Powers, standing in front of him like she was shielding him from us. She had eyes especially for Phoebe, watching hard and listening hard to her.

The first thing Phoebe asked after they were introduced was why Mamie had gray lips and streaks of gray stuff on her cheeks. "It looks like grease," she said.

"That's graphite," I told her. "Mamie kisses Powers."

"Of course she does," said Phoebe. She looked at each of us. "It fits."

I tried my best to explain that Mamie thought of Powers as her teacher, that she could never learn so much from any of us but that from Powers it stuck to her like honey in her hair.

"It's her brain chemistry," said Shepard, like it was that simple.

Phoebe said to Mamie, "Does Powers kiss you back?"

"He luffs me so," she answered.

"Oh dear, she does sound like an idiot," said Phoebe quietly.

"She's a genius," Shepard replied. "Often difficult to recognize the species, when filtered through the plebeian mind. I myself have been a genius since birth and have had to struggle to make others understand me."

"I can see that," she said. "I'm very sorry."

"No apology needed. The mundane mind is something I'm used to. It has never been able to appreciate me. Mamie knows what I'm saying. We have great deformability of the brain. Which is a perfect definition of genius, believe me, if you will. We have vision."

Phoebe sounded sincere when she told him, "Actually, I think I do believe you." She looked Mamie over carefully. "She makes me think of a golden bear, a sweet Goldilocks-type of bear."

"I know what you mean," I said. "She's all kinds of things, a golden bear and a golden horse and a golden ox and sometimes just a golden girl."

"Like a fable," said Phoebe. "Like a fairy tale. Look at her face –

pure as summer sky, eyes like sapphires, a mouth sort of like a frog's, except she's got lips. And she's got freckles too, little tomboy freckles. Look at her hair, it's like . . . like . . ."

"Like tiny flames," I offered.

"Yes, like that, the curls licking up like that." Phoebe studied Mamie more, studied and studied. Then she said, "I can see why you might love her. Where on earth did you find her?"

Shepard looked at me behind Phoebe's back and put his finger to his lips. "She is a mystery, pure and simple," he told Phoebe.

"A mystery?"

"She appeared one day out of another dimension, in a blaze of light emerging from a crack in the universe."

"And she rode me on her back," I put in. "Rode me up and down the street. Then she followed me home like a stray dog."

"An immaculate inception from the crack of time," said Shepard, rolling his eyes like a pious preacher.

"A gift fwum Gott," said Anna.

And Phoebe said, "Whatever you say. But you may be onto something as extraordinaire as this handbill says. She does have an aura like a movie star."

"Hers is natural," I said.

"Uh-huh," Phoebe answered, biting her lip, her eyes narrowing in on Mamie, concentrating on her hard. "Has she really been examined?"

"Yes, a doctor came here and examined her from head to toe," I said. "Said she was healthy as a horse."

"Who was he? Where from?"

"Doctor Jacob from Superior."

"Came all this way?"

"I called him in," said Shepard, giving me a shut-up look. "He's a specialist."

"I see," she said, biting her lower lip again and giving us the see-through eye, like speculating whether she should believe us or not. "And Doctor Jacob was baffled, you say? What baffled him, exactly?"

Shepard turned his attention to Mamie. "Now, Mamie. 'There is something in this more than natural, if philosophy could find it out.'"

Mamie answered with a change to Hamlet's voice, "'I am but mad north-northwest. When the wind is southerly, I know a hawk from a handsaw.'"

"Amazing!" Phoebe cried. "How did she do that?"

"Precisely what the doctor asked," said Shepard, raising his eyebrows at Phoebe. "And that is a mere nibble of what she can do."

"Well, I'm impressed! She gave me goose bumps," said Phoebe. "My dear, you are very, very talented."

"Then you see what we have here?" asked Shepard. "You appreciate that this genetic aberration must not go unrequited, yum yum?"

"Everybody round here thinks she's a gyp and a faker," I said.

"Dey tink she fool dem," said Anna.

"Fake? How do you fake that? That was Laurence Olivier's voice. How do you fake that? Fake, my eye. Let me hear more. Say something else, Mamie."

"Ahem, Miss Bumpus. She cannot do it without me," said Shepard. "I exhumed her talent. I disinterred it from the traumatized regions of her abused soul, yum yum. Without Don Shepard, she produces no evidence of thespianism."

"Make her do Hamlet again, please."

So Shepard got her going, and Mamie did some big chunks from *Hamlet*, line after line rolling out like thunder. And all the while, Phoebe stared and stared and shivered. When it was over, she told us, "God, I'm goose bumps from head to toe. This really is a story. I mean a *story*. I want to see more. I want to learn everything about her. No detail is too small. Show me her whole act, Mr. Shepard."

So we did the whole thing. We got Mamie into her robe, and we put Powers's light on her as she stood on the stage with Shepard in the shadows. Shakespeare, Shaw, all those writers she knew came tripping out of her mouth in the voices she had learned. Phoebe was crazy for it and wild about Mamie. She said she was going to stand this town on its ear, going to wake up all these clods and teach them the possibilities of the human spirit, make them see the complexities of the brain – Mamie's brain that had such power to recreate what it saw and heard. Shepard yum-yummed everything Phoebe said. I'd never seen him so happy. By the end of the performance, he was sobbing into his hanky.

"My goodness, he's such an emotional man," said Phoebe.

"He says he's very sensitive," I answered.

After Shepard had pulled himself together, we went over to the house to have a drink and celebrate. Shepard laid out beer with splow chasers, and we all toasted Phoebe Bumpus, who was going to bring the power of the pen to bear and create the legend of Mamie. Shepard had to cry a bit more over it.

"What *is* wrong with that man?" Phoebe whispered to me.

"Don't mind me," he told her. "It is my, ub ub, my curse to have the soul of a poet. I was thinking now how hard I've struggled and how my dear old friend Amoss struggled with me. He's gone and cannot enjoy the triumph – ooooh boo-hoo-hoo, cruel fate. Please don't make fun of me. It is that all my feelings are at my fingertips; my heart is on my sleeve. It is a mixed blessing, for it is what fires my genius and makes me want to, ub ub ub, blaze like a comet, bringing the light of knowledge to all the wanton ignorance I see, ignorance looking through a glass darkly, yum yum. And yet I know I sometimes look like a fool. Mixed blessing, genius."

He looked at Mamie above the hanky he held, and suddenly he said, "Mamie, will you marry me?"

She snorted and made a "Phoo" sound, and told him "Nup nup nup."

That brought another flood of tears. It seemed like he was having a pretty good time. I think we enjoyed it as much.

The five of us spent the day together, drinking and talking, mostly talking about how dense everybody was in Temple. We learned that Phoebe was a college graduate from some little college in Minnesota and that this was her first job on her own away from home. She had been a copyeditor at first but now they were letting her be a reporter, and if she did good, they would make it permanent. She was only twenty-three, and she wasn't married and never wanted to be some damn man's slave.

The more she drank, the more friendly she got. She wanted us to know she really liked us, that it usually took her a while to warm up to people but we took her in right away. We were different and she liked the difference. She hoped we liked her. Of course, we said we did. We'd have given her anything she wanted right then, given her the house, if she wanted. She was a wonderful, big-hearted girl who appreciated Mamie's talent as much as any of us. And she got more wonderful as the day wore on. By the time night came, I was sure I was in love with her.

We ate a bunch of hot dogs and had potato chips and pickles with pork rinds, all of it washed down with beer and splow. And by the time it got good and dark, we were good and drunk, hadn't ever felt better. We played the radio and sang the songs that came on, whether we knew the words or not, sang into each other's faces, sang solos and duets – some sounded so beautiful they made us cry. Anna seemed to get more and more lovey as the songs came and went. She put herself on Shepard's lap and sang to him, kissing his nose in between breaths.

She told him if it wasn't for Soren she would let him look up her dress. Shepard blinked slowly and smiled like a Cheshire cat. He had a look in his eyes like he thought he was Don Juan. After a time, I saw his hand petting Anna's ankle. Next thing it was lost up inside her skirt, petting something that made her squirm and sigh.

Then Mamie got to feeling no-rainy and plucked me off my chair, where I had been leaning close to Phoebe, trying to tell her how much I loved her teeth and that I didn't care a sot how her ears stuck out. Mamie took me away and plopped me on her lap and crooned mystery words in my ear, like Anna was doing to Shepard. Pretty Phoebe came over and kissed me on the mouth, a big wet kiss. She kept saying how much she wished I was older. Her eyes were bloodshot; her voice was steamy. Now and then I'd catch sight of her running her hand over her little oranges and looking at what Shepard and Anna were doing. Shepard asked her how long she thought it would be before the story came out. Phoebe looked at him sourly, like she didn't want to talk about it just then. Mamie was kissing on me, and Phoebe started pinching my legs, saying, "Tut-tut, did I hurt the little boy? Did I hurt him? Did I? Tell me, little boy, are you little?" I hardly felt the pinches. I wanted to tell her it was okay, but about all I could manage was a grin.

"Roll Out The Barrel" came on the radio and Mamie wanted to dance. She dumped me on the floor and started kicking up her legs. Anna jumped up and joined her. The two of them hooted and crashed across the room. The rest of us joined in the hoots, calling out for the cows to come home. After that a waltz came on, and Phoebe pulled me to my feet and danced me in a circle. Anna grabbed Shepard and waltzed with him. She looked strange, so tiny a thing holding on to him, trying to see his face over his belly. Finally, he lifted her up and locked his hands under her bottom while she straddled him and they shuffled along.

Sitting back with a jar of splow, Mamie was eyeing me and Phoebe. We were hardly dancing at all, just rocking in place, and Phoebe kept kissing me and sticking her tongue in my ear. Mamie saw it, and she cocked her head to one side and watched. Another time and sober, I suppose I would have been embarrassed, but I felt a sort of grudge against Mamie right then, at the way she had cut me off and given herself all to Powers. Serves you right, I said inside my head. I kissed Phoebe back and tried to kiss her neck, but her sweater got in the way. A couple times I tried to push it down a bit with my chin, but it didn't work. Then finally she stepped back, pulled it over her head, and unhooked her brassiere. Tossing it after the sweater, she pulled me up tight against her, locking her lips on mine. Amazing what splow will do to a woman's conscience.

She wouldn't let me go, and it wasn't that I didn't want to do what she wanted to do, but I wasn't feeling good all of a sudden. The pork rinds and hot dogs were doing things to my belly. I was feeling hot and queasy and thinking about Amoss. And damn Phoebe kept wanting me to kiss down her neck. Which I did, but the churning inside kept me from enjoying it. I remembered Amoss threw up blood. When Phoebe pushed my head down far enough that my lips touched one of her nipples, I knew I couldn't stand it. I broke away and ran to the toilet, wrapped myself around it, and heaved. Afterward I rested my cheek on the cool bowl, feeling what a miserable excuse for a man I was. Phoebe came in and caught me by the hair, lifting my head back so I had to look up at her.

"I want you," she said, her voice husky. Her hair whipped my face. I could see her ears sticking out like moth wings.

"I want you too, baby," I said. My head was swimming in her hand. I couldn't hold it still. She let go of my hair and my head rolled back into the toilet. It seemed like there was nothing I could do about it, and there was nothing I could do about her.

Some time during the night, I woke beside the toilet and heard snoring in the living room. I got up and staggered out to find Mamie gone and Phoebe asleep on the couch. Shepard sat in the big chair, head thrown back, mouth as wide as it would go, and snoring loud enough to rattle the windows. To my right I saw Anna sprawled out on Shepard's bed, her feet hanging over the edge, her skirt pulled up hiding her head, pink underpants showing. I turned back and washed my face under the faucet, took a big drink, and hawked all the crud out of my throat. My mind was focusing in on Phoebe, how slim her arms, how small and cute her oranges were, how her tongue felt pushing inside my ear. I was wishing I hadn't spoiled it by drinking so much. I told myself to go tell her how sorry I was. So I did. I went to the couch and ran my hand over her hair and gave her a kiss on the neck.

"Phoebe, Phoebe, wake up, honey," I said to her.

She turned her head and looked at me through angry, half-opened eyes. "Touch me and I'll punch your lights out," she snarled.

I climbed into my bed and got under the covers. I thought to myself that it was all Mamie's fault what happened. If she had stayed with me instead of switching to Powers, I wouldn't have made a fool of myself for Phoebe. Mamie wouldn't have cared if I got drunk and threw up, but Phoebe would probably never forgive me. I felt miserable, felt like an idiot, a real stinker, lonely and stupid.

Speaking in Tongues

A few days later, Phoebe Bumpus's story was on the Entertainment and Life page of the paper:

Idiot or genius – you decide

Don Shepard said he had a Phenomenon Extraordinaire waiting for us at the Artlife Theatre. And you know what? He wasn't lying. The phenomenon is a girl named Mamie Beaver. Remember that name, Mamie Beaver. She is an uncannily talented young lady, eighteen to twenty years old (she doesn't really know her age) who I predict will be famous some day.

What is so exciting about Miss Beaver? I'll tell you. She has an unexplainable ability to memorize lines of spoken script, script from films she has seen, and not only to memorize them perfectly, but to mimic just as perfectly the voice of the actor or actress who spoke those lines. It is not just a talent I am talking about. It is a phenomenon bordering on the supernatural.

I sat dumbfounded while I watched her play role after role from certain movies that have been shown at the Artlife. First she was Hamlet, then she was Horatio, then Ophelia, the king, the queen, the garrulous Polonius; and she was Major Barbara from Shaw's play; she was Blanche Dubois from *A Streetcar Named Desire* by Tennessee Williams. She was even Stanley Kowalski yelling "Stella! Stella!" And she was Stella. She opened her mouth and out they came. Voices not her own, but her own. Words she could never dream of saying, let alone words that she could understand – not this bumpkin girl who showed up from a crack in space and was classified by Dr. Jacob of Superior as having the brain of a five-year-old. And yet he is wrong, I think. I doubt anyone can say exactly where she fits in the intellectual scheme of things. But the brain of a five-year-old? It can't be. So how do I explain it? I don't. Except to repeat what Don Shepard said by way of explanation: "Chemistry. It is all brain chemistry."

Please understand this. Mamie Beaver cannot even hold a normal conversation with you. She stutters and stammers so badly that she must keep her sentences extremely short. She cannot read or write, not a word! She knows no mathematics, not even that two and two are four. Time and again she has been called an idiot, but not by those who know her. Perhaps you think I have been taken in by a trick. I assure you I have not. Mamie Beaver is just what the advertisement says she is: a Phenomenon Extraordinaire. Onstage all her defects disappear. The depthless blue of her eyes becomes filled with understanding and intelligence, the bulky awkwardness of her body (she must be six foot three and over two hundred pounds) evaporates like mist in the sun. And there you have her – a compelling and graceful figure, flowing with the changeability of a human chameleon.

Can this be genius like Don Shepard says? What else can it be? Unless you want to believe in the supernatural and that some holy spirit has descended upon her. Both sides, I am sure, will have their advocates. But for me the only question is, can genius reside side by side in the mind of a moron? an idiot? Well, perhaps to our limited senses and understanding, she seems to be a moron or an idiot. Seems, I say, but only seems. Maybe we see her as such because we, you and I, are the brain-damaged ones. Don Shepard says she is Evolution Accelerated. If he is right, then our opinions of her have to be wrong. So perhaps she is the future, a goddess of a thousand years from now, when all mankind will be interchameleon. Anyone out there working on a doctorate in psychology might want to study the wonder of Mamie Beaver and tell us if she is from some future time warp, a crack in space, another dimension, or just out of whack. Tis a mystery.

In the meantime, readers, treat yourself to a performance that will leave you filled with a baffling admiration for what can only be called, for lack of something more precise, a chromatic aberration of great art – a change in the position of a flaming heavenly body.

Go see Mamie Beaver. You won't regret it. Now playing at Don Shepard's Artlife Theatre. Call for show times.

Phoebe Bumpus was almost right about her story making Mamie famous – almost. For a few days she was famous in Temple. People came and paid a dollar to see her. They filled the Artlife. They even bought books and a painting or two. They bought popcorn and drank apple juice, and they didn't complain that we didn't have Coke and candy bars. No one said a thing about double features or war movies or cowboys and Indians. The people came, they sat, they watched, and they clapped politely when the show was over. And when they left, you could hear them talking to one another about what a phenomenon they had seen and repeating some of Phoebe's best phrases: "Her big body does just evaporate like mist in the sun." "Oh, yes, and isn't she compelling and graceful?" "It borders on the supernatural, that's what I'm saying." "Dumbfounded. I'm just dumbfounded." Stuff like that. Some came back for another performance, letting their friends know that they had seen Mamie twice or three times, and wasn't she just too amazing for words?

So at first we all thought we were right there on the edge of something big. Shepard couldn't have been happier, nor could Anna or Phoebe. Phoebe came by all the time to see how big the crowds were. She kept predicting that Mamie would get such a following that we would have to get a bigger theater. And we might even need a press agent name of Phoebe Bumpus, yeah. Get ready, she said, because when things got hot, we would have to move fast. We were ready for the hot things. We waited for the signs of the big time on our doorstep: newsmen from Milwaukee, television reporters, major magazines hounding us, Hollywood, New York calling, Ed Sullivan. We waited. And we waited.

And sure enough, none of it happened. In fact, the crowds began to thin out again, and within about three weeks we were damn near where we had started – not quite as bad, but close. And when the crowds dropped off, Phoebe almost had a fit. She cursed the fate that had planted her in such a backward town as Temple. She even wrote another article about Mamie, telling the people that they were too ignorant to know what was in their midst. But she said the paper wouldn't publish it. She got demoted back to copyeditor. When she told us that, she cried and asked us to forgive her for leading us on into thinking she had the power of the pen, the power to make silk purses out of sows' ears. She promised us that she would find a way yet to make Mamie famous, even if she had to write a book about her to do it. She went away that day vowing she would never give it up.

The roller coaster ride we were on finally leveled off after a few weeks. We were into spring, April almost over, and the balance in the weather seemed to be like the balance in the Artlife. Every Saturday came a group of people, about fifty of them – men, women, and children. A lot of them I recognized from the book-burning, the old followers of Robbie. They gave their attention to Mamie all the while she did her act, and they would smack their kids if they got bored and acted up. They would tell the kids to sit still and see the sign of God's Holy Spirit and be grateful for the witness. More and more they would get caught up in her act, and a man here or a woman there would shout out something like, "Yes, Lord!" "I hear you!" "I hear Jeee-sus talking!" That kind of thing. It really got Mamie going, really made those words roll off her tongue, so hard that Shepard sometimes lost his place and couldn't keep up. But that worked too, after a while, because the people were starting to memorize the words themselves, and so if Shepard lost his place, someone in the audience would shout out the next line. As the Saturdays wore on, the people began to drown him out altogether, just taking over his whole role, making it them and Mamie. She liked it, and he got mad about it, purple-ear mad. But the people didn't care, and there wasn't much he could do about it. It was their dollars that kept the whole thing going.

And once they had it all their way, the people got selective about what they wanted to hear. They would call out those lines that would bring the right words from Mamie. She went crazy for it. She would run back and forth across the stage and point to one section or another, and the people in that section would shout out a line like:

"'Thou know'st 'tis common – all that lives must die, passing through nature to eternity.'"

And she would answer, "'Aye, madam, it is common.'"

They liked those lines a lot.

Another set they liked to share with Mamie was Hamlet talking about suicide. The people would take a line of it, then Mamie would take a line of it:

"'Or that the Everlasting had not fixed.'"

"'His canon 'gainst self-slaughter! Oh, God! God!'"

"'How weary, stale, flat, and unprofitable.'"

"'Seem to me all the uses of this world.'"

This set would end for sure with a bunch of them yelling, "Yes, Jeee-sus! Hear him now! Hear the words of the Lord!" Plenty of loud hallelujahs would get mixed in too.

And so it went, from one play to the next, characters bubbling out of Mamie's mouth like a river over its banks and flooding over the people, so that they swam all together in a kind of waters of inspiration, their voices rising like a heavenly chorus, a holy echo that bounced off the walls, back and forth, from Mamie to them. Words floated everywhere. I had never seen people so alive and on fire as Mamie's followers. I had never seen her so fired up before either, not even when we did the no-rain or played drowning man. This was different. This stage-thing with the people below and her above just made the sparks fly. The people had the glow of a hunter's moon, and Mamie burned like a little sun. Who could help getting caught up in that?

That's how it went every Saturday. The same people came and the same kind of ritual took place. And it got more and more perfect.

April went away. May came and made things even warmer. Trees, grass, flowers, and bushes – warm colors, best time of the year – warm enough to start planting a crop but still cool enough to keep the flies down. It seemed like with the warmth came a growth in the number of Mamie-followers. The fifty became eighty; the eighty became a hundred. It got so we could count on the Artlife being full for both Saturday and Sunday. During the rest of the week, we showed movies, the kind that other people wanted – John Wayne stuff. And we had a fair business, all right. We were making money, more money by a long shot than when Shepard had stuck to his ideas about what art was.

He had done some soul-searching, he said, and had come to conclusions about what went wrong. "I gave them too much credit," he said. "I forgot that no man of the common ilk will care to use his brain, if he can contrive any way at all to let it rest. This leads to a phenomenon of the worst kind, where men who have a rage to say something profound have nothing in their heads. They have nothing to say. And so they fall back on old platitudes and clichés, spouting meaningless religious dribble to make themselves feel important. Humph! The people despise all intellectual labor. It hurts them sorely to think. And even if thinking were easy, they would be content to be ignorant rather than trouble their minds with thought. But my brilliance will prevail! I have a plan! I will create the First Church of Art! These Christers wish to pull art down to themselves. They cannot bear the mental effort of rising up to art. So be it. I will give them art as simply as the church gives them the dogmas by which they wander thoughtlessly through life. If that's how it must be, then why not learn a litany from the great writers of the ages rather than from some tired old tome like the Bible? It is what they are doing already, and we shall encourage it. We shall keep it up. And slowly but surely, the people will be given more and more. They are naturally dull, but it will soak into them, inculcate them to the core at last. And the day will come when they will cry out not 'Praise Jesus,' or 'Hear the words of the Lord' but 'Praise Shakespeare, praise Shaw, praise Herman Melville!' Melville is next. I have the movie *Moby Dick*, and Mamie is learning it. She shall add it slowly to the litany. How crafty I am. How stupid the people who thought they could push me aside. Before they know it, they will be worshipers of art! Their minds will turn against the inspissated gloom of Christ, yum yum.

"And I will find my destiny in this as the founder of the First Church of Art. Noble Donald Samuel Shepard, who took men away from worshiping the irrational blood of Christ and gave them the *anima mundi* of art, the great collective memory of the world 'to sing / To lords and ladies of Byzantium / Of what is past, or passing, or to come'! All was chaos and mob superstition till Shepard came and set the world right. I will show them that man himself makes miracles of art, 'Monuments of unaging intellect.' So bless my memory with a tabernacle. This scheme came to me in the night and told me I shall be raised to stupendous heights!"

After telling me how he had it all figured out, he changed the act just a bit. I didn't take a dollar at the door anymore. Instead, between the time Mamie had finished with *Hamlet* and was getting ready to do *Moby Dick*, I passed a collection plate, just like in church. And the people filled it up.

Everything but *Hamlet* and *Moby Dick* was dropped from Mamie's sermon, and Shepard formed it just the way he wanted it. Like when he had her do Melville, he slipped it in so smooth the people hardly noticed a change of beat. "Call me Ishmael," he prompted, and Mamie gave the speech about deep November in the soul. The speech had the same melancholy-Hamlet woe in it, and the congregation leaned forward to listen in a sort of rapture, and when it was over they gave Ishmael a soft amen. From then on *Moby Dick* was part of the litany, and in no time at all the followers were alternating lines with Mamie.

Shepard also got more of a part, because he held Mamie back each service until after he made a speech. He would come out into the light and say, like a preacher or a prophet: "Behold a miracle of our time. Behold the art of Mamie Beaver. Behold the incarnation of the Supreme Creator's beneficence and pleasure, for she is an idiot whom he has made to speak in tongues. Let this be a sign to those who believe, 'they will speak in new tongues.' Behold, little people in search of holiness, Mamie speaks in the tongues of the greatest artists of all time. It is the pleasure of the Great Creator to give us the zenith of art from the lips of a moron. Through her we have received a litany which combines the best of his message for the indoctrination of all mankind; yea, even to those poor players strutting and fretting for an hour upon the stage. From here the word will go forth that the *anima mundi* has given us the First Church of Art. And now I give you the symbol and the crown, the witness and the prophet – Mamie Beaver!"

And out she would come. The followers would go crazy, screaming and crying and praising. And when the show was over, they didn't ever want to leave. They would stand up, holding hands and singing out, "Oh ye damned whale! Oh, ye damned whale" over and over, while it echoed back to them off the ceiling and made a wave of words in which the people seemed to swim in an ecstasy. And there was Shepard in the middle of it, standing onstage next to Mamie, holding his hands out over the crowd like a pope giving a blessing.

It wasn't long till so many people were coming that we had to go to two services on Saturday and two more on Sunday. The people stood in the aisles, and the collection plates overflowed. And I lived for the weekends, for Saturday and Sunday and all the excitement of the services, all the money pouring in, all the happy people taking part in the loving. It was the best time of my life.

Old Scores

From Monday to Friday, things were pretty dull. We would show whatever movie we had, and a few people might come, and we might break even three nights out of five. But it didn't really matter, because we had plenty of money to spend.

Then one night, we had a movie nobody came to see called *Battleground*, so Shepard closed up and we went for beer and hamburgers at Charlie's. There were two guys there I recognized from Amoss's funeral, the friends of his named Cody and Jim, who were men of the trains. Except they had been laid off. They were playing pool when we came in. Neither one acted like they remembered us. They both looked grumpy. The man named Cody was short and thick, with sloping shoulders and heavy arms. He had a fat face and a scruffy beard and deep-set eyes. A cigar was stuck in his mouth, which kept bobbing up and down as he chewed it. He kept whispering something to Jim and jerking his thumb in our direction. Jim had to bend down to hear because he was a foot taller than Cody. He looked like an egret with its long neck and tiny head always dipping toward the ground. Cody liked to tap his finger on Jim's chest while he talked. Jim kept slapping the finger away and bending down to listen.

A lot of mumbling went on between them, and a lot of glancing over and eyeing Mamie and sniggering about her. Out loud Cody would say, "Thorn's scorn," and both of them would snicker about whatever it meant. We kept to ourselves, but it was hard not to notice how disrespectful they were acting toward Mamie.

Anna Gulbrenson interrupted whatever was going to happen with Cody and Jim. She came in huffing and puffing about Soren, saying she finally did it, finally broke his television. She ordered up a shot of splow to celebrate, but Charlie was out – said he had ordered a case and it should be coming in pretty quick. So Anna sat with us and had beer and a hamburger.

"I bweak dat gottdamn telewision," she told us for the fifth time. "I smash it goot. He don't vatch no mo. I tell to him he is not a hoosband to me and I sick of it. He a big baby! Cwy like a baby feeling sowwy fo itself. He says, 'Dey bweak my back and tell me to go die now. I not goot for nutting.' He say dat all da time. I sick of it! I vant a man! I bweak da telewision and tell to him he don't luf Anna and so he can go to hell!" At that, she started bawling, grabbed her skirt and sobbed into it.

When it was over she said, "Bah, he vas sooch a stwong man one time. All gone, all gone. Vhut he seeing now is a ghost of Neil, dat fwiend vhut died. Ghost coming ewery night vhen he sleep, so he don't sleep. He vatch telewision! So sick of him!" She hooked an uppercut fist in the air and made a noise in her throat like she was spitting Soren out.

Anna drank her beer while we sat with her, staring at her like lumps on a log. Even Shepard had trouble finding something to say, but finally he came up with a subject.

"Anna, darling," he said, leaning over and taking her hand. "I have some tremendous news you must hear. In fact, you all must hear this. You know how we are growing at the Artlife. We are bulging at the seams, so to speak, and funds are pouring in at a precipitous rate, yum yum. Such affairs should not vex us, I think. Indeed, as I have observed before, an idea whose time has come is more powerful than any whim of the body to resist it; the idea devours, absorbs and destroys all degenerate opposition." He snatched his hand back from Anna and motioned us to lean in closer. In a quiet voice he said, "My First Church of Art has the potential of being a tyranny, tee hee, more tyrannous and absolute than any Christer church that ever was. Once the worship of art takes hold of our little Temple here, it will explode across the state, then the nation, then the world – proselytizing in the name of the greatest achievements of mankind, yum yum, tee hee. Once such an idea takes hold it will dominate the mental life of every thinking being. Yes it will! And listen – it will save us from the destructive lust for damnation feeding the fires of Christendom, yum yum yum. And now we teeter at the cusp of infinite expansion."

Leaning even closer, till his nose looked like the craters of the moon and his dogteeth the fangs of a vampire, he said, "Heh heh heh, guess who's going to preside over the construction of a New Artlife, a greater more capacious edifice to the religion of art. Humm? *Moi*! Yours truly. The Shepard himself. I've been negotiating in private with several members of the church, and together with the filthy rich Cunninghams backing us, we have purchased the five acres of woods next door. Construction begins in two weeks. What do you think of your Shepard now?" He sat back and looked us over, blinking slowly, like a cat about to start purring.

"Vee get wich as sin," said Anna.

"For the cause," said Shepard. "All is for the cause."

"Do you think I'll make enough money to buy a new Chevy from the Cunninghams?" I asked. I was thinking again about how great it would be to drive home in a brand new pickup. Christian went away a dumb little kid and came back a big shot.

"Chevy, my eye," said Shepard. "We're going to purchase a fleet of Cadillacs, my boy. Long black ones with whitewall tires."

Anna got up and pushed herself into Shepard's lap. She petted his nose and kissed his chin. She said if he played his cards right, she would get rid of Soren and marry him. She said Soren used to be a hell of a man, but now he wasn't, so Shepard could have her if he wanted. He cuddled her like a little stuffed toy and told her she brought out the beast in him.

I saw they were going to spend some time playing with each other, so I got up and went outside. I was curious about what Soren was doing, since he had no TV to watch and he was all by himself except for Chee Chee. I went over there and looked in the window, and I could see him sitting in front of the TV, staring at a black hole, all jagged at the edges. He looked pretty beat. While I stood there, Mamie came over and looked in the window for a minute. Then she went inside, so I followed her in. There was a smell like a piece of burnt hose in the room. Soren didn't look up but just stared at the hole. Chee Chee came out of a back room, her tail wagging. When she saw it wasn't Anna, she bopped around and yapped at us, then came over to give us each a good sniff.

"Sure a mess," I said to Soren about the television.

"Anna did it," he said softly.

"She's over to Charlie Friendly's," I said.

"It's good for her. Let her stay. She's right, I'm not the kind of man for her anymore. She needs somebody that cares."

I didn't know what to say. I thought about telling him what she and Shepard had been doing, but I didn't want to add to his troubles. If it were me, though, I thought I'd probably want to know, not want to look like a big dope to everyone.

After a few seconds, he said, "I've been seeing my friend's ghost, Christian, my buddy Neil. If I sleep, he comes and talks to me."

"What does he say?"

"He says he's cold and he hates it. They buried him in a green coffin, and he never wanted that. He wanted to be cremated. That's what I want too. We talked about it once, and he said he couldn't stand the idea of being put in a box and stuffed into the cold ground and left down there in the dark forever and ever. That just gave him the willies. He wanted to be cremated."

"Well, then he should've been, I guess. Who put him in the ground that way? Didn't they know?"

Soren gave a hard little laugh and looked at me for the first time. "Yeah, he should've been," he said. "You're right. But right has nothing to do with ritual. His family buried him the way they thought he should be buried, with a priest doing mumbo-jumbo things over the coffin. What did Neil know about the right rituals to get him into heaven? The family knew. They took care of him."

"But now he's cold and hates it, you said."

He smiled at me, just a little smile, like he was sorry for me. "It's just a dream," he said. "What's in a dream?"

Right at that minute I didn't know why, but I sure liked him.

Mamie had bent down and was petting Chee Chee and listening to us. She looked at me and said, "Kritch'n. Anna st-st-stuuu-pid, yaay?"

Real quick I compared Shepard and Soren. Anna was too tiny for one and too sexy for the other and too old to be such a flirt, but I didn't know if that made her stupid. I asked Mamie, "What do you mean, she's stupid?"

Then Mamie looked at me like I was stupid. It was a surprise to see her looking at me that way, like a whole lot of thought was going on in her head. She stood up and said, "Oh, Kritch'n." And her voice had exasperation in it. It was her voice too, not one of the roles she played.

"Well, excuse me for living," I said.

She shrugged me aside, took hold of Soren's wheelchair from behind by the wheels, and lifted him up and headed out the door with him, with Chee Chee behind, yapping her little head off.

"What you doing?" Soren asked. "Where you going? Put me down, Mamie. Goddammit now, put me down!"

But she wouldn't put him down. She snaked him out the door and right down the ramp. He was cussing, and Chee Chee was taking nips at Mamie's pantlegs. Soren yelled at Chee Chee to sic Mamie. Chee Chee clamped down on her pants and hung on and growled, which made Mamie laugh. She dragged the dog along, skittering her across the pavement, and all the while Chee Chee was acting like she could tear Mamie to pieces. Even Soren couldn't help but laugh a bit, in between cuss words.

"That's my little wolf," he said, looking over the edge of his wheelchair at her. "Kill her, Chee Chee!"

She hung on all the way to Charlie's, until I opened the door and we went in. When Chee Chee saw Anna back in her own chair across from Shepard, she gave a yelp and jumped up on Anna's lap.

"Vhut you do to my Chee Chee?" said Anna. "My poor baby-vun. Kiss Mama." The dog squirmed and licked Anna's face, while Anna looked past her to Soren, looked at him like he had done something bad. Mamie set him down next to Anna, close, but he turned his wheelchair sideways to her and looked away.

Shepard told us that while we were gone Cody and Jim had challenged him to a game of pool. He had been waiting for Mamie to come back and be his partner. The four of them got pool cues and chalked them up. Cody was saying he was Kiss-of-Death Cody and he never showed mercy.

"You're just Cody to me," said Shepard, looking down at Cody, who was nearly half Shepard's size.

"I'm the kiss of death, quick as a rattlesnake. My stick is poison," he answered back, chewing his cigar like it was a piece of Shepard.

And Jim got in on it, saying, "And I'm the mongoose. Call me Mongoose Jim, cause I'm quick as a rattlesnake. No, I'm quicker, by god."

"My ass," said Cody. "I'm the only quick-as-a-snake round here."

"I'm the mongoose. Mongooses are quicker'n snakes, and everybody knows it, Cody. I saw a picture in a book once, a mongoose killing a cobra. It was neat."

"You're no goddamn mongoose, Jim. You get any slower, you'll be backing into yesterday."

"Ah, bullshit."

While they fought about it, Mamie racked the balls and ran the table. When Kiss of Death and Mongoose caught on to what she had done, they punched each other.

"Pay attention to the game," said Cody.

It went on for a while, with the guys just watching. Mamie hit fifty in the pocket without a miss, and Cody got really steamed. He chewed his cigar to a nub and rubbed the blue chalk till it turned to powder in his hands. "That's it!" he said at last, when Mamie just wouldn't miss. He threw his cue on the table and stomped off to the bar. "I oughtta break her nose," he said to Charlie.

"Yeah, sure," Charlie answered.

"She'd kill you in a minute," said Mongoose Jim. "Remember what she did to Thorn?" Mongoose dipped his head and snickered.

Cody's tone was full of scorn. "Well, she didn't let us lag for break.

Now, what the hell is that, Jim?" He furrowed his brows and scowled like he'd never heard of anything so dirty in his life.

Mongoose Jim dipped his head like a long-necked bird, agreeing that Mamie hadn't been fair.

Ordering a beer and pretzels from Charlie, Cody swung round on his stool away from having to look at Mamie, and his eyes lit on Soren, who had a look on his mouth like he had swallowed a raw clam. He was looking back at Cody.

"What you looking at?" said Cody.

With a dead-level voice Soren said, "Not much, I'd say."

That stopped Cody cold. Jim chuckled about it. "Hey, I think he just insulted you, Cody," he said.

Cody came off the stool and scuttled over to the table, walking almost sideways, like a crab. He leaned over across my chair to say something to Soren. I smelled his cigar, like a twist of spoiled brome, and a kind of gym-sock odor coming off him.

"In a wheelchair, I see," he said in a sneery voice. "At's why you got such a big mouth. You think I won't crack you one just cause you're in a wheelchair."

He took the cigar out of his mouth and flicked ashes on the table. Chee Chee, who was curling her lip at Cody, made a leap off Anna's lap and snatched at the cigar. Cody jumped back and dropped it on the floor, where Chee Chee pounced on it and worried it into bits and pieces. Cody turned to Mongoose, who was pointing at Chee Chee and roaring with laughter.

"That ain't funny, you stupid ass!" Cody yelled.

"I think it's funny as hell," said Mongoose Jim.

"I oughtta squish that goddamn dog. Oughtta squish it, that's what. Oughtta squish this old cripple too. Would if he wasn't a cripple. You think you're privileged, don't you, mister? You think you can act like a wiseass and nobody'll chop your nose cause you're sittin in a wheelchair. I don't give a shit about that crap!"

"Privileged?" said Soren, like he couldn't believe his ears. "In a wheelchair is being privileged? You stupid little runt."

Cody threw his arms back like Soren had shot him. "Gaaa!" he stammered.

"Sowen, he beat you face, you . . . you stubby!" said Anna, shaking both fists at Cody.

"Stubby? Runt?" he shouted. "I don't take that shit from nobody!"

A pounding noise came from behind us. Charlie had a sawed-off baseball bat and was hitting the bar with it. "Knock it off, Cody," he said. "Leave the man alone."

Cody sneered and said, "Yeah, you're right, Charlie. Ain't no glory in kicking ass on a cripple. Even if he does deserve it. But you better watch your mouth, buddy." He turned like he was going to walk away, strutting away like he had settled it.

"You sonofabitch!" said Soren, which froze Cody in his tracks.

"Am I suppose to take that?" he said to Charlie.

Soren rolled himself up so his legs were under the table, then he put his arm on the table, cocked it, and said, "I'd love to get out of this chair and oblige you, but I can't. But nothing's wrong with my arms, Cody. Put up or shut up now."

"What? Arm-wrestle? Can you believe this guy wanting to arm-wrestle me?"

"I can't believe it," said Mongoose. "Cody's good at arm wrestling."

Cody put his fists on his hips. "They call me the Tiny Titan of Temple," he said. "I'm maybe the best arm-wrestler around here, next to Bob Thorn, and shit, he outweighs me by sixty pounds. Pound for pound, I'm the better man. Look at my forearms. Look at my wrists. Look at these bear claws I got for hands. You mess with me, Soren, and I'll break your goddamn arm off."

"You don't know Sowen," said Anna, patting her husband on the back. Her color was high, her eyes shiny, like sunlit water. Her voice had a tremor in it from excitement. "You don't know Sowen. He beats dem all. He beats ewyone. I seen him. I seen him. He is a wiking! No stubby like you beats a wiking!"

"Look who keeps calling me stubby," said Cody, scorn oozing out of him. "Your little legs don't even reach the floor, baby. Look you guys, look." He grabbed Anna's skirt and threw it up, so we could see her feet didn't touch the floor.

"Looking up my dwcss!" she shrieked. She kicked Cody in the belly. He stumbled back and caught himself on another table, just as Chee Chee dashed in and bit his leg. Then Chee Chee ran back and jumped into Anna's lap. The two of them looked at Cody full of challenge.

He limped around and swore he was bleeding.

"Let me see," said Mongoose Jim.

"Get lost," said Cody. "Lot a help you been."

"Well, you sure ain't making friends here."

Charlie banged on the bar some more. We looked at him. "Sit down and wrestle him, Cody. Let's get this shit over with," he said.

"Then if I have to I will," said Cody.

Cody sat across from Soren and put his arm up. Charlie came over to referee. He put a folded dishtowel under Cody's arm because it was shorter than Soren's. When everything looked fair, he told them to have at it.

Soren's arm started to go over with Cody's on top, but he managed to stop six inches from losing. And he hung there, hung and hung there, his long, deep-lined face getting red as ketchup, the veins in his neck pumping up more and more. In his temples you could see his pulse racing. He looked like his head might shoot off his shoulders. His eyes were closed tight, like he didn't want to see himself lose.

Cody was grinning and saying, "He's going. He's going."

But he had to quit saying it, because Soren's arm wasn't going down anymore, and pretty soon Cody's face was getting red too. Charlie had to yell at him not to grab the table underneath with his other hand. A minute passed, then two minutes, and the arms stayed like they had been carved that way – Cody's on top, bearing down so hard the tendons in his wrists looked like bowstrings; and Soren's on the bottom, tendons looking the same but holding steady. Another minute passed, and Cody was beginning to pant and grumble. Soren was taking deep breaths and letting them whistle out. His eyes were still closed, his face gone from ketchup to scarlet. The arms raged against each other like mad boa constrictors.

Mamie had watched it all from the back by the table. Then she came up behind Soren, put her hands on his shoulders, and said in his ear, "Sarn-Sarn, hmmmm – hurry-up money."

"Broke my back," he said through clenched teeth.

A baffled look settled over Cody's face. "What's she sayin that for?" he growled. "They're cheatin."

His arm was coming up slow, like all its strength was seeping out some little hole. He was gasping and trying to grab the table again, but Charlie wouldn't let him. The arms came straight, and then Cody's started going over. "Hey! Hey! Hey!" he said, watching his arm fall. And when it was almost down, he jerked it away and stood up.

"You did something!" he said, pointing his finger at Mamie. "I'm sick of being cheated. She cheats at pool and now this!"

"What? What did she do?" asked Charlie.

"How am I suppose to know?" said Cody. He went back over to the bar, rubbing his arm up and down and mumbling something.

"You just lost, that's all," said Mongoose Jim. "Hey, he's a tough old bird, ain't he?"

"Gives me the creeps, same as her," Cody told him, jerking his thumb at Mamie. "I'll tell you right now, she did something to him. I could feel it."

"Aw bullshit, Cody," said Charlie.

"Bullshit yourself, Charlie. She broke my concentration."

"Yeah yeah."

"Sonofabitch, some friends I got," Cody complained. He went back to the pool table and started cuing the balls.

Soren wrapped an arm round Mamie's waist and gave her a hug. "Mamie, I'll shoot the next man who tells me you're an idiot," he said. "That was the smartest thing you could have said to me."

She bent down and hugged him back, nodded her head like she knew just what he meant. "Yaay, Sarn-Sarn," she said.

Anna got her hug in next, hugging Soren hard and telling him how proud she was of him, and telling him too she was sorry for breaking his television.

"You had a point," he told her.

Shepard watched them making up, and he was close to having tears in his eyes, but not because he was mad and sad about it. "It's wonderful," he said. "I've never seen you two enjoying conjugal bliss before. It appears more profitable in you both than its abstinence witnessed. Love is the wisdom of fools, you know? How melancholy to think of you without one another – in misery's darkest cavern, hmmm?" He rubbed his nose on his sleeve until it shined like an apple.

A couple minutes later, the back door opened and Bob Thorn came in carrying a case of splow. He set it on the bar. He looked just the same as he had at the school – big chest, big stomach, sideburns down to his jaw. "I got two cases if you want them, Charlie," he said.

"Yeah, I'll take them," said Charlie. "I got a gal here can drink a case all by herself." He pointed to Mamie.

Thorn glanced at her first, then did a double take. "You," he whispered. "Well, Jesus Christ."

Mamie put on her friendliest smile for him, like she was really glad to see him.

Cody started cackling like a witch going to cast a spell. He left the pool table to come over and elbow Thorn in the ribs. "Remember her, Bob?" he said. "She's the one whipped your ass. They tell me you was walking on your ears. Did a little ole girl set you on your head?"

"Fuck off, Cody!" Thorn told him. He pushed Cody away, all the while keeping his eyes on Mamie, like he thought she might jump him. "Where'd she come from?" he asked.

"You don't know about her?" said Cody, smiling crooked at Mamie. "She's the goddamn pheenom everybody talks about. Shepard's parrot."

"The one the Robbinites turned to," said Mongoose Jim.

"Her? Those fartfaces?" said Thorn. He looked at Shepard. "I thought you said she was working for Snowdy."

"She was, Bobby. But Teddy threatened to kill her. Don't you know he shot Ben?"

All of them looked surprised and said, "What?"

Charlie asked, "Is he dead?"

"No, he lived through it," said Shepard. "They put Teddy in Camelot."

This was all news to me and Mamie too. I asked him when he'd found out. He said a long time ago.

"Well, they kept that pretty hush-hush," said Charlie.

"Best place for the little bastard," said Cody.

Everybody seemed to agree that it was. I think things would have been all right then, because the tension was out of the air from talking about the Snowdys. But Cody had a plan, you could tell. He wanted to get something going between Thorn and Mamie.

"Hey, you know what I heard?" he said, putting a sly look on his face. "I heard that Bobby Thorn said if he ever come across the two-ton Tessie who kicked his ass at the school, he was gonna stomp her like he would a spider. That's what I heard."

"I heard that too," said Mongoose Jim.

"You don't shut up," said Thorn, "I'll stomp you like a spider." He looked from Mongoose Jim to Cody, threatening them but keeping his eyes sliding back to Mamie.

"Well, it's what you said, goddammit," Cody told him.

"Yeah? Well, you kick her ass, Cody. There she is. You're always talking about how tough you are. There she is. Kick her ass! Go on!"

"Hey, ain't my fuck'n fight."

"Well then, shut up!"

"Jesus, what's the matter with you guys? Everybody's getting sore at me tonight."

Soren and Anna wanted to know what was going on, what had happened between Mamie and Bob Thorn? When I told them what she had done to him, dragging him around by the ankles and all, they laughed about it and so did everybody else. Except Thorn. He hunched his shoulders and went back to sizing up Mamie.

Cody laughed the hardest and said, "It still tickles me to death to think of her hauling you round like a sack of taters. It's funny, man!"

"You think it's so funny, huh? You don't shut up, I'm gonna pound your head until you're laughing out your asshole, Cody!"

"Oh yeah, sure! Pick on me, Bobby. I ain't but half your size."

Thorn grabbed Cody by the shirt, lifted him up close, and said into his face. "You don't know nothing, Cody. That broad ain't human. She's half gorilla. Fucker could whip Marciano. Now I don't want to hurt you, Cody, but you better shut up." He shook him a bit and set him down.

Cody's voice was real quiet then. He said, "Sure, pick on me."

"You guys knock it off now," said Charlie. He was rolling his little bat back and forth under his hand.

Thorn turned his back on us and pulled a jar of splow from the case. He opened it and drank deep. A couple more times he drank, and we were all so quiet we could hear the gurgle of it going down. Then he slammed the jar down and turned back, glaring at Mamie.

"Don't do it," said Charlie.

"Don't listen to Cody," said Mongoose Jim. "He's always that way when he ain't got a job. He's pissed at the railroad and he takes it out on everybody."

"That's got nothing to do with it," said Thorn. "It's her and me."

Still smiling at him, Mamie bent partway into the same monkey crouch she and Thorn had used on the school lawn, arms and legs out, ready to wrestle.

"Whoa," said Thorn. "Look at that! She wants to try me again."

Cody said, "I hope she eats you, you sonofabitch."

"She doesn't mean anything," I told them. "It's play to her, that's all. She likes it."

Suddenly Thorn reached over and snatched Charlie's bat away. Charlie yelled at him, but Thorn shook the bat and told him to stay out of it. Then he waved it at Mamie and said, "Come on, hippo. You're messing with Bob Thorn now."

Shaking from head to foot, Shepard stood up and held out his hands, like he was pushing Thorn away. "Please put the bat down, Bobby," he said. "She doesn't mean any harm. She's as innocent as a child. She doesn't know what she's doing."

"Go fuck yourself, Shepard," Cody said. "It's too late for that kind of crap. Sic him, Mamie baby. I'm with you."

Mamie came around the table in her blocking crouch, shuffling back and forth in front of Thorn.

"Gawd, she ain't afraid of me at all," he said.

"Sic him, Mamie baby. Use him for a mop!" yelled Cody. And just then Thorn turned and swung at Cody, who jumped back into Mongoose Jim, knocking him flat on the floor. Then Cody stayed out of range.

Mongoose Jim said, "I'm staying right here till this is over."

Soren shook his fist at Thorn and told him to fight fair. Anna was yelling too, and Chee Chee was barking and growling. And when Thorn took a step toward Mamie, Chee Chee jumped off Anna's lap and went for his legs. He swung the bat at her, but quick as a cow's kick Mamie dove in and grabbed the dog. The bat came down with a whump across Mamie's back. It sounded like someone beating a rug. And with the dog in one hand, Mamie sprang back up, caught the bat in the other hand, and twisted it out of Thorn's grip. He shrank away from her. There was pure disbelief on his face. For a second the room was quiet as death.

Mamie gave Chee Chee back to Anna and put the bat on the table. Then she went after Thorn. He saw her coming. "Whoa, gal!" he yelled, but it was too late. Catching him by the wrist, she jerked him toward the door. He planted his feet, but she just hauled him along like he was on wheels, rolling him out the door, with him hollering "Whoa!" the whole time. "Whoooooa!"

"What's she gonna do to him?" asked Charlie.

"I gotta see this!" said Cody.

We all had to see it. We hurried out to not miss anything. But it wasn't quite what we expected. Least of all, I guess, was it what Thorn expected. Mamie still had him by the wrist, but she had turned her back on him and pulled him tight against her. She was coaxing him to mount up. Slowly he did, his head turned to us, the whites of his eyes glowing in the moonlight. She caught him with her hands under his legs and away she went, galloping off with a snort and a whinny, heading toward the woods. Thorn was looking over his shoulder at us, saying, "Jesus, Jesus, Jesus," each one getting fainter, until they disappeared into the trees.

Cody leaned over to me and said in an amazed voice, "Do you think she's taking him there to kill him?"

"She might," I said.

"Oh, Crystal, not a chance," Shepard said. "Poof poof, she's playing with him, you know that."

I shook my head. "When it comes to Mamie," I said, "I don't know a thing. And the more I'm with her, the more stupid I get."

Shepard poof-poofed me, but I meant it. A faint cry reached us from somewhere in the woods, a cry like cowboys make when breaking a horse.

"You hear that?" said Mongoose Jim. "What a wild sound."

"She killed him. I feel it in my bones," said Cody.

The night was quiet, except for a breeze rustling the big elm in front of Shepard's, and we waited – Soren in his wheelchair, the rest of us standing and looking off where the dark line of the woods started, like feathers held against the starry sky. We waited and waited. It was a minute, then it was two, and all our eyes stared at the woods. Chee Chee gave a little yip, then another, hearing what took us another second or two to hear. There was a kind of rustling sound, and a dull pounding sound, and a sound that twigs make when they crack. It got louder and louder – a whooshing and a booming and a cracking.

"What the hell?" said Cody. "It's a stampede."

"That's just Mamie," said Shepard proudly.

And there she came, she and Thorn, Thorn clinging to her back and her big legs churning like the haunches of a mule. Thorn waved his hand at us, crying out, "Gawd, oh gawd, ain't she wonderful? Ain't she great?" She pulled up in front of us, snorting and blowing and stamping and sweating, her face excited and happy, and his face too. They both looked like they wanted to run some more. He jumped off though, and held her by the hair, like he was holding reins. "Ain't she wonderful?" he said again, his face beaming with a sudden love of her.

She pulled at the reins and sucked in lots of air.

"Where'd you go?" asked Mongoose Jim.

"We thought she killed you for sure," said Cody.

"Naw, she don't mean no harm. She rode me all the way to the tracks and back. She jumped a log you wouldn't believe, a good three or four feet over – and me on her back! It was like magic, like a magic carpet or something, like she had wings. A four-foot log and me on her back! Jesus, I wish I could buy her. I wish she wanted to buy me."

He couldn't get enough of praising her. He said his heart was smitten with love of her. Even Mongoose Jim and Cody were taken in by the way he carried on. They reached out almost shyly to stroke Mamie, to pet her hair and her back. They listened to Thorn like he was telling them he'd found a mountain of gold.

Carnival and the Girl without Eyes

After he fell in love with Mamie, Thorn tried to be a part of everything she did, except she cut him off where her closeness to Powers was concerned. He didn't get to stay in the booth with her and Powers, but she allowed him to be near any other time he wanted, at Charlie's or at Shepard's.

Times when I was in the bar with them and other people would come in, Thorn would always work the conversation to his night ride in the woods with Mamie. It got larger and larger in the telling, having Mamie leap over logs no less than ten feet high, and having her bounce twenty feet through the air like a kangaroo, and having her run so fast she left a pack of wolves in the dust. He bragged of her ripping the bars off the jail, and he even turned his own defeat at the book-burning into a proof of her wondrousness – that she could throw him, one hundred ninety pounds of the toughest player in the history of Temple football, toss him like a feather and drag him like a toy. He was proud of her. And especially he was proud that he was part of her life now. He was, he claimed, her personal bodyguard, because powerful as she was, she didn't understand danger or really know how to take care of herself against those who meant her harm. He knew the ways of the dog-eat-dog world and he would protect her from it with his life. He said to put out the word to the lowlife sonsabitches in Temple that Big Bob Thorn was Mamie Beaver's badass bodyguard, and God help the imbecile who tried any funny stuff.

He was there every weekend for her four services. He stood in the wings while she did her act, watching her and watching all the people, the Mamieites, he called them, ready to knock sense into any of them who might get over-rambunctious and want to come up onstage with Mamie, or hug her or pet her or act one-on-one with her, which happened sometimes and always spoiled things a bit. Shepard had always talked the huggers into sitting down. He was mild in handling the situation compared to Thorn, who grabbed them by the collar and hauled them with their heels dragging on the floor. After two or three times of seeing that, the people quit getting stagestruck, as Thorn called it.

One Saturday, after her last service, he came over to the house with us, saying he had a present for Mamie. Phoebe Bumpus was there too. She had come to take Mamie and me to a carnival that had set up a couple miles out of town. When Thorn heard what we were doing, he said he was coming along to keep an eye out for Mamie. A lot of lowlife sonsabitches hung out at carnivals, he told us.

In his hands was a box from Montgomery Ward. He shoved the box at Mamie. "Here," he said. "This is something you could wear to the carnival, if you want."

Mamie snatched it away from him and tore it open. Out tumbled a new dress. "Oh, p-p-p-retty," she said, holding it up.

It was pretty. It was yellow, like marsh marigolds. It had puffy sleeves and a low neckline with a lacy border. As Mamie held it up, her face glowed pink with pleasure. And Phoebe was excited too. A sly look came over her face.

She said, "Come on, Mamie dear. Let's do something with you." She dug in her purse and brought out some makeup, lipstick and rouge and eye shadow. "This ought to do it," she said. "Yeah, and Christian, you go down by the ditch and pick me some flowers for Mamie's hair. I saw a bunch of them coming by this morning. Hurry up now."

I did what she said, and I brought back some purple alfalfa buds and some white clover buds and some dandelions. Mamie and Phoebe were in the bedroom. Phoebe made me hand the flowers in without looking. After about twenty minutes, she came out and said to us: "Gentlemen, may I present the butterfly escaped from its cocoon? I give you Mamie Beaver, ta da!"

Mamie came out, trembling at her own beauty. We all sort of gasped to see her looking like that. She looked like something an artist would paint and call it "The Spirit of Spring," or "Colors of the Country Girl," or "The Milkmaid Fairy." Barefoot she was, with the dress just covering her knees and showing off her strong ankles and calves. The dress had a full skirt and a white border at the hem. The waist pulled in tight and showed Mamie's nice healthy hips and the healthy little roll in her tummy. The top of the dress gave room for her bosom and let just the crease at the top of her breasts show, along with her neck and the collar bones, all smooth as cow's cream. The sleeves were puffed up like yellow clouds over her shoulders, which had the effect of making her seem slimmer and softer, like you would expect a spring fairy to be. And she was crowned with the flower wreath.

"A divine metamorphosis," said Shepard, taking out his hanky and dabbing at his eyes.

"She looks like she should have wings," said Thorn in awe.

"She looks like a movie star," said Phoebe.

I offered that she looked like an overgrown leprechaun. It was the flowers braided into her hair that made me think of something from the deep forest, something like a leprechaun, which I saw as redheaded and fair with freckles like Mamie. The only thing I would have changed was that Phoebe had put junk on her face that she didn't need. Her lips were red enough on their own, and her cheeks had their own rouge, and she sure didn't need eye shadow to make you look at her eyes. I didn't say anything about it though. No matter what, Mamie was a gorgeous sight.

"What do you think about it, Mamie?" Phoebe asked.

Mamie was very pleased. She threw her head back and whinnied.

Thorn tried to imitate her, but where she sounded like a filly, he sounded like a mule. It didn't matter though. He stepped up to her and gave a bow. "Mamie," he said. "I'd be honored if you'd go to the carnival with me and let me show you off."

"Yaay, Booby," she answered.

Shepard said he had meetings to go to, so just the four of us went. We drove out to the place past town where the carnival was set up. It was a nice warm day and a lot of people were there enjoying it, lots of families having picnics on some farmer's pasture, lots of kids running by chasing each other or racing each other from one carny ride to the next – the hammer, the rocket, the ferris wheel, the pony ride, the merry-go-round, the whip, the earthquake, and some other things.

We paired off – Phoebe and I, and Mamie and Thorn – and strolled along looking at things.

"She's so pretty, Christian," said Phoebe to me, as we passed a booth with a sign overhead: SOUVENIERS – CURIOS – ANTIQUES.

I thought she meant Mamie. "It's hard to see past the farmeralls and see what a real beauty she is," I answered.

Phoebe chucked my elbow. "I mean that," she said, pointing.

She was pointing at the souvenirs, curios, and antiques, which I thought were pretty gaudy, if not downright ugly. But Phoebe meant something in particular. She pointed past all the stuffed animals and ash trays with different states painted on them, past all the straw hats stacked up with CARNIVAL TIME IS ANY TIME printed on them, past all kinds of plastic stuff – pink and breakable things that my mother would call doodads or knickknacks. Pa would probably call them crap. But Phoebe pointed at a row of chalky, six-inch statuettes of women, half-naked women with small breasts and flat bellies and noble faces all the same – all with vacant white eyes. Next to them was another row of six-inch women, only they were clothed in robes and were meant to be the Virgin Mary. But the faces of the naked ones and the robed ones were exactly the same.

Phoebe touched a naked one. "This is Aphrodite, the goddess of love."

"Venus," I said.

"Or Aphrodite. Same thing, you know?"

"And this one's Mary, the Mother of Christ. See the faces?"

"Yeah, people prayed to statues of Aphrodite back in the time of Socrates and those guys."

"People pray to the statue of Mary too. My mama has one in her bedroom, a little one like this that she lights candles to."

Phoebe pulled her hair back and turned so I could see her profile. "Any resemblance?" she asked.

Phoebe didn't half look like Venus or Mary, but I said she was just as pretty as they were.

She chucked my elbow again and laughed, "Flattery will get you everywhere," she said. Her laugh made me feel warm inside, and I wondered if I should kiss her. She was flirting with me, I could tell, showing me statues of Venus like that.

While we were eyeing each other, a man pushed by us and up to the counter. "Gimmee one a them straw hats," he said to the girl.

"They cost two dollars," she told him.

"Gimmee one ennaway," he said, and pulled some rumpled bills from his pocket. He put the hat on with the CARNIVAL TIME facing forward. The hat pushed the tips of his ears outward and made him look like a hick. Phoebe burst out laughing, trying to stifle it with her hand but not succeeding, and the man's eyes darted at her. He looked her up and down, dipping his head like a vulture sizing up where it should take a bite. Phoebe got behind me and laughed into my shoulder.

"Funny, missy? Funny?" said the man, pecking at her with his sharp nose.

Phoebe stopped laughing. I took her by the arm and pulled her away into the crowd. When I looked back, the man was still standing in the same spot, his angry eyes glued to Phoebe's backside.

"He likes your rear," I said to her.

"Don't look at him," she said. "Goddamn me and my giggles. They always get the best of me. Did you see that face? Like a mean vulture. Those eyes! Dirty eyes, dirty thoughts in them."

"You shouldn't have laughed at him," I told her.

"I never mean to, but when something strikes my funny bone, I can't help myself."

We stopped at the freak show and marveled at all the weird-looking people. They had the usual fat lady and the bearded lady and the dwarf, and a legless fellow who walked on his arms; and a guy who could look at you with his legs folded behind his neck. Another one they had was called the Alligator Lady. She came onstage wearing a purple robe with a hood, so that all we could see was a dry nose and one eye peeking out. She didn't look at the customers but kept her head down and her eyelids lowered, while the carny barker explained that she was the offspring of a woman who was raped in Florida by an alligator. Phoebe and I snickered about that, but some of the people seemed to think he was telling the truth. At least, their faces didn't change any that I could see, faces staring up at the guy like he was a scientist or a politician never known to lie.

"And now what you will see," he told us, "is a throwback to those ancient times when our ancestors still lived on both land and sea, and they had the skin of alligators. This is once in your lifetime that you can seen evolution in reverse. It won't come again like her. So step up on the stage, folks, and for one little quarter come look at the wonder of prehistory. One quarter to see the child of a human and an alligator. One quarter to see a sight that has bamboozled the world!" He turned to the woman in the robe. "Step inside the box, Alligator Lady," he said. "And take your clothes off."

She lay herself down in a box that looked like a coffin, and then the man reached in it and pulled off her robe. "There she is," he declared. "The Alligator Lady naked. Come on up and see. Give me a quarter there, friend. That's it, come on. Don't be shy. She wants you to see. You come too. Give me that quarter. Don't miss the sight of a lifetime. Come on . . . Come on!"

I had to admit I wanted to see what was naked in that box. Phoebe said she wanted to see it too. She took my hand and pulled me up the steps. We gave the man our quarters and got in line. The men and women going by and looking down into the box were quiet and respectful. They shook their heads and made small noises, like they felt pity for the Alligator Lady. When we finally got to look inside, I was as disappointed as could be. She was nothing but a woman with some badly dried out skin, the skin of someone who had spent fifty years in the sun getting all the moisture baked out of her. She had dark, shining splotches all over her, with borders of dead-white and flaky skin. What she reminded me of mostly was not an alligator but a giraffe, with patterns of white and brown running over its hide. And she wasn't even naked either. She wore a two-piece swimsuit with cherries printed on it.

"It's a gyp," I said real low to Phoebe.

"Poor thing," she whispered. "Got some kind of skin disease."

We hurried off the stage to get away from her. We had a good mood going, and I don't think either one of us wanted the Alligator Lady to change it. As we walked along, I watched the ferris wheel going round, and there in a seat were Mamie and Thorn, like a bright marigold next to a weed. I waved at them, but they didn't see me.

"Hey, look at that guy," said Phoebe. She was pointing at a strongman who was picking up a ball weight that had 500 LBS written on it. His muscles popped like knotted rope as he lifted the ball to his waist and put it down. Then he posed for us, lifting his arms and showing off his biceps and turning so we could see the muscles in his back. Phoebe liked him.

"Oooo, he's so strong. Look at those muscles. What a man," she sighed. "What about you, Christian? How big are your muscles?"

She gave my little bicep a squeeze. It was embarrassing. "Not so big," I said.

"But very hard," she replied. She must have known I was jealous of the strongman, because she added, "You wouldn't want to look like him anyway. Really, he's kind of ugly – so lumpy."

I agreed there was something ugly about him, with all those red muscles and the wormy veins sticking out, and the awkwardness of his movements, no fluid in them at all. Mamie was as strong as he was, I was sure, but she moved gracefully, like an animal, a bear or a moose. I mentioned to Phoebe that Mamie was as strong as the strongman.

She thought about it, "I know, but wouldn't it be just awful if she had to make her living as a freak? She's lucky she found you. I wonder if she knows it?"

I felt warm for Phoebe again. I said, "Do you remember at Shepard's when we danced? I'm sorry I got sick. I would have given anything not to be."

"Well, actually, I was too smashed to remember much about that night. I've been hoping I didn't make a fool of myself."

It was a nice way she had of letting me off the hook, and I liked her all the more for it. We stared into each other's eyes, and I could feel something was happening between us. She took my hand. "Let's walk," she said. "Let's see what we can see. There's a show here I heard about from one of the reporters. There's this blind girl in a bikini who looks like Marilyn Monroe. Let's see if we can find her, and then I'll tell you a secret."

So we did. We walked to the edge of the shows and came to a tent that advertised THE SULTAN'S HAREM. Inside, it said, were the most beautiful women of Arabia. Along the front of the tent were three cartoony-type portraits of long-haired, big-breasted women, smiling and sexy. Their names were written in sequins at the top of each portrait: Dew, Dawn, and Aphrodite. The paintings were chipped and sun-bleached but the name tags looked new.

"This must be it," said Phoebe.

The carny barker was standing at the entranceway, persuading us that we should invest a quarter to see a million dollar's worth of beauty.

"One quawta! Just one-fowth of a dollah to entah the Sultan's Harem and see the prize possessions of Arabee. They walk, they wiggle, and they dance. They will show you the ancient dances of the desert, and you will be amazed and astonished at what you see." He raised one black brow and leered at us.

"Heh heh heh," he laughed.

"Heh heh heh," we answered.

"And they do it all for you and juss one-fowth of a dollah. So step up now, the show's about to begin. I can hear the music startin." He cupped his hand round his ear and made like he heard the music. "Yep, it's startin," he told us.

Then we could hear it too, a steady beat of drums, the sound filtering through the canvas – dum ta ta dum ta ta dum.

"And here comes golden Aphrodite to find out what's keepin you all."

He pointed to the entrance and there was a surge forward as a woman in a yellow robe appeared. She sure wasn't an Arabee. She looked more like a Minnesota Swede. Her face was pale and she wore a lot of black eyebrow pencil and blue shadow and scarlet rouge. Her lips were as dark as blood from a vein. She stood just a moment, not looking at us, the sun sparkling off her short, swept-back hair, and she made me think of what a yellow sun-ray might look like if it came alive for a second, dazzling us like Venus coming down. And when she turned to go back inside, the people standing there followed her like they were hypnotized. They had their quarters ready.

I had my doubts about going in with Phoebe. I didn't see but two other women in the crowd. But she didn't care. "Come on," she said. "I want to see this."

Inside, it was pretty close. To our front was a waist-high stage, about ten feet long and half-curtained by two shabby red shower curtains hung on a pole that sagged in the middle. The tent was too hot and airless. It stank like canvas and sweat and tobacco – and like there were things rotting in it.

"Bring on the dancers! Bring 'em on!" yelled a voice behind us, raspy with age.

"Yeah," bellowed another. "Bring on the babes!"

"Let's see some Arabee cunt," said a man behind me whose voice was low and nasty and not meant for the whole audience to hear. Phoebe winced and took hold of my arm.

The carny man appeared from behind the curtain. He paced up and down the stage in white pants and a white shirt with rolled-up sleeves that showed he had milky forearms heavy with black hair. His nervous fingers wiggled at us like fat worms. As he bent toward us, the crowd hushed. He licked his lips and grinned. His face seemed to be saying what a bunch of idiots and hicks we were. I wondered how many like me, like us, had stood before the carny man day after day, waiting to see the harem, with him knowing that it didn't matter if they were from Arabia or not – or even who they were. Maybe they could have been machines, just so they had the right fleshy parts. And he knew it. He stared down at us and sized us up – city people looking for a kick, farmers wanting to see a behind that wasn't cow, miners wanting to see something besides the land and the forest getting stripped; and there were clerks, no doubt, and college kids and factory workers and whatnot, just a mulligan stew of northern Wisconsin.

He finished his introduction with a waving of his fingers and a side step offstage. "And here they are, ladies and gentlemen! First, for your delectation and delight, welcome Dawn and Dew!"

He scurried behind the curtain, while a few people clapped. Then we heard a scratchy sound of a phonograph record and the same monotonous dum ta ta dum of the drums came on, followed by Dawn and Dew. They came from opposite ends of the curtain, not dancing but merely walking with an exaggerated hip roll that was greeted by hoots and whistles. Dawn and Dew wore what looked like silk underpants, dyed blue and red, and brassieres with the top half cut off but covered by a gauzy blouse. Their bellies were bare. Around their ankles were chained bells that tinkled in an innocent kind of way. Above their blue and red costumes were faces with wide oval mouths and yellowy teeth, dark eyes with dark slashes for eyebrows, and curly, piled-high hair the color of cinders. They passed back and forth above us, parading their big boobs and flared hips, while the drums beat and some of the men in the audience growled or squealed or brayed like donkeys.

The guy behind me said, almost in my ear, "Now that's what you call well-worn pussy. Look how broke down they are."

There was a boy about my age or a bit older standing next to him. "Shut up," he whispered to the man. I glanced at him. He was staring at Dawn and Dew with eyes on fire, looking at them like they were movie stars glittering up there like on the screen, flawless as angels.

The man laughed, but he didn't say any more nasty stuff.

The carny barker started coaxing us to clap, "C'mon, people, you got to wahm these girls up if they're gonna really get into it. You got to show some appreciation. C'mon now, let's give 'em a hand."

He clapped and we joined in. There were a few whistles, a few rebel yells.

"C'mon, citizens, you can do better than that. Got to do better than that if you're gonna wake these girls up. The louder the noise, the better they dance. Now, let's hear it for Dawn and Dew!"

Again we clapped and whistled and yelled. The one woman in red bent over and waved at us from between her legs. Someone howled like a coyote; others clapped, whistled, and wailed.

"That's the way!" coaxed the carny.

As long as we made a lot of noise and showed we were having the time of our lives, the girls bent and dipped and wiggled. But after a bit, it got monotonous, and no matter how the carny urged and the dancers strutted and kicked, fewer and fewer of us clapped like they wanted. Seeing it wasn't working, the carny man stopped the music and the dancers disappeared behind the curtain.

"Don't leave, citizens!" the carny man shouted. "No no, I've got another one back there who can't wait to come out here and dance for you, and believe me now, she ain't as shy as Dawn and Dew. She'll show you a whole lot more of what you're lookin for! Now, who's gonna stay and see little Aphrodite, goddess of love? She's only fifty cents, good people, and she's worth a million. Who's gonna stay? Juss pass 'em up, folks. Fifty cents. I got change."

A few left, but most of us gave him the fifty cents. Phoebe said she wasn't about to miss the one she came to see, even though it was a robbery. I had watched her while Dawn and Dew did their stuff, and it seemed to me, she was enjoying it as much as any of the men there.

She had been looking just as hard at those spots the men looked at hard, and her face was flushed and sweaty too.

Aphrodite came out, and we worked our way forward close enough that we might have touched her if we'd wanted to. She had taken off her yellow robe and was wearing only a thin yellow halter and what were no more than two little bits of yellow cloth covering her patch and rear end. When she walked out there was a roar from the crowd, and I felt myself getting squeezed forward by the people trying to get close to her. It would have been funny to me if I hadn't been a part of it. But I felt my blood pounding too, as I looked up at her, and there was even a feeling in my throat like I wanted to howl. Instead I just gasped and gave a moan and stared with all my eyes at her legs swaying in front of me and her rotating pelvis in its thin, yellow cloth.

But as I stared, I became aware of a flaw in Aphrodite, goddess of love. She had a scar on her belly, a waving scar that ran up out of the yellow patch to her belly button, a trail of old pain that proved she was merely human after all and had suffered once, that she had not been just lowered from the gods or picked ripe off a tree. The scar was so out of place in my fantasies about her that I felt like I had woken up from a dream. She was real, and suddenly I wanted to see her eyes, to see what she was thinking about us. I tried to find her eyes, but I found only the blue and black shadows beneath her brows and the long, fake lashes curling from what I came to see as eyeless eye-sockets, little slits of ink. I tried to look closer, feeling nearly frantic about my discovery. Her head rolled downward for a second, then back up, but I caught at a glance the dull cream-colored balls of blindness, purely blind, no pupils, no iris. I grabbed Phoebe's arm and shook it and shouted into her ear, "She's got no eyes, Phoebe. Blind as a bat."

"I know," she said. "She's the one."

The carny man was getting on us to clap louder again, saying that Aphrodite's feelings would be hurt if we didn't show how much we loved her. I looked back, and it seemed that most of the men were in some kind of a trance, staring at the blind girl with eyes that were in love and lust at the same time. There was something desperate about the way the men looked, as if they wanted her but knew in their hearts that nothing like her would ever come their way – only in dreams. There she was, in eye-reach and no more, a beautiful blond girl, glistening like a raindrop in the sun. Just a shimmer and she would be gone, leaving nothing more than a memory to make them dissatisfied with anything waiting at home.

She went away, and we clapped and roared for more.

"Ain't she the most beautiful thing you've seen walkin?" asked the carny man.

We shrieked and hooted and whistled.

"You mean you want her to come back?"

We shrieked and hooted and whistled.

"She'll come back if you want her to, and she'll show you a whole lot more of what you're lookin for. She ain't shy. You want that?"

Yes, we did.

"Aphrodite don't like to wear no clothes. She don't feel right with 'em on. She thinks clothes cover up her best features."

Everybody laughed at that.

"But the law don't allow her to dance up here like she'd like to, folks."

We booed the law.

"But don't despair, good people. Stick with me, and I guarantee you'll see all you want of little Aphrodite. She's got her ways. And the law can go to hell!"

We agreed.

The carny man leaned forward. "What about it, citizens? Is she worth a dollah? Will you ever see anything like her again in your natural life?"

Nobody left. He went up and down us collecting dollars. "Thank you, thank you, thank you," he kept repeating, while he snatched dollar bills from us with his thumb and forefinger, like he didn't want to touch us.

This time she wore a yellow skirt that came down just midway on her thighs. She had yellow pasties over her nipples. Her breasts were hard-looking and scarcely bounced at all as she walked onstage. She stepped within three feet of the edge and stopped. The drum beat began, and she began to kick with her right leg, low kicks at first that sent her skirt riding upward. I was crushed against the edge of the stage, as the people pressed forward to get their fifty-cents-add-a-dollar peek.

"Eeeeee-haaaaa!" someone yelled in a raspy, half-strangled voice.

I looked back and saw the man in the carnival-time straw hat, his head thrust forward on his long neck, the adam's apple bulging, his nose pecking at Aphrodite. And he was watching her like he would love to make pudding of her and slurp her down. She was kicking above us, kicking higher and higher, the skirt lifting.

"Come on, baby, let me see that wet hole!" the vulture-man snarled.

Her leg faltered for a moment. Then it got going again, so we could all look at what a dollar-fifty bought. Phoebe was looking like she didn't have one of her own and it would be all new to her. Her mouth was open and her tongue was licking her lips, and her eyes were reaching under Aphrodite's tiny skirt. I turned my attention to the leg kicking away the pretense of the skirt and showing us a bluish split framed in light brown hair. There it was, the dollar-fifty secret. As I saw what I had hoped to see, I felt shamed and sexy at the same time. I forgot everybody around me and stared for all I was worth, wanting, I knew, to burn the picture of it into my brain, every tendon stretching, every bit of pinkness showing, all the glistening of the flesh. I said to myself, Christian Foggy, this will never come again. Take its picture! I was in a fever. We were all in a fever. The heat swarming over us was suffocating.

And when finally the leg quit going up and up, and the girl without eyes had slipped forever behind the curtain, I blinked and shook my head in wonder at who I was and what I had learned about myself and Phoebe Bumpus. There was a feeling that I had changed in a permanent way, that the no-rain with Mamie was an innocent thing compared with Aphrodite's dance inside my head. I felt shabby and old, like I had a scar on my brain.

The show was really over. The carny man had no more to offer us, and he threw back the exit flap and walked away. We filed out, and I, for one, felt like we ought to hurry up and get some distance between us and the Sultan's Harem. But as I started through the door, Phoebe touched my hand and told me to look behind.

"There's that guy," she said.

The vulture-man was leaning on the stage and talking to someone behind the curtain. In his hand was a roll of bills. I saw dainty fingers come out and pluck the money away. Then the vulture-man climbed up and went on all fours, dipping his lean body under the skirt of curtain that hid what he was about to do.

"No amount of money," said Phoebe, "would tempt me to let him touch me. How can those girls do it? Can you imagine him?"

I didn't want to. I headed toward the center of the carnival and took Phoebe on some rides, the hammer and the octopus, and tried to get the good mood back that I had lost in the tent. It was on the ferris wheel later in the day that Phoebe finally told me who Aphrodite was.

"Her real name is Mickey Baker," she said. "She's been blind since birth. My friend knew her parents. He was raised next door from their house. Mickey was easy, he said. Ever since she was just a little kid, all the boys came around to do it to her in her basement. But when she was only thirteen, one of them made her pregnant, and then her father found out and went nuts. My friend saw what happened that day. He was in his front yard and heard yelling and screaming, and here comes Mickey out the door and her old man behind her with a knife. God, how would you like to be blind and have someone chasing you with a knife?" Phoebe shuddered and waved her hand like she had a knife and was stabbing something. "What a nightmare!"

"Chased her where?" I asked, seeing her with her blind eyes running through midnight like some poor chicken about to get its head chopped off.

"She ran down the street, screaming bloody murder, and her old man with his butcher knife was screaming that he was going to give her an abortion. Cars were running into trees to keep from hitting her, and people were standing with their hands over their mouths, just watching the whole thing. It must have been a sight. Can you imagine? Then I guess she fell and he jumped on top of her. He put his butt right on her face and held her down with one hand and slashed up her belly with the other hand. And then somebody came out and shot him. My friend said he was a quiet guy, a guy you'd never think would go crazy like that. It's the quiet ones you've got to watch."

"God, that's awful," I said. "Poor Aphrodite."

"Stupid father. What a way to act. What gets into men sometimes, especially about their daughters? Men get crazy about their daughters, you ever notice? Like part of their harem, I think. Must be a stag instinct."

I didn't know what got into men, but I didn't think my pa would ever do something so awful to Mary Magdalen. John Beaver would do it to Mamie, maybe, but my pa was different.

"I saw the scar," I said.

"Yeah, me too. She must feel it every day, every single day, and know she drove her father crazy enough to get him killed. Heavy burden, Christian."

"Poor Aphrodite," I repeated. "She couldn't even see where she was going."

We got off the ferris wheel and walked out past the tents to where some people were still sitting on blankets near the pasture. We sat on the grass, making sure to keep away from the cow-pies scattered here and there. I told Phoebe it was a wonder Mickey Baker didn't die that day too, getting her tummy ripped open.

"The baby died, of course," Phoebe said. "But it's just as well, because it was a monster. I saw it. My friend took me over to the hospital and showed me where they kept the thing in a jar of alcohol. Christian, it was like something from outer space. Six inches long. White as bone. You could tell it was female, but a freak. It would have had no kind of life. Its head was huge and round as a pie pan, probably like Mamie's must have looked, with inflammation of the brain or something. And this thing had no eyes, Christian. None at all. There was just skin, a sheet of skin covering where her eyes should have been. She would have walked through life blind and probably would have been an idiot. It was ghastly. It was pitiful."

I chewed a sprig of timothy and gazed off across the pasture to where some cows were grazing and minding their own business. The sun was going down and making the sky a shrimp color. A clump of dandelions was nearby, Mamie's weed that always reminded me of the time at the Brule with her running through the meadow like an overgrown fairy. The music from the carnival was behind us. It was peaceful everywhere, and girls without eyes didn't fit in. But I had seen her, and Phoebe had seen an eyeless baby with a pie-pan head floating in a jar of alcohol.

"Where is God?" I asked, more to the sky than to Phoebe.

"Oh, who knows?" she answered, like it was a boring question.

As evening came on, we went back to the carnival and found Mamie and Bob Thorn. They were at a beer stand, next to the dance floor, and the band was warming up.

"Some shit-kicking music coming on," said Thorn. "You want to stay?"

We decided we would. We sat on the edge of the dance floor and drank beer and told each other all we had done. They mostly went on the rides. Thorn said Mamie was like a two-year-old running from one ride to the next. Phoebe told him about us seeing the sideshows, but she didn't tell the story of Mickey Baker. Her mood had changed since the telling, gotten quiet and thoughtful.

The lights came on and the band played some slow music. Phoebe pulled me to the middle of the floor and we danced, rocking slowly in a circle like we had done the night at Shepard's. Mamie and Thorn danced too, and I felt a twinge of jealousy about it. Mamie was caught up in her new prettiness and the attention of Thorn, and she was all but ignoring me. It seemed a distance was growing between us. She and Thorn made a more natural-looking couple than she and I made, that was for sure, but I felt I had grown beyond caring about looks. It was the inside Mamie, the soul of Mamie, that I was beginning to miss. But I had Phoebe in my arms, thin, curvy Phoebe with her cute mouth and beautiful teeth and moth-wing ears, all of her leaning into me and warming me enough to push Mamie out of my mind for a while.

The band played a couple of waltzes that coaxed the people to come out and shuffle across the floor. Then they struck up the first polka of the night. Mamie recognized that kind of music from before, and she knew what to do. She and Thorn stole the show. People saw them coming whirling like a pair of giant tops, whooping like locomotives coming through, and got out of their way, which was a wise thing to do. Round and round they went, Mamie's yellow skirt flaring out and bright as the May moon, her powerful legs showing off the life in them; and Thorn, almost a match for her in size, hanging on and spinning for all he was worth, the wonder of what he had in his arms showing in his eyes. The people clapped and the band picked up the tempo and boom boom boom went Mamie and Bob Thorn, the length and the width of the floor, sending little shocks up our feet every time they hit the boards. There was plenty of whistling and hooting for them. It reminded me of being in the Sultan's tent and how the audience carried on so that Aphrodite would lift her leg.

"Go, baby, go!" "Faster, honey, faster!" "Look at 'em go!" "Faster, faster!" "Look at them legs!" "Eeeeee-haaa!" "Waaaa-whooo!" And a shower of clap-clap-clapping in time to the beat.

The difference to me was that I didn't feel guilty about being part of it the way I had with Aphrodite. This was joy. This was happy.

Phoebe was coming out of her mood. She was leaning against me and bumping me with her hip, keeping time with the clapping with her bump-bump-bumping. And I was bumping her back, saying to myself in the midst of it all, For heaven's sake, don't get sick and spoil it this time!

When the polka was over, the audience gave Mamie and Thorn a big hand and gathered close to them, saying it was the best polka they had ever seen, that it was like seeing something professional. Some of them reached in to touch Mamie. It was something I had noticed a lot of times – people loved touching her; and it was no wonder, with the way that such a glow came off her, a kind of dew of life shining on her skin. She was like life at its shiny best, the way racehorses shine running down the track or cows shine, full of alfalfa and grain, udders heavy with milk, as they rise in the morning. Mamie Beaver: big, strong, sexy, pretty, fresh, loving, awesome, holy, and good. Touch her and maybe some of it will rub off.

It was midnight when we got home. Thorn had been kissing on Mamie all the way home and saying they were going to get married. She was drinking splow and giggling about it but not saying, "Nup nup," like I expected her to. When Phoebe pulled the car to the curb, they got out and walked away from us without even saying good night. They went to the Artlife arm and arm. Phoebe said they made a perfect couple and that they would make marvelous, giant babies.

I opened the jar of splow to take a drink, but she snatched it away from me. "You don't need that, honey," she said. "You've got something better tonight."

We went inside into the bedroom and kept the lights off. The moonlight coming through the window made Phoebe's skin look blue and her lips as dark as those of the harem girls. She pushed up against me hard and said she didn't understand herself, because every day I was on her mind making her want to rob the cradle. She was pressing and pawing on me, sucking my fingers and lips and licking my neck. I wanted badly to take a shower and soap it up with her. When I mentioned it, she said, "Are you kidding? The aroma is the best part. We don't want to wash it off." She opened my shirt and sniffed at me. "Yummy, you smell so sexy, you young thing. You're making Phoebe Bumpus feel all oily. Naughty naughty baby."

She suddenly pulled her blouse off and did a funny thing with it, rolling it up and tying it around her head, blindfolding herself.

"What're you doing that for?" I asked.

"Shush, shush, shh, don't talk, youngster. Don't say anything to me. Breathe. Let me hear you breathing, okay?"

With tender fingers she felt over me, ran her fingers over my face, feeling my eyes and cheeks and inside my mouth, and all the while sighing, "oooo, oooo."

"Phoebe, what's going on?" I asked. "Let's take a shower."

But she was for having her way. "Trust me," she said, unsnapping her brassiere and letting it drop. "Nurse me," she said. So I did nurse her awhile. She shimmied out of her jeans next, then pushed my head down further and said it again, "Nurse me." I didn't want to, but some part of me did, some part of me went wild for what she wanted. The aroma came out and filled my body with itself, and I no longer wanted to take a shower. The dew of her seeped into me and tasted sweet, like

I had never imagined it would. I glued my mouth to her for what seemed like an entire whirl of the world but was too short at that. And then she pulled me to my feet and helped me with my clothes, and when we were naked she did to me what I did to her. Her lips were nasty, and awful fine too, and afterward she said, "Lead me to the bed." Which I did. Fire was in me, and thunder and lightning, and she was storming too, yelling out at each stroke, "Here's the darkness! Here's the pit! Eyeless! Eyeless!" She rose like a wave beneath me, drowning me in herself, and no Mamie to save me.

When it was over, I felt weird, like I didn't belong to the body that had done those things. I lay beside her, imagining myself a piece of damp wood rotting on a beach. The question turned over and over in my mind, Is this what grown-up people do? Or is it a sick thing? It came to me that I had learned something important about women, maybe – that they played a game with sex, played at the borders and over the borders: Mamie with her no-rain dance; Phoebe and her girl-without-eyes. There was a feeling of slipping toward Camelot in it. And I wondered if it was good or bad that I had learned so young the power of a woman in heat and the things a fellow would do, like his will had turned to water; things that even my pa didn't know, I was sure; things that maybe most guys didn't know; things that wet the mind down worse than any proof of splow; things about the aroma and taste of women and their fantasy worlds.

Phoebe took off her blindfold and looked at me smiling. "Robbing the cradle," she whispered. "Little boys in basements. I must be a pervert, ooooo . . ."

Robbie and the Riot

It was the first Sunday in June. The construction of the New Artlife was going good, and three acres of the woods where Mamie had romped with Thorn had been bulldozed flat. Backhoes had come in to make trenches for pipes and the foundation. Soon the workers would be laying pipe and pouring cement, then the walls would go up and the roof, and Shepard would have the Artlife of his dreams – a huge glass and tamarack and brick building with two-thousand seats in it and a stage and a screen to beat anything Temple had ever seen.

Once the construction started, Shepard spent all the time he could watching the men work and giving orders to them and rubbing his nose happily. If any of us came around him, he would chatter about all his dreams about the theater to be, the great center of culture in Wisconsin, a beacon of hope in a drab world full of tiny-minded bores incubated by circumstance and mediocrity. He would offer them a stimulation they could not resist – the stimulation of the mind, from his own creation and farsighted genius and warm love, with Mamie Beaver as the central symbol of who he was and what his destiny had to be. While he told us of these visions, his hands would clap for himself; his fingers would poke and pinch the air, slashing it, making rectangles and triangles and squares, as if forming from space itself the thing he called the center and the beacon and the monument, the invisible temple where the religion of art would fly out and gobble up the world. All the converts would go out and capture more multitudes for Mamie to mesmerize. The church coffers would overflow, and with money would come fame, television, books, radio, film – all the things necessary to carry the litany of art across the country. There were no limits. It was all going to happen. He knew. He knew.

But on that first Sunday in June, it all changed. It was a warning when things started out strange, a warning I picked up on, but there was nothing I could do. The first service was crowded, as usual, but there was something different about the people, about the way they looked and the way they acted. On the west side of the aisle were lots of them I had seen enough times to know they were sort of tried-and-true members. Some were the book-burners who had come around to seeing life Shepard's way, but they weren't many. Most of the book-burners had left after it got clear to them what Shepard was trying to do – that is, trying to get them to worship the great things that men had done rather than the things of God. So the majority of the people were not connected with burning the books; they had come into the fold later, after Phoebe had written the article about Mamie. They were people Shepard had nicknamed the Intellectuals because of the way they took to the art litany and showed they believed in what he was trying to do.

On the east side was another bunch, different from the Intellectuals. I recognized a lot of them too, the book-burners who I thought had dropped out of our church. But they were back and had quite a few people with them I had never seen before, and most of them were carrying big, black bibles, holding the bibles in their hands folded up against their chests, like shields. I caught up with Shepard before he went on and pointed out what was happening in the audience. He gave the east-siders a piercing, down-the-nose look and decided he knew all about them.

"Humph, they're Christers," he said. "Christers on the verge of conversion, on the verge of sliding over the cusp into the life of the mind. The bibles are their armor against Mamie's message. Poof poof, it isn't going to work. Once they've sat through the service, any of them with an IQ one jot above moron will know the Bible is mere ancient vapor. Art is the living symbol of the soul and the aegis to protect them from their abysmal ignorance, yum yum – the aegis to protect them from abysmal ignorance." He ran his left hand over his mouth and sucked at his fingertips one at a time, like he was getting the last bit of flavor from the words he used. Then he said, "We will call down fire to light our altar. Fire will bring them into the fold." He hurried off to get Mamie ready. I could hear him saying, "Fire! Fire!" and see him poking the air with his finger as he lumbered along.

But in my belly was an uneasy feeling about the people filling in the east side. For one thing, they weren't being nice to everyone. They were telling certain persons here and there to get out of their section, that they had it reserved, which wasn't true. It had always been first-come first-served, like in any church. The unwelcome ones were always civilized about it and apologized for being on the wrong side. They would go find themselves seats in the other section and tell the person next to them what had happened, which, after the word got around, made the west side look at the east like they were a great puzzlement. Everybody seemed to be on edge. There was a lot of whispering going on on both sides.

I went up the aisle to the main doors and stood there feeling prickly. In a minute the front door opened and a woman came in, along with someone dressed in a monk-type robe, covered up from head to foot, so I couldn't see if it was a man or a woman. But it was tall, and I figured it to be a man. The woman I recognized to be Lulu, the one who had burned *Samson Agonistes* and had told the others to burn Shakespeare because he was so depressing. She escorted the robed person in, and the east side made room for them in the front row. My skin got more and more prickly.

The lights went dim, and into Powers's eye came Shepard to give his introduction to Mamie. Both sides were polite and listened to him. Then he brought Mamie out. She wore her yellow dress and had fresh flowers in her hair. Behind her in the shadows was Bob Thorn, watching out for her. She opened her mouth to say something, but a guy on my left, on the east side, cut her off, shouting out, "'Before my God, I might not this believe without the sensible and true avouch of mine eyes.'"

"Whhaat?" said somebody.

"Is that from *Moby Dick*?" a woman asked.

There was a minute of grumbling and asking what the hell was that "avouch of mine eyes" stuff?

Mamie stared at the east side with her head cocked, her eyes puzzled, looking like she was trying to remember what was the next line to what the man had shouted. It didn't come to her, so she just said what came to mind.

"'Call me Ishmael.'"

And the people on my right sighed with relief and settled into the give-and-take of the lines about having no money and wanting to see the oceans. But the ones on my left said nothing. One of them close by was flipping the pages of his bible with his thumb.

Mamie took up her next response, "'Whenever it is a damp, drizzly November in my soul . . .'"

And again, when it was time for the audience to reply, only the west side said what they were supposed to. They went back and forth, Mamie and the Intellectuals, talking about paths to the sea and the magic of the water, where the water is a mirror where every man sees himself. It was soothing the way they said it, and for a while things went along fine, except the Christers stayed shut-mouthed. Then Mamie hit the part where Stubb tells Ishmael, "'If God ever wanted to be a fish, he'd be a whale!'" And the Christers mumbled and made noises like they were disgusted with such a notion. Some of them even shook their bibles at Mamie, like they wanted the bibles to see what a liar she was to say that about God being a whale.

One of the west-siders named Arnold told the Christers to shut up, and then he cut to the next scene himself and shouted out what Ishmael says about Queequeg – "'Better a sober cannibal than a drunken Christian!'"

The east side really erupted then. A lot of harumphing and huffing and calling Arnold an infidel and a humanist. Mamie had to raise her voice extra high to get her next line heard. In the voice of the preacher in *Moby Dick*, she told them, "'And God created a great fish to swallow Jonah,'" which calmed the Christers down. And it even got approval from both sides when she came to the line, "'To preach the truth in the face of falsehood.'"

And so it went, and it was like walking a tightrope of words back and forth. The people on the west side held to the normal litany. The ones on the east liked some things but didn't like most. I had a feeling we would never get to *Hamlet*. The two sides were giving each other dirty looks, and their faces were swelling up with anger. The pressure kept building until the part came where Mamie was Captain Ahab saying, "'God hunt us all, if we do not hunt Moby Dick to his death!'"

"'Death to Moby Dick! Death to Moby Dick!'" the Intellectuals sang.

And following them came a familiar voice crying out, "Sweet Jeee-sus Christ, I've heard enough of this! I will not hear more!"

The man in the robe leaped on the stage and threw his robe off. His long hair and beard flashed like tinsel in Powers's light. His hands reached out for us; his eyes burned into us. And sure enough, it was Robbie Peevy himself come back from the dead.

"Oh no, not him," I heard someone say.

The other side started chanting, "Robbie! Robbie! Robbie!"

He was his old self, oozing with righteousness, soaking up the love of the Christers.

"Jeee-sus called me back to you. Jeee-sus sent a message to me, told me that you were in trouble back here. Told me there was blaspheming and apostasy going on!"

"Amen!" the Christers answered.

"Told me that some of you were headed for hellfire damnation."

"Amen! Amen!"

"Told me, 'Robbie, go ye back in the name of Christ's love and seek ye my lost sheep and bring ye them back into the fold, for I am their good and true shepherd, and their eyes are blinded by an evil *Shepard* carrying the beacon of hell's infernal light!'"

"Tell 'em, Robbie! Tell 'em!"

"Amen! Amen!"

"Oh, sweet Jesus!"

Robbie crossed the stage to where he could look down on the Church of Art members. His face was showing his sadness for them, how sorry he was that they had been taken in by the evil shepherd. "And so I am here for you," he said, sweeping his hand across the air to show he meant them all. "I am here for you – yes, Jeee-sus! – here at the request of your one and only savior. Jeee-sus is the way!"

The people in front of him stayed quiet, but the Christers went wild: "Amen, Jeeee-suus is the way!"

"The way! The way!"

"Tell 'em, Robbie! Give 'em the word of the Lord!"

"Sic the heathen, Robbie! Sic 'em, Jesus!"

Robbie backed up and put his arm around Mamie. She was standing in a frozen beam of light, her eyes staring up to where Powers was, like waiting for him to tell her what to say.

Robbie squeezed her and told the people, "And Jeee-sus has a special love for this one! She is his Holy Fool! His Holy Fool, misused and sore abused by a false prophet preaching the divinity and omnipotence of man!" He pressed his lips together and curled them out, like such disgusting words were going to make him puke. "This precious child of Jesus has been made into Satan's pawn, made to do the devil's work. God forgive the corrupters of such a sweet soul. God forgive them, for I cannot!"

"Kill the false shepherd! Kill the evil one!" someone shouted.

"Shut up, you fuck'n moron!" yelled someone else.

Shepard moved over to Mamie's other side and looked at Robbie like he was swamp water come to life. "Thou art the evil one," he said. "In your immeasurable stupidity is boundless evil and boundless suffering for the world! It is contemptible that an intellect of my magnitude must needs lower itself to even speak of you. Phooey!" He made a wet noise with his tongue and curled his upper lip, showing off his two teeth and his gums. He took Mamie's arm and tried to pull her away from Robbie, but Robbie held on tight.

"This . . . thing!" Shepard said next. "This thing can't even tell you what it was he saw just now, that's how stupid he is." He looked again at Robbie. "Tell us, moron, what does it mean – the phrase that had you protesting so vociferously – 'Death to Moby Dick'?"

"It wasn't just that," said Robbie, "but I can tell you what it means. I'm not stupid. Just substitute the name Moby Dick for the name Jesus Christ. That's what it means – it's saying death to Jeee-sus! It's the same thing as calling out to Satan to come on and snatch your soul away. Death to Jeee-sus! That's what it says." Robbie looked out on us, and we could tell he was pleased with what he said.

Shepard raised a finger to get our attention. "That's what I would expect from an evangelical cretin – a superficial interpretation. Death to Moby Dick is death to evil, death to the malevolent spirit pervading this miserable world. This pusillanimous cretin with all his amens and Jesus-is-the-way simplicity aids and abets that evil spirit. Its name is ignorance! Ignorance is the only evil!"

"Ignorance of God leads to evil!" said Robbie.

Shepard rubbed his nose viciously and glared down it at Robbie. "It says death to evil!"

"Death to God!"

"Evil!"

"God!"

"Eeeeee-villll!"

Thorn stopped it by coming up and jerking Robbie away from Mamie. "It's all bullshit," he said, and he threw Robbie off the stage into the arms of the Intellectuals, who didn't want him and tossed him over to the other side. The people went to screaming at each other, throwing words at each other like they were punches that could knock somebody out. Some of the Christers were chanting again, "Robbie, Robbie, Robbie," while others on the west side were saying "Mamie, Mamie, Mamie." Mamie herself stood like a bird in a cage, not looking at Powers anymore, just watching back and forth the words fighting.

Robbie pulled himself back onto the stage, where he was going after Mamie – I think to pull her off. But Bob Thorn started chasing him round and round, from one side to the other of Mamie. He kept a step ahead of Thorn for a while, and the people on both sides watched and laughed about it, but finally Thorn lunged and knocked Robbie down flat on his face. Thorn picked him up by his collar and the seat of his pants and threw him off the stage again. He hit in the aisle and rolled himself into a ball. The Christers tried to pick him up. One of them said, "He's bleeding! His forehead's gushing!"

"Oh, you sinner!" shrieked another.

"Kill him!" said someone.

"Kill them all! Kill the evil shepherd!"

"Kill the false prophet!"

"Kill the hoo-manist bastards!"

And the other side was saying to kill the Christers – "Kill the goddamn Christers!"

"Kill those chuckleheads!"

"Kill them cretins!"

And so it went, louder and louder, until it all blended together and you couldn't tell what was being said. It was just a big, ugly noise.

Thorn came to the edge of the stage and was screaming something too and spitting on the Christers. Some of them went after him, trampling over Robbie, who was still trying to keep himself in a ball. More Christers followed, rushing the stage, where Thorn waited in his tackler's pose to beat them up. The first ones up got smacked back, and more came, cursing and clawing their way up, and he kicked them and punched them and tossed them, but there were too many and they finally pulled him under. And they went for Shepard too. He saw them coming and fainted dead away, ka-boom! – right in back of Mamie. At the same time, the west side got pulled into it, and in no time at all the two sections were beating each other. Women kicked and punched, same as the men. Men punched men and men punched women. Little kids got whacked and little kids ran around biting the legs and the bottoms of anyone they could reach. Everybody wrestled and pulled hair and tore at each other's clothes. And a furious cussing – "Bastard!" "Bitch!" "Cocksucker!" "Cuntlicker!" – was everywhere.

The woman named Lulu ran past me, crying out, "This isn't what I meant, Jesus! I wanted to save the faith!" She went out the door, sobbing like her heart was broken.

Another woman, with patches of hair torn out and a bloody nose, ran up to me and told me to call the police. Behind her, a woman with a split lip and a dress torn open down the front grabbed the first woman by the hair and pulled her screaming bloody murder back into the crowd. Just in front of me was a man getting bitten on one leg by a kid and being kicked in the stomach by another man. A woman was being chased up and down the back rows by a man with a belt who was calling her a fat twat. He caught her finally at the door and whipped her with the belt. She turned on him, screaming, "Goddamn you, Howard, we're suppose to be on the same side!" And she charged him and knocked him into the seats. Another woman crawled out from the battle and up the aisle at me. Her clothes were all gone except for a hanging nylon on one leg. There were marks on her from her shoulders to her knees that looked like everyone had been biting her. She grabbed my shoulders and shrieked that she couldn't stand it anymore. Throwing her head back, she screamed so loud it made my ears ring. When it was over, her eyes rolled up in her head and she went backward in a heap, hitting the floor with such a thump I thought she must have killed herself.

The war raged on and on, up and down the rows and the aisle and in the seats and in front of the stage. Thorn was on the stage in front of Mamie, bleeding from his mouth, his shirt torn and scratch marks down his arm, but at the ready to defend her, though no one was even paying attention to her anymore, nor to Shepard, who was lying like a dead whale behind her. As for Mamie, she wasn't looking at the people anymore. In her hands were flowers she had pulled from her hair, and she was sniffing them and twirling them in the light. In front of her the crying and the screeching, the punching, the kicking, the biting, the ripping and the roaring were still going on, but all of it was nothing to her.

Finally the people wore themselves out and couldn't beat each other anymore. Their voices were hoarse, and they could only throw sissy punches. One by one they sank into chairs or onto the floor and sprawled out. Then there came nothing but panting and moaning and bawling. The people looked like a mess of bloody rags and bones lying about.

A voice rose up out of the center of the bodies. It asked, "What the hell happened?"

Moaning and whining answered him.

Bob Thorn took Mamie by the hand and led her offstage. Shepard stirred and checked out the condition of his nose. The naked lady in front of me opened her eyes and said, "Where am I?" A man crawled past her and told her she ought to get some clothes on, which made her faint dead away again. People crawled on all fours toward the bathrooms and brought back paper towels soaked in water to clean up their bloody brothers and sisters. There was no way to tell which was the west side and which the east. They were all hurting pretty badly together. In the middle of them, I spotted poor Robbie, still curled up like a baby in a crib. I dragged him out and saw he was bleeding from his nose and mouth and a gash on his forehead. One eye opened and he looked at me. "Christian," he said weakly, "I think my ribs is broke."

¶ I helped Robbie over to the house, and as we were going in Shepard came up behind us. His voice was shaking with anger.

He said, "What on earth are you doing, Crystal?" He followed us into the bedroom, where I put Robbie on the bed.

"He's still my friend," I told Shepard.

"I'll not allow it. I'll not have that fanatic under my roof. I refuse it! Did you see what he did to my disciples? They are destroyed. Someone should knock that factious dog in the head!"

"You're the fanatic," said Robbie, pointing a bloody finger at him.

"You are the fanatic," he answered, pointing back. "I cannot hold services with you and your ilk around. Wherever you go is chaos!"

"Shepard, he can't go anywhere now. Look at him," I said. "He thinks his ribs are broken."

"Serves him right, the scoundrel. Humph!" Shepard stood awhile and chewed his lips and stared at Robbie. Robbie was pitiful to see, all bloody and worn-out-looking, his eyes and mouth pinched with pain. Shepard was mad, sure, but it was hard for anyone with a heart to look at Robbie and not feel a bit sorry for him.

"He's got to go as soon as he's better," Shepard said at last. "Now let me go see if I can salvage something of what we've built."

I got hot water and towels and got Robbie cleaned up. I wrapped one of the towels round his head to catch the bleeding. But for the rest of him, there wasn't much I could do except clean the wounds and let them dry up. Nothing at all I could do for the ribs. Later on I made him some tomato soup and gave it to him along with a glass of splow. By sundown he was feeling much better, his face not so crooked with pain. He liked the splow, drank a second glass, and said it made him feel kind of numb. He slept awhile, and I got a chair and a book and sat next to him reading. In a couple of hours he woke up and said I should never go to California.

"It's full of goofs and demons," he said. "I felt them in the air. I saw them all around. It was like with my friend, the holyman I told you of. The demons crashed his motorcycle – he was surrounded by demons, just like that. And they're gonna get me, Christian. They're coming here, sniffing me out. I feel them coming, feel them in my soul, coming, like that."

"You'll be safe here," I said. "No demons want to mess with Mamie and Bob Thorn."

"You don't know what I went through in California, Christian. Demons. I threw my best scripture at their heads. All my inspiration. All my Christian love. No effect. I might as well have preached to a pack of seagulls. Nobody listens to nobody out there. Everybody's got an opinion, but nobody listens to nobody." He was quiet for a minute. Then he said, "Seems like nobody listens to nobody round here either. I'm laying here thinking maybe Wisconsin is California in some ways. Like that fighting in the Artlife there. If I'd had more chance to talk, there wouldn't have been that fighting. Nobody listens out here either, like that, yeah. And I'm wondering, where do I belong, Christian? I feel low. I feel like the Lord has forsaken me. Shepard's right. Everywhere I go is chaos. People get hurt. Nobody listens."

I leaned over, so I could look at him. His eyes were wet with tears that ran over and hid in his beard. Pale as a ghost he was. Skin and bones. I felt bad for him.

"What did you come back for?" I asked. "Demons drive you out?"

"Lulu wrote and told me what was going on. Said souls were being lost to humanism. The way she described it, I knew I had to come back and try. Humanism is a cancer on the soul. Kills it. I had to try."

"But nobody listens," I said.

"Nobody listens."

I wasn't going to tell him what I really thought – that he never listened either. It was just his style that caused riots. It didn't seem to me that anyone could *talk* a middle ground with him. Everything was black and white.

"We'll get you fixed up," I told him. "Get you fixed up and on your way. Wouldn't want the cops coming to take you off to Camelot."

"I can't go," he said. "Christian, I can't run off now. Got to stay and save some souls. Can't leave them to go down Shepard's path. It just goes to darkness. The people need Jesus, honey. They can't make it in this world without him. It's Jesus what makes them behave, makes them follow the precious path of good. Jesus *is* the way, Christian. Without him life is hopeless, nothing to live for; everything is just an ugly joke without Jesus. He gives us the reason for all the suffering. Because of him, I know my wounds have a purpose. I know that nothing in my life happens by chance. Think of living under chance! Why, I don't see how you can stand it. But Jesus tells me nothing happens by chance." He sighed and rubbed his ribs. "I'm thinking maybe they're just cracked a little."

"A little cracked – that'd be a lot better," I said.

"Tell me something. What has Shepard got to offer to compare with Jesus?"

"It's complicated. Get him to explain it. He says that great art soothes the savage beast in man. It makes men sane. And he says it makes men understand they've got a soul much greater and grander than the old simple soul of a peasant groveling at the feet of a master. He blames all the wars on the fact that no one knows just how great their soul is. Don't ask me to explain it. My mind can't keep up with his. He's a genius."

"Great art! Art making men sane! Poo! What is art? It ain't nothing but what some smartass teaching college says it is, all written up in some book or something. You know what art gives to people? You know what it does for them? Gives them nothing, a big nothing, except maybe makes them feel stupid cause they don't know what's so great about it. A big black hole and nothing in it for most of us. Art gives you nowhere to go, nothing to pray to when you're down. Art ain't nothing to give people in place of Jesus. Why can't he see that? If he's a genius, why's he so stupid? Art can't match the wonder and mystery and love of Jesus. And you know what else it don't give them? You know what art don't give?"

I didn't know.

"It don't give hope. Show me a world that can live without that. Shepard's stupid if he thinks it can."

Made sense to me, the hope thing. "Yep," I said, "you've got something there."

Mamie came in, looking fresh and pink-cheeked, as if she had just come from a nice Sunday stroll. She bent over the bed and brushed Robbie's hair with her fingers.

He caught her hand and kissed it, and he said, "Jesus, am I glad to see you again, Mamie. I thought so much about you when I was gone. Thought about you every day." He kissed her hand some more. They stared at each other. It made me think of a sunflower staring at a lily.

"Mamie's always liked you a lot," I said.

"And I *love* her," he answered. "God has touched her, and you can tell it. Purity shines from her. She's an innocent soul, God's Holy Fool. God wants to use you, honey. I'm sent to tell you, beware the anti-Christ."

"Anti-Christ," she repeated. "Anti-Christ, anti-Christ."

"She likes that word," I said. "You can tell when she likes a word."

He told her to say, "I heard a holy one speaking," but she just came back with "Anti-Christ" again.

"No, no," he said. "Don't say that no more."

"Anti-Christ."

"Please, honey. It hurts me to hear it so much."

She quit saying anti-Christ, and she cocked her head and gave

Robbie a look as if she was reading his mind. There was a sort of sweet understanding in her eyes, the kind a mother has for her goofy kid. "'I heard a holy one speaking,'" she said softly.

"That's it, that's my girl. That's my Mamie. I'm going to teach you the whole bible. Then we'll show 'em. I'm going to teach you chapter and verse, and I'll take you to every city and you'll stand tall and speak the bible. You'll be a living, breathing bible, a holy miracle. Mamie the idiot speaks!"

She giggled and poked Robbie in the rib with her finger. He cried out in pain.

"Oh!" she said, jerking her hand away.

"Somebody jumped on his ribs," I told her.

"Jumped him?"

"In the Artlife. The fight today."

"It's okay." Robbie took her hand again. "You didn't know, honey."

"You didn't know, honey," she answered. Then she stood up and stretched and yawned.

"Where you going?" he asked, clutching at her dress. "Don't leave me. Stay here with me. Listen, listen, I got this feeling, and I got to tell somebody." He was talking fast and trying to pull her back down. "The voice has come and told me if I fail at this, if I don't win you for the Lord, then my time is through. You and me, Mamie, chapter and verse. 'In the beginning God created the heavens and the earth.' Say it to me. Tell me that you know it."

She slipped her dress away from him and at the same time said in a kidding kind of voice, "Mamie the idiot don't know it." She turned round and left. She went into the bathroom and closed the door.

"I'm the suffering idiot," whispered Robbie.

"She's been getting that way more and more," I said.

He asked me what way, and I told him, "Independent sort of. Saying what she wants to say, doing what she wants to do. Shepard's got no control really. Mamie makes up the litany now."

Robbie thought about it. His brows knitted together and his big eyes got small. His lips thinned out. He stroked his beard. "If that's so," he said, "then I'm too late. And if I'm too late, I'm done for sure. Something's come and told me. Something's come and whispered in my ear. There's no place left for me anymore. I'm just a ghost-in-waiting, just a ghost-in-waiting. I've come back here just a ghost-in-waiting."

"Quit talking stupid," I said.

He looked up at me, his eyes sharp and desperate. "It's the truth, honey. I'm not playing no joke. Just a ghost-in-waiting. Now look here, listen up. You're my friend. You and Mamie – you're my friends. Don't leave me here, honey. Don't let 'em roll me into a ditch and – and have the ants eat me! Don't let 'em do that. Or don't let 'em do things to me neither – cut me up, look at my brain to see why. Don't let 'em cut me up for science! Oh Jesus, not that! Don't let 'em, Christian!"

"I won't. I won't," I told him. His face was awful, red like a cock's comb and twisted up. "I'll take you to the farm," I said. "I'll bury you in a nice place."

His face settled down and he looked curious. "Where's that?" he wanted to know.

"Next to the Brule, right near the edge of our pasture. Nice place. You can hear the river going by, soft and whispery, like angels talking."

"Like angels going by," he sighed. "That's more like it. The river of time. That's the kind of place for me. You mean it, huh? You promise me, honey?"

"Sure, you bet."

He was quiet for a second, looking up to the ceiling and stroking his beard like it was a pet cat. "That'll be just fine," he said. "Angels talking, whispering river talk, and Robbie shushing by, Robbie gone to water."

Then he wanted some water, said he was hot. I touched his forehead, and it was sure burning up. I figured with such a fever it was no wonder he was talking so weird. I got him some water and put a cold cloth on his forehead. He mumbled for a while, and then he cried and mumbled. Then he just made faces, and finally, after a time, he went to sleep.

Mamie was still in the bathroom. I put my ear up next to the door and couldn't hear anything. "You fall in?" I said. There was no answer. "What're you doing?" I said. It was quiet as dust. I couldn't stand it, so I opened the door for just a peek, and I saw her standing in front of the mirror, concentrating on herself, making faces. She was smiling and batting her eyes and looking at her left side and her right side; fluffing up her hair, pulling it back, shoving it forward, making bangs; and doing funny things with her mouth, like she was surprised, then pouting, then mad, then moony, then kissing the air. It reminded me of things I'd seen Mary Magdalen do, and I wondered what was next. She'd probably want to marry Bob Thorn and have kids. The idea made my ears burn. I whispered the door shut and went back to sit by Robbie. He was snoring through his nose, which I thought was probably a good sign. I leaned back in my chair and took up my book where I had left off. It was a strange story, scary in spots, and like looking into the dark side of people's souls. It was called *The Possessed.* About some nuts in Russia, misfits, and some believed in nothing and others believed in something, but I couldn't tell exactly what. All it seemed was that everybody was tortured inside and the pain just paralyzed any good sense they might have had.

Armageddon

It was close to sunset on a Wednesday, three days after the riot, when something happened that I had been fearing in the back of my mind ever since Phoebe wrote the first story about Mamie for the newspaper. Robbie was still in bed. Shepard, Mamie, Thorn, and I were in the house, sitting and listening to Shepard complain about the ways of the world. He said he figured the Artlife experiment was over, because not enough people wanted to keep it going as the Church of Art, but a lot of them were ready to make it the Church of Jesus Christ. The people wanted to buy him out and to go on with the new church next door. He growled about how he should have known better than to think he could break the time-honored hold of mysticism and ignorance on the hearts of men, which had enslaved them since the first bare-forked animals stood on two legs, and he should have known the Rock of Ages had always been stronger than the Rock of Reason. He should have known. *He should have known*. He told us things were going from bad to worse, a bad sign for sure.

We didn't know how right he was.

There came a knock at the door, and I went to answer it. I opened the door, and what I saw made my stomach fall and my scalp get prickly. Standing in front of me in his farmeralls and chore jacket, a red baseball cap on his head, a wad of chew in his cheek – was John Beaver.

"Close yer mouth, soggybuns," he said in a husky voice. He was grinning at me like a monster in a nightmare.

I could only stare and stammer. I tried to say Mr. Beaver, but it came out, "Missss . . . ai-yi-yi."

"Shet yer face," he ordered. Then he shoved me aside and came in.

Mamie was sitting on the couch next to Thorn. Shepard was in the big chair.

Beaver said, "Sure nuff, it's her; it's my Mamie-girl. Come on to Pappy, Mamie. Pappy's here to fetch you home."

"Booshit," she said, her voice seething with hatred. She stared at John Beaver like he was an ugly spider.

"Now, Mamie," he said, a hard edge in his voice. "You know I been patient with you and this little fuckhead here. I been real patient. Real patient. Even let you crack my head open, that's right. But you better know that I run outta patience now. Patience and me had a partin of the ways." He turned his head a tad and spit a brown wad on the floor. It splattered and made dots on Mamie's bare feet. "Patience and me had a partin of the ways," he repeated. "So let's get that big ass a yers off that couch cause I got tickets for a bus ride home." He looked at me. "Had to come on a bus," he said, looking insulted by it. "Know why? Cause of you, you little worm. Fuck'n wrecked my pickup."

"But but I heard you had it running, Mr. Beaver. You had it in Plato that day," I said.

"Dumb fuck, don't remind me of that day. I'll stomp you right here and now. It ain't runnin no more. You wrecked it, and that made it get old and die. Yer fault, fluffyfuck, you fuck'n punkin-headed piss-ant curse of my life."

"Yessir."

"Damn right." He turned back to Mamie, who hadn't moved. "Mamie, don't make me drag you outta here."

Shepard stood up. He tried to suck in his belly, but the effort was too much. "So!" he said.

Beaver looked him up and down. "So?" he answered.

"So you are the proud father of this prodigy. I have taken her under my wing. I have uncovered her hidden talents. I am Don Shepard." Shepard bowed.

Beaver spit on the floor again. "I don't give a damn if yer the mayor of Milwaukee. And I'll tell you what – I know about you, about yer using my little girl here. I know all about it."

"He taught her to run a movie projector, gave her a trade," I said weakly.

"Big fuck'n deal. I taught her farmin. She don't know nuthin without I didn't teach her. Movies, shit. What the hell is that? No goddamn good for nuthin." He sneered at Shepard. "What else you teach her, fatso? Teach her to ride yer pud?"

"Me?" Shepard's nose flushed like a tomato. "I-I-I've taught her nothing of the sort. I've been her mentor, sir. To me she came, a waif, a pitiful and homeless orphan. I taught her a trade, you . . . you hooligan. I would think you would thank me."

Beaver cackled like a warlock. "You know somethin, chubby, you got a nose like a ugly wart. Ick, makes me want to squash it."

Shepard's hands flew to cover his nose. Beaver kept talking. "Folks round here tell me yer the brains a this sorry-assed outfit. Yer makin a reg'lar fuck'n mint, they tell me. I say yer exploitin my dotter, you fuck'n wartnosed tub of lard. Folks tellin me yer makin a freak show outta her, a reg'lar carnival."

"Lies! Contemptible lies!" Shepard answered from behind his hands.

Beaver stuck his finger in his ear and twirled it. "Did I hear this here fatass right? Did this fatass call me a liar, Foggy?"

"I don't think he meant you, Mr. Beaver," I replied.

"Am I a liar, puppybutt?"

"I'd never call you one, sir."

"But yer one, ain't you."

"If you say so, sir."

"Got big plans for you, fluffybum."

My heart was pounding so hard, I felt like I was going to choke and die. Beaver looked wild as an ax-murderer leaning over a pot of body parts. The light coming through the window hit his face and made it seem like all the creases in it were scars, old blue scars from his victims who went down fighting. I knew he had plans for me; he didn't have to tell me. My guts were loose with knowing.

Shepard was trying to keep a brave tone of voice, but his belly was quivering. "I never taught her to ride my pud," he said with muffled dignity.

Thorn, who had been watching John Beaver all the while, finally stood up. He flexed his shoulders. "You a troublemaker?" he said.

Beaver sized him up. Beaver was half a head taller. "Yep, I'm trouble all right. More trouble'n you want, gorillaneck."

"I'm a gorilla?" said Thorn, sneering at Beaver. "You're the fuck'n gorilla, man!" He wasn't scared! Bob Thorn wasn't scared! I was so happy he wasn't scared. Shepard was too. He took courage and lowered his hands from guarding his nose.

"Actually, I believe the law would say that Mamie is old enough to decide for herself where she wants to live," he said. "You cannot force her to go with you."

"Shet yer face, wartnose. I'm the law for her."

Shepard looked at Mamie and his voice got stubborn. "Mamie, you want to live with me or your father?"

"You, Shep," she answered softly.

"There's your answer, Mr. Beaver. The law – "

"I don't give a flyin fuck about the law! I told you to shet up, you blubber-bellied ton of shit!"

Shepard's lips worked all over his gums, but no words came out. I saw tears welling up in his eyes. I sure didn't want him crying and giving John Beaver something more to cackle about. Beaver crooked his finger at Mamie. "Blud of my blud. Yer mine. Yer all I got, and I'll kill the motherfucker tries to keep you from me."

Thorn's voice was tight, coming through clenched teeth. "You don't own shit round here, gorilla. You try to fuck'n take her, I'll knock your fuck'n head off."

"Had nuff of you," said Beaver. His big fist flew out and clubbed Thorn on the side of the head. Down he went, quick as an ox with a bullet between its eyes.

Shepard scurried behind the big chair and held it between him and Beaver. "O father's wrath, don't hit me like that. I have a delicate brain!" he cried.

Beaver looked at him with surprise, then broke out howling with laughter. He slapped his leg and pointed and screamed, "Delicate brain! Delicate brain!"

If things hadn't been so serious, I would have had to laugh myself. Shepard looked the opposite of what anybody would expect from the size of him – a girl inside a galoot, a plum-nosed, mustached, toothless, raggedy-headed giant with the heart of a bunny. To be so big and so scared wasn't really funny, but the way he looked and the way he said "Delicate brain" made it slapstick funny, in a sad sort of way. A hysterical giggle rose in my throat. Beaver roared himself half-sick over it. He got so carried away, he ended up bent over and coughing and choking and having to spit out his whole wad of Redman.

Finally he caught his breath and straightened up, wiping his tears away. "Blubberbuns," he said to Shepard, "nobody give me such a good time since Roy Shift got a butt full of buckshot for stealin turkeys. Weee! I tell you what, you tryin to get me to laugh myself to death, right?"

Shepard got brave again. He stuck out his dogteeth and told Mamie to get up and throw the sonofabitch out.

Beaver quit smiling and told Shepard that Mamie was trained to have respect for her papa. "Didn't I teach you the Bible says to honor me?" he asked her.

"Yaay, Papa," she answered. And she stood and set herself to fight him.

"Mr. Beaver," I said. "I tried to tell you once before that Mamie is the one who knocked you out at the river, not me. And you wouldn't believe it, remember? I think you're going to see now."

"Shet up, fartface."

"Well, I think so, sir. Mamie's got supernatural strength, like Samson. You've just got the strength of the devil."

He looked at her. "You break my head that day, Mamie?"

"Yaay, Papa."

He thought it over. Then he told us, "Well, I always wondered how a runt like Foggy could hit hard nuff to knock me out. It took a Beaver to down a Beaver. But you know, you did dishonor to the commandment, Mamie. Kids what don't honor their parents don't get a long life, it says."

He inched toward Mamie. They were of a size, but she was slimmer. Seconds passed as they stared into each other's eyes. I saw Beaver make a fist, and before I could shout a warning, he had already swung on her. But she was so quick, with panther reflexes, like the time Mike Quart tried to hit her with the trench shovel; she feinted left, just enough that Beaver's fist caught nothing but air. Then she caught him by the collar of his coat and used his momentum to spin him over onto his back. He went down across the coffee table, flattening it with a bang and a whoosh. Thorn, lying next to the table, knocked heads with Beaver. Thorn let out a groan. Beaver's mouth was open, trying to catch the wind knocked out of him.

Mamie didn't miss a beat. She grabbed his legs and hauled him out the door and bumped him down the steps. She whirled him one time and let go so he skittered across the lawn and hit the elm tree, the dead half, and a branch broke off and smacked him good across the shoulders. Before he could get his wits, Mamie grabbed him once more, pulled him up, and wrapped her arms round his waist. She shuffled with him to the street and threw him in the gutter. She kept after him while he tried to scramble away, rolling him, pushing him, dragging him.

Shepard and I were going wild, yelling our heads off, telling her to pulverize the bastard. Robbie came limping out, holding his ribs, eyes full of concern, "Will she kill him?" he said. Nobody answered him. We were too busy telling her to do just that.

"Squash that turd!" hollered Shepard.

Across the street, Anna and Soren came out, Chee Chee behind them, barking in a serious way and taking off after John Beaver and worrying his ankles to shreds. Mamie kept him flat on his face, dragging him across the asphalt by his collar. Anna and Soren caught the fever of the fight and started yelling at Chee Chee to cat John Beaver. But he was fighting her off with kicks, and a lucky one caught her full in the face, sending her in a roll that ended with Chee Chee on her side, little legs churning the air, searching for escape. A weeping yip came from her, like she was half-killed.

Anna cried out and rushed for Chee Chee, coming to the rescue.

Mamie stopped dragging John Beaver and rushed over to the dog. It was all Beaver needed to get away. Off he went in a running limp, stopping just long enough to snatch up his red cap and jam it back on his head. When he was about a block away, he turned around and shook his fists at us and hooted and snarled like a frustrated werewolf. Mamie took off after him, which got him loping along again. He disappeared at the corner, and Mamie came back.

"What kind of thing was that?" asked Soren.

"Vas dat man wobbing you?" asked Anna. Chee Chee was cuddled in her arms, whining profoundly.

"That was the living breathing nadir of mankind," said Shepard. "A walking, talking, merciless Attila. An incarnated Mars." He touched his thumb and forefinger to his temples, as though he was bringing forth great thoughts. "The Spencerian-Darwinian survival-of-the-fittest thing itself, yum yum – Neanderthal-tainted chromosomes."

"It was Mamie's pa," I said. "He punched out Bob Thorn."

"One stupendous punch," said Shepard, with a kind of gasp of appreciation for so much power.

"A tough-looking critter," said Soren. "Being his enemy would make me nervous as hell."

"He's the devil," said Robbie. "I know him."

"She make da dewil vit him," Anna declared, kissing Chee Chee, who was still whimpering.

I told Mamie she had done a good job.

"Yaay, Kritch'n," she said. "But poor Booby." She touched the side of her face where Bob Thorn had taken Beaver's punch.

"It was a doozy," I said.

We went back to the house to see how he was. We found him sitting on the couch, a red lump covering the left side of his cheek. We tried to give him sympathy about it, but he was having none of us. He glared like we had done it to him.

"Don't talk to me!" he said, hissing at us.

"He sure caught you a good one," I said. "You gonna be all right?"

"Yeah, you damn right I am. Because I'll tell you people what. I've had enough of Beavers to last the rest of my miserable life. I'm through with Beavers. Fuck'n killers. Law ought to lock 'em all up! Ought to shoot the fuck'n savages!" He stood up and staggered past us to the door. Shepard reached out to help him, but Thorn said, "Don't fuck'n touch me, nobody." At the door entrance, he looked back and growled at us. "None of you people is human. Bunch of friggin Camelot freaks!"

"Booby," called Mamie.

"Don't Booby me, Mamie Beaver. You been the fuck'n baddest luck on me I ever had in my life. You been more misery than you're worth. You beat me up. Your old man beat me up. Goddammit, I ain't been beat up but twice in my life, and Beavers done 'em both. I stay round here, I'll get killed for sure." He touched the lump on his face and squinted in pain. "Ouch, shit, this sucker's gonna be sore." And he left, saying ouch and shit with every step he took down the stairs.

When he was gone, Mamie reached out her hand and touched the screening on the door. There was a wondering and a hurt in her face, in her eyes especially, like the fixed eyes of a baby who'd got slapped for the first time.

"Booby," she whispered, running her fingers down the screen.

"It's okay, Mamie," I told her. "Kritch'n is still here. Kritch'n is always here for you." I pushed myself between her and the door and made her hug me.

"Kritch'n luffs me so," she murmured.

We went out on the porch and sat together on the steps. Mamie reached out and took hold of the dead branch that had fallen on John Beaver. She snapped twigs off it as we talked.

I asked her, "Mamie, who do you love? Do you love Powers?"

"Yaay, Kritch'n."

"More than me?"

"Nup, you more."

"And what about Thorn?"

"I luff Booby."

"More than me?"

"Nup, you more."

"Then how come we aren't together like before? We don't no-rain anymore. And you don't even get jealous of me and Phoebe. What's so more important that all you've got time for is Powers? You've been away from him only one day, when we went to the carnival, and then you were with Bob Thorn, and then right back to Powers. What gives?"

She thought it over carefully before answering. "Kritch'n, Powers teached me. Time gone for me knowing nothing. Now time to know what Powers teach. Booby touch me one day. Phoebe touch you. But Kritch'n – hippa-weee – me and you, ever and ever, yaay! Powers luffs me so, teached dumb Mamie dumb is dead. Yaay? Time to learn now, Kritch'n, time for making up ABCs. Yaay?" She showed me the smooth branch, all the twigs and bark gone, the vanilla shine of the wood underneath coming through. The branch looked alive again.

I patted her head and told her I knew what she was saying, and I would just stick by her and behave from now on. I told her also not to worry, because she would never be the old dumb Mamie again. She was as far beyond that as the stars were beyond the loony moon.

A strong feeling of contentment came over me then, and I was half glad that John Beaver had come and driven away Bob Thorn and caused Mamie and me to remember what we had been through together and what we meant to each other. It seemed funny that we had to be reminded by the likes of John Beaver stirring up our old fears, but if fear is what it took to make us understand one another, then I was willing to let it live at the edge.

Inside the house we could hear our friends chattering about Beaver and Bob Thorn, saying one was a monster and the other a jerk. Shepard held out that we had given Beaver a taste of wrath he wouldn't soon forget. Anna said his ankles would be awful sore, thanks to her hero Chee Chee. Soren said again that he wouldn't want that guy for an enemy.

"Vanquished!" declared Shepard. "He is vanquished! Come in Mamie and Crystal. We must celebrate."

We went back in, and Shepard brought out some jars of splow.

"Not for me," said Robbie. "The devil is never vanquished. Only fools think it so." He shuffled off to the bedroom and closed the door.

"Mystic moron," said Shepard. We all sat down, and he passed out glasses of splow and toasted the vanquishing of John Beaver.

Holding up his glass, he said, "A plague of pollywogs and crickets on him – Moses, chapter none."

"Bweak him ass," said Anna, lifting her glass.

"From the doctrines of demons, Lord save us," came Robbie's muffled voice behind the door.

"Skoal," said Soren.

Mamie and I sat quiet.

Shepard went on. "May he forever be the summa cognizant symbol of fear vanquished by valor, yum yum."

"Bweak him ass," added Anna.

"Skoal," said Soren.

Another sip. Another toast. "May the gods of cowardice and confusion disable him."

"Bweak him ass."

"Skoal."

"May the forte of panoramic lameness infect his feet."

"Bweak him ass."

"May the terrible lightning of Mamie's wrath retool his *rodentia* pattern of thought, ho ho ho."

"Bweak him ass to pieces."

"We met the enemy and he was ours. We broke his ass!"

And on it went, Shepard and Anna mostly, acting like John Beaver was dead and they had done the killing. After a few more toasts, I had had enough and told them we were celebrating too early where John Beaver was concerned. They didn't know him like I did. I added that Thorn might be the only smart one among us, getting out while the getting was good.

"Thorn, poof poof," said Shepard. "A consummate coward at heart. Some bodyguard he turned out to be – a glass jaw."

"We'd all have glass jaws if John Beaver hit us," I answered.

"Mamie beat him too bad," said Anna. "He not coming back."

"You don't know him. He keeps coming. We beat him once real bad, so bad we thought he was dead. But he's not like us. It doesn't scare him like it would us. He doesn't get scared enough to quit."

"Poof poof, he ran away like a rabbit. You saw him. He is a goblin with antediluvian genetics at work on his will, yum yum. His overwhelming fear of Mamie's fire will keep him away."

"That's stupid," I said, which made Shepard's jaw drop. "A couple of minutes ago you were calling him Attila and Mars and the thing in itself. Now you think he's just a goblin? You don't know a thing about him. He skins minks alive for pleasure. He was going to scalp Mamie once. He's a nightmare, I tell you."

"I saw the devil in his face," came Robbie's filtered voice.

"Shut up, Robbie," yelled Shepard. "Who cares what you saw? You Christer fanatics are all the same, always throwing inkpots at the devil. Just listen to me. I will put my powers of second sight to work." He paused and stroked his nose, like he was stroking a crystal ball. "Yesss, and now my powers tell me that the worst of all futures await those who run away. What, after all, has it gotten us so far? Hmmm? John Beaver, you say, came on and on, and you stared over your shoulders, searching for his evil form rising from the horizons of all your days, yum yum. Tell me, would you really want to continue such a pattern ad infinitum, ad nauseatum? Deep down you know you would not. The troll has found you here and would find you anywhere. So now you should face him once and for all and turn the stench of fear into the aroma of victory, yum yum. We shall slay this dragon together as one, I promise you. We'll get Thorn to come back, and we'll hire Cody and Mongoose

Jim as bodyguards – they need jobs, you know? They'll jump at the chance. Let John Beaver face such a formidable wall if he dares! What I am telling you has the bona fide wisdom of a prodigy behind it. And I have no motive but your best interests in my heart."

I wasn't completely convinced. But I had to admit there was something in what he said about looking over my shoulder for Beaver all the days of my life. I tried to tell myself that if Thorn came back and Cody and Mongoose Jim were with him, and of course invincible Mamie herself, John Beaver wouldn't have a chance. They would slaughter him!

"It is time to take a stand," I told Shepard.

He toasted my courage and said I wouldn't be sorry. His genius coupled with his second sight were never wrong.

Wasn't anything more I could do, so I let it go. I stood by the door and looked out, watching for the troll, or the dragon, or whatever he was, and behind me, Shepard tied his tongue round another curse to lay on John Beaver.

"Let the ferret cunning of his mind be made a rotting placenta of doom!"

"Bweak him ass."

¶ A day went by and another. Then Friday came, and I was beginning to hope that Beaver knew we had bodyguards and was afraid to come back. We hadn't been able to find Bob Thorn, but Cody and Mongoose Jim had jumped at the chance to earn a few bucks by guarding Mamie. One or the other was always with us, though I didn't have much faith in Mongoose Jim; he kept saying he had back trouble and so he would have to depend on brass knuckles if this guy Beaver came looking for a fight. Cody was proud of being a bodyguard and said he was born to kick a bad Beaver's ass. It made me feel safe when he talked tough like that, but the most safe I felt was when I was with Mamie herself, who I knew could kick a bad Beaver's ass.

Beginning the same night that Shepard talked me into staying, I took my blankets and slept in the booth with Mamie and Powers. We slept on the floor, with Powers above us, rigid as a palace guard. Those two nights were good nights for me, with Mamie hugging me up close, cuddling me in her big arms, wearing me out with the no-rain. I no longer wondered if I might love Phoebe Bumpus. It was only Mamie I loved. It had always been only Mamie.

Then that Friday came. Shepard had come back from the post office with a movie he said would get the people back to the Artlife again and get them wanting to play the roles with Mamie once more. He called himself an irrepressible optimist, yum yum. He had been way down in the dumps about the riot, and the people giving up on him, and the Rock of Ages winning. But now he knew it was all temporary, a slight setback. The movie he had would retrieve those poor souls tied in the confines of Saint Paulian doctrine, bitter hard boob of the mystified past, and get them all headed in the direction of the universal truth that art represents. He was bouncing with confidence. The movie he had was *Gone with the Wind,* and he was holding a special preview for us, for me, Soren and Anna, Mongoose Jim, and Mamie, and dippy Robbie could come if he wanted.

We gathered inside at noon to watch, but Shepard had to give a speech first. He said we were sure lucky to get to see one of the masterpieces of cinema. He said the role Clark Gable played was no Hamlet but was still the personification of a fable brought to life. All of manhood, from Alexander the Great to Casanova, bloomed in Gable as Rhett Butler. This would make us see an instant truth about the ember of instinct in all men, the entelechy, yum yum, that haunts the dreams of heroism, however unheroic the Homo sapiens' dreaming. As to Vivian Leigh, she was dainty perfection, whose Blanche Dubois was priceless but whose memory was made immortal by the role of Scarlett O'Hara. And *Gone with the Wind* would stand for all time as the epitome of artistic and romantic expression of Darwin's survival of the fittest and Aristotle's acorn growing into an oak tree. "The entelechy which drives the acorn drives the fittest to survive, the Rhett Butlers and the Scarlett O'Haras and the Mamie Beavers of this world. For our Mamie, my second sight sees visions of greatness beyond anything your puny minds can imagine. I see the mighty oak she is to become! The beauty of Scarlett, the strength of a hundred Rhetts. And when she unfolds her wings at the epiphany of metamorphosis and stands before the world, resplendent as Psyche from regions of holy land, I say, when that butterflication occurs, Christ himself will step aside in awe, and the true deity of man will come forth – come forth and recognize Mamie as the future! Mamie Beaver – Messiah! Yum yum!" Shepard's face was purple, his lips and cheeks were trembling, his eyes popping. "I've had the vision!" he cried. "I've had the vision. And when genius has a vision, you better listen. By God, the Second Coming is Byzantium!" He gave a few ahems and yum yums and trailed off into a mumble.

"He's cwackas," whispered Anna to me.

"It's been a strain," said Soren. "It's telling on him."

"Blasphemous bastard," Robbie muttered.

Shepard raised both arms and stared at the booth. "And now, on with the show! And imagine, if you can, if your minds will let you soar one-tenth of the way to Mamie and me, what this place will be like when Mamie does *Gone with the Wind* – Yummy!"

The lights went off and the movie came on, with beautiful music and lots of violins. GONE WITH THE WIND read the screen.

But suddenly the words got wobbly and blurry. The words bounced back and forth from one edge of the screen to the other. Shepard was still onstage and he shouted to the booth, "Steady on, Mamie! Steady down!" Then all hell broke loose. The movie went dancing off the screen and darting all over the curtains from one side to the other. Then we heard a crash, and the light of Powers went out. Terrible noise and darkness were everywhere.

Shepard shrieked, "There he is!" and pointed at the booth.

"Vhut's dis? Vhut's dis?" cried Anna.

"Sounds like it's time to do my job," said Mongoose Jim.

"He's here," said Robbie. "The demon has returned." His voice was strangely calm.

I jumped out of my seat and ran up the aisle, across the lobby, and up the stairs to the booth. The door hung on its side, cracked in two. John Beaver was next to the projector, stomping on it. Mamie was getting up from the floor behind him. He turned, and in his hand was a cylinder thing that filled his palm and stuck out about two inches above his thumb and forefinger. It was Powers's eye, the steel tube holding the lens, and John Beaver was using it like a little club to hit Mamie and knock her down. He stomped on Powers's body some more and broke pieces off, throwing them over his shoulder. Robbie and Mongoose crowded in behind me.

"Shit," said Mongoose, "where's that goddamn Cody when you need him?"

I felt like a spell was on me. I stood alongside of Robbie unable to move. Mamie was up again and she charged John Beaver. She knocked him over hard, smashing him into a wall so hard the wall crumbled, and plaster and white dust fell all over both of them, turning them into ghosts. He cussed and growled, picking himself out of the wall. Mamie didn't follow it up. She turned her back on him, and stared down at ruined Powers like she was in shock, just stared and stared. Beaver got his feet under him and came roaring back at her. They wrestled like two mad bears, till Mamie flipped him over her shoulder and onto a pile of scrap. Then she staggered back and leaned against the wall looking at me, blood cutting the plaster dust on her face, her eyes like an explosion of blue poppies. I hit Mongoose Jim and told him to get some help. He took off out the door yelling, "Call the cops! Call the cops! Oh gawd, where's Cody?"

Beaver got up again, and he had the piece of Powers in his hand. He came after Mamie. He lunged, and at the same time Robbie lunged. It was so quick I hardly saw Robbie do it – lunging at Beaver and catching the force of Powers's eye – boom! – smack on the top of his head. Mamie caught the falling Robbie in her arms, leaving herself wide open for Beaver's next swing, which caught her on the left side of her head and dropped her. I had no idea I was going to do anything at all, but I found myself gone crazy and leaping on Beaver's back and tearing at his hair and ears and biting the top of his head. He reached back and plucked me off, tossing me to the floor like he was getting rid of a clot of mud. I almost fainted, but I managed not to and managed a weak kick at him. He grabbed my leg and started jerking me around the room, banging me into pieces of Powers. "Mamie!" I cried. "Mamie!" Somehow she pulled herself up and took another run at Beaver, caught him up between the legs and rammed him back into the wall again. Another hole appeared and white plaster dusted down.

Just then Shepard came in. He took one look at Mamie's bloody face and his eyes rolled up in his head and he went over backward, hitting the floor with such force that the boards dimpled and dust rose like a fog. I jumped up and went after Mamie, took her by the arm, and pulled her away from John Beaver, who wasn't dead yet, not even knocked out. Mamie walked a couple of steps with me, then collapsed next to Robbie. "No!" I screamed. "We've got to run!" But she wasn't listening.

John Beaver got up slow, weaving like a drunk, the lens hanging in his hand. I couldn't stand to have him hit her anymore, and I threw myself over her, pleading with him, "Please don't hit her anymore. For the sake of Jesus, don't hit her anymore!" I was half-growling, half-crying, hugging my Mamie and snarling over my shoulder at him, wishing I had a gun to blow his mink-carving brains to kingdom come. And then far off I could hear the sirens. He heard them too.

He stopped in his tracks. The murder left his eyes. He listened. "Juss like a rat in a trap," he said breathlessly.

"Coming to get you, John Beaver," I said. "Coming to kill you."

"Shet yer puky face," he told me, "an get off'n her. I ain't gonna hit her no more."

I stood up off of Mamie, but she wasn't moving. Her eyes were open, looking at me, but nothing moved. The white powder sifted down and made a little outline of her form on the floor.

"You hurt her real bad this time," I said.

Then he did a funny thing, funny for him, I mean. He tore off the tail of his shirt and wiped the blood off Mamie's face. "Beavers can take it," he said, almost gently. "Can't we, Mamie? Look what you did to me." He pointed at the white worm scar wiggling down the middle of his hair. "There's a hard-won trophy that won't never go away. Yer tattoo, Mamie. Jesus, she don't look so good." The sound of the sirens was getting louder.

"Coming to get you," I said again. "You're a killer now, John Beaver." I pointed to Robbie.

"Damn fool. Who is he?" Beaver wanted to know.

I thought for a second I should tell him that Robbie was a holyman who said a demon was coming to kill him, but I said instead, "He was our friend, a preacher. You killed a preacher."

"A preacher? Shit, you might know it. But the dumb bastard jumped in hisself where he had no business to be. What the fuck kinda pa would I be if I didn't fight for my dotter? I never cared for nuthin but her, Foggy. But you think anybody's gonna give a good goddamn?" He was almost whining. He hefted the lens in his hand, and I thought for a minute he might hit me with it and I shrunk back. But he jammed it into his pocket and said, "What the hell is goin on anyway? I've kilt everthin I ever loved."

I was surprised to hear him say such a thing. It was like the time he'd said the butterfly was pretty – just not the kind of thing that should come out of his wolverine mouth. The sirens were really getting loud, just coming up the block. He grabbed me hard by the hair and twisted my head back, his face right on top of mine. "Don't think it's over yet, fartybum!" he yelled. Then he pushed me away and ran out the door. In a second I heard Anna and Soren shouting at him downstairs and heard the sirens right out front.

Anna came up and gasped when she saw what had happened. "Did dat dewil kill dem all?" she asked.

"Did he get away?"

"Out da back, like a scawy cat," she said. She went over to Shepard and slapped him on the cheek. "Look at dis blubber! Call dis a man? Vake up, you. Vake up!" She sat on his belly and slapped his face more. He broke wind. "Ach! listen to dis! Vhut can you do vit such a one?"

The police came, and then an ambulance and a doctor. The doctor bent over Robbie with a stethoscope and said matter-of-factly that he was gone. He moved to Mamie and examined the side of her head. "Oh god," he said. "Skull fracture for sure. It's a wonder she's conscious."

"Beavers got hard heads," I explained.

He packed the wound and wrapped gauze around it, while two other guys in white uniforms came in with a stretcher. One of them stared down at Shepard and whistled and said, "Doc, how the hell Harley and me supposed to carry this walrus? Look at the size of him."

"Stretcher won't hold him," said the one called Harley.

They loaded Robbie on instead and went out with him. The doctor held a bottle of something under Shepard's nose and woke him up. First thing he said was, "Where's Caliban?" He was rolling his eyes. I told him Caliban was gone. "Prince of darkness," he murmured. "Robbie's right – Satan lives."

I held Mamie's hand and told her she was going to be just fine, that the doctor would fix her right up, never fear. She moved her lips, trying to tell me something, but nothing came out. I bent my ear close to hear, but nothing came out. Nothing. "Tell me, Mamie," I said. But she couldn't.

There was no room in the ambulance for me, so I had to run all the way to the hospital. By the time I reached there, Mamie was in the operating room and Robbie was in the morgue. After a time a cop came by and wanted to know all about John Beaver. I told him the whole story, starting with finding Mamie on the Brule and ending with the fight in the booth. It took a long time to tell. The cop wrote stuff down at first, then just stopped and listened. Shepard and Anna came and they listened too. When I got finally to the part about Robbie jumping in front of Mamie to save her, Shepard interrupted to say he didn't really like Robbie much, "Camelot-bound, you know, a latter-day Savonarola but noble nevertheless, noble . . . what he did." Tears started down his cheeks.

I finished my story with the warning that John Beaver still had the lens in his pocket and wouldn't think twice about breaking another head with it. After that the cop questioned Anna and Shepard. Both of them nearly talked his arm off. They were jabbering away when the doctor came in and said the operation was over. He didn't know yet how Mamie would do – the first twenty-four hours would be the key. "She could die, or she could come back an idiot, or she could recover all the way. Can't tell much yet till the brain swelling goes down – if it goes down."

I was allowed to go to her and sit by her bed. She hung on to life, hung on in a little white room, in a white bed, with her head dressed in white bandages covering her down to her eyebrows. A white tube was up one nostril and a brownish tube up the other, both gurgling, and a machine behind her was wheezing, making breathing noises, and every once in a while beeping softly. A nurse came in now and then to clean out the tubes.

My mind was almost numb, but I had an idea that if I stood by Mamie and massaged her up and down the way she had massaged Jewel the cow, I could work the miracle on her and bring her back. So that's what I did, all the while hoping I had the healing touch. The blow on her head had made her eyes swell up horribly. Such big eyes. The swelling making her face look sort of like she came from outer space – some Martian with the eyes and mouth of a frog, the head of a ghostly pumpkin full of breathing tubes. I stayed awake and massaged her, working my hands over her feet and legs, her belly and breasts and arms, and back down again, then to the other side.

The doctor came in later that night. Then a new one came in the morning. The new one listened to her heart, and I could tell by his face he didn't like what he heard. I went on massaging. He didn't know my Mamie. The day passed and night came again. I couldn't feel my hands anymore. I was in a daze, moving on automatic, up and down, side to side, forcing myself to stay awake and keep going. If I kept my hands on her, I knew she wouldn't die.

On Sunday I woke up hearing voices from far away, coming through the window. I was under the bed, curled into a ball. "Oh no," I moaned. "How could you fall asleep?" Pulling myself up, I saw that Mamie was still alive, tubes still gurgling, machine still wheezing, beeping softly every few seconds. I looked out the window and saw a huge crowd of people gathered together. Shepard was there, and Anna, and Soren in his wheelchair, Cody and Mongoose Jim and Charlie. Bob Thorn was there. Dozens and dozens of people, all the Intellectuals and the Christers I knew, mixing with each other. Phoebe Bumpus waved to me and blew a kiss. Lulu was holding a sign that said PRAY FOR MAMIE. Some of the people were singing, "Go tell it on the mountain." Some were shouting out, "Call me Ishmael!" and others were calling out verses from *Hamlet*. The people weren't getting in each other's way, and what they were singing out didn't really clash like you might think it would have. It sounded more like a huge prayer, like two ways of praying made into one, two kinds of scripture making up one. For some reason, I thought about Pa, how all my life he had been quoting Shakespeare and the Bible and Emerson, and it had always seemed that he was quoting just one book. Right then I told myself that Pa was what I wanted to be, a man who could balance all the forms of truth.

The people stayed outside for about four hours, singing and quoting whatever came to mind, celebrating The Book of Mamie, each in his own way, each in her own way. And then they broke up and went home, leaving the world quiet again. I went back to Mamie and put my hands on her and massaged my heart out. Her skin was cold. That night she died.

Raising the Dead

The night Mamie died, I went back to the Artlife and up to the booth. I gathered all the pieces of Powers round me and laid myself in the middle, the gear cover for a pillow. In the dark I saw myself like a dead soldier in a foxhole, arms and legs sprawled over mounds of shrapnel. My thoughts were on Mamie and Robbie, dead; and on dead Amoss and almost-dead Ben Snowdy. A feeling sat inside my belly, like a black monster with tentacles running up my arms and legs and into my head. It was the monster of death, and it told me that I was going to die some day, just like everybody else. *I* was going to die. My parents, my brothers and sister, all my friends – everything living was going to die. No getting out of it. It would come one day, and you'd have no say in the matter. It would show up and put you to sleep forever. Stars and planets and the sun would go on shining, but you wouldn't be there to know it. "Me too," I whispered. "Just like you, Mamie. And Robbie. And Amoss. Nothing'll warm them up ever again." She had been so cold. She had made my hands cold. That is death, the endless cold. It was hard on me thinking such a way, but I couldn't help it. Death was real inside me, touching all my parts and warning them not to count on growing up or anything, not to waste a second of my life, because even if I lived a hundred years, it was nothing and would be too soon to die. I was alone. I would die alone. That's what it was. Nobody did it for you. Nobody kept it from happening. My hands didn't keep it from Mamie. If Mamie could die, anybody could die.

"Poor Mamie," I said. "Poor, poor Robbie. Poor Robbie, poor Mamie, poor Amoss, poor Christian Peter Foggy. Poor me, poor me." Without knowing it was coming, I started crying a real gusher, huge sobs and moans, worse than any crying I could ever remember doing. It practically choked me, but I couldn't stop. I felt like a tiny boy in a dark dungeon, left there like in a grave and nobody coming, no Mamie to save him.

"My heart is broke," I cried out. Then louder, "My heart is broke!" It made no difference. My words went out into the dark, and back came only silence to sit on the ruins of blue-edged metal ringing me round, all the pieces of Powers shattered like Humpty Dumpty after his great fall.

I woke the next morning with a plan to put Powers back together again. I laid him out like a giant puzzle and moved the pieces here and there to get an idea of how they fit. I could see that the gears and wheels had no serious injuries. Mainly, it was the big sheeted stuff, all dented and bent, that would need some torch-warming and a ball-peen hammer to straighten them out. I started with Powers's foot and set it back on its rollers. Then I fit the leg back on, only it was cockeyed and wobbly and had a split seam that would need brazing. I switched to the main box and traced the course where the film ran through. I could see how it was supposed to be, and little by little I fit bushings and gears and wheels back together. I spent hours at it and could see the possibility of really bringing Powers back to life. I would need some tools, some delicate screwdrivers, and long-nosed pliers, and slim wrenches – three-eighths and five-sixteenths, for sure – and cotter pins, screws, washers, and nuts. But I could do it, I thought; I could make Powers hum.

I went over to Shepard's, ate some breakfast, and took a long hot shower. I scrubbed myself raw, especially my hands, which still felt like they had Mamie's death on them. When I had finished, I put on clean clothes and went over to Charlie's to find out what was going on. All the gang was there, including Bob Thorn. First thing Charlie said was, "Your old man's coming. He called here just a while ago and said to tell you to sit tight. He'll be here in a few hours."

"He knows about Mamie and John Beaver?" I asked.

"Sure does. Everybody knows. There's a statewide manhunt on. Word is out they're going to shoot to kill."

"Take no prisoners," said Cody gruffly. "Sonofabitch is lucky I wasn't there. He'd be dead now."

"I went looking for you," said Mongoose Jim.

"Let's not talk about what you did," Cody answered shaking his head in disgust.

"Funeral's today," said Charlie.

"Naw, already?" I asked.

He told me sure enough and that the Cunninghams and Christers had taken over everything and were going to bury Mamie and Robbie together at the entrance to the new church. Shepard raised his head from his glass and moaned about the Christers making themselves a shrine for pilgrims, the worst kind of infantilism he had ever seen. Everybody agreed it was a typical religious notion – to make Mamie and Robbie into martyrs and give the faithful a place to pray to them.

"Bad as ancestor worship," said Shepard. "Next thing they'll be working miracles."

I thought about what I had told Robbie, that I would bury him at the Brule. But getting made into a shrine seemed like a much better idea, one I thought he might appreciate more than sleeping at the edge of a pasture. Or would he? What was it he wanted? *Angels talking, whispering river talk, and Robbie shushing by, Robbie gone to water.* I had promised him that. And what about Mamie? She belonged back home, next to her mother, didn't she?

"Who do these people think they are, burying Mamie there?" I said. "Nobody asked me about it."

"They didn't need to ask you, Christian," said Charlie. "No kin to claim Mamie, and it's either the shrine or up next to Amoss on the hill. Shepard and I offered to pay for the hill, but the Cunninghams and the Christers have more influence."

"Cunninghams' money won the day," said Mongoose Jim.

"They'll turn Mamie into a cult," said Shepard.

"They ain't stupid," said Cody. "A Robbie-Mamie shrine's worth a million bucks to this town."

"It'll be the Lourdes of the North," added Shepard with a sigh.

At eleven we all went over to the site where what was once the woods was mostly cleared out and the church foundation laid. Twenty yards in front of the foundation were the graves. Both coffins were made of steel – a gray color, like cold ashes – and each had a ring of yellow chrysanthemums arranged on top. The coffins sat on slings over holes about twelve feet apart. The Christers formed up in a circle around both graves. An architect stood at the edge of the crowd with us and told us he was hired to design the entrance. He showed us a sketch he was making that had a pointed archway overhead, under which the people would walk, passing the graves on each side, the graves being covered by smooth slabs of stone.

Shepard scorned the design. "Like the resurrection of medieval gothic," he said sourly. Which made the architect sniff.

"Go on," said Cody. "Before we put a match to it."

The architect hurried away with his sketch to the far side, losing himself in the crowd. One of the Cunninghams started talking to the people, telling them how brave and holy Mamie and Robbie were in life, and how lucky they were to die for what they believed in. "There is no better death we could ask of God. God has given his faithful servants a priceless gift. Given them martyrdom!"

"See, what did I tell you!" whispered Shepard. "Martyrs!"

"And a boy once lost, given over to Camelot as crazy, and yet he was made to speak and to witness and to save souls. And a girl as pure as the driven snow, born an idiot and having the power of Christ descend upon her, making her speak in tongues for the enlightenment of the faithful. How good is God, amen."

"Amen!" roared the crowd.

"It is all proof of the power of Jesus. Blessed are the righteous who preach the Word, for they shall rise up brand-spanking-new on the Day of Judgment!"

A number of hallelujahs and amens followed. Then they all chanted the Lord is my shepherd psalm. Some held up their arms and hands to the sky, weeping and moaning. Others hugged each other. One woman threw herself on Mamie's coffin and sobbed. The sling underneath slipped up toward the head of the coffin, and down went the footside and the weeping woman with it, coffin and woman tumbling into the grave. She really wailed then. Another woman close by fainted and had to be carried to the edge of the crowd. Two men held her, one by the shoulders, the other by her feet. And alongside came a little boy in a blue suit, hanging on to the woman's skirt and saying, "Whatcha doin that for, Ma? Whatcha doin that for?" And meanwhile the lady in the grave got dragged out. You could tell she was frazzled. Men had to carry her off too. Then it was like an infection, one after another of the women started shrieking and fainting. At least half a dozen had to be carried away. Someone hollered, "Before God I might not believe this without the true avalanche of my bleeding eyes!" Which brought more cries and tears and shouts of "Oh ye damn whale! Oh ye damn whale!" and other portions of the litany.

Shepard told me he was leaving before the people made him puke. We followed him back to Charlie's.

Inside the bar, we sat glumly and drank splow with beer chasers. Everybody kept saying it was a sad and stupid day. We could hear the people down the block going on and on for better than an hour more before they finally buried Robbie and Mamie and went home. By the time the last shovel of dirt was piled on, I was feeling no pain.

Neither was Phoebe, and she wanted to dance. So Charlie put some music on the jukebox, and I danced with her. She said she had been missing me. She rubbed on me, but I was too fuzzy-headed to care. Finally she gave up and turned her attention to Cody. He was glad for it, waltzing her over the floor proudly, like he had won her from me. "She knows a livin man," he said.

A while later Pa showed up. I jumped at him and gave him a kiss on the face, which caught him up short and made him laugh. "Don't get mushy on me now," he said, roughing up my hair. He sat with us and told how the whole North was out hunting for Beaver, but the wily bastard was giving them all the slip.

"I wisht I could've got my hands on him," said Mongoose Jim.

"Go on," said Cody. "You had your chance. He wouldn'a got away if I'd been there." He twirled Phoebe round, making her hair fly. The jukebox sang, "Gonna live fast, love hard, die young, and leave a beyootiful mem-oo-ree."

"Well, he's wanted for double murder now," said Pa. "It's the kind of thing you expect when you live like he did. Hard justice eventually has its way. It's in the Over-Soul's scheme of things."

"I hope they kill him," Shepard blurted out savagely. "A sacrilege, a desecration, a profanation. Goddamn the man!"

"It won't be easy to catch him," Pa told us. "He got to Oulu in a stolen car and slipped off into the woods. Those are thick woods to squeeze through, you know? They got an army after him, but I got my doubts. Beaver's an animal. He knows how to move in the wild."

Cody and Phoebe sat down, and Cody said he was going to go out and track the sonofabitch himself. Bob Thorn, who had been pretty quiet, said he was ready to go when Cody was. Mongoose Jim was ready too. They passed the splow and drank to the hunt.

"Gonna get snockered," said Cody.

"Snockered," Mongoose Jim agreed.

"He was her bodyguard that day," Cody reminded us, pointing at Mongoose Jim.

"It would've taken every goddamn man here to stop him," Mongoose Jim yelled, shaking his fist at Cody. "Get off my back!"

"I would've stopped him!" Cody showed us his fist, holding it up to Phoebe's jaw. "Pow, like a sledgehammer." Phoebe looked at me and rolled her eyes. Cody wasn't the one for her; I could have told her that.

I held my glass up and gave a toast, "To Mamie and Robbie."

"The warp and the weft," Shepard added.

We drank. Smoother than mineral oil, warmer than whisky, the splow went down and made a nice whirlpool in my belly. It burned out the monster and left a glow. I told myself that this time I would keep it down and keep up with the rest of them. In Mamie's memory, I would drink splow and not get sick. Anna and Phoebe tapped their glasses on the table, and Charlie filled them up again. I tapped mine, and he filled it. Pa, watching me, didn't say anything; he just kept a small, sympathetic smile for me.

Round and round the splow and beer went, everybody filling up and sloshing it down. Even Chee Chee got her own ashtray full to drink, and she liked splow better than she liked beer. In a short while we were feeling more optimistic. Anna was on Soren's lap. Phoebe had switched to dancing with Bob Thorn. Cody and Mongoose Jim were matching each other drink for drink and saying what friends to the death they were. Pa and I talked, and I filled him in on what happened in the booth – the battle Mamie put up to save Powers, the bravery of Robbie, and all that. Shepard said it was the war of the Titans, colossal and overwhelming.

We talked a lot about Mamie, how she could drink splow like it was water and never get drunk; how she pulled the bars off the jail to free Robbie; and about her and Bob Thorn running through the woods with him on her back (that had made him a fan, he said); and the time she wrestled him in front of the school and he thought he was having a nightmare. Mamie stuttering and stammering, and then smoothing it all out when she quoted the movies; Mamie in love with Powers and getting graphite on her face from kissing him; Mamie as Ishmael and as Hamlet and Blanche Dubois and all the others (Shepard sobbed over what a Scarlett and Rhett she would have been); Mamie as everything, an idiot and a genius. And dead now. In a metal coffin with yellow flowers on top. In the ground next to Robbie. Like Amoss (O Amoss, cried Shepard, my one true friend). In the dark. Solid black. Cold. Robbie and Mamie and Amoss. Dead people.

The feeling was coming back, the tentacles growing out from the monster in my belly. Then Pa chimed in that there was more in heaven and earth than dreamed of in our philosophy. His instincts told him that Mamie and Robbie had become particles of the Deity and were better off than we were.

I put my head between my hands and snuffled. Shepard joined me, then Anna and Phoebe, and finally Chee Chee too, whining and worrying.

"I should've kicked his ass!" cried Mongoose Jim.

Cody punched Mongoose in the eye and told him he was a royal fuck-up. Mongoose rubbed his eye and agreed with Cody and hoped we would all forgive him.

Thorn cried out, "I shouldn't've run out just cause that bastard kicked my ass. But it was hoomiliating! Ah gawd!"

I peeked at Pa. He was filling his pipe and keeping on his sympathetic smile.

"How would you like to be me!" Thorn continued. "I was the number one bodyguard round her, and the fucker flattened me like a toothpick. How would you like that on your mind for the rest of your life? I'm used to being a hero. Now I'm a skunk."

"You think you got it rough," said Mongoose. "At least you stood up to him and took his best punch. I was in the booth. I was the one on duty. Try livin with that, fellas."

"Try livin in this shittin town," said Cody. "Try raising a family without a goddamn job or nuthin."

"Live with ghosts and your back broke for hurry-up money," said Soren. "And no goddamn TV."

"Vhat a vorld!" wept Anna.

"Woe, woe . . ."

Listening to them complain made me quit my blubbering. An idea came to me all of a sudden. "Well, let's do something about it," I said. "Why should we take this shit?"

"What you want to do, son?" said Pa, patting my head.

"I want to dig up Mamie and Robbie and take 'em home, Pa."

Everything got still, and my friends all looked at me like I was either out of my mind or a genius. Seconds ticked by. Then I told them how I had promised Robbie a place by the Brule and how Mamie belonged there too, next to her mama.

Again, the seconds ticked by.

"We could do it," said Cody grinning.

"It's an idea all right," said Bob Thorn.

Shepard rubbed his hands. "Think of the multitude praying to a pile of concrete and dirt."

"And we could watch 'em from here," said Cody.

"Yeah," Mongoose Jim agreed.

"Splow has made you all goofy," said Charlie.

"Yeah, somewhat," said Pa. "But there's a feeling of righteousness in it. Mamie does belong with her mother, not in this city with a cement slab over her and – "

"Better than having her as a relic for Christers!" interrupted

Shepard. "It'll be Canterbury Mamie, I tell you, dunces on their knees, metaphysics for mystics, atavism, dark labyrinthian rites of passage, yum yum, and unevolved reason. They'll dig them up one day, mark me, and steal their bones and worship the tatters of their clothes and sell their snot-rags as relics, their boots as shrines. It is the nature of the beast to want rabbits' feet, clovers, horns, icons, dice, pebbles, beads, Ave Marias, potions, feathers, and crosses – or Mamie Beaver's thighbone."

"I like this," said Phoebe.

Thorn pounded the table. "I'm for digging them up and letting the Foggys take them back to the farm." We all agreed it was the best thing to do. We drank on it.

Phoebe told a story of a woman from Racine, a rich one who wanted her Thunderbird buried with her when she died. They buried her in it, with her sitting up behind the steering wheel.

"It's paying your last respects," she added. "You do what the dead wanted."

We toasted last respects, and Anna told us she wanted Chee Chee buried with her when she died. We toasted that. Anna put Chee Chee on the table. The dog was drunk and couldn't hold up its hindend.

"That mutt can't hold its liquor," said Cody.

"She dwink you unner da table," Anna told him.

Chee Chee wasn't fighting it. She put her head on her paws and went to sleep.

Cody told Anna he liked her for having so much sass. Anna batted her eyelashes at him. She said, "Mans like you alvays vant to look up my dwess ven I dance. Bad boys you be. I slap you face, but not too hawd. Sowen vus like dat, ya." She sighed and looked at Soren with goopy eyes.

"You still got legs worth fighting for," he told her.

"Look my legs!" she cried. She threw Chee Chee off the table and climbed up. She raised her skirt and we saw up close her pair of milky legs, fat at the ankles but not bad-looking. She started to dance and the table quaked. We held the table upright while she did a cancan, humming it and lifting her skirt and jerking one foot up, then the other, till she lost her balance and went tumbling over the side into Shepard's arms.

"Okay, okay," she said, breathing hard. "It . . . make . . . Sowen so mad . . . dat you look . . . up my dwess."

"Inspiring, inflammatory," said Shepard. "More splow for Anna, our gifted one!"

She petted his nose and kissed the tip of it.

Soren reached out and goosed her. "Ya ya!" she cried.

We toasted her great legs; we toasted Soren who beat up all the mans looking up her dress; we toasted her underpants; we toasted her eyes, her accent, her sass. Then she took out her teeth and yelled, "And to my teef!" So we toasted them too.

It was just past the toast to the teeth that I began to feel I had gone too far. It was like my butt was sinking through the chair and everything I saw was floating in water. It seemed I couldn't control my words. I tried to say again, "To Anna's legs!" But it came out, "Oo wana's eggs." When I heard myself, it made me laugh. I pulled on my lips to try and shape them up, but they kept bouncing back in the same offset way, like warped rubber. I tried to focus on Pa, but he kept dodging me. I saw two of his crooked fingers pointing at me. I heard him say from far off, like a voice from a barrel, "That boy has himself a snootful."

"Snootal," I heard myself saying.

They were laughing at me, but I didn't give a damn. Fools. I tried to tell them so. "Wu foozzz," it came out. I looked at Phoebe perched on Thorn's lap. I wanted to smell her. I sniffed at her, and she wagged her finger at me and said I was "naughty naughty." Leaning her mouth next to Thorn's ear, she told him something that made him laugh. I didn't care.

Looking down, I saw Chee Chee asleep between Pa's chair and mine. It occurred to me that Chee Chee was the only one who knew what she was doing, and it would be nice to curl up like her and get some rest. I decided that's what I would do, get some rest. But when I tried to get up, I found myself sliding down instead, slipping over the edge of the table, slipping away, slipping out of my chair, my knees touching the floor, my chin resting on my fingertips hanging on to the edge of the table, slipping away, slipping away – and then no more table. I was a warm blob of mud squirming over the floor between the feet of all the fools who couldn't stop laughing.

I heard someone say, "Let him sleep it off."

Then I heard Shepard's voice saying, "We've got to do the polka in honor of Mamie!" Chairs scraped, feet pounded the floor, and the Beer Barrel Polka song filled the air. I opened one eye and saw them all dancing, except Pa, who was sitting, smoking his pipe, watching the fools dancing like Indians and bellowing, "Roll out the barrel!" I wished I could do it too.

The rest was a whirlpool.

I woke up clinging to a broad back. Sweet night air soothed my face. My eyes were itchy, my mouth dry. The body beneath me was galloping and whinnying like a horse. For a wild moment I thought Mamie and I were going off on another adventure. Voices behind us yelled, "Giddup! Haw! Haw!" There were trees on every side, leaves and twigs brushing us, a huge trunk ahead with the moon shining on it. We tried to jump the trunk, but I felt the lack of power as soon as we left the ground, and I knew we wouldn't make it. We hit and pitched over, flying, tumbling through the air, somersaulting into the leaves of old winters gone by. I lay on my back, watching the shimmer of the trees above me and the stars beyond. I said to myself it was sure enough a drunken dream.

"Sonofabitch," cussed Bob Thorn.

He was on his belly, face in the dirt, cussing and giggling at the same time. "How you figure she did it?" he said. "Where did the power come from?"

"I dunno," I answered. "I thought you were her."

"You kept calling me Mamie and pinching my muscles," he said. "You wouldn't stay off me. So I thought I'd give you a ride." He pointed back to the tree trunk. "That's the same log she took me over that night."

"We didn't make it," I told him.

We got up and made our way back, coming past the church foundation and onto the grave robbers. Cody said, "I knew you couldn't last. You fell, didn't you? We heard it."

"Sounded like a gut-shot moose," said Mongoose Jim.

"I'm no Mamie, I admit it," said Thorn.

Pa told us to keep the noise down and get the job done. He was digging along with Charlie. The dirt was flying. In about fifteen minutes we had Robbie out, and in another twenty we had Mamie. We loaded both coffins in the pickup. It wasn't quite wide enough, so we had to arrange them in such a way that they tilted up on the sides of the pickup bed and leaned against each other in the middle, forming a sort of *V*. Cody and Mongoose Jim went over to the workmen's gangboxes. They slid a pair over to the grave holes and dropped them down in. Then we all hurried to fill the dirt in over them.

"Hail to thee, holy gangbox. To thee we pray, heh heh," sang Shepard.

"I'm sure glad I'm in on this," said Cody. "Does my heart good. I'm coming to services every Sunday to see 'em pray."

"Me too," said Mongoose Jim.

"We got to go," said Pa.

I asked Shepard if I could have the pieces of Powers to take with me. He said it was a hunk of junk and I was welcome to it. So I had Pa pull up to the Artlife, and we got Powers and loaded him into the *V* of the coffins. Pa brought out some rope and tied everything down.

"Hope no cop stops me," he said. "This'll be hard to explain."

I said good-bye to my friends, gave them all hugs, and told them to come see me sometime. When I got to Shepard, he threw his arms around me and sobbed, "First Amoss and now Mamie. No one will know how I've suffered. Take her gently, sweet prince. Tend her with love. And think of me alone, a hollow, tortured genius, his farsighted mind, his unique eccentricity desiccated in the fiery furnace of old-time religion. With her I had a chance of creating a new mythology. Think of me as a comet that had a brief moment of oneness, its message written across the fiery sky, yum yum. Across the fiery sky, hmmm, and poof – gone to cold slag upon the rock of time. Think of me with a jar of splow in my hand and the memory of what could have been breaking my heart. Think of me, Crystal. Ub ub ub, don't forget old Don Shepard."

Anna and Charlie pulled him away from me and told me to get going. As we headed down the road, I looked back and saw my friends standing in the middle of the street looking after us, dark silhouettes against the ragged forest, and the skeleton of the church in the distance with its two burial mounds pointing the way in the wash of a full moon, a pumpkinhead in a pumpkin moon, a Mamie face with crater eyes watching over all.

Resurrecting Powers

It was close to five-thirty when we drove into the yard. The lights were on in the house, and I knew my brothers were dawdling at the table, having their toast and coffee. Mama would be shuffling back and forth in her robe and slippers, holding the pot and telling the boys to wake up. They would be hanging their heads and yawning and rubbing their faces. Mary Magdalen would be coming out of the bathroom, bright and sunny Mary Magdalen, and she would tell the boys how worthless they were and what a wonder it was that they even knew how to milk cows. They would hiss and grumble at her, and she would bully them until they would hurry with their coffee just to get away from her. And I thought about how when tomorrow morning came, I would be sitting with them, everything like it was long before I left. The adventure was over.

Then they came bursting out the door, five inkblots flowing toward us through the ground fog, as we sat in the pickup watching them. They surrounded us and started howling at the top of their lungs, "They're here! They're here!" The yardlight came on, and the inkblots became my brothers, waving their arms and kicking up their heels like a herd of bull calves showing off.

"Hang on," said Pa. "They got us cornered."

The door opened on my side and someone hauled me out and shook me back and forth. Then the rest of them were punching me and pinching me and yelling "Christian! Christian!" so loud I thought my eardrums would break. Calvin pulled my nose and wiggled it, then grabbed my ears and jerked on them like they were bellropes. Cutham yanked my arm one way while Cush yanked on the other, like they were trying to pull me apart. Calah had a hold of my hair, pulling my head back so he could look down into my face and scream, "Christian!" Cash was pinching me till I kicked his shins and made him hop and fall. Then everybody was stepping on him, and he was holding my ankles and crying, "Look who's here! Look who's here!"

Finally Pa got out and bellowed at them to leave me be. Mama came out, and when they saw her, they threw me into her arms and grinned. She gave me a solemn look and told me I was never to go off like that and worry her to death again. Mary Magdalen caught my neck and squeezed me close. She said she was glad to have me back. She had almost forgotten that Mama had once given birth to a human boy. My brothers made faces at her and told her she was the one wasn't human.

Cush jumped up on the coffins and started stomping up and down. "What's this here?" he asked.

Cutham banged one with his fist and cried out, "It's hard!" Then he hit it again for the insult of hurting him.

Calvin called the twins a pair of morons and told them they didn't know coffins from mailboxes. Cush and Cutham got solemn, both pulling their lower lips inside out and staring at the coffins in awe. I told them Robbie was in one and Mamie in the other.

"Dead!" said Cush.

"Oh, for pity's sake," said Mary Magdalen. "See what Mama and me have to put up with?"

Calah asked, "How come you brung 'em?"

"To bury 'em here," said Pa.

That made sense to everybody. They nodded their heads like they had never heard of such a good idea. Cash fingered the remains of Powers and asked what was all the junk?

"Yeah, what's this stuff?" said Cush, hoisting up Powers's foot.

"Untie the rope. Let's take a look," said Cutham.

"What is it? What is it?"

"Shut up!" hollered Pa. "Give a man time to speak, for crying out loud."

The boys shut up and looked sore at Pa. He took some deep breaths, then told who Powers was and that Mamie had loved him and so Christian brought him along and was going to put him back together, and we were all going to plant Robbie and Mamie down next to Mary Beaver at the Brule. My brothers bobbed their heads up and down, like it all made perfect sense to them, uh-huh.

"A real for-sure projector?" asked Cash. "For movies?"

"You gonna show us movies?" Calvin wanted to know.

I declared I was. I told them I had a friend in Temple who would send us *Hamlet* and *Moby Dick* and all kinds of movies.

"Hot dog!"

"Neat!"

"We like you, Christian."

My brothers gathered round and petted me like I was their favorite hound. Mary Magdalen said not to count on the movies working any kind of magic on the boys like they had on Mamie. I told her it couldn't hurt to try. The brothers were untying the rope and hauling Powers off to the machine shed, treating him carefully. When they came back, they wanted to know if they could see in the coffins.

"We never did get to see this Robbie fella," said Calvin.

"And we should say good-bye to Mamie," said Cash.

"Do you all want to look?" asked Pa. All of us did, even Mama and Mary Magdalen, so Pa said it was okay, and my brothers hauled the coffins out of the pickup and dropped them side by side in the drive.

"They're heavy!" they complained.

"Made of stainless steel," said Pa. "Cost a bloody fortune."

"And poor little Mary got cowhide," Mama told us.

We got tools and unbolted the lids and lifted them off. There lay Mamie and Robbie, each in a cocoon of white sheet. Pa pulled the sheets off their heads, and we could see Mamie's face. All the swelling was gone, and except that she was skim-milk pale, she looked the same as in life. She had her frog smile on, like she was dreaming something funny. And Robbie didn't look half-bad either, except he had a blue ridge across his forehead where Beaver had crushed it. Otherwise he looked as peaceful as could be, his blond beard and hair fanning out and starting to catch the first rays of the sun just peeking over the garage.

And it was the sun that did something strange to the bodies. Wisps of ground fog were rising around the coffins, and the sun shot through the fog and turned the coming light into a rainbow that seemed to hover over the coffins and shoot a shimmering shower of gold inside them, glittering over the bodies so intensely that we were all blinded by the light.

Mama cried out, "Holy Mary Mother of God!" and dropped to her knees. Mary Magdalen joined her and they started murmuring something together that was like a foreign tongue, a chant of some kind that put goose bumps on the goose bumps I already had.

My brothers stood frozen with their mouths open and the word "Gawwww" coming from their throats. Pa was the only one could speak and make sense: "Like a glory," he said breathlessly, "turning them into pure energy, a jillion midget stars rising up. A regular filigree of sun-spangled atoms! Rising to the Deity! Who's gonna fear it now?"

"Gawww," repeated my brothers.

Then it was over. The fog swam away and the light fell in normally, but for a few more seconds we stood waiting to see if the glory would come back. When it didn't return, Calvin asked softly, "Can we bury 'em now, Pa?"

"After chores," said Pa. "Get the lids back on and take care of the cows."

"After chores," said the twins in awe.

"Let's hurry!" said Cash.

We did. There was no messing around. We bolted the lids back on and loaded the coffins in the pickup, then went to the barn and did the milking and cleaning in record time, and not one squabble either. After chores, we took the tractors and shovels and drove to the grave site. We used the front-end loader to make two holes, finishing them off with the shovels. By the time we were done, Pa and Mama and Mary Magdalen had come in the pickup. Pa brought ropes, and we put them under the coffins to let them down easy.

We stood over the holes, and Pa opened the Bible and read the part Mama pointed to about the Son of Man coming with his angels to repay every one of us for what we had done. When he had finished that part, he looked up and raised his voice so it boomed above the swishing of the river. "The Deity sits in the bosom of Nature and is the Lord Over-Soul of all visible and invisible. In every spirit he dwells and connects that spirit with its father-earth and mother-sea, and the salt of the sea is in its veins and the minerals of the earth in its blood, flowing from the beginning in an endless cradle of time, through and through the world over, the union of brotherhood everywhere. Return then, Robbie Peevy and Mamie Beaver, to the bosom of creation whence you came, and one day we will all join you there, and it won't be calamity no more than the rising of a drop of dew."

Pa looked at each of us as we said amen and stared back at him, proud of him that he could say such wonderful things. He looked tickled with himself and satisfied. Mama leaned her cheek against his shoulder and made the sign of the cross. Mary Magdalen dropped a rosary on top of Mamie's coffin. It made a snapping noise as it hit the lid and slid off.

Calvin said respectfully, "That was good preachin, Pa."

"Yeah," all my brothers agreed.

Pa let himself be praised for a second, then told us there was no more to do for Robbie and Mamie but to bury them. He said to hurry up and get it done and get to the house for breakfast, as he was starved. Mama and Mary Magdalen went with him back to the house, and the rest of us started filling in the holes.

It shouldn't have taken long with all six of us at it, and we did get Robbie's filled right away with no trouble, but before we got Mamie's half-filled, the twins started acting up, throwing dirt at each other, which got the rest yelling at them and then at each other. Then it wasn't just Cush and Cutham throwing dirt, it was all of us. From throwing dirt, we went to wrestling, and right off I got thrown into the grave and nobody would let me out. Next thing, Calah stood up on what was left of the mound and told us he was king of the hill. "Oh, yeah?" was our answer, and the brothers dove for him. I stayed put and let them fight it out. In no time, there wasn't any hill left to be king of. Most of the dirt was managing to get kicked in on me, so that for a few minutes I wondered if I would get buried with Mamie and nobody would notice. The brothers had their blood up and went on wrestling, hill or no hill, and none of them listened to my yelling that I was getting buried alive. At last, though, they got tired, and then I told them they should have listened better to what Pa had said about brotherhood and such. They stopped trying to get in a last punch or a choke on one another and turned their attention to me in the hole.

"Shut up, you little shit," said Calvin.

"You don't be tellin us what Pa said. We got ears," said Calah.

"Yeah, Christian buttface!" hollered the twins.

Cash kicked dirt on me and said I wanted to get back to being Pa's pet. Then Calvin said I had gotten out of more chores than he could shake a stick at and it was time I started earning my keep.

"Mamie's your gal. You bury her," he added.

"Yeah!" hollered the twins.

Calah gave me the finger. Cash kicked more dirt on me. Then with a righteous "Humph!" they all marched away, saying I hadn't changed a goddamn bit, still the same smartass turd I always was. They climbed on the tractors and roared off, leaving me to climb out and shovel as fast as I could and finish Mamie's burial.

Some nice and slow and drizzly days came on, just the thing a farmer needs to get caught up on machine and barn repairs, and just the thing to turn the pasture and the hay field into a sea of green. It was then I got to spend time with Powers, and piece by piece, gear and belt and wheel, I got him back together. Pa did the wiring for me and helped braze all the split seams and shrink with torch and water all the wrinkled metal. He went into Duluth for supplies one day and brought back a lamp that fit in the place of the shattered lamp, although we had to fashion a new socket for it. Then we put the leg back on the foot, screwed it down, and mounted the main box on top and the arms for the reels, for which we had had to invent some spring-loaded belts made of old inner tubes. Last thing, I plugged the socket in and flipped the switch. The hum of Powers filled the room, all the pieces of his transmission turning in the right directions and the lamp glowing inside.

We stood back and admired what we had done. A little bit of paint and Powers wouldn't look half-bad, we decided. Only thing missing now was his eye, and Pa figured we could probably order that at the same place he had bought the lamp.

It had stopped raining and the sun was out, so we slid the big door back and let the light flood in. Powers stood there, somewhat the worse for wear but looking like he could still do the job, given an eye and some film. My brothers came by, carrying posthole diggers and a shotgun, ready to go make fence with Pa and me. They wanted to know when they were going to see some movies and if they would get to see cartoons and some three stooges. "None of that crap," said Pa, which damped their enthusiasm.

We went to the close end of the pasture to make a new fence for a plot of trefoil that Pa wanted to try. He told me to go check on the graves real quick to see if they had sunk in with the rain, so while my brothers got started digging holes, I ran to the far end of the pasture to see what Mamie and Robbie were going to need.

It was as I got close to the graves that I saw something wasn't quite the way I had left it. Something was added; a new thing, like a tube, was sticking out about six inches from Mamie's sunken mound. I slowed down and went forward at a walk, trying to focus on what the tube was and scared half to death that I already knew. When I saw I was right, I lost control for a minute and turned round, screaming at Pa and my brothers, "John Beaver! John Beaver!"

They came running. In Calah's hands was the sixteen-pound sledge hammer. Cutham brought the twelve-gauge. The rest carried shovels and posthole diggers. The boys ran right by me, shouting "Where is he? Where is he?"

"In the woods!" I hollered. "Probably watching us right now."

They stopped and looked suspiciously at the woods. "How you know?" asked Calvin.

I pointed to the lens in Mamie's mound. "That's Powers's eye," I said. "That's what John Beaver killed Mamie and Robbie with."

"Gaw," they all said, looking at it.

"It's the murder weapon itself," said Cash, fingering the lens.

Calah stood next to me, hugging the big hammer. "Don't you worry none, Christian. We'll fight for you," he said gruffly. Then he shouted towards the forest, daring John Beaver to come out.

"Big scaredy-cat!" yelled Cutham.

"Stinking rat!" yelled Cush.

"I got traps in there, John Beaver!" Calvin hollered. "Bear traps!"

"Cut your leg off!" yelled Cutham.

"And your weener too!" yelled Cush.

"Boys, boys," said Pa, finally catching up and out of breath. "Take it easy, boys, make a guard line here and keep your eyes peeled."

They formed up between the river and the graves. Cutham started marching back and forth with the twelve-gauge on his shoulder. Cush tried to grab it from him. "Get the hell away from me," yelled Cutham.

"My turn," said Cush.

"Back off, Cush," ordered Calvin.

Pa was asking me what made me think John Beaver was around.

"The lens, Pa," I said pointing to it. "Powers's eye. Beaver took it with him that day."

Pa called Cash over and told him to run quick and call the sheriff. Cash took off like a greyhound. The rest of my brothers scoured the river's edge up and down, nudging each other and pointing here and there, nervous as mice. Next thing the boom of the twelve-gauge broke in the air, and a crow fell out of a tree, bumping branches all the way down. Cutham lowered the twelve-gauge and looked at us sheepishly. "I thought it was him up a tree," he explained.

"I told you I should have the gun!" yelled Cush.

"Gimmee that shotgun, Cutham," said Pa, marching over and snatching it away.

While he was giving Cutham hell, I went up close to Mamie's mound and looked at the lens squatting there, a dark tube against the red earth, looking almost like a grave marker for leprechauns. I pulled it out and took it down to the Brule. I washed it in the water and dried it on my shirttail, then looked through it and saw that for all the banging it took, it wasn't broken. It magnified the trees, making them fuzz for giants such as John Beaver crashing through them at the edge of what passed for a civilized world.

And it struck me then that I had lucked out. I had the thing I needed, the last part, the eye to see through to see what Mamie saw and light up the wall of the shed with movies and get from them what magic Mamie got, and maybe even get more of the magic in me, get it living in me the way it lived in Mamie and the way Jesus lived in Robbie. All that in me and maybe I would know something, and maybe I would have visions of Mamie – Mamie as Hamlet, Mamie as Ahab, Mamie as Ishmael.

Mamie as me? As me, Mamie?
Yaay, Kritch'n.
You and me, Mamie?
Yaay, Kritch'n. Hippa-weee!

"Hippa-weee!" I hollered down the river. "Hippa-weee!" I yelled, holding Powers's eye up for Pa and my brothers to see.

"Hippa we?" said Pa, scratching his head.

"Hippa we?" said my brothers.

"Yaay, Pa. Yaay, brothers," I answered. "Mamie says 'Yaay and hippa-weee!'" I tossed Powers's eye into the air and watched it cartwheel slowly, catching the sun and flashing quarter-size dots of light at my face, beads of Powers coming down like fire into my hands.